Praise for
URBANTASM

"*Urbantasm: The Dying City* is a novel of wonder and horror — but I don't mean that in any traditional sense. Though preternatural elements impinge on the story here and there, what really fuels both the wonder and the horror is Connor Coyne's uncanny portrayal of early teenhood, when every dimly understood new vista promised ecstasy untold, and every wrong move or unintentional difference could mean social death — or worse. This is a tough, tender, and unsettling rumination on coming of age in a dying industrial city, and I'm both eager and terrified to see what happens next."

— William Shunn, author of *The Accidental Terrorist*

"The first volume of Connor Coyne's epic novel *Urbantasm* imbues a neglected part of America with an azure luminescence. Portrayed with sensitive and romantic candor, this tale's young protagonists are never despairing but perpetually haunted. Coyne understands that to survive is to be wounded, and *Urbantasm* illuminates the shadows of a nation that has always exploited the defenseless and the forgotten."

— Jeffery Renard Allen, author of *Song of the Shank*

"The fate of Flint, Michigan can often be hard to believe. Yet Connor Coyne skillfully captures the tarnished essence of a thinly veiled Vehicle City — known as Akawe in *Urbantasm* — with a compelling blend of noire and Rust Belt magical realism."

— Gordon Young, author of *Teardown: Memoir of a Vanishing City*

"Combining an ongoing love of noir atmospherics with memorable character development, Connor Coyne's *Urbantasm* takes readers into a vivid and utterly authentic world of adolescent angst, yearning, fear and love. Coyne's teenaged narrator John Bridge is a brilliantly shaped character, both wise and deeply attentive to the world on the inside and painfully awkward, vulnerable and intrepid on the outside. Perhaps the greatest treat of all in *Urbantasm* is Coyne's writing, which with all senses intensely engaged, is remarkably original and full of heart. His rich, often disturbing, and loving evocation of the urban landscape where his struggling adolescent characters wander honors the 'dying city' – and suggests, in fact, it isn't dead at all, but pulsing with stubborn, surprising, and resilient life."

— Jan Worth-Nelson, author of *Night Blind*

"While I appreciate the universal chords in *Urbantasm*, it is the delivery, the writing style, that engaged me. The writing propels this story. So do the characters as they reveal themselves through the writing. Coyne's fluid prose is the perfect vehicle to carry an epic allegory. The wordsmith in me particularly enjoyed the stylistic change-ups he would throw."

— Robert R. Thomas, *East Village Magazine*

"Incandescent prose illuminates the darkest underground passages of a town ruined by an auto company, where gangstah drugs turn everything dreamy, mysterious, and deadly. And you can't look away, sentence by gorgeous sentence, from the drama caught writhing and screaming, squinting its eyes against the light."

— Tantra Bensko, Author of *Glossolalia: Psychological Suspense*

"Connor is a great writer. His ability to create amazing characters in a richly painted fictional background is something to be truly admired... This is a coming of age tale, crime story, thriller, suspense novel and a use of fiction to condemn and glorify urban decay and corruption... From a pure storytelling perspective, this is a fantastic read. Realistic characters in real peril and dealing with real-life situations... Then a bizarre pair of sunglasses is found and things get — weird. It's breathtaking writing. I feel *Urbantasm* is destined to be a classic."

— Bryan Alaspa, Author of *S.P.I.D.A.R.*

"*Urbantasm: The Dying City* recognizes that adolescence is magic — your understanding transforms, you are consumed by desires of and just beyond your body, you know your friends in a way you didn't before. Coyne combines this magic with the sociology and cartography of Akawe, Michigan — a 'dying,' but by no means dead, incarnation of 1990s Flint — and a pair of strange blue sunglasses to pull seventh-grader John Bridge and his friends towards something raw, complex, and new."

— Gemma Cooper-Novack, Author of *We Might As Well Be Underwater*

"Urbantasm is a coming of age story told with such specificity that it becomes universal. A tale of first kisses, contrived plans for new identities and the utter confusion that comes from being thirteen years old."

— M.L. Kennedy, Author of *The Mosquito Song*

"In *Urbantasm*, Coyne presents his dying city as a place of warmth, humanity, and friendship, as seen through the eyes of young people more wise and thoughtful than their world is willing to admit."

— Amanda Steinhoff, Author of *Lily and the Golden Lute*

URBANTASM

THE DYING CITY

URBANTASM

a novel

BOOK ONE:
THE DYING CITY

Connor Coyne

GOTHIC FUNK PRESS

Flint, Michigan

GOTHIC FUNK PRESS
gothicfunkpress.com
Flint, Michigan

URBANTASM: THE DYING CITY
Copyright © 2018 by Connor Coyne
All rights reserved.

Edited by **Hosanna Patience**

Designed and Illustrated by **Sam Perkins-Harbin**
forge22.com

ISBN: 978-0-9899202-3-0

Printed in the United States of America

10 9 8 7 6 5 4 3 2 1
First Edition

for Jessica

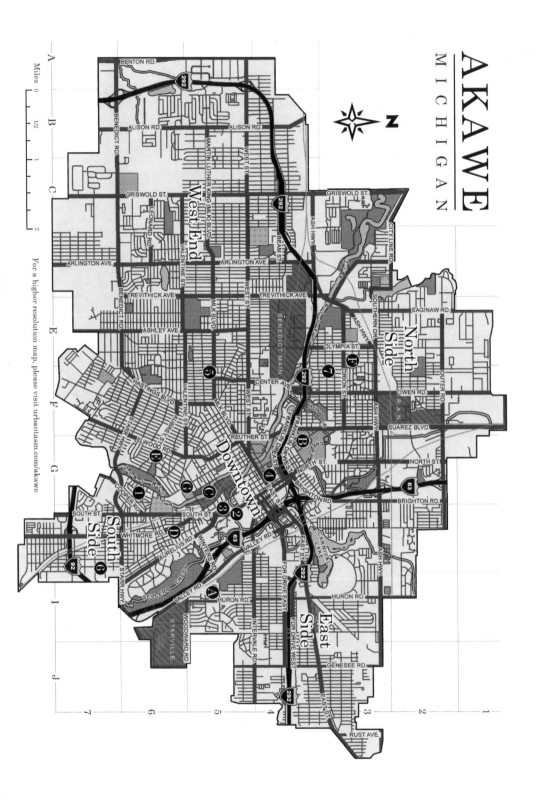

LEGEND

1 - Ashburn Heights

2 - Cartierul

3 - Cellarway

4 - Downtown Akawe

5 - Hastings Corridor

6 - South Side

7 - The Os

A - Beckford Junior High School

B - Campus Akawe

C - Old Benedict

D - Radcliffe Junior High School

E - St. Brendan Church and School

F - St. Francis Church and School

G - X Automotives Institute

I have to become the Antichrist.

I realized this one night when I was standing on an overpass looking down through a chain-link fence onto the expressway below. Blue neon light shined off icy puddles. The gutters were flush with slush. Empty houses, ragged wrecks, hung out on tiny lots to my left and right. Beneath me, the cars that this city had built were leaving it – some of them forever. Across from me, on a rusted trestle, a freight train slowly passed, bringing in the parts for more cars.

As the train moved on through, I thought about Drake and about how God had fucked him over. How he'd fucked us all over. Then I thought about the house with Jesus graffitied on its side. Orange skin, blue eyes, green thorns. A welter of wounds. I clenched my jaw and my teeth squeaked together. Across from me, the train wheels squealed.

If I wanted to save my friends, I would have to murder God.

2

This is mostly my story, but I'm gonna start out by telling you about what happened to Drake. Just so you know – just so you can see right off the bat – what a bastard God could be and why a lot of us had it out for him.

In the summer of 1993, Drake had just turned sixteen.

He was going to be a junior, and his horror-show-of-a-life finally seemed to be turning a corner. He'd been living with his dad and sister in the trailer park when his mom finally moved out of her little house in the Lestrade neighborhood. She'd given it to Drake's dad. She knew damn well that he wasn't going to pay any rent, but she didn't care as long as he kept the kids. Now Drake would have empty houses next door instead of empty trailers. He, his sister, and his dad had filled a couple dozen Hefty sacks with all their stuff and dropped them in the trunk of their scraped-up Benedict.

One trailer over, Sapphire watched, leaning back against the bent wall, her narrow eyes shaded behind her too-big sunglasses. She was a white girl, also sixteenish, with hair so light it glowed like tallow dripping from one of my mother's candles. Blue eyes too, quiet laughter, nervous all the time, but silently thrilled to be growing up as fast as she could.

"I ever gonna see you now?" she asked.

"See me at school," Drake said. "Summer's done next week."

"Suck a dick," she said and laughed.

"Come over to my new place tonight. Come over, what, nine? Bring DeeDee. I'll get Jamo and TK. Drinks from my dad. We'll bust up that hospital like we said. I got gold now, you know. Crazy gold."

And he did. Drake wasn't a Chalk – fuck those racist fucks – but they were a North Side gang wanting to sell some coke and E out on the East Side, and Drake was their man. Okay, their middleman. EZ set the whole thing up. Drake hated the Chalks but he liked the money and he also liked EZ. How could you not like EZ, talking the way he did? Dude had magnetism.

Even before Drake had unpacked all his shit at the new place, even before the sun had dipped behind the swampy trees shadowing the creek, EZ pulled up in his moon blue Starr Slipstream. A sweet make and model for a blue-collar beater. Rust patches shaped like Martian mountains silhouetted against a dusty sky. EZ called Drake over to the window.

"You straight over here, D?" EZ said. "This all new to you?"

"Naw," said Drake. "I got all the fiends back on Ash and I'll get some here too. See my moms lived here years. Lestrade

Hood. I know it. Every street. Every liquor store. Every squat the kids go to fuck."

"What about you?" EZ asked. "You gettin' some, D?"

"Not now, you know," Drake said.

"But you got plans on that."

"I don't..."

"You better stitch it up then. If boys don't fuck they die." EZ grinned without parting his pink lips. Crows feet in the cracks of his mellow yellow eyes. He was white-ish, but he had some black in him, too. It always struck Drake as funny when black kids joined up with the Chalks.

Now EZ leaned out of the car, looking forward, turning to look back, taking in the whole street with its tidy ranches and its burnt-out wrecks. "Le Strayed," he said, the tip of his tongue probing his teeth like he was rolling a Werther's.

How old is he anyway? Drake wondered. Older than Drake. Younger than Drake's dad. It was hard to tell.

"You know," EZ said. "Jesus was a fool to crawl up on that cross. God made the devil. Devil is God's tool. Hammer in his hand. And the devil offered Jesus all the kingdoms of the Earth, and don't you think that was part of Yahweh's plan too? What you think woulda happened if Jesus had just said 'yes?' I bet we wouldn't be slumming in Akawe."

Akawe is the name of this city.

6

A poor city. A beat-up city. A car-making city an hour's drive from Detroit, but then the cars it made left, along with the money, along with the people. Akawe.

"I don't know," said Drake. "I ain't religious."

EZ laughed. "No, you ain't," he said. "Here. I got something new for you to test for me. Make some night special. Full of secrets."

He beckoned. Drake leaned in through the open window. In EZ's palm, a sandwich bag with five white pills.

"What's that?" asked Drake.

"A new thing," EZ said. "Chalks call it O-Sugar. Kinda like E. Kinda not. Try it out. Give it some time. Don't go to sleep. Gonna see the world through God's eyes. Feel like Jesus would if he'd said yes to his good friend the devil."

After EZ signed off, Drake helped his dad and his sister unpack until the sun went down and his friends came over. They all sat on the front porch, passed a 40, smoked up, and put the pills of O-Sugar on their tongues and swallowed. They talked about music and cars and love and sex.

About big old TK who had built a Frankenstein sedan from the soldered guts of four different cars.

About DeeDee, sad-in-her-heart that this boy Shawn would never see a woman in her like she saw a man in him. "He's on varsity, you know," she said.

Then, there was skinny Jamo with his horn-rimmed glasses. He kept farting. He said he liked the kids' urinals best because that way his dick didn't brush the puck.

Drake didn't talk much, though. He kept looking at Sapphire – her eyes, her face, her perfect nose – and he felt her laughter run his spine like blue notes down a keyboard. She was a song he hoped he might play some day, but not in a crude way. He hoped he was a conversation she might have.

The kids' hearts started to glow in their chests with a slow, soft burn. That was the beer talking. They walked down the driveway to DeeDee's Aubrey.

They left Lestrade and crossed the expressway into Anderson Park – brick houses, neat lawns, where the mayor and the college presidents lived – but even these exalted ones couldn't keep St. Christopher's Hospital open in crumbling Akawe. The hospital towered in the midst of the neighborhood, full of empty-dark windows and stern staring statues.

DeeDee parked on a side street of prim Cape Cods and the kids walked the last half block to the hospital complex. Above them, the moon waxed, and the whole sky – the everything – seemed to unfurl and offer itself to Drake, limpid and tender. *Is that the O-Sugar? Or just the weed?* Drake swelled into the wide space of that raw and thrilling moment.

TK led them across the cracked parking lot to the loading dock.

They hauled up the service gate, slipped inside, and descended into the fluorescent-lit basement. There were seven buildings in St. Christopher's, but underground tunnels connected them all. After hitting a few dead-ends, the kids found their way to the central building. The six-story main building with a floor plan shaped like a giant cross. As they climbed, floor by floor, moment by moment, the shadows around them expanded with opportunities, with regrets redressed, and the future converging upon their pasts. Infinities of little universes hid in the dark corners of that empty space, clear of matter but clouded with tension, ready to emerge.

By the time they reached the roof, they all felt dizzy and disoriented. Before, their yearning spirits had stretched into each new second, each new room. But now that the potential for movement threatened actual motion – now that acceleration accelerated – they put their hands in their pockets and tried to slow down. The speed of everything was getting weird on them.

"Babies, I gotta sit down!" said Jamo.

They all sat.

"I feel like, like sad and sore," said Sapphire and she plucked at her hair.

"Hold my hand, Saph," said DeeDee, and they all held hands.

Far off, the sound of a train rang out and, at that moment, the city lights opened wide like eyes, and the stars glowed and exploded, and heat spilled like syrup from above. Dust and clouds, spinning and shining with lightning and friction. Planetoids and asteroids whirling with volcanoes down jets of solar steam. As the train whistle sang, its sound was compressed, compacted, tonally shifted upwards, higher, with panic. As the pitch got higher and higher, Drake felt better and better, and it terrified him. He climbed on top of himself – palms pushing down on his head – to hold his soaring heart in place, but the shadows everywhere slid up convex hypotenuses from the streets below. They weighed down invisible tightropes that connected to the tallest buildings Downtown. Everything kept turning bluer and bluer. Turning to blue and purple.

The shadows swung their arms. They were the remnants of that abandoned place, humanoid, with blue coins replacing their eyes. They had flown away when their owners checked out and went home or died at the hospital. Now, they returned, suctioned in, pulled back toward the points of departure.

But as the shadows converged and became more humanlike, Drake's friends had been reduced to matter and residuals. TK and DeeDee and Jamo and Sapphire had all lost their eyes and their ability to speak. Their faces had become smooth planes of flesh and, finally, pure fields of electricity. Small blobs, data balls, started to grow and divide. Oxygen bloomed. The kids floated – *impossible!* – but happening, and as they did the lights got brighter and brighter, heightened and compressed, flattened and overheated.

"Sapphire..." Drake tried to say, and he leaned toward her, straining to see her features again. He wondered what had happened to him and his friends. What was happening around them. On every side. He imagined their height, sixty feet up. The death it represented.

Then, as if in response, space *itself* pressed in and Drake felt himself stretched out over the edge of the building. He fell. He was falling. Yellow-blue parking lot lines dropped away behind him and approached. They got small. The last thing he saw before he hit were black streaks of grypanian spirals, dotting away and multiplying.

The sky was a dome, but the parking lot was deep.

3

When Drake woke he saw his sister sitting at his side.

His first words were a cliché: "Where am I?"

"Proctor Hospital," she answered. Her brow was furrowed and she tugged the sheets up over his shoulders. "You went up to the roof of St. Christopher's with your friends. Then you all jumped. Why did you jump, Drake?"

"We didn't jump," Drake said. "Are they... okay?"

She answered with her wide, wet eyes. "It was so high!" she finally stammered. *Sapphire is dead,* he thought. *TK is dead. DeeDee is dead. Jamo is dead.* Words with meaning. He understood. But the thoughts seemed too far off to feel. Antarctica far. Drake thought he would feel the meaning soon.

"We didn't jump," he repeated. Then: "Where is the center of the universe?"

His own question surprised him. *Is it 'cause nothing nowhere was holding still?* The question didn't surprise his sister, though. Nothing he said ever surprised her.

"Times Square?" she answered.

She's kind of dumb. New York isn't the biggest city in the world. Not even close. Tokyo's bigger. Mexico City's bigger. And there are other cities: trading cities, factory cities, cities that started out as dirty shacks and crossroads in the wild. Rome. Berlin. Jerusalem. Buttfuck backwaters. Meanwhile, huge cities eventually get buried by the desert. Babylon. What makes a city? Roads, right? And people? Travelers who decide to settle down at the crossroads. Crossroads where they bury suspected vampires because the shape of the intersection suggests the crucified Lord? Crossroads that would have been shaped like eggs if their branching paths were blue ribbons pulled back and taped together where they met? Easter eggs? And at what point do crossroads become a city? What makes a city live? Why have cities at at all? Why have crossroads? Why should space be more important in one place than in another?

"No," said Drake. "This is the center of the universe. It's where we are."

"You mean Akawe?" she asked.

"Yeah," Drake said. "Akawe. Michigan. Akawe, Michigan, is the center of the universe."

Akawe, the home of X Automotives, the fourth member of the Big Three. The second-largest American automaker.

Akawe, where they used to build four of Brand X's five lines: Valentines, Benedicts, Aubreys, and Starrs. For style, size, speed, and savings. Huge factories with names like "Benedict Main," "Starrville," and "The Old Benedict." Metal fabrication, engine assembly, robotic systems and system maintenance. Money and jobs, prosperity and productivity.

The productivity of trains that sang into town seven nights a week. The prosperity of hospitals that saved boys who jumped.

In Akawe, six hundred miles west of Times Square, on the Zibi River, on the East Street bridge, nobody pops champagne corks under a fountain of confetti on New Years Eve, but thirsty winos suck off their skirted rosies to keep themselves warm. Drake could look down into that water any time he passed and he'd see mooneyes looking up at him, mergansers watching from the bank, spiders crawling along the rusted rungs. Meanwhile, the water rolled on, dragging silt through stargrass and cattails – everything precious, everything ours – to the Shiawassee, to the Saginaw Bay, to Lake Huron, to the St. Lawrence, and finally the wide, deep Atlantic.

As far as Drake was concerned, all addresses in the world fanned out from this one point in the heart of Downtown Akawe. North Side, East Side, South Side, and West End. Drake's ambulance had crossed the bridge when it had carried him from the dead hospital to the living.

It was on the North Side – a neighborhood called the Os – where Drake had met EZ for the first time, in the front yard of some nasty house EZ's dad owned. Drake had been dealing in his trailer park, cutting some product with caffeine, boosting his profit, and EZ had figured it out and had been impressed. "You're an entrepreneurial motherfucker," he had said that night. "You ready to make some real money? Can't get out nowhere on that nickel and dime shit."

Stars spun round on cold nights. Afterward there was an explosion of light. Millipedes and moss. Mites and spiders. In the Os, white trash and brown and black trash sit on the curbs and porches and in the yards. Most of the street names start with an "o."

"Oh no," Drake said from his hospital bed. What if the trees killed everything by giving them too much shade?

It was on the West End – really half of the whole city – drawn out along the factories, the mass of black neighborhoods, tamaracks and tabernacles, where EZ had sent Drake to meet up with Ziggurat. Ziggurat was with the Demonik Mafia, and they were rivals to the Chalks, but EZ had wanted the two gangs to make an alliance. He asked Drake to set up the meetings. Middlemen have their uses. So Drake had picked up Ziggurat in his mom's Aubrey, and together they ripped through the West End, wind cutting through their hair as they went. *That neighborhood has a girl's name. What was that neighborhood's name?* Drake wondered. *Was it Sapphire?*

Then he imagined Sapphire hitting the asphalt headfirst. Her rusted ruins, her ruined nose, her crushed skull... *but that's not right.* Drake couldn't keep it straight. The lights were blue overhead, vibrating where they hung, buzzing through the night while the moon glowed through the walls. *What happened to Sapphire? Did they burn her or bury her?* Drake was crying now but his thoughts still felt far away.

The neighborhood's name was Shelley with its rusted ruins and wheat fields. Drake groaned in his hospital bed. He knew that his hands were clenching the sheets, but he couldn't feel his feet at all. He had no idea what they were up to unless he looked. Sitting still. Still sitting still. The hallucinations hadn't stopped. The drug hadn't died. Drake's mind cruised Shelley and Arlington on the West End with Ziggurat and then past the sprawling Benedict Main factory complex. They cruised the Fender where the mom and pop shop meets the stop and rob. *Stop pop or I'll blast you, bitch.* And then, south of that, the Hastings Corridor, its Gothic mansions, its sycamores and guns. Cockroaches and dinosaurs. Flies and sharks.

It was on the East Side – in Lestrade – where Drake lived with his dad and his sister. There, rotting houses pressed up against the manicured lawns of alabaster-bricked ranches and Carnival Lake mirrored on out toward a treed horizon. Fogs and frogs. Murderers hid blue bodies – blue bones – out in the cattails. But then again, Lestrade also sang other kinds of blues from golden throats. From the Treemonisha Club where, during the golden age, you might have caught Dizzy or Bird, Miles or Trane. Flowers and snakes. Lestrade had once been the wealthier black neighborhood, so of course the city had to slice it up with two different interstates. That house. That mural. Orange skin, blue eyes, pink skies, and all the pain, pain, pain.

Once, Drake woke up to see the nurses painting him hot pink and sky blue. Fucking Chalk colors. He clawed at their hands with his bitten nails, but the nurses were only trying to draw his blankets up over his body. He always threw the covers off while he was sleeping.

One day, Drake pushed out of his bed to take a shower to rinse the mercury and paint off, but he fell from his worthless legs, ripped his IV out, and started vomiting up shreds of flesh and blood. It was the beginning of a long and bitter gray winter. The volcanoes had something to say. Drake felt his throat flecked with dust, but the O-Sugar was inside him now. Swept beyond his blood. Nestled in some corner of his brain. After that, they restrained him in his bed.

Drake had never spent much time on the South Side. That's where I lived. Old, brickish, inner-cityish neighborhoods with names like "The Cellarway" and "The Old River District." The Old Benedict. The first of the factories. Cartierul, the Romanian neighborhood, was squeezed into a ravine cut off from the rest of the city, in the shadow of the South Street viaduct. At the bottom of the ravine, a levy had been raised against Sellers and Carnival Creeks as they merged and flowed toward the river. Cartierul, always flooded, always contaminated, where my parents lived when I was born.

Just south and east of that, up on a hill, the Whitmore Street District, where my parents had moved when I was four. Broken roads with bricks under the crumbling asphalt. Shake-sided, stucco-dusted houses too big for poor people like us to heat. It overshadowed the X Automotives Institute to the west – the engineering incubator – where sad students walked about wearing engineers' goggles.

Drake clenched his fists as his mind raced through Akawe, inventing truths and sometimes finding lies. To him, every engineer was a Satan with horns, and their eyes had been replaced with blue coins and sunglasses. They glided over the city on vast span bat wings and Drake scoured every neighborhood asking: *Who did this? Who did this? Who did this?* It was, he realized, a meaningless question. What did he mean by "who" and "this"?

Was it EZ and his O-Sugar? The gangster and his toxic drug?

He ain't been here to see me, Drake noted.

Was it X Automotives, the company that had built the town and then had ruined what it had created? That had turned its back and wandered off, stranding the people who had made it wealthy?

They giveth. They taketh away, he reflected in a rare moment of bitter religiosity.

Or was it Akawe itself, this place, this point in space, this crossroads crossing, this city that had robbed him of everything and had given nothing back? Nothing worth keeping?

The Zibi River?

The State of Michigan?

Day by day, week by week, with debt piled upon granite debt, the doctors stitched Drake's face back together. His spine had been snipped and he'd never walk again, so the therapists taught him to use a wheelchair instead. Drake's dad had gone to jail for stealing a car. His mom never came by, but her not giving a shit wasn't any kind of news to him. Drake's sister came by after school each day, and she'd sit by his side for two or three hours. She'd work on her homework for a few minutes before giving up and turning on the TV. Whenever he woke, she was holding his hand.

"Someday, I'm gonna move away from here," he'd say.

"Away from dad's house?" she'd answer.

"No. Away from Akawe. To a big city."

"Like Detroit?"

"Like New York."

Life, he felt, was too dangerous in Akawe, near the center of the universe. Better to take shelter in the anonymity of the margins.

4

A month later, when Drake finally went home to the house in Lestrade, he noticed that far-away things were tinted strange colors: blues and grays and purples. Brightness didn't matter. It was all about distance. The stars never returned to normal. The sun looked strange for a year. After just a week, though, the moon reverted from a vibrating azure to its plain, pitted self. Still, he sometimes caught it rising over the side-yard, looking inside out with a waxy white mouse tattooed upon pitted black skin. Imagine a rat with human teeth. Imagine a whale with legs.

Drake lay in his bed and slept all day because he was tired and didn't want to think. He slept all night and had dreams about blood pouring from the shower fixture while he sat on the tile floor. The drain would be clogged with crimson clots, and as the blood rose, Drake would try to kick the door open. His legs wouldn't move. He tried to hold his breath, but...

Sometimes he got calls. When he did, his sister carried the telephone down the hall then stretched the cord over to his bed so he could hold the receiver taut to his mouth and ear. It was the hospital and universities, together and separate, a bureaucratic Gordian knot. They kept calling him in for studies, to answer questions, the cripple bus honking its horn as he struggled into his donated wheelchair and rolled on out.

It was hard to roll out. His dad was out on probation, but he hadn't built a wheelchair ramp yet. Just three steps from the porch to the walk, but they were steep steps, like the slick walls of St. Christopher's, and deep, like the parking lot, and Drake just couldn't...

What is O-Sugar? the researchers asked him when he'd arrived. *What are its effects?* His bloodwork had found atropine, scopalomine, and MDMA, but there was something else... a secret ingredient. What was it? An adulterant? A reagent? Some sort of industrial solvent? Where did it come from? Who made it, and how?

Law-enforcement called a lot, too, first the police and then the FBI. Sometimes they came in person. *What is O-Sugar?* they asked. *Who gave it to you? Was it from Arlington or Hastings? The Demonik Mafia or the Satan's Masters?* It wasn't one of the gangs from the Os, that was for sure. They couldn't put together something like that. The Os were for glue sniffers and thinner skimmers.

Drake told his questioners as little as he could. He kept EZ's name from them. He told them some Chalks had given him the drug...or maybe was it the Undertakers? He didn't know what, he didn't know how, he couldn't understand what had happened to his mind and his soul. He'd remained heart-cold since the fall. His quintessence had been buried and was slowly petrifying beneath the parking lot of St. Christopher's. Everywhere Drake went, everything seemed to be coated in blue apathy. But when he thought about his friends taken away – stripped like copper from the cracked-up houses on either side of his dad's – a hard seed of hate began to bloom within him. That blossom made Drake feel alive again, in a compacted sort of way. He didn't want to leave Akawe anymore. He wanted to stay and slit death-deserving throats. Wounds inflicted, not received. Forgiving blood on his hands. A bright-voiced singing bird, blurry red.

From time to time, the public defender's office called. DeeDee and Jamo's parents were trying to sue everyone. Drake's mom, his dad, the city, the Catholic Church, each other, and on and on. Then the medical bills. Then the collection agencies. Drake didn't have any money. Neither did his parents. *Nobody has any fucking money!* And once or twice, he was woken when reporters called, because sometimes Akawe makes national news over shit like this. A hippopotamus and a little man and woman, sweaty and stupid. Drake could always tell when it was a reporter calling because the phone would ring fifteen, twenty times before they gave up.

Sometimes, when he woke to the sound of the phone, he'd count out a year of his life to each ring. He had been three when his dad lost his job at X, four when his parents got divorced. When he was five, his dad had had the nervous breakdown and his mom wouldn't take Drake or his sister, so they lived with his grandma for two years. Then she died. Choked on a fistful of popcorn. Drake found her body the next morning, curled on the floor with one hand gripping her throat and the other clawing spiderlike into the tufts of the carpet.

After that, their dad took them back. They moved into the trailer park. The next three years had probably been the most normal, but then the whole thing with Leigh had happened, and they moved to another trailer park. By now Drake had gone through a carousel of schools: Frost, Trevithick, Elm, and Grigorescu. Walpole and Beckford Junior Highs. Northern and Eastern High Schools. Everyone at Eastern would want to know about O-Sugar. *What is O-Sugar?* Drake would be heading back after Christmas. He wasn't looking forward to it. He didn't know what he was going to tell them. What he was going to tell his friends' friends. What he was going to tell anyone.

"What is O-Sugar?" he asked the anvil-headed gray shade sitting on his dresser.

It shook its heavy head. Drake looked inside himself again. Tightened mental fists around his heart. The fascinating glow of hate. His anchor. His whole life. Everything else was fucked.

5

Months later, the hallucinations finally faded.

The horror though? That never faded. Drake still imagined his friends' ghosts following him through his day – when he woke, shaved, brushed his teeth, wheeled down the wooden ramp his dad had finally built.

The cold within him? That didn't fade either. The drug had knocked Drake out of step with the rest of the world. He always noticed a pause now, a gap in his thoughts, while life around him moved on according to some inaccessible rhythm.

Since hate was all he had left, he fed it and nurtured it. He put his palms upon it and it seemed to purr. To vibrate. He felt a bloody soak in the squeak of others kids' sneakers. He heard the ghosts aching for revenge in the winter wind that whistled around his house. He heard their rage in the lowing of the distant train. He started to make his plans.

To set ties and lay down tracks for the next revolution.

FIRST REVOLUTION

TIME

6

But like I said, this story doesn't *really* start with the fall of Drake and his friends. It's about *me* and *my* friends, and it begins with me standing on the South Street viaduct on the day before I started junior high. My name is John Bridge. I was just a week from turning thirteen. It was the end of August, 1993. A hazy evening. I was wearing sunglasses. I was thinking about Kiara and waiting for Adam.

On the phone, Adam had said that he had a plan. *A plan for what? For rap?* That summer he had spent a lot of time rapping for whoever he could get to listen. He had even given himself a stage name: "Emcee LeFly."

"It's like French," Adam had said. "Everyone knows the French are fly."

I heard a firework crackle in the neighborhood beneath me. A startled heron leapt off a low branch and flapped away along the creek. Squirrels scratched up through the trees. I looked down on it all. The viaduct, supported in the middle by sharply-slanting earthworks overgrown with weeds and small trees, spanned the small neighborhood from forty feet up. *Cartierul,* they called it. I could look down into the windows of the tallest houses there. I saw the ruddy sun sinking toward the Old Benedict factories several blocks away, and they stretched their shadows toward me. They moved like the distant creep of winter, like a spring storm ages away, but this was still summer, still heat, and I felt a little dizzy.

That May, while I'd been under Kiara's spell, I'd gotten bored with homework and had started skipping school just to walk around my own neighborhood. The other hundred sixth graders at Truman Elementary bored me. So did the video games I played with Adam. The RPGs I played with Bill. The bike rides I took with Chuck. I was tired of field trips to the Detroit art museum so we could squint up at the stone-carved lamassu. All that childish shit. That was before Adam had noticed the "Sold" sign in Kiara's front yard. *She* never called to tell me about it.

While I'd never gotten to find out what would've happened if Kiara had agreed to go out with me, I'd been certain it would've involved serious things, adult things, things that would have spiked my blood through me like gasoline set alight. But now that Kiara was gone, my interest in the old stuff hadn't returned. I knew that I wanted something new, but I didn't know what that meant. *Gotta get some not shitty clothes? Get some real cologne? Get a girlfriend? Someone who won't move away without telling me.* Good ideas, I thought, but they usually ended in a question mark. I didn't know what I was looking for. Just something grand and far-away. Something to tell me that I could become more than I had been in the past.

I *did* know that there were 800 kids spread across two grades at Radcliffe Junior High School. They didn't all come from my neighborhood. Some of them were preppy kids from Bellwood and others were gangbangers with the Reapers and the Satan's Masters. Most of them would just be poor and smooth soled like my other friends, but they'd still be new to me.

Adam arrived on his bike.

"Hey John," he said.

"What up?" I asked him.

He hopped off. "Some dude drove his car into the overpass on Intervale and splatted all over the place. I just heard about it on the radio! Want to go see?"

"Not really."

"Why not? You got somethin' better to do?"

I didn't. That was the problem. I wiped the sweat from my brow.

"You shouldn't go alone," I said.

"We gotta hurry," Adam said. "They clean up fast!"

7

It was only a five minute ride to the place where Sellers Creek and Carnival Creek merged beneath the Intervale Road bridge, itself curving beneath the massive pylons that supported the eight lanes of I-63 overhead. It was a huge space where I never went. It creeped me out. The ambulance had already come and gone. A tow truck was dragging off the shattered car... a silver Celica. A cop saw us and shook his head.

"Dammit," said Adam.

"There's still glass," I said. There was glass everywhere, actually.

"Dammit. Is that blood?" He squinted at a stain on the road. Then, giving up on that: "Hey, what you humming?"

"One of my father's records," I answered.

Blue Rondo à la Turk.

"Jazzy," Adam said. "You listen to jazz. Why?" He looked serious.

"You said you had a plan?"

"Hey! You know how you said I shouldn't go here alone? Like you didn't even want to come out – to see the accident – hey, that's cool of you John. See, I think you're right. Two are better than one. We don't get jumped when we go together. If I fall off my bike in the road, you make sure I don't get hit by a car. If I was alone, anything could happen! That's why I wanted to tell you about this plan."

"Okay, so what's the plan?"

"Not 'the plan,' John. The Plan! See, I was gonna do it myself, but I want you in on it. You remember last year when Kiara said you could kiss her and you stuck your tongue down her throat?"

"But I didn't! It didn't happen like that —"

"And that girl at summer camp gave me a blowjob?"

"Adam, I don't want a picture."

"It was dope!"

"I get it. Stop talking about it. Her name was Britney. You said so."

"Yeah, Britney." He grinned. "I'm talking about it because it's part of the Plan. I was thinking about it the other night. We aren't assholes. Like Chuck. I like Chuck, but he's kinda an asshole. You and me? We're players."

I cut a laugh.

"I mean it," he said. "You are the mac daddy and I am the daddy mac."

"I just... with me, it was sixth grade camp. It was just... then."

"Look," Adam said. "We're starting over from shit tomorrow."

"What does that even mean, shit-for-brains?"

"Nobody knows us! Okay, practically nobody. Three elementary schools feed into Radcliffe. If we want to make a name for ourselves, now's the time to do it."

I need to describe Adam, because you're going to be seeing a lot of him. He still had another seven months of being twelve ahead of him, but of all my friends he was most determined to grow up fast. A short white boy with a fast and scissoring voice. His straw-colored hair looked like someone had stuck a bowl over his head and just cut around the edge but there was no getting around those cold blue eyes. Half of the girls in our class wanted him. He knew this, too. Their wanting it and his knowing it made him a dangerous kid. Even though he was bird scrawny with chicken legs.

Okay, me? Sure, fine. You're going to be seeing even more of me than Adam. I was a white boy, too. I wasn't fat. Just a little short. I took after my father in that way, though he wasn't fat either. He had a beer belly though. And I had kind of thin eyebrows like my mother, and dark eyes, but girls liked my looks alright. They didn't like my attitude, though. "Pissy," they said. I had black hair. In seventh grade I parted it on the side so it looked stupid. Now that I'm sixteen, I part it in the middle.

Adam spoke: "A lot of assholes – assholes like Chuck – want to be popular. I don't just want to be popular. Popular ain't enough for me. I want everyone – popular kids, loser kids – to want a piece of me. Because then I can do what I want."

I laughed at him. "No way. You're not a thug. Or a playa. Just call Britney, see how busy she is."

He shook his head. "Listen, John, we get there, we got game 'cause we had it last year. That's your French kissing. That's my blowjob. We use *theze skillz* to get girlfriends. Eighth grade girlfriends. Hot girls. Popular girls. Dumb girls. They'll go for it. Trust me. Because we'll be gaming it up."

"We don't got nothing they want!" I said.

"Right. I know," he said. And he grinned. "That's why we dump their asses. Right? See, that's the Plan! We run our mouths, talk a good game just the first few days, we ask dumb bitches out, they say yes because we're new and exciting and... game... and then we dump them before they know we're not thugs or gangsta or whatev. After that we can be whatever we want and we'll still get respeck!"

"You're crazy, Adam."

"No, I'm *loco*. That's what the señoritas say. And we'll have some of them at Radcliffe tomorrow, too."

"It won't work."

"It will. I'll help you out. You'll help me. All those other jocks and thugs? They all think they're princes and shit. But why would you want to be a prince when you could be a king?"

He was shaking his hands in the air like a freak, but the shadows they cast out into the underpass were even freakier. A few feet beneath our feet the water rolled along on its long and languorous journey to the ocean.

"I think you're out of your mind," I said. "Anyway, I don't like it here. It's like a place where things come to die."

8

By the time I rode back across the viaduct, the rectangular shadows of the Old Benedict had run down Cartierul, climbed up the slope, and leapt into the air over the rest of Akawe. The winds, westerlies, had died away. Sometimes they brought rain and storms across the state from Lake Michigan. I could imagine blueberries, sand dunes, and the cool currents of distant Chicago. Without the wind, I was stuck with the stink of Akawe: ozone, exhaust, and wildflowers. Lots of vacant lots had eventually become prairies of honeysuckle and coneflowers. Black-eyed Susans. They sheltered bumblebees and cottontails. Deer mice held court on the exposed porches of abandoned houses. Bats roosted in the empty attics.

I rode back to my house – 1012 Agit Street – a little slip on a triangular block, a steep little hill that linked Whitmore Road and South Streets while they converged on a point just to the north. South was down and Whitmore was up and both were filled with auto body shops and party stores and boarded-up restaurants and live-in motels filled with prostitutes and disabled old people. Agit Street was residential.

My own house was a lot like the other boxy, blocky bungalows, stuccoed with a broad, open front porch that ran the length of the first floor. The house stood out, I guess, because moss had grown all over the shingles. It also stood out because the house to our west and the two more behind it had been demolished. My parents had bought the lots for a song. A thicket of weedy trees grew in the back, but we had a glorious view of the river valley and the neighborhoods on the other side. A silver maple grew on the median between the sidewalk and the road.

I put my bike in the garage and went inside.

"John, where have you been?" asked my father.

After the cooling twilight outside, our living room felt bright and hot.

"I went out with Adam," I said. "I told you."

"Didn't I ask you to be home by 6:30?" called my mother from the kitchen.

"Sorry. What time is it?"

"Almost an hour later. What were you two doing?"

"Just riding our bikes. Jeez..." I stopped myself; I didn't want to push my luck. Not on the first week of junior high.

"I can microwave some spaghetti for you," she called. "Go sit down at the table."

I went into the dining room and took a seat at the scratchy wood table. My father followed me. His name was Mark. He had red hair. Strong arms. Something between stubble and a beard. He'd brought his newspaper but I didn't have anything to read, so I glared out the window. Our driveway bumped right up against the neighbor's house: Archie with all his pit bulls. His walls blotted out the darkening sky, but I saw a naked incandescent light through one of his windows and it shone out fierce like a second sun. There were sixteen houses left on Agit Street. Ten of them occupied. One had burned down. It was nice to see a little light next door. My mother, Theresa, came in with a plate of spaghetti and garlic bread and a glassful of water. She was tall, cool, with dark hair and eyes, her mouth somehow warm and frowning at the same time. Tensely relaxed. She was the opposite of my father. She set the food down in front of me and took a seat.

"Can I have pop?" I asked.

She gave me her look, and I let it drop.

"John," said my father, "we really want to be happy about tomorrow. You're growing up, and I'm proud of you, and I –"

"I'm proud too," interjected my mother.

"It's a big day," my father said. He smiled. They'd staged this thing. Like an intervention. That's why they were pissed I was late.

"But," I said.

"It wasn't exactly what we wanted. You remember last year when we took you to St. Patrick's school?"

"That was like an hour drive –" I said.

"It was a half-hour drive," said my mother.

"I went to Parson Junior High, here in the city," said my father. "It was pretty good back then. Now they're gonna close it in the next year or two. You wait. Radcliffe is better off, but it's nothing special."

"Okay?" I asked.

"Your grades," said my mother.

"We really wanted to send you to St. Patrick," said my father. "Your mother thinks we can't afford it. Turns out she's right. They've changed shifts on me four times in the last three years. Half of that's been swing shift. I don't know how much longer I've got with Tool and Die. And we owe more on this house than we could sell it for today. So yeah, we can't afford the school."

"You have to get better grades this year," said my mother. "It's just the work, John. These classes are easy for you."

"The kind of job I have isn't going to be there for you when you get out of high school. You're going to have to go to college – a good one – and if you're spending the next six years in the Akawe schools, that means you have to be at the top of your class."

"So?" I asked.

The question startled them. I wasn't sure exactly what I meant by it either, but it wasn't much of a pep talk they were giving me.

"So don't blow it," said my mother.

Six years was a long time. Six years of boring, hard work seemed even longer. Anyway, nobody I knew was thinking about college yet except my cousin Michael, and he was the last person I wanted to copy. I caught some movement from the corners of the room. A fragile breeze probed at the curtains. Just past them, that naked lightbulb – its stark yellow fire. This time I didn't imagine the sand dunes or blueberries. I didn't imagine Chicago. This time I breathed in Akawe. Its bitterness and spice. A hint of bitumen. West End santería shacks and throbbing bass. Maybe the habeñero scent of the Os. Shit was happening out there. Nothing was happening in here. Grades were deadly, but the city was awake.

"Oh, by the way," said my father. "O-Sugar."

"What?" I asked.

"You ever hear of it?"

"No."

"I guess it's a drug. I don't know. I just read, last night, five kids from Eastern got doped up on O-Sugar and jumped off the roof of a hospital."

"Proctor?" I asked. *How did they manage to get onto the roof?*

He shook his head. "No. St. Christopher's." I'd been born at St. Christopher's. It'd been empty for years. "Just tell me if you hear anything about it. We don't have to tell you to steer clear of that stuff, right?"

"No. Obviously."

"Adam... concerns us sometimes, John," said my mother.

"Why did they jump?"

My parents looked at each other.

My father splayed his hands like this was the greatest mystery in the whole world.

9

My window gave a little scream when I opened it that night.

The screen was torn. I knew the bugs would get in, but it was too hot out to keep the window closed. Not that there was much comfort in opening it; outside was hot as hell, too.

I lay down on my bed, on top of the covers, then got under them, then got on top again. I heard my parents moving around downstairs, talking. Probably talking about me. My mediocre sixth grade grades. It's not like they had anything else worth talking about. Nothing exciting going on in their lives. My mother kept trying to turn some part-time work with Michigan Radio into a full-time gig and it kept not happening. My father was always reading up on new training or apprenticeships through X Auto, but they never took his applications.

I reached over and took a baseball off the nightstand and tossed it to myself in the dark. I waited for my parents to shut up, but they didn't. The noise they made was distracting. That low murmur in the background. I got up and felt around on my dresser until I found a cassette and put it into my alarm clock tape player. The red bars said it was 10:15. Cannonball Adderley clicked in. With Miles. "Somethin' Else."

Works for me.

A breeze?

It wasn't.

The heat settled in for good and I couldn't stop clenching and unclenching my fists.

The wood-panel walls were so dark that my room turned cave black at night, but a few things stood out against the darkness. My Miles Davis poster. My father was devoted to St. Trane, but I preferred Miles's growl. He just always sounded like he was playing angry – that fierce brass bell – but there was an ache in his music, too. This was a man who wouldn't come out of the rain. A man who would wreck his voice to make a point. I'd seen old pictures of Juliette Gréco. Grace and beautiful. He left her and Paris to come back to the U.S. to shoot up his life and beat on his wives. To play Detroit. To play Akawe on the way to Chicago. *Maybe I want something new,* I thought, *but I don't want his life.* I couldn't play the trumpet anyway. My father had bought me a pawn-shop trumpet for my tenth birthday. I'd tried it for an hour before tossing it in the closet. Now it had a lot of dust on it.

Miles's eyes were angled toward the far wall, so I rolled over to follow his gaze. It fell upon my Japanese fan, tilted out with slight formality. My mother had bought it for me at a flea market. It was her protest. She had gotten it after she'd had an argument with my father over a certain poster in my room. Not the Miles Davis poster.

The fan looked real. Was it? *Real what? Really a fan or really from Japan?* It was a cheap fan. *It probably isn't from Japan.* It was supposedly made from hinoki – cypress wood –

and tied together with string. Ivory white painted with a vibrant purple iris and tapering swords of grass. Right now, of course, they were just dark splashes on a glowing arc. For the first time, I thought about actually taking the fan off the wall and waving it in my face. I imagined how ridiculous that would look. *Anyone saw that, no one'd want a piece of me. Do I want someone to want a piece of me?* I imagined Kiara, her slick black hair wrapped back in a ponytail. Her cutting laughter. Her angry girl's chin. I imagined myself giving her my Japanese fan as a gift, her grateful appreciation. But she'd vanished on me, so fuck her. *She doesn't deserve my fan!*

My father's model airplanes hung four feet above me. World War II models with propellers. They were traveling far out over the world. Seeing things. Tunisia, Italy, France, the Philippines. Papua New Guinea. I couldn't see my father's attentive care in the dark. His perfect detailing. I saw silhouettes. Motionless propellers. *I wonder if O-Sugar would make someone jump from those planes.*

And then there was Strawberry Smash. This was the poster my parents had argued over. *Really, mother should have been more upset about Miles.* The poster pictured a glow of a woman in a bikini. She was at a bowling alley and her arm was swung back with a heavy ball in her grip. Ready to roll it toward the pins. "Strawberry Smash!" the poster said. You saw the girl from the angle of the lane. She was a terror, a blue-collar Kali with her tied hair, painted nails, sharp teeth, hungry eyes. Adam bought it for me as a joke for my twelfth birthday. My mother told me to take her down, but my father took my side and she stayed.

I had put the poster on the wall facing the foot of my bed. It was the last thing I saw before sleep each night, the first thing I saw each morning. She smiled cutthroat, but I imagined her lips pursed and blowing. A warm breeze, but cooling – any motion in that stillness meant relief – moving across my face and sweaty forehead. *Am I sweating now?* Smash didn't sweat at all. She hung there, permanently kinetic between lean and lunge. Only the ball and her backflung arm kept her from diving out of the poster and onto my bed. Dark as it was, I could see her shapes if I looked closely. I looked for a long time. *She would never leave me without even calling.* The heat was slowly building and building. Then, a mechanical snap and the tape player lapsed into silence.

"But I'll never meet you," I mumbled to Smash. *I want someone to want me*, I thought. *Do I want to want someone?*

Now the clock said it was after eleven. The house was quiet. My parents had finally gone to bed. I let out a slow breath, and stars crowded my vision. I felt like throwing up. I tugged at my undershirt, and it was soaked with sweat. I lifted it off anyway. I sat up in bed again, near the window.

I raised the screen and leaned out into the night. The air was as still outside as in, but at least I could hear interesting things. Cars boiling away in the heat. A wino giggling off on

South Street. The moths beating themselves against the sick yellow streetlights. A distant grumble of thunder. Right in front of me, our silver maple.

"Adam's a jackass," I said. "Who wants to rule Radcliffe Junior High?"

The leaves hung limp before me.

You have to get up in seven hours but you're standing here talking to a tree.

I took a deep breath and went back to my bed. I imagined the tree. I imagined my house, what it must look like from above. Shivering like a mirage. No, simmering. No sun up, so it would have to simmer in the vague glow of expressway lamps reflected down from mossy clouds. A matrix of suspended temperature. Nitrogen cycles. *Will they talk about that tomorrow?* The waste of Akawe. Human slag. The losses of a city untended. Dissolving into dirt. Burying itself. Bleeding out germfood, ammonia rot, and other pollutants. Carbon cycles. *Someday, the leaves will blow off the trees, and the trees will fall over and go down into the river. To the lake. The ocean. And in the ocean, the waves will heave and pitch and drive our trees to the heavy black bottom. They'll be buried there until death changes them into something dense and dark. The continents will shift, the drills will descend, and we'll draw forth black gold to fuel the cars Akawe makes in 200 million years.*

The ceiling seemed blue above me.

Everything seemed blue.

Not tonight, I thought. *Not right now.*

There had been times, throughout my life, when everything looked bluer than it should have.

I knew that only happened some of the time, because if it had been all of the time I would have thought that it was normal. Mostly, the feeling would come and go, fading in and out, vibrating, then dissolving. The older I got, the less often it happened. Kind of like dreams. Or, I mean, like nightmares.

And that's not a bad comparison, because, when I was little, most of my nightmares had been about blue things. Blue ghosts. Their images, blue and bluer, glowing, sometimes green, occasionally purple, but mostly blue. Our backyard – its vacant lots overgrown with young cottonwoods and cattails – trembled in blue expectation and blue leaves danced up from the dirt to alight upon the branches. Bright blue propeller seeds spun upward toward their mothers in the springtime. I was four then. It had been a really messed up year. We'd left Cartierul and moved onto Agit. My Aunt Ellie had died, and my father spiraled out of control for a while. Once, he whipped me for calling him "Mark."

And I remember standing in the driveway of our new house on the day my Aunt Mabel and my mother told my father that it was time for him to climb into the car he had bought with his own money – a car he had possibly helped build with his own two hands – so they could take him to a rehab center to dry himself out.

As I stood there, listening to the sound of my father crying and protesting through the window, along with the soft murmur of my mother's voice and Mabel's louder annoyance, I knew that the things around me had turned blue. The stuccoed paint of our house. Our neighbors' aluminum siding. The clouds in the sky and the pavement underfoot. I knew that I was seeing the world in a new way. Seeing old things made new again, so new that they glowed blue. The blues told me that life is motion. Time is travel. Loss is learning. It all felt like so much – this blue shivering – and I felt so dizzy that I had to lie down on the dusty back walk.

My father got into his car on the passenger side and my aunt drove him away.

"John," said my mother. "Why don't you come inside now?"

In the weeks that had followed, my mother quit smoking. She enrolled in classes at the community college to finish her Associates. I was studying too. I watched the blue rain climb back up into the clouds. I saw the blue lightning flashes that followed the undulating rolls of thunder. My mother made me sweet tea with lemon wedges, and the blue aftertaste buzzed on my tongue for hours.

The air had been cool that year. It had hummed with dark electricity. I could touch it and taste it, and it filled me with a fast, expanding fear of destruction. Late at night, the blue glow of the TV leaked out from my parents' room where my mother watched the news alone.

X Automotives to Close Benedict E, F
Cut 4,000 Akawe Jobs

Double-Homicide at West End Bar

Akawe Infant Mortality Rate Highest in the U.S.

I remembered all this.

And I must have been dreaming by then, because I also remembered something I had never experienced: the blue banshee cry of a passing freight train, sliding higher and higher, and a boy, falling through blue, story after story, and crashing into a concrete parking lot. I suddenly woke, gasping for air like I'd been under water for way too long.

"Why would they jump?" I asked out loud.

10

When morning came, it stirred me with goose bumps and cool air breathing through the ripped window screen. The sky had just started to purple in the east. Out in the grass, mist became dew. A breath of honeysuckle. It was six o'clock. *It's the first day of junior high!*

I got out of bed, put on some jeans and a t-shirt, and opened the door. I heard low voices from my parents' bedroom, so I hurried past, down to the kitchen, and poured myself a cup of coffee from the carafe my father kept in the fridge. They didn't like me to drink coffee, but I liked it, and after a restless night, I needed it. I finished the mug in one bitter gulp. *In less than two hours, I'll be there.*

I hurried into the downstairs bathroom. Locked the lock. Ran the water. *Everything has to be perfect.* I was in there for a long time. I got out and looked at myself in the mirror. I forced my hair to part on the side then rubbed in plenty of gel to keep it that way. My face looked okay. There wasn't much I could do about my fat lips, so I practiced holding them in to make them look thinner. Biting my lower lip between my teeth. It worked but I couldn't smile. That was okay. I didn't smile much anyway. *Should I smile? What will people think if I don't smile enough? What will they think if I smile too much? They'll probably think,* that dude has fat lips.

My mother knocked on the door. "John?" she said. "I have to get on the road just a few minutes after you. Could you hurry up in there?"

"It's the first day of school," I said. "Sorry, but you knew that."

"I was trying to be polite," she said. "It wasn't a question."

I put on chapstick and deodorant. I still didn't have any of my own cologne, so I rubbed on some of my father's. Musk, it was called. At first, I couldn't smell it on myself, so I put on some more. Then my hands smelled musky, so I washed them and washed them again. My mother started banging on the door.

"Okay!" I said. "Jesus."

"You're welcome, your highness," she said, coughing as I passed her.

"Breakfast is just about ready," called my father from the kitchen.

"I'm not." I wasn't.

"It'll get cold!"

"Good! It's getting hot out!"

I hurried back to my room and got dressed. I'd figured this part out the day before. I put on a black polo shirt and some thick brown cords. I wasn't an athletic-looking kid, so I figured the best I could do was to look serious and grown-up. Like it would offset my shortness, right?

Why did they jump? I wondered again. The question distracted me from my other doubts. *It couldn't have been suicide. Not for five of them at once. That's like some horror movie shit. It had to be the drug that made them do it. But what kind of drug would make a bunch of people so crazy they'd do something like that?*

I unpacked and repacked my backpack to make sure that everything was there and sorted right: the frosted blue space maker with scavenged pens and pencils, Flexgrip Ultras, Sharpies, and a couple yellow highlighters. Paper clips, paper punch, protractor and compass, stapler, calculator, padlock, erasers, transparent tape, index cards, and playing cards. My five-subject Wired, college-ruled, rigel blue. My Celestial Seasonings, Earl Gray black. The olive-colored JanSport backpack my Grandmother Richter had bought me as an early birthday present, even though I'd told her I had wanted the black one.

"John!" called my father. "Hurry up!"

Smoking gets you cancer and booze gets you drunk, he had told me many times. *Pot gets you sleepy and smack gets you dead.*

I put on the backpack.

I guess O-Sugar gets you out-of-control. But shit's out of control to begin with. Who needs a drug to make it worse? Who wants that? I don't want that. I want what I want. I want what I want. I want what I want.

"Fuck O-Sugar," I said.

I looked at myself in the mirror. The look worked, especially because the shirt and cords ran well with the backpack. *They're all earth tones.* But I wasn't done yet. I still had to pick out a pair of sunglasses. I had a lot of reasons to wear sunglasses. Sonny Rollins wore them. So did Tom Cruise. It was still summer, so they wouldn't look out of place. If I could get away with wearing them inside, it would make it easier for me to hide any nervousness. *I'm not nervous,* I told myself. Plus, sunglasses would make me mysterious. Everything about me would be memorable. Distinctive yet distant and unphased. I finally settled on a set with dim gray lenses set into bright green frames. It would go with my backpack. It would be like the emerald sunglasses that Nero wore when he watched the gladiators fight to the death. *I am nervous...*

"Why am I worrying?" I asked myself. "It doesn't get me anything. Why not enjoy it? We're all gonna die anyway."

I looked at myself in the mirror a moment longer, because once I left, I wouldn't see myself again until after I had been a seventh grader for a day.

I pocketed my sunglasses and went down to breakfast.

11

Outside, some sparrows scratched for sunflower seeds among the shells my father had left scattered in the dirt. I shifted my weight, adjusted my backpack. It was too full and I didn't even have textbooks yet. The sun was up now and if the morning twilight had given some relief from the smothering heat, the air was already billowing out into another white blister of a day.

I walked up the hill to Whitmore Road. On the corner, the gravel parking lot of Sal's Tires was empty. Across the street, no lights on in the boxy wooden bungalows, but I did see a little kid in a second story window looking out at an overturned red wagon in his dusty front yard. A Radio Flyer. The kid looked at me. I put on my Nero shades and looked back. He waved. I turned south onto Whitmore. I wasn't waiting for a bus. Radcliffe Junior High was just a five-minute walk from my front door.

If I had asked, my father probably would have given me a ride. But 1993 was the year when X Auto would finally put the Benedict Honor out of its misery, and I'd rather walk to school than arrive in a craptastic geriatric car like that. X Auto was in the middle of a do-over, frantically trying to paint over the wreckage of the last decade's mistakes. The heavy Benedicts sputtered along, unable to settle on any vision or style, to choose between wealthy retirees and class-conscious boomers.

Aubrey and Starr made a dozen or so compact models, but none of them did well against the imports. And the legendary Valentine division – the "I'm loaded" cars – was still waiting for people to forget the Memento, its shitty compact executive model that had been born and died in the 80s.

A lot of people were fed up with the American automakers right then, but nobody was as pissed off as we were in Akawe. Line-workers, who took the blame for shitty quality instead of the suits and engineers, railed against XAWU, the X Autoworkers Union, for failing to link up with the UAW and get them a better deal. *Organize! Organize!* Not that the UAW was doing much better with its Other Three. Plants closed. Manufacturing musical chairs. By 1993, more than half of Akawe's X workforce had been slashed. 50,000 jobs gone.

I passed another dozen bungalows, their own sloppy piles of trash spilling out onto the road.

On the other hand, we had a Democratic president for a change. He was already planning to take on health care reform. For a year, the economy had been getting better – everywhere but Michigan, at least – and the auto industry *had* to bounce back at some point. Right? With all the colleges in Akawe – Southern Michigan U, the X Automotives Institute, Akawe Community College – there was even some hope that manufacturing might morph into high technology, and then *we'd* lead the march toward the New Economy.

But I mostly had other things on my mind. People wrote books. I was way beyond *Goosebumps* and *Fear Street* by now, but Toni Morrison may have been a step too far. According to some Norwegians, she gave life to an "essential aspect of American reality," and so my mother bought me a copy of *Jazz*. She also wanted to take me to see *Schindler's List* when it came out, and I could just tell that that was going to be a fun night. But *The Fugitive* had made me lean forward in my seat, and *Jurassic Park* had blown my mind.

"Holy shit!" Adam had yelled when the T-Rex ate the lawyer. He pissed off half the audience, but the other half laughed.

I passed "Ernest's Earnest Transmission," with an ancient sign for 9-2-12 Electrics.

The Tigers swung a winning season. U of M had just barely lost to North Carolina in the Big Dance, and I was still dancing to Janet and Michael, but only in my bedroom with the door and curtains shut. When Dizzy Gillespie died, my father hired a trumpeter from the plant and invited a dozen of his buddies over for a small wake. I listened to my father's old cassettes – bop and cool jazz mostly – but my friends were listening to different music and, here and there, I caught that too. Bill Chapman, my oldest friend, liked Genesis. Quanla liked TLC and Elizabeth liked ICP. Adam was into scuzzy rap and Ace of Base. My father had told me just about everything I knew about music, but it was Adam who gave me mix and radio tapes with Domino and Snoop Doggy Dogg, Dr. Dre and Ice Cube, Kriss Kross and House of Pain. The Red Hot Chili Peppers. I didn't know these groups really well – which song matched up to which singer – but I knew some of their hits, like *Whoomp! Run to you. Said I loved you, but I lied. Love shoulda brought you home*, but have you heard *both sides of the story?* And DJ Jazzy Jeff with Will Smith, the Fresh Prince. A lot of my friends had started getting CD players and Adam and I got them to give us their cassette tapes instead of throwing them away.

Once a week, I wanted to be a kid again and watched *Animaniacs*. Late at night, Conan O'Brien made my mother laugh, but he annoyed the shit out of me. We didn't have cable, so my father didn't get to see a *Star Trek* space station, but he could see an underwater "space station." *Star Fox* was the coolest shit I'd played since *Battletoads*, but Rosa Farrell was still the hottest.

The sun shined full in my face.

Global Warming came up once or twice in sixth grade. Computers learned to talk to each other over a phone line, which was... weird. Romania continued to shift democracy along its shoulders. The Czech Republic and Slovakia politely got a divorce. The split-up of Yugoslavia was a lot less amicable. Sierra Leone. Algeria and Somalia. Afghanistan. Tajikistan. The Rwandan Civil War wrapped up, so that was nice. I knew about these things because my mother talked about them at her "job" then brought them home to work through at our dining-room table. Afterward David Koresh torched his congregation and some asshole decided to bomb the World Trade Center. So yeah, there had been frictions, factions, crimes, dramas, and strifes, but in '93 they were local and limited. Like everyone was busy sorting out their part of a big tangled mess, and *no worries, we'll sort it out.*

Akawe did make national news that summer when a man threw his brother's severed head into a reflecting pool right as the opening night of *Madame Butterfly* was letting out next door. But over all, our poorness, our violence, our confusion wasn't high on anyone's list of priorities. America was watching TV and discovering a brave new world of denim and flannel and bomber jackets and gypsy tops. Most kids I knew wanted to be rapping Angelinos or dirty Seattlites. They worshiped the sun and the rain, respectively. That was 1993.

We forget the little things. The bulbous cars, the posturing raps, the global calm or "calm," but these little things, moment by moment – that's what made it what it was. 1993 is still too close, too recent, for me to really say that I understand it. Maybe in a few years, in the new millennium, I'll be able to tie these strands together and hang some meaning on them. But right now I still don't know what they're all about.

12

The school was three stories high with pointy arches and windows and took up an entire city block. Red and purple bricks, steaming in the sun, extended on either side of a jawed entryway at the base of two turrets. Fat battlements blunted the turrets against the sky. Behind the sprawling school was its just-as-sprawling parking lot and, across the next street, a bunch of shoebox satellite classrooms they'd built right before the district's enrollment went down the toilet. A few of the windows were covered with plywood.

I had heard, from Adam and Chuck, from my father and Aunt Mabel, that there were secrets under the school. Tunnels and pipes and cellars. Rusted ladders linking basement to roof and gray catwalk mazes that connected attic crawl spaces. Seventeen hidden hives and paper wasp combs. Seven cabinets stocked with Mercurochrome. Between the crusted boilers, a catacomb, and, further on, caverns that joined the school to the sewers.

I walked right up to the entrance. The heavy dark wood doors, pen and pocketknife scarred, had been flung wide. The halls beyond boiled with hundreds of students. But first I had to walk through a second gateway – a faded plastic metal detector – as an already tired-looking security guard looked on. *I'm going to school*, I thought. *I guess I'm going to battle.*

I walked through. The machine immediately beeped.

"Try again," said the guard.

I backed up and walked through again. The machine beeped at me. *Is it the staples or the paperclips or the compass? I wondered. Is it the padlock?* The guard was waving his hand impatiently. A line of kids was starting to stack up behind me.

"Hurry up, retard!" one of them yelled.

I took off my backpack and started fumbling for the zipper.

"Just go, just go!" said the guard.

I slipped my backpack on again and went in, joining the crowd.

13

I found Room 127B at the end of a narrow, windowless hall where a single fluorescent light flickered feebly in the darkness. I had to make my way by running my hand along the wall. I was late but I wasn't the only one. There were only about twenty kids in the room and no sign of the teacher.

I spotted Adam right away, sitting on a desk, kicking his feet. Chuck leaned up against a wall next to him, and Elizabeth sat in one of the chairs. Adam's hair was different than it had been yesterday. Now it was a thin, pink, bubblegum color.

"What the hell did you do to your hair?" I asked.

"I did it with Kool Aid!" Adam answered.

"Why pink? People're going to think you're a faggot."

"That's what I told him," said Chuck. Tall, lean, and sullen, with an angular face, dark black skin, and his head shaved almost bald, Chuck was the one-of-these-things-is-not-like-the-others in our group. He was my best friend after Adam. Chuck didn't speak a lot. He made his words count.

"Some guys might think I'm a faggot," said Adam. "But I'm not trying to impress dudes. I'm trying to impress bitches."

"I'm impressed," said Elizabeth sarcastically. She was a white girl, tall, lanky, awkward, with big hips and thick calves. Kids laughed at her, at the black bristles that stood out on her pale arms and legs. She had long, messy hair and watery blue eyes. Not Adam's type by a mile.

"See what I mean?" Adam said.

By now it was five minutes past bell, and most of the kids were waiting at their desks, but the chalkboard had a smooth, untraveled look to it. The closet door hung open, and inside it was dark and empty. It didn't look like anyone had been in this classroom since last spring.

"Where's the teacher?" I asked.

They shrugged.

"Mr. Kolin, right? Science?"

"Or somethin'," said Chuck.

I sat down.

"Adam —" I began.

"The Plan!" he said. "You *in?*"

The world opened up to me then. I saw, all at once, that the plan was so much smaller than everything I wanted and yet so much bigger than anything I had planned myself. I'd caught some hints in Miles's glare from my wall as he played, in Strawberry Smash's feral grin, and in the cautionary tale of five teens who'd handed their free will over to a new drug. I didn't want anyone or anything ruling over me. I had to start somewhere.

"Why be a prince when you can be a king?" I asked him back.

"Schwing!" Adam answered. "You're awesome, John. You da man."

"What are you talking about?" asked Elizabeth.

"Nothing," I said.

Chuck's silence was noisy with questions.

Adam sat down next to me.

"The hard part," he muttered, "is knowing who's in eighth grade and who's just coming from the other elementaries. We got seventh graders from Truman, Wilson, and Anderson here."

"So wait, won't your plan work with popular seventh graders?"

"No! Because the popular eighth graders lord it over the popular seventh graders. But if we date and dump popular eighth graders, ain't nobody gonna lord it over us."

"So how was your summer, Adam?" asked Elizabeth.

"It was great!" Adam said, almost yelling. "John and I were ho hunters. Weren't we, John?"

Over the summer, Adam and I had spent one morning calling random numbers in the phone book, telling people that we were "pimps in practice," that we'd collect a bounty on "hos on probation," and generally smack a bitch if she got lippy when she was delivered into our careful custody. Then, Adam had put on his older sister's fake furs, so she kicked us out of her apartment. It wasn't a situation I much wanted to explain.

"There were Indians," rapped Adam. "They called them Arapaho. But John and me, we always smack a ho."

Chuck glared at me. I shook my head. I looked around the classroom. Nobody else was noticing my ass of a friend. They were all in their own loud conversations. Without a teacher, people broke out their cards for poker and blackjack, got up, walked around, laughed, and told jokes. A few kids got up and left. A girl went and sat on the teachers' desk while her friend braided her hair. Two boys climbed onto their desks and started removing the ceiling panels, one by one, while other kids watched the deconstruction.

"Do you spell it H-O or H-O-E?" Elizabeth asked. "Because I'm never sure."

"A ho's a ho, that's all I know," Adam answered.

"Man, shut up!" said Chuck.

"Chuck Chuck, cluck cluck, you're just pissed because I didn't invite you to be a part of my plan!"

"What has he had to eat today?" asked Elizabeth. "Pure sugar?"

"Sugar with a side of crack," I said.

"No doubt," said Chuck.

"Naw," said Adam. "I had ginseng and cocaine with my Frosted Flakes."

Chuck stepped forward and punched Adam three times in the shoulder. Adam started laughing, but then winced and clutched his side.

"Damn, Chuck, that hurt!" he said.

Chuck, quiet as he was, had earned a red belt from a dojo in the Os, and he never stopped reminding us.

These were my Truman Elementary friends. Over the years, as the other kids had all left Agit Street one family at a time, as I went to church less often and lost touch with the nursery school kids, these three friends had stayed front-and-center for me: Adam Miller, Chuck Coppo, and Elizabeth Furrier. It was perfect that we all shared the same science class.

"What plan you keep talkin' about?" Chuck asked.

"I don't want to tell you," said Adam, rubbing his shoulder.

"You do want to tell me," said Chuck. "That's why you said it in the first place."

Adam explained the Plan.

"Adam, you're retarded," said Chuck. "John, I didn't think you'd go along with this shit."

I shrugged. "I'm ready for a change, you know?"

Elizabeth didn't answer. She put her hands on her desk, and put her chin on her hands, and studied us.

14

In second hour, in Mrs. Anders' lit class, I ran into Selby Demnescu.

"John," she said. "It's been a time! Whassup?"

Selby and her four brothers and sisters had been my neighbors down in Cartierul. When I was four, my family moved and her family stayed behind. Nobody really got their family tree, including Selby, but there was enough African in her that she got followed through stores by security. The Demnescus were Romanian too, and her parents had spoken Romanian at home until her dad died in a construction accident, again when I was four. And then their neighbors whispered that they had some Romani – gypsy – blood, which seemed to be more of an issue in the neighborhood than their African history. It was a weird situation, the Demnescus and the Cartierul Romanians.

Selby had pale brown skin, slight eyebrows, and deep set eyes – serious, dark eyes – and actual breasts. She was a little thick around the waist, yeah; the kind of seventh grade girl a seventh grade boy would notice. But everyone noticed her voice. It was horrible. Old winos living under the bridge had smoother voices than Selby, which was strange, because when I thought back to when Selby was a little kid, I never remembered her having had a rough voice.

"Stuck around here all summer," I said. "Watched some TV. Hung out with Adam. We got a plan."

"What do you mean you got a plan?"

"Got a plan to get down some girls' pants."

"Ha!" Confidence and anger. "John, you're hilarious. You're full of shit."

"Wait and see."

"Maybe you should stop scarfing Twinkies if you want to be a playa."

"You ain't skinny neither!"

"I ain't trying to get in nobody's pants, but I still could if I wanted. You'll try and try, but it won't get you nowhere. Trying just don't work."

"Sorry. I don't mean to sound like an asshole."

"Don't say you're sorry. You're just being who you are."

"Selby!" came a voice from across the classroom, honey to Selby's gravel. "C'mere. What's the fight? What's the deal with John?"

It was Quanla Adams. Another friend from Truman. She was cute enough, a slim black girl with her long hair usually tied back. The main thing I noticed about her were her huge, expressive eyes. I figured that Old Testament prophetesses had to have had eyes like that: terrifying because they saw so much. Quanla's eyes had seen a lot of movies. She was obsessed with them. Especially horror movies where the virgins survive, but the promiscuous kids have their entrails slowly pulled out through gaping wounds as they helplessly watch and wail.

"I ain't sayin'," said Selby, and she stood up and crossed to sit next to Quanla.

But I didn't want Quanla to know anything about the plan. Quanla seemed pure and clean to me. Selby was something else. *Shit! They tell each other everything.*

"Just kidding, Selby," I said. "I went to a few Tigers games. With my parents. That's all I've been doing."

"Whatever, John," said Selby. Quanla shook her head at me.

Mrs. Anders was talking now. She was a slight black woman with graying hair. She stood ruler straight. All business. The classroom of thirty kids sat mostly quiet, although Selby and Quanla managed to whisper occasionally. Mrs. Anders' own hard voice, her stern eyes, gave rules for covered textbooks, for cursive writing, for attendance and papers and answers and essays. "You'll have three hall passes per semester, but you can earn another pass for each marking period without any missing homework." Humanities and divinities. "You should complete your reading assignments by Friday so that you can focus on your homework over the weekend. I won't give a lot of homework during the week. Mostly just reading." The kouroi in the gym and the korai whispering in the corner. "If cars and trains and airplanes had hands and were able to draw with their hands and do the same things as men, cars would dig out the shapes of gods to look like cars, and trains would dig them to look like trains, and each would make the gods' bodies have the same shape as they themselves had."

Mrs. Anders stood chalkboard erect before young men and women and would have neither prevail unrighteously over their homework. *How the hell is this just one class?! This is an insane amount of reading!*

Meanwhile, Selby and Quanla whispered in the corner, and I worried about what they might be saying.

15

Third hour was a wash. Gym class. Not only were there not any eighth graders to scope out – there weren't any girls at all. My guess was that a lot of these dirty kids had skid marks on their Hanes. I wasn't looking forward to finding out during showers. That's the last I'll say about that.

On the other hand, fourth hour math with Mrs. Norman was something else. After welcoming us she started giving us a history lesson. Nothing about pluses and minuses and *x*es and *y*s. She told us about Thales who lived in 600 B.C. and thought that earthquakes might be caused when large waves struck the floating earth.

"Space," Thales said, "is the greatest thing. It contains all things." The glowing Pyramids of Giza that rose high threw gloomy shadows past Thales. How tall was the summit? Seeing that his own shadow was about as long as he was tall, Thales realized that the same must be true of the pyramids. He could figure out their height by pacing out the length of their shadows.

"This was the beginning of geometry," said Mrs. Norman.

It was the first class I shared with any eighth graders – *Will eighth graders in remedial math be more gullible?* – but I realized I'd have to study them carefully so I didn't seem like a staring creep. I was sitting in the last row, so I could see everyone, but they all had their backs to me. They were all quiet and still, listening to Mrs. Norman talk.

"Unfortunately," she said, "we won't be able to take much time to talk about Thales or Archimedes or Pythagoras in this class." Each year, most of Mrs. Norman's students had come from schools that were far behind in their math curriculum; we would have to spend the first six weeks reviewing everything we were supposed to have covered in sixth grade. Then, in the winter, we'd have to spend another six weeks preparing for the Michigan Educational Assessment Program. Mrs. Norman encouraged us to go to the library and check out a book on early Greek mathematics.

"I know you probably won't," she said, "but I like to let my students know that math began with storytelling and questions."

16

The day was half over, and so far, nothing catastrophic had happened. We hadn't sorted ourselves into new cliques yet. There were too many strangers here, and the many divides we'd glimpsed at the end of elementary school – black homes, white homes, whole homes, fractured homes, big homes and cookie-cutters – were all erased for the moment by uncertainty. The seventh graders walked down the halls wearing expressions of generic anger and anxiety, glances voguing from side-to-side like the eyeballs of carnival skulls. Our posturing was so generic that it was tough to tell us apart.

When I got to lunch, I found Selby and Quanla at a long table near the entrance.

"Can I sit with you?" Quanla was asking.

"Better than my brother," Selby said.

I sat down as well. They noticed me, barely; I caught a glimpse out of Quanla's eye. They got out their sack lunches, and I realized I hadn't packed mine. *I'm an idiot.*

"John, don't you have lunch?" Selby asked.

"I forgot it," I said.

"Want my apple?"

"No thanks. I ain't hungry."

"John," Quanla was saying. "You were supposed to call me this summer. We were gonna go see *Jason Goes to Hell*, remember?"

"Sorry, I forgot. Things were messed up with... with Adam."

"They were?"

"Yeah. CPS finally took him from his dad's."

"What about his sisters?"

"What about them? I mean, Carla's got her own apartment. I think Ophelia stays over there most days."

"Doesn't Adam stay with them too?"

"No, he's living with his grandpa now. Most of the time, I mean."

"Which grandpa? The policeman?"

I laughed, dully. "No, the racist."

"Oh." Quanla shook her head.

"Who's racist?" Adam asked, setting down a can of pop.

"Your Grandpa Miller," I said.

"Yup. Racist like Tennessee. Not like Mississippi"

"Same difference," said Quanla.

"Word. John, we sitting here?"

I looked at Selby, at Quanla. "That okay?"

"It's fine with me," Adam said. "Watch my shit, I gotta go stand in line."

Adam left.

"Is he okay?" Selby asked.

"It's nothing new," I said. "It's always something with Adam."

Quanla rolled her eyes in an exaggerated sort of way.

"I don't know why you even waste time with him," she said. "He's just a little creep who loves to act like he got game, but he ain't got none."

"You see his hair's pink?" asked Selby.

"It's kind of hard to miss," I said.

"You spend a lot of time together," Quanla said. "Like you're boyfriends. No, you didn't forget to call *Adam* last summer."

"Nope," I said. "He's a good little bitch."

Selby snorted.

"Now I think of it," Quanla said, "you didn't call me neither, Selby."

Selby set down her food.

"My mom was keepin' me home," she said. "Anyway, I'll have more time soon. My ballet scholarship didn't get renewed for this fall. I won't be dancing no more."

"What?! You can't quit!"

"I can't do nothing about it. I don't got no money for that class."

"Man, that's bogus. Well look, hey, we gotta go down to Detroit, because Darius has a friend there, and his dad's opening a restaurant, and they're gonna have music at it – like live music – and they're gonna get us in free."

Chuck sat down silent across from me and started eating. He spread a napkin in front of him. He took out a plastic knife, an orange jelly packet, and two slices of toast. Chuck was obsessed with toast.

"I bet that makes Darius happy," I said, "having to drag you two along with him."

"Nothing makes Darius happy, 'cause he don't have a girlfriend."

"Do you gotta girlfriend, John?" asked Chuck.

"'Course John don't have a girlfriend," said Selby. "You ain't skinny, John."

Chuck grinned.

I turned to Quanla.

"So, what, you're not inviting me? What kind of music?"

Quanla grinned and eyed Chuck. "Hey Chuck, you want to go to Detroit with Selby and me?"

"No thanks," said Chuck.

"Oh, fuck off," I said.

"Don't tell me that!"

"When we gonna go?" asked Selby.

"I don't know," said Quanla. "See, I haven't asked my parents about it yet. I'd like to go on a weekend sometime later this month."

"Just make sure you tell me first. My mom's making me do cross-stitching with her, and I need to make sure we won't be doing that."

"You're gonna pass up dinner with me and Darius for cross-stitching?!"

"You know if I tried to go, she'd just lock me in my room. You know how she gets."

"Bitchy," mouthed Quanla.

"This summer we did three motherfucking quilts! It took forever. I think she got up every night and undid them so we'd have to start over in the morning."

Nobody spoke. They all ate their food. I ate nothing.

"Well," said Quanla. "My summer was good, at least. In July we went up to Muskegon, and we went along the lake. That was fun. We were in the town, and I saw this boy who looked like Denzel Washington. I was fanning myself as he went running by."

This caught Selby's interest. "He went running by?"

"He was running a race or something."

"Fast enough to run from Selby?" I asked.

Selby glared.

"Selby and Quanla run fast enough to get away from you and Adam?" Chuck asked.

"Shut up, Chuck!"

"What is he talking about?" asked Quanla.

Chuck smiled and wiped the crumbs from his mouth.

"Nothing," I said.

Quanla glared at me, misunderstanding. Which was fine with me: I wasn't sure how these two girls I'd known my whole life would feel about Adam's plan.

"John and Adam have a plan," said Chuck.

"Shut up!" I said.

But Chuck told them everything, and Quanla punched me in the shoulder.

"You can go to hell," she said. "We don't need friends like you, John. Or friends like you Chuck, who snitch on their own friends."

Chuck shrugged an elaborate shrug that he turned into a stretch, and folded his arms behind his head.

"Anyway," Quanla went on, "we got all these older boys, to choose from. We've got eighth grade boys, ninth grade boys, tenth grade boys." She stabbed her palm with her index finger for each number she passed. "Maybe we can find some older boys, who won't be dipshits when they come over from the high schools."

"What they gonna come over here for?!" I asked.

"To pick up their brothers and sisters, dipshit! In their cars! 'Cause they can drive! C'mon Selby, we shouldn't have let him sit with us. Let's get away from these boys that keep chasing all the other boys away."

"Bye," I said.

They left.

I glared at Chuck.

I didn't hit him because Chuck could kick my ass.

Around us, the cafeteria raged with noise, laughter, jokes, and shouts, but I still heard a soft, heavy voice from the table right behind me.

"I'ma spit your food, faggot."

A large lanky black kid leaned over a chubby white kid sitting at the table behind us. The big kid growled the saliva up his throat like he was about to hoc a loogie, but he laughed instead.

"That your cousin?" asked Chuck in a low voice.

I nodded. The sitting kid was, indeed, Michael, my cousin, chubby cheeks and sunspot freckles and curly, putti hair.

"The other kid's Jay Flighting," I said. "He's from my hood. We all fucking hate him. He trashed Adam's bike and broke his finger once."

"Damn."

"Yeah, his dad died burning down a crackhead's house, but don't say nothin' about it. He'll fucking kill you and light your corpse on fire. He's crazy, man."

"Go away," we heard Michael whine. "I'm eating."

"Eat my spit, faggot," said Jay.

I couldn't see it, but from the sounds and the disgusted look on Chuck's face, it was easy to picture what was happening: a bead of cloudy saliva falling from Jay's mouth and landing in a blob on Michael's spaghetti. I looked over my shoulder in time to see Jay laugh and leave the cafeteria. None of the monitors seemed to have noticed what had happened, but Michael caught my eye. I shrugged and turned back to

Chuck. I could hear my cousin picking his tray up and throwing it in the trash.

Adam got back with his own tray full of spaghetti.

"I thought we were eating with Selby and Quanla?" he said.

"They didn't like the Plan," I said.

"You told *them* about the Plan?!"

"Chuck did."

Adam spluttered for a minute, waving his arms around like semaphore. Then he spotted Selby and Quanla, two tables away.

"Selby! Quanla! I'm sorry about our Plan! I hope you know I love you very much!"

They ignored him.

Adam went on: "Chuck's just mad 'cause I was with his mom all night, and the bed kept thumping the floor, woke him up. Thump thump thump!"

Chuck grabbed the back of Adam's shirt and pulled him down.

"Shut up about my momma."

"Ow! Jesus!" Adam rubbed his neck. "That's the second time you hurt me today, Chuck. Anyway." He started eating. "While I was in line, I figured out who I'm going after. She's got to be in eighth grade, and man, she's hot."

"So who is it?"

"Blonde girl, tall, alone, halfway up your side. Just don't stare too hard. I don't want her to see us yet."

I knew who he meant as soon as I saw her. White girl. She was reading a paperback and her long, straight hair fell back, a rich honey-gold, like out of a magazine, her face narrow. She wore slim blue jeans and a tank top, and her skin was a bit browned from the summer sun. She leaned forward. Tiny glasses perched on the tip of her nose. *She looks lonely,* I thought. I couldn't have guessed her age, but she seemed much older than me.

Chuck laughed out loud.

"Hey," snapped Adam, "don't laugh at me. I'll get with her. I got further than you have."

"Not with her," said Chuck.

"I'll get her number this week."

"No, you won't."

"I'll put on some moves. Tell her how beautiful she is. I'll promise her a lot of fun! She's not worried about my age. She loves me!" Adam was on his feet, actually angry. His face was turning the same color as his hair.

"No, she doesn't."

"Why not?!"

"Sit down, you... short... asshole! You want to know why? I'll tell you, Adam. Her name is Sara Lupu, and yeah, she's in eighth grade. For the second time, in fact. See, I know because my cousin Kerm has been obsessed with her three years. And if that ain't enough to make you piss your pants, think about this: Last year the police caught Sara Lupu up on the roof of the school at night. Your girl, Adam – she was up there getting her freak on with another girl!"

17

After lunch, I went off to my Foreign Languages class with Miss Mika in a bright room on the third floor where water dripped from an orange-stained ceiling panel into a bright yellow bucket.

Miss Mika seated us alphabetically, so I was at the back of the first row. Far from the teacher, close to the windows. Near the front of the third row sat Sara Lupu. She spoke with a friend who had big curves, copper-colored hair, freckles, glasses. Way more my speed than Sara. But I had no idea what to do about it, and I had no idea what Adam thought he was going to do, either. Everyone who had hooked up at Truman had known each other for years. *How do you hook up with someone you've never even met before?* I mean, it obviously happened all the time. *But how?*

"¡Hola!" said Miss Mika like she was yawning for a doctor. "Mulishani." "Γειά σας." "你好." "Yo quiero..."

Drip went the water into the bucket.

After that, I was back in Mrs. Anders' class for Language Arts, which was interrupted by a middle-aged black woman in a floral dress. She walked in carrying a pile of books for Mrs. Anders and gave her a lingering kiss on the cheek before leaving again. Gasps and giggles all around, while Mrs. Anders glared at the woman, her hands shaking with pale anger.

Finally, with six out of seven classes murdered, I left the school and got on the stuffy-hot bus to ride over to Beckford Junior High on the East Side for my Social Studies magnet with Ms. Ropoli.

18

Just one other Radcliffe kid followed me through the halls to Room 121.   The desks ran down one edge of the room, along the back, and up the other side in a U formation two rows deep, so that the middle of the room was open.

Every inch of wall was covered by the flags of many nations and states (but no sign of Ohio's burgee), travel advertisements, and posters. Kaleidoscopic corals waved in the salty swell. The Lake of the Clouds reflected the back the sky. A dense mass of nshima steamed on a porcelain plate. A cluster of laughing children followed puppets along Sighișoaran parapets, the river foamed up through the Tarbela, the blue depths of Tahoe hid its bodies, and spotted desert sheep slipped along the sudan. Hans Nursamat climbed the Matterhorn, an antique aqua hatchback sweltered in the streets of Punta del Este, fog licked the trunks of California redwoods, and healers sat with handmade drums outside of Great Zimbabwe. Below Ulm Minster, the Danube ran cold but still not as frigid as winter on the Altiplano. Sorcerous salt crusted the bleak shore of Antelope Island and Ojibwa dancers swung in motion in the tall grass of Wanuskewin. The Pyrenees rose stark and sublime over the haunted pirates' castles of Languedoc. And then: a lima-bean green Valentine Avalon guzzled gas down Avenida Francisco de Miranda in Caracas. A young punk sucked a broad stein of beer froth in the Black

Forest. Javier Méndez hit a homer. A happy panda. The Parthenon soaked in alabaster light by night. Devil's Tower loomed over an ocean of Ponderosa pines. The Pantheon and El Capitan. UOB Plaza. Solfatara. Bank of China Tower. Volcano. Tokyo Tower. Stromboli. Woodmen Tower.

And when the walls had become too crowded to hold any more of Ms. Ropoli's posters and flags, they spilled upward, onto the ceiling, stapled to the foam panels: Scott's Hut, the glittering depths of a Hohburg Hills rhyolite quarry, and the foamy mist that hung above the polished gemmy surface of the Champagne Pool.

The windows were open and a breeze from outside carried in the tricky scent of close-mowed grass mingled with the subtle acid of particulated plastic; the Starville exterior paint plant was just one block away.

I heard someone rummaging in a closet to the right of the doorway. A petite white woman emerged, maybe in her late twenties, wearing a black blouse and gray skirt, with black eyes and dark hair with red highlights. She set a couple of jewel cases on her desk.

"You're late," she said.

"The bus was late," I said.

"I'm Ms. Ropoli. Who are you?"

"John Bridge."

The other kid murmured something.

"Speak up!" Ms. Ropoli barked. "Can't hear ya."

The kid repeated himself.

"Great to meet ya, John, Terrell. Go ahead and sit down."

The window seats were already taken, so we sat across the room. Ms. Ropoli stepped into the center.

"Excuse me, excuse me. Hey, listen!"

The class quieted.

"Great. Thanks. So you're seventh graders. What do you think?"

Silence for a moment. "Sucks!" said a boy.

"Great, well that's a start. Okay, now we are expressing ourselves. Anyone else?"

A little nervous laughter. Otherwise, silence.

"Well, it's nice to see you are all... withholding judgment until you have more perspective. That's good. Perspective is important in my class. So is expressing yourself... important. And not rudely or anything like that, no, but what you think. Right?"

Nobody spoke.

"Well, that's too bad," she said. "You have to learn to... um, articulate your thoughts a bit better if we are to continue. Anyway, I do have rules. I'll tell you most of them tomorrow. Don't be lazy. That's one. No slouching. That's another. 'Leaning' looks good for daydreaming, but I think it's just a half-assed kind of lying down. But today you can talk and just try to stay cool from this heat and get to know each other better. Talk, talk, talk! And relax."

The class broke into clamor. Ms. Ropoli turned on several oscillating fans, two directed toward the classroom and a smaller one on her desk. Then she noticed the jewel cases.

"Wait, wait, wait!" she said. "I'm sorry, I forgot to ask. Should we listen to the Moody Blues or Pink Floyd today?"

I wonder if I could try the Plan out on her, I thought.

"John Bridge," she said. "No slouching!"

19

I still don't remember exactly why I decided to walk home instead of taking the bus. Looking back, I wonder if the day had just been so full of sounds and smells that a sweaty bus ride back to Radcliffe would've pushed me over the edge. Then again, I knew that my parents would be asking me a thousand questions as soon as I got home, and this was my only chance to process the day alone: I didn't care about the classes, I hadn't made a fool of myself, but I didn't know what it all *meant* and I didn't know what to *do* either. *How am I even going to meet an eighth-grader, whether it's Sara's friend or somebody completely different?*

I had only gone a block when I realized I had made a mistake: it was too hot for walking, but the buses had already left. This was the kind of trip I only ever made on wheels. It had never seemed like much of a distance that way. Now that I was on foot, I realized that I had miles to go.

I crossed the parking, leaving both Beckford and the Starville factories behind me. Valley Road ran from the inner-city hoods of the East Side south toward the factories, sunk between I-63 on one side and the rails on the other. No sidewalks there, and not really any shoulder either. Just hot pavement, chicory, and witchgrass. For the first time that day I was happy to be wearing my thick cords because they brushed the weeds aside. On the other hand, I was sweating fat slugs.

Am I halfway home yet? Half of halfway? I felt dizzy. There weren't any clouds. The sky was milky blue overhead. I put on my Nero shades and it turned gray instead.

What I need, I thought, *is to really impress people. Like that kid that said "sucks" in Ms. Ropoli's class – only something sharper and better than that. Like some motherfucker starts talking trash, and I kick his ass.*

Winters Road ended at Valley against a row of four metal pipes thrust out of the ground from the edge of the pavement. About eight feet up they angled into the face of a concrete retaining wall, the image of pipes extending from a monstrous organ buried beneath the earth. So we called them "the Pipes."

Because of all the traffic here – from the factories and Eastern High School and the expressway – the Pipes had become ground zero for Akawean graffiti. Sometimes it was gorgeous and sometimes it just looked like some dumb kid had slopped pails of paint around. That day, someone had written in a delicate purple script: "R.I.P. D.D. We Love You. Tho I walk in the Valley of the Shadow of Death, I will Fear" but someone else had painted over this message: "Fuk D that hoe." "H-O-E," I muttered to myself. "I'll tell Elizabeth."

Miles picked up his trumpet like it was a hunger. Maybe I need to pick up my trumpet again. Learn how to play for real this time. Or maybe I need to pick up a hunger.

A car cranked past me at high speed, turned up Winters Road, and from there onto the 63 entrance ramp. I spit. I wiped my brow. I turned away from the Pipes, into the sun, and started walking along Winters.

Nobody cares whether I can play the trumpet or not. I've got to learn how to play guitar. Or how to rap like Adam. Or do karate like Chuck. Or skateboard...

It couldn't have been that far to the expressway underpass, but the stretch of brown grass and green sky felt like a desert running off toward an endlessly receding oasis. Damp ruts cut through the mud on my side where someone had pulled over to dump a trunk's worth of stinking trash. Rotted meat, I guessed, from the stench and the cloud of swirling flies. I felt like I had bricks strapped to my back and my pants and shirt were soaked in sweat.

Is some female going to be my O-Sugar? Take the Plan out of my hands and make me do what she wants so I can make her want me? What if I have to show I want something in order to get something? That's what I did with Kiara. It didn't get me nothing, and she forgot all about me. If you show someone your hunger it's like they know you. Own you. It's like your death because you told them you need them, and they know that they don't even give a shit.

The words sounded melodramatic as I heard them in my head, but I still felt their truth. Their resonance echoing in the repeating clip of five kids launching themselves off of the hospital roof.

Is some hunger going to be my O-Sugar?

Eventually I reached the underpass, and its dry shadow swept over me. I could hear cars, trucks, semis clattering over my head. I walked a bit farther into the dark and took off my backpack. I leaned against a concrete support. I breathed in the dry, dark air. My eyes slowly adjusted, and I was able to make out all of the expected things you see under the expressway: empty plastic bags pinned against a column, ground out gravel, a few uncapped plastic bottles half-filled with mystery liquids.

One dark corner was filled with a heap of ratted blankets, but as I stared at them I realized that they weren't discarded. There was a person over there, sleeping in the shadows, surrounded by a sprawl of trash. I'd never seen a squat quite like this before. Rays of dirty clothes, ragged sheets, glass bottles, cups, forks, knives, torn bags of bread, empty bags of chips, shoes, socks, and plastic beaded jewelry spiraled out from the figure. The cleaner, more valuable things seemed to be at the periphery, while I only saw some soiled scraps and rotting food heaped up around the sleeping figure. Flies buzzed. I now caught a stench worse than the rancid meat I'd passed before. It was the stench of shit, of rot, and of something worse that I didn't have a name for.

I stood, quickly, then knelt and slipped my backpack on again. I started walking as quietly and quickly as I could, veering into the road to keep myself out of the circle of debris. In the dark, it was hard to do this, and I heard something crunch beneath my feet. I stopped and looked down. It was a pair of sunglasses. I hadn't broken them when I'd stepped on them, and that alone was amazing. These weren't ordinary sunglasses, either. The lenses were blue and they seemed to radiate a deep glow. An ultrablue. There was so little light to reflect in there, it seemed almost supernatural to me, that glowing. They seemed holy to me. Like they belonged in a reliquary. I picked them up.

I walked out of the shadow on the far side of the underpass and held the sunglasses up to the light. They looked less magical now, but still special and antique. Anomalous, and not only because of where I had found them. I was quite sure that these were the only sunglasses like this that had ever existed. They were teashades, like a number of pairs I had owned through the years, and I had owned a lot of sunglasses. But the wire was thin and gold, while the lenses were large and thick. As I studied them, I realized that they had been cut, very carefully, from the bottoms of glass bottles. The bottoms of the lenses were shaded green, the tops purple, while the larger centers were blue. *Who would've spent so much time – gone to so much trouble – to make a pair of sunglasses like these?* I held them up by the handle so that they swung sideways and made an eight. They were beautiful.

I was still just outside of the underpass. I didn't know that the figure in there was sleeping. Maybe he was waking up. Maybe he was already awake. The sunglasses had been on the edge of the road. If I had almost broken them by stepping on them, it was really amazing that a car hadn't crushed them already. I didn't see why I should put them back. I wasn't going to wake up some drunk-and-high-as-a-kite homeless asshole to give him back some sunglasses. He obviously didn't care about them. He obviously didn't need sunglasses like these when he was sleeping under piss-streaked blankets surrounded by his own shit. He had more important things to worry about. Hell, the sunglasses probably didn't even belong to him. Maybe he stole them or maybe someone else lost them. They were so different from all of the other trash in the underpass that they couldn't have belonged to the homeless guy. I wasn't stealing. I was taking something discarded and making it valuable and treasured again.

I put the sunglasses in my breast pocket and hurried west along Winters Road.

20

When I finally got home, the same sparrows I had seen that morning were pecking around the porch. My father had thrown some moldy bread out for them but they were ignoring it. I could hear his records playing Billie Holiday in the living room. My father was always a sap for Lady Day, and especially the early stuff. I liked her later stuff more. Today, she had a date with a dream, and maybe I did too. I wrapped my hand around my new pair of sunglasses and looked at the hopping sparrows again. *Your lives are so much shorter than mine,* I thought, *but I've still changed more than you have today.*

And then the totality of everything I had seen since the morning – girls, boys, thugs, teachers, textbooks, and temptations – surged up within me and I felt my heart beating fast again.

It had been one day of seventh grade. I had another 179 ahead of me.

21

The next day went a lot like the first. It was hot out but not white blisters.

In Science, Adam told me that he had tracked down Sara's locker and left her a note. Meanwhile, Mr Kolin, the science teacher, didn't show up, but an office aide did. She had dropped by to ask him why he hadn't submitted his attendance sheets for the first day. We told her that he had just stepped out for a moment. "Hmm," she said, eyeing the pile of ceiling panels leaning neatly against the wall. When the bell rang, nobody knew what was going on.

In Lit, Selby and Quanla were still pissed off about the Plan and not speaking to me, but that gave me a chance to check out some of the other girls in Mrs. Anders' class... they were all seventh graders, but I still didn't know how I was supposed to meet any eighth graders when I only shared two classes with any of them, and I was starting to think that Adam's obsession with the theory of the Plan might keep us from carrying it out in practice. I did see a blonde girl with a kind of anger that I liked. She didn't seem to think much of me though. When she caught me looking at her, she laughed under her breath and leaned in to whisper to her friends. Mrs. Anders gave us our first reading assignment: "The Secret Wives of Walther Smitty."

Gym was gym.

Math was math.

Then, at lunch, Jay decided to share Michael's table again. They were the only two sitting there. I couldn't hear what Jay was saying, leaning over, a few inches from Michael's face, but it had an effect on my cousin. Michael was visibly shaking, looking down, and trying to eat, silent. Once, Jay laughed, sharp, in Michael's face.

"Why you let him dog your cousin like that?" asked Chuck.

"Because my cousin's a salty fatass," I muttered back.

I fell asleep in Miss Mika's class. She either didn't notice or didn't care. Back with Mrs. Anders' we talked about punctuation, but the kids in the back were muttering back and forth. They were wondering if they should listen to their teacher if she was just a snooty dyke.

My favorite part of the day was the bus ride from Radcliffe to Beckford. The crazy driver blasted through stop signs and breezed through red lights, and as the big bus lurched over potholes and swung around corners, we all laughed at it, like little kids. We enjoyed the wind ripping through our hair. There was a white girl a few seats up confidently talking with her friend. She had light freckles and a sort of airiness about her, and I thought, *she's a possibility.* There was another girl, a black girl, with a huge afro, reading near the front of the bus and nodding along to something noisy on her Walkman. There were too many different girls everywhere, and I was looking at them, but they didn't seem to be looking back. I was so sure it was because I was short or dressed wrong. It didn't occur to me that it might have anything to do with the way I was sitting and staring at them.

Ms. Ropoli had a headache and phoned it in that day, inviting us to get into small groups to talk and handing out a few decks of cards to help us along. She *did* tell us not to bother covering our textbooks, as we wouldn't be using them at all. We could plan on reading a lot of newspaper articles. I wondered what the Beckford admin thought of Ms. Ropoli and her newspapers and headaches.

I rode the bus home that day.

When my parents asked about school, I told them that I liked Social Studies, that Math was a drag, that Gym was a joke, and that Mrs. Anders was already giving way too much homework. I didn't mention that the Science teacher hadn't shown up yet. They seemed happy that I told them more than they had expected and asked me what I wanted to do for my birthday that weekend.

"I don't care," I told them.

They asked again.

"Just take Adam and me to Don Pablo's for lunch this weekend."

"But you're turning thirteen!" said my mother.

"Yeah, and I don't wanna make a big deal about it, okay?"

"You know, Bill called yesterday. You could invite him. Find out how he's doing at his school."

"It's just a day, okay?"

They frowned. I did Mrs. Anders' homework and covered my other textbooks with Hamady sacks, and that was the end of day number two.

22

The next day, at lunch, I sat and ate my chips, felt the breeze from a distant oscillating fan, saw the liquid beads of reflected sunlight fixed upon the ceiling. I heard Jay as he leaned over the table behind me and hissed something at Michael. I had my back to them, but when I strained I could hear his words: "What if I killed your mama? Or what if I fucked your mama? Fuck her first or kill her first – that's one dead bitch." Something in the way Adam poked at his food while this was going on, the way Chuck stared at me, toast in hand, waiting... it started to bug me. *It's not my fault my cousin's a pussy. I don't take shit like this. Come on, Michael, say something to him. Tell him to fuck off. Hell, say anything.* I heard a snotting sound from behind me, and I realized Michael was about to cry. *Too much*, I thought.

"Why can't you speak up, Jay?" I said. I looked over my shoulder, just a little. "Why you gotta whisper? Way your voice sounds, it's like you got a dick stuck halfway down your throat. But I guess you don't notice, you're so used to that."

I didn't say it very loud, but people pick up on things fast. Kids stopped talking. Everyone at the tables around us was looking at us, at me. I saw Quanla and Selby turn in my direction. Hell, I could see Sara Lupu watching, with a sort of bemused, half-distracted smile. *Damn, she's hot!* I set my sandwich down, and kept talking:

"Maybe someone took a shit down your throat, mess up your voice like that."

By then, I knew Jay was standing right behind me. There were dozens of kids watching now. They wouldn't stop a fight. They'd love to see a fight. Of course there were a couple faculty monitors peppered around the room. If Jay did anything, he'd get suspended. But I didn't think Jay would care about that. I didn't think he even cared if he got expelled. It didn't matter. I was in control. He could fuck me up ten different ways, but I wouldn't turn around, and I wouldn't look up at him, and I would do whatever it was *I* wanted to do, as long as it wasn't what *he* wanted me to do. *I don't want nobody ruling over me.*

"I see a little bitch who wants to get raped in the shower," he said.

I laughed. This was my moment. Had Adam gotten any eighth graders to notice *him?* Well they were certainly noticing *me* now.

"You just want someone to drop the soap," I said.

I waited for Jay to smash my face into the table.

That's when Chuck stood up and ruined my moment.

"Don't beef with us, Jay. That's John's cousin over there. You fuck with him, you fuck with John. You fuck with John, you fuck with me. See, we got friends. You got friends? No, you don't got nobody. But I do. I got my belt in my backpack and my dad's got a gat back home. Your dad got a gat? Oh yeah, right, I forgot. Maybe you better just drop this."

I felt the heat on my back float off me and fix on Chuck, and then I did look up. Jay was leaning forward a bit, like he wanted to jump, but there was nowhere to jump *to*. So instead he breathed very loudly, two, three times, then croaked, "Fuck all y'all," and stomped out into the hall.

Chuck glared at me.

"That was stupid," he said.

He sat down and started eating again.

The other kids had gone back to their lunches. It hadn't been a fight, but the showdown had been better than nothing.

"You're welcome!" I snapped over my shoulder, where I knew Michael was sitting.

23

Once upon a time we found ourselves across the bridge from Belle Isle, and I wanted my friends to go check it out for me – the forbidden palaces and gardens – but they were all afraid. I got hard on them, so they went off on an expedition, with Eurylochus leading the way. There, in the midst of twisted thorns and massing green we saw a huge conservatory with a great glass dome and a stenchy lily pond and a leash of fallow deer. But the deer weren't skittish at all. They tried to nip some food from my friends' pockets, nuzzled their heads up against my friends' warm coats, and everyone was laughing and happy like it was fucking *Bambi* or *Fantasia* or something.

A beautiful woman named Birdie came out of one of the greenhouses and offered my friends a snack of honeycomb, but she weirded out Eurylochus, the way she seemed to look him up and down, so he hid in the wild hedges with the foxes and rabbits. When the other kids ate the honey, Birdie laughed between her cunning teeth and waved her hands like a dancer, and hexed everyone who had eaten into wild deer.

Eurylochus escaped unnoticed and ran back to the Warehouse District and told me what he had seen.

"Come on!" I said. "I know who this is! The day has come. She's a part of the Plan."

"I'm not going to stand up to that woman!" Eurylochus said, and peed his pants.

"Go to hell," I said, and I ran out onto the island alone.

But before I got to the conservatory, Hermes descended, dripping bread crumbs.

"Holy moly," he said. "I got this one."

"Where did you come from?"

"You're out of your depth. I got a black belt and my dad's got a gat, and I'm gonna make that asshole my bitch and that bitch my girl."

"You can't! She'll cut up your nutsack! Anyway, this ain't even your story!"

"Shut up," he said. "I'm going to put my sword against her throat."

And that's what he did.

Fucking Hermes.

"Hey," said Sara Lupu after Foreign Languages the next day.

"Huh?" I said. I'd been noticing her friend as she left class. I'd finally caught her name: Patricia Perez. She *was* an eighth grader and she was *all* attitude: when Sara called Patricia's yard trashy, Patricia had said, "You got a trashy mouth and mom, so shut up, Sara."

"What's your name?" asked Sara.

"John," I said.

"I'm Sara."

"Yeah."

"And you told off that kid, Jay?"

"Yeah. I did that."

"And then your friend kept him from kicking your ass."

I couldn't think of any clever words to say. "No."

"I mean, he stood up for you."

"He stood up is all."

"Yeah, he did." She smiled for a coy, elusive moment, then handed me a note with Adam's name on it.

"Adam?!" I said.

"You're friends, right?"

"Yeah, we are, but I thought you..."

"Could you give him that?"

I shrugged. "You're friends with Patricia right?"

Sara laughed with scorn. *Still pissed about that trash comment, I guess.* "Yeah, she's my friend."

"I'll give Adam this note. You tell Patricia my name, okay. Tell her I live two blocks from Jay and he's been running from me for years."

I hoped that Patricia would hear this and not Jay, but then Jay hadn't even come to lunch that day.

Another laugh. "I will," Sara said.

I slipped the note in Adam's locker before catching the bus to Beckford. He'd always been better with girls than me, but I didn't see how he was going to convert a lesbian.

24

When I saw Adam at lunch the next day, he told me that Sara had written him back.

"She wants to get with me," he said. "She wants to meet up with me this weekend."

"Not on Sunday," I said. "We're going to Don Pablo's for my birthday."

"Man, I wish I had wings. I'd fly over to her house, and peek in her bedroom window, and do all sorts of stuff with her."

"Yeah, but you ain't got wings."

"No, I don't." Adam thought a minute. "I got words."

"Words ain't wings."

"My words give me wings. Winged words."

"How's that work?"

"My words give wings to my mind and take me high. I've imagined Sara Lupu head to toe."

The Plan was back on track. At least for Adam. I was wondering what Sara had told Patricia about me. That I was a young badass who had stood up to a stone-cold psycho? Or that I was a short, fat-lipped dipshit who had been saved by his badass friend? Chuck caught me in the hall just an hour later.

"You're going to meet me at Adam's dad's house after school, and that pink-haired little bitch is gonna meet me too!"

"Adam's dad's? He's not even supposed to go over there —"

"Yeah, I know that. Just be there."

25

Adam's dad's latest place had been down on Gurruwiwi Drive, a few blocks from me but closer to Aurelius Road and the Bellwood mansions beyond. On Kris Miller's block, it was all cookie-cutter bungalows with different colored shutters, some red maples, and tiny mowed lawns. It was one of the nicer parts of the South Side, though now things were starting to slide. Adam's dad was part of the sliding. His house had mint-green shutters and shake siding. It also had plywood over the windows while the front door yawned wide. Adam was sitting on the porch and, when I got close, I saw Chuck and Elizabeth hanging back in the doorway. Adam's face was pale.

"What's goin' on?" I asked.

"My dad's not home," Adam said.

"No," I said. "Doesn't look like anyone's been home a long time."

"I thought they'd give him longer."

"Jesus, Adam, he had to have been evicted a long time back for it to look like this!"

"I was staying here just two months ago!"

"They board them up when they're empty to keep the scrappers out," said Chuck.

Adam sniffed. "It didn't work this time."

A woozy, tinny rhyme rattled out from Elizabeth's headphones: hypnosis, mesmerism, trauma, paralysis, and terror. The Insane Clown Posse.

"Could you turn that shit off?" I said.

Elizabeth glared at me but clicked off her Walkman.

"They're geniuses," she said.

"What is going on?"

"Let's start walking," said Chuck, and they picked up their backpacks.

"Walking where?"

"The Butt Hut," said Adam with a rueful grin.

"What? I didn't come out to this crack house just so I could walk all the way to a... strip club! What's going on?!"

"She didn't think the note was from me!" said Adam. "She thought it was from Chuck!"

"What?"

"Let's start walking," repeated Chuck, and he started back up the street, toward Whitmore Road.

We followed.

"Sara Lupu," said Adam. "See, she got me mixed up with Chuck. When she got my note!"

"How'd she get you mixed up?"

"Because I mentioned you in my note, and I guess she has a class with you? Well she saw you and Chuck step up on Jay and...you know! Got us...mixed up!"

I had to smile at the idea that anyone would get skinny, white, pink-haired Adam mixed-up with tall, black, close-cropped Chuck.

"So did you tell her? About the mix up?"

"I told her," said Chuck.

"So what's the problem?"

"The problem," Adam said, "is that she told some people about it... about how the guy who stood up to Jay Flighting left her a note, and she wants him –"

"I thought she was a lesbian."

"So did I," said Chuck.

"All right, Chuck," I said. "That's cool. She's got a friend named Patricia and –"

"I don't wanna see her, John."

"But she's so hot!"

"Excuse me!" said Elizabeth.

"Oh, don't wig out, Elizabeth? It's not the same with you, okay?"

Elizabeth's glare disagreed.

"I told you," Chuck said, "my cousin Kerm's wanted to get with Sara a real long time."

"Three years!" said Adam.

"And now he thinks you're asking her out?" I asked.

"Yeah," said Chuck. "He's pissed."

I laughed. "He doesn't know her that well if he doesn't even know she's not a dyke."

"It ain't funny. He *will* kick my ass, and he's got friends in the Reapers."

"Oh!" I said, exaggerated. "Yeah, better run scared from the South Side Reapers!"

"You should," Chuck said. "They're rednecks with guns. I'd rather deal with the niggas on my block than trash packin' heat."

"So just tell him it was Adam. She's still got the note, right? Hell, have *her* tell him. If she knows you don't like her, she don't got nothing to lose."

Chuck shook his head.

"Why not?"

"It's complicated... I don't want to explain..." he trailed off.

We'd reached the end of the block, and houses and yards were smaller and dingier than before. We'd have to cross Whitmore to get to the Butt Hut, but Chuck looked down side streets for another way to go. He turned left onto Farner Avenue, which ran parallel to Whitmore.

"That's the wrong way," I said. Chuck kept walking. "That's totally the wrong direction. You'll never get there that way."

"Chill," Chuck said. "I know how to get there. I just don't want to walk past Radcliffe."

"Why not?"

"He thinks his cuz'll be looking for him there," muttered Elizabeth.

We hurried to catch up.

"Is it really that bad?" I asked.

"Yeah," Chuck said. "I'm not supposed to know he likes Sara. I know 'cause I was at his house this summer and I heard him talking about it on the phone. I mean, I... was listening in on the call while he was talking to someone else. That's when he said she was a dyke. But he found out I was listening in. He was already pissed off at me about that."

"What, you think he thinks you went and told her about it?"

"I don't know," said Chuck. "He don't like me. Not even when we were kids. I think he's just lookin' for a reason to fuck me up. Now he's got it."

We walked in silence for a while. I kept trying to figure out a way around or through it. If it was just a misunderstanding, it would be easy to work things out. But if Chuck was right – if Kerm Coppo really was just looking for an excuse to make his cousin an enemy – then the only options were fight and flight.

We finally reached Whitmore Road a ways down, without ever having come within a block of Radcliffe. The traffic passed and we crossed the street. Now we were on my side of Whitmore.

"Say 'bye' to the skanks, 'hi' to the stanks," said Adam.

"Say 'hi' to the mange," I said. "Fucking dogs over here. My father carries pepper spray when he's out. He got me some but I left it at home."

"Ha."

As we walked, I couldn't help but feel bad for suburban kids whose experience inhaling the great fragrances of the world – its signatures – were limited to chopped grass and lilac bloom. The American ghetto, on the other hand, was a shifting kaleidoscope of odor, scent, and stench ranging from the wretched to the divine. My own neighborhood was a great case in point: in just a few blocks, I'd caught traces of mildew, mothballs, animal sweat, spilled beer, Diesel fumes, air fresheners, ginger snaps, the reek of pot and patchouli, crusted dry dog shit and melting hot dog shit, crushed cloves, sprawls of trash, dirty diapers, gasoline puddles, the icy bite of sprinkler mist clinging to a rusting rail, chopped weeds, stale grease, crumbling plywood and stagnant sawdust, the molding paper of discarded phone books, burnt oil, matted mattresses, damp cloth, Swisher spice and cigarette smoke, streams of aerosol haze, the webby wetness of a lost umbrella hung from a chain-link fence, the tarry residue of spent asbestos, brick dust, woody soot, crisping leaves reduced to ash, singed sticks, the savage spark of snapped pine branches, body odor, paint thinner, maggoty beef, honeysuckle perfume, fried fish and chicken, floods of molasses-thick barbecue sauce steeped in crusted black pepper, rotted apples, spent fireworks with a lick of sulfur, acetone, Barbicide, enameled acrylic, and some sickening thing buried under a pile of soiled laundry. Lavender blooms we crunched under our tattered sneakers and kicked up into invisible clouds that we imagined to be thick and purple.

"So what's at the Butt Hut?" I asked.

"I can't go home 'til this blows over," Chuck said. "Adam thought I could stay with his dad. If he ain't at the house, Adam says that's probably where we'll find him. I wanted you there for backup... and to let you know how your plan has fucked things up."

"Adam's plan," I said.

"Hey!" said Adam. "We're in this together."

"I don't know," I said. "I don't think you're doing it right."

"I *am* doing it right! I can't do it wrong. It's *my* plan, dammit!"

"I'm going after Sara's hot friend. You're the one who decided to go after the not-lesbian Chuck's spaz cousin is in love with."

"You're going after her fat friend? How's that gonna make you popular? Do you even *understand* the Plan?!"

"Shut up!" snapped Chuck.

"Man," Adam went on, "she's got, like, fat rolls on her sides, I just know it."

I laughed. I took the shades from my pocket and put them on. They were the blue bottle shades I'd found on the underpass on the first day of school. They cooled the world around me, and the whole situation seemed trifling and stupid.

"Okay, Chuck, fine," I said. "We'll go to that titty bar. Maybe we'll even get to see some while we're there."

"Excuse me!" snapped Elizabeth. "I'm right here! This whole time, okay? Do you want me to leave?"

We turned onto Dickinson Avenue, a side street connecting Whitmore Road to South Street. Halfway down the first block the sidewalk ended. A haggard hemlock – too little space and time to grow – arched up over the downward-sloping street.

"Come on, Chuck," I said. "You could take Jay. You can take your cousin, can't you?"

Chuck shook his head.

"Kerm is into some shit," he said. "The Reapers, remember? He ain't a gangbanger, but he runs with some. I paged him a few hours ago. We talked. He said he'd find me at home or school. He's out looking for me right now. I think he probably brought his friends."

That took the smile off my face.

"So what's gonna happen?" I asked.

Chuck looked up and down Dickinson. He clenched his hands and jaw. He was looking around as if trying to see in all directions at once. He wasn't just nervous; he was afraid. I'd never seen Chuck afraid before.

"You think it's going to happen soon?" I asked. "You think he might find you... even before we get to the bar?"

Chuck laughed. "Rednecks and guns, John. What the hell do I know?"

"Can I say something, please?" asked Elizabeth.

She was obviously fed up with us, though I couldn't tell why.

"Yeah," said Chuck.

"You said your cousin's got a pager. Let's go to John's house. He's a lot closer than the bar. Call Kerm. Tell him you're sorry. Not about Sara, which was just a mix-up, but about listening to him on the phone. And you weren't hitting on the girl he wanted, and tell him you're going home, but you don't wanna start nothin' with him. It wouldn't look cool for him to pick a fight after you told him that."

Chuck shook his head.

We started walking again.

"No," Chuck said. "He don't believe me. I don't know, maybe he does. He don't care. He wants to beat me up. 'Cause then I'll know."

"Know what?" Elizabeth asked.

"That he can beat me up. That he's always a better...now and before. Always. Know he's better."

"So your best answer is Adam's dad?!" said Elizabeth. "Adam, why did the state take you from your dad?"

Now Adam laughed. "Um, bad food, electricity turned off, water turned off, bad clothing. Safety hazards and unsanitary household conditions. And they got him for no seatbelts in the car, but he said I never rode anywhere. Moderate neglect. Oh, that and all the drugs. Drugs he does. Drugs he deals –"

"And this is the guy who's gonna protect you from your cousin, Chuck?"

"So you think I should go to your mom, Elizabeth?" Chuck asked. It wasn't a serious question.

"No, duh. Weren't you listening? I said we should go to John's parents. They're cool and shit. They'll have some idea of someone they can call or somewhere you can go."

"I don't know –" I started, but it wasn't necessary.

"No," said Chuck. "I'm gonna face this like a man."

Now it was Elizabeth's turn to look incredulous. "Oh, yeah, great, you're twelve, Chuck! You gonna face your cousin and all his friends, and you don't know they ain't packin' heat? You keep talkin' about it! And you're gonna get you killed, or beat up, and maybe John and Adam 'cause they're stupid enough to follow you. Well, I ain't gonna follow you. Fuck that shit!"

Elizabeth stomped off ahead of us toward South Street.

"How are you going to get home?" I called after her.

She spun around to face me.

"I'll find a pay phone!" she snapped.

As Elizabeth continued toward South, the rest of us continued at a slower pace.

"I wish you would have told me all this sooner, Chuck," I said. "Like this afternoon. I could have thought about it."

"I didn't have time."

"Did you know it was gonna be like this? Like us just sneaking from one place to –"

"It's been fast, man. I don't even know."

While Chuck was talking more than usual, Adam had been quiet for most of the walk.

"What you thinkin', Adam?" I asked.

"You know me. If someone looks at me wrong, I scream and piss myself. I feel sick right now."

The neighborhood between Whitmore and South – the Stanky South Side, Adam called it – was chopped up by overgrown railroad tracks and empty strip malls. One of the tracks crossed Whitmore out by city limits, and then cut every east-west street in half over the next two miles before crossing South Street just north of Ashburn Cemetery. The tracks used to stop outside the Old Benedict, which was a great place to put a fine establishment like the Butt Hut. Now the factory was gone and the bar scraped by on a dwindling crowd of loyal patrons like Adam's dad.

We got to the place where Dickinson Street crossed the tracks. I remembered, dimly, when trains had taken this route, sometimes blocking Whitmore and South as they rocked slowly forward, then backward, then forward again, so slow with their monumental freight, pissing off the growing line of motorists. I couldn't remember when the rails had been pulled up, but the track was already overgrown, with tall grass in the sun and belladonna choking the shade.

We turned off of Dickinson and onto the tracks. We were almost halfway to the bar.

26

The farther we walked, the less I liked it. The cottonwoods loomed so far above us that the afternoon sun got lost in their branches, and even though there were houses and backyards off to either side, the bushes grew so thick and dense that I couldn't see much. A stink of stagnant water rose on both sides, and mosquitoes started landing on our hands and arms. We smacked at them and they exploded, leaving tiny smears of bright blood. The crickets sang louder than the traffic, and we could only tell that South Street was somewhere ahead of us because every so often we saw a white pickup or rusty hatchback crossing in the distance.

"Things are fucked up the last month," Chuck said. "Several dudes with the Undertakers did a job on Hastings."

"The Undertakers?" I asked. "I thought they were over in the Os. What they doing on the West End?"

"Seems Kid Zero made a truce with the Chalks, and all those Undertakers take their orders from him. If they ain't fightin' with the Chalks, I guess they think they can move in on the Masters."

"That's crazy."

"Yeah, no shit. So that's a gang war going on and since the Masters are in my hood there's drama even without my cousin tryin' a kick my ass. Like they all gonna pop off any moment. Then that shit at the hospital!"

"What happened to the hospital?"

"Been all over the news. Bunch of kids from Eastern High took some drug that went bad and they jumped off the roof of St. Christopher's."

"Okay, yeah, I did hear about that. O-Sugar right? I didn't know it was a big deal."

"Are you for real?! It's all over! They all died, except this one guy."

"You catch their names?"

"News didn't say their names. Why? Who you know at Eastern?"

"Nobody," I said. "Selby's brothers, I guess. I was just wonderin'. You think it was the drug? Or suicide? I mean, why do you think –"

"Jesus, John, I dunno. Fiends do all sorts of crazy shit."

Purple clouds, swollen with rain, had quietly moved over the sun. Now the wind tunneled down the rail line from north to south and beat cool against our chests. It swept the mosquitoes away. Now the leaves gliding against each other were louder than the crickets, and I couldn't hear the cars at all. It was like we were in the countryside. When the wind died down, we heard the sound of running feet coming up behind us. We all whipped around at the same time.

It was Elizabeth, her face red and flush, waving her hands to get our attention.

27

When she caught up with us, Elizabeth put her hands on her knees, breathing heavily.

"Five guys," she panted. "Up at South and Dickinson. I think they're looking for you Chuck."

We all stared at Chuck.

"We should have stayed on the road," he said. He looked at me. "Okay, we'll turn around and meet them by the houses. Maybe –"

"Chuck!" came a harsh voice up ahead of us, from South Street.

"Fuck," hissed Chuck.

Three figures, bigger than us, taller than us, were picking their way down the tracks in our direction.

"Chuck?" said Elizabeth.

Behind us, two more were coming up on us from Dickinson.

Chuck smiled. He laughed.   "I'm retarded," he said. "Why did we go this way?"

Adam started trembling. He held his own hands. "I can't fight," he said. "I'm too small."

"I gotta beef with you, nigga!" The same harsh voice. Kerm Coppo was walking fast. His two friends – maybe teens but they sure seemed to have adult-sized bodies – hanging just behind him. "Little bitch start shit," Kerm barked. "listen in on my shit when I'm on the phone! Little bitch start shit talking shit behind my back?!"

Chuck had started moving forward too, but more slowly. "I didn't start shit with you, Kerm. I didn't say shit neither. I told you, she saw me take out that kid Jay. She thought I was him," he said, gesturing to Adam.

Kerm was talking too, faster and faster: "You bring your little faggot friends for backup? You think your little faggot friends gonna save your ass? I brought some friends too, bitch." And Chuck's voice merged with Kerm's, both of them talking too fast, talking at the same time, words on words, and they came to a stop, inches from each other. Kerm's other two friends were closing the distance behind us.

"I ain't gonna fight you," said Chuck. "Not over some bitch I don't even want, I don't even know her, who the fuck is she?"

"You bring your fucking faggot friends like you gonna jump me, but I brought my friends and we gonna jump you you fucking faggot."

"Who you calling faggot?"

"You a motherfucking faggot dick bitch."

"I don't gotta take this."

"You a fucking faggot take a dick in yo ass."

"I don't gotta take this."

Chuck swung first. Kerm leaned back from the blow, but too slow and took it on the face. Then Chuck's arms cut a quick, sharp arc around Kerm's waist, though this didn't look at all like one of his karate moves. But Kerm, bigger and taller, got his own grip around Chuck's arms. They swung around, for a moment like they were dancing, then Chuck planted his foot and pulled back, and they both went down in the dust and rolled off the ridge into the weeds. At first, I thought that Chuck had the edge, but then he was on his back, his feet were kicking out, trying to get a grip on something, to push off. Kerm wedged his left forearm against Chuck's throat, and as Chuck tried to pry himself free, Krem's right arm went up and cut down, driving his fist into the side of Chuck's head. It sounded like an apple falling out of a tree and hitting the dirt. Kerm hit Chuck one two three times. Adam screamed. I had thought I was just a bystander, but now I saw two of the kids coming at me, huge wearing black shirts that concealed their sweat stains. That would hide my blood stains, I figured. Out of the corner of my eye I saw Adam make a run for it. Elizabeth had backed up against a tree. Then, Chuck managed to slip out of Kerm's grip, stumble to his feet, bleeding from the nose, plant his legs and crouch down a little, ready to spring, ready to fight.

Between two poplars, I caught a glimpse of a chain-linked fence and someone's backyard beyond. Maybe I would've stayed and fought if I was thirteen – a teenager – but I still had two more days of being twelve. Or maybe I was just chicken shit, but I hadn't picked this fight.

I ran down the ridge, grabbed the fence, and leapt over.

28

My feet hadn't even touched down on the other side when the dog was at my heels. Its mouth hollowed open with foam and rage. It would've ripped my leg open if it hadn't run the wrong way around a clothesline pole and cut its chain short. I hurried along to the edge of the next yard, which was ringed by a wooden privacy fence. I was up in the air and about to come down on the other side when I saw another dog, larger, with blue eyes, snarling and leaping up at me.

"Jesus!" I yelled, and hunched down on the top of fence. I wobbled for a moment, then found my balance, crawling forward toward twinned gates leading to the front yards while both dogs followed me below, howling and snapping and waiting for me to fall. It hurt, putting my full weight on the pointed stockade posts, so I just focused on each step as it came. Finally, I reached the end and jumped down. I was covered in sweat and my arms and legs were latticed with raspberry scratches. Blood pooled in my hands and legs where I'd crept along the fence. I could hear, not far off, shouts coming off from the fight and then the sound of police sirens.

"Jesus shit," I said.

The dogs were still barking at me, right on the other side of the gate. I aimed a kick at the first dog's face through the fence links, and it leaped back then lunged forward at me. The latch almost jumped out of place, but the gate stayed closed. I put my hands up and walked slowly backwards while the two dogs continued their frenzied barking.

"Okay," I said, and turned and walked quickly down to the street, glancing into windows to see if anyone inside the houses had heard or seen me. I didn't see anyone. I knew this street. Pitcairn Street. I was just about four blocks from my own house, but I hadn't realized it sooner because I'd never walked home before through abandoned rail lines and feral dog backyards. I brushed my palms on my shirt. Blood streaked. It was a white shirt. My heart was pounding but there wasn't anything else I could do now except start walking home.

The sky had started to clear. This was one of the nicer blocks. Trimmed yew in the small front yards, little bungalows with aluminum siding, white pickups in many driveways. Mowed lawns, a few American flags, young trees. The sirens had died over on South, but the dogs kept howling, and a man came down one of the driveways up ahead. He stopped at the sidewalk and looked at me.

At first I thought he must have lived in the house, which looked just as plain and decent as all the others on that block, but he kept looking at me. Then I recognized him as one of Kerm's friends. Except I had figured that Kerm's friends were high schoolers, and this guy looked a lot older than that. Tall and wiry and all serious. He grinned. *He chased me?* He didn't seem to be breathing hard.

"What?" I yelled, and I was surprised at how ragged my voice sounded.

"What's your name?" he asked, his voice resonant beneath the howling of the dogs.

"What's yours, faggot?"

"Easy now," he said.

There were more than two dogs barking now. Several others had heard the excitement and joined in the song, though I couldn't see any of them. They were locked away behind fences and doors. I started to walk backwards, slowly. The man started walking toward me.

"Stay where you are," he said.

I stopped. He continued walking, long strides closing the distance fast, his eyes fixed on me. Black stubble stuck out of his chin. His whitish face framed brownish eyes with red rings. He started to run toward me. I turned off to my right and ran through a vacant lot, under a spreading elm tree, and scrambled over another chain-link fence into another yard. There was a mad dog there, I don't know what kind, shoving its face against the window screen and snapping at me in jarring, blank rage. I turned toward it and fell onto my back. I thought the thing was about to smash through the window and come after me.

I looked back the way I had come, but the man was gone. I got back on my feet and ran on through the yard, climbed onto another fence, and jumped from there onto the roof of a low shed. I looked down into the next backyard and didn't see a dog, although now they were barking all around me on every side, like this wasn't a neighborhood of humans anymore but of hungry dogs. I jumped down and twisted my ankle when I landed. I hurried, limping, toward another gate, toward the front yard. I got to it. I didn't feel like I could climb another fence, so I groped for the latch. Then pain shot up the back of my leg. A tiny dog with a fuzzy snout had locked its jaws on my ankle. I shook my foot and the dog let go, yammering at me. I had the gate open and I slid out. I closed the gate behind me.

I limped down to the next street. The houses here were a little rattier than they had been a block over, their lawns more ragged, and each house was perched on a small hill with stonework holding the dirt back. I wasn't any closer to my house than I had been before, but I was closer to Whitmore Road with its churches and businesses and people.

I saw the man walk down another driveway, three houses ahead of me, just as he had before, not breathing hard, not having broken a sweat, as if he owned all the houses in the neighborhood. As if he could come and go as he pleased. He stopped when he reached the sidewalk.

"Where did you get those sunglasses?" he called out.

I had forgotten that I'd been wearing them.

I didn't answer, but the dogs did. They howled and roared and moaned and whined and hissed and wailed at us.

I took the shades off. I put them in my pocket.

The man turned his watch so that it was reflecting the sun in my eye, like a mirror. I squinted and looked down. The man laughed.

He knelt down, like he was going to tie his shoes, but he wasn't wearing shoes. He was wearing boots. He was pulling a short knife out of his boot.

My mind went smooth and white, like all thought had been cut away. Like this was a movie about some other kid being chased, and from now on I had no control over what that kid did.

The man stood and started to walk toward me again.

I glanced over my shoulder. An old pickup was up on blocks in front of the next small, tan house. I ran to it and grabbed onto the metal antenna. I bent it down and up and down and up and it snapped off in my hand.

The man kept walking toward me.

I held the sharp end out toward him.

He stopped, just one house away.

"Where did you get those sunglasses?" he asked.

"Just leave me the fuck alone!"

"Do you want to fight?"

"I ran away from the fight, dumbass."

"And I followed you."

Now I was backing toward the house, mindful of the little hill, trying not to stumble as I went. *If I slip it's all over.*

"Someone," I yelled, my voice shrill and breaking, "is going to hear those dogs and come and see what's going on. And they're going to see some tall faggot threatening me and they're gonna call the cops."

"Most definitely. What's your name? Where did you get those sunglasses?"

"Leave me the fuck alone!"

"I'll find out. I'm always able to find out."

"Fuck off!"

I dropped the antenna and ran up the driveway of the tan house. *No fucking dogs, please. No dogs.*

There weren't any dogs.

I made it through the backyard and over the privacy fence into a small meadow behind all of the nearby back yards, but not connected to any of them, nor to any street or alley. I'd never known that this place existed. Scared as I was, I decided to come back and check it out another time. Now, though, I hurried across the field and hoisted myself over a red shadowbox fence into a small backyard made smaller by a large tool shed and an above-ground pool with a couple of little kids in water-wings splashing around in the water.

They stared at me as I stumbled past them.

I made it down the front driveway, and found myself standing on Whitmore Road. I saw people. I heard traffic, laughter, screams, and thudding bass from teenagers blasting rap from their parents' sedans. I was just a block away from

Radcliffe where some kids I probably knew from class lounged in the shade and talked about their weekend plans.

I looked and looked but I didn't see the man with the knife.

He was gone now, and even the dogs I'd woken were starting to settle down.

I crossed Whitmore Road so I could walk near the school. I went slowly, checking every alley, driveway, and window as I went. I wasn't far from home now. I knew I'd make it back okay.

29

The first thing I saw when I got home was Elizabeth sitting on my parents' couch. Her angry expression startled me, so I just said, "Hey."

"What the hell happened to you?" asked my father, who was standing at a side window, peeking through the curtain.

"Um," I said. "I came home a different way. I jumped a fence and a dog came at me. I didn't see him. I fell trying to get away."

My father dropped the curtain to glare at me. "Well, that was stupid. Are you okay?"

I shrugged.

He lifted the curtain again. "Yeah, I thought so," he muttered under his breath. "Archie's dog is shitting in our yard again." He moved to the front door and opened it. "Archie!" he shouted. He looked back at me, "We'll talk about this later." He stomped out of the house.

When the door had closed, I turned to Elizabeth.

"What happened?" I asked.

"What happened?! You and Adam ran off and left Chuck and me with his cousin and a bunch of Reapers!"

"I didn't pick that fight," I said.

"Oh, and I did?!"

"No, you didn't..." I didn't want to apologize, but I didn't see any way around it. "I'm sorry."

"You should be."

"So what did happened? After...I left."

"Well after you and Adam took off, the cops showed up and everyone else ran for it, except Chuck and his cousin. They kept fighting until they got broken up. Then they said they were cool with each other so the cops took off. You know I was the only girl there? And I was the only person who wasn't being an idiot. I mean, boys are idiots."

I didn't know what to say. I wanted to tell someone about the man with the knife, but not my parents, and Elizabeth didn't seem too sympathetic right then.

"So what are you here for?" I asked.

"Calling for a ride."

"Couldn't find a pay phone?"

"Just shut up, John!"

30

The moment Elizabeth left, my father flipped his shit. It wasn't that I had wrecked my clothes... although that certainly didn't help. No, it was because he'd just gotten a call from the school saying that Mr. Kolin would be reporting for work the following week.

"So what, you just didn't have anyone, any adult at all in that class all week?!" he said.

"No, just Monday and Tuesday. Then we got a sub."

"You didn't tell us!"

"I didn't think it mattered."

"You didn't... and how are you supposed to learn science if you don't have a teacher?!"

"We don't do much the first week anyway. Just cover our textbooks."

"You don't get why I wanted to send you to St. Patrick's?"

I shrugged.

Then he told me that I was going to be spending the night at Michael's house the next night.

"What?!" I said. "You didn't ask *me* if I wanted to!"

Now it was his turn to shrug. "Michael's your cousin, John. He's had a rough first week at school. He doesn't make friends easily. I also told Mabel he was free to come to your birthday party. It's your birthday, John. Why don't you call up some of your friends? Invite Chuck, invite Bill to –"

"I'm not having a birthday party!" I snapped. "I'm having lunch with Adam at Don Pablo's!"

"Well, it's going to be at least four, because I told Mabel that Michael could come and that he could bring his friend."

By then, I was angrier than my father. I didn't want Michael at my birthday meal, and I certainly didn't want whatever math geek he'd conned into coming along. I wanted to shout at him. Instead, I crossed my arms and smiled.

"I thought you said that fatass didn't have any friends."

That got me sent to my room. I went without another word. Normally, I would have been pissed off about my "party" all night, but something larger was looming in the background. For starters, I had run away from a fight. I had left one of my best friends, alone and outnumbered by a bunch of older kids. I had left a girl alone with a bunch of boys. *Is that the kind of person I am?* It wasn't the sort of badass move I had imagined for myself... I couldn't fight, or at least I didn't think I could fight, but I hadn't thought I was chicken shit, either. Then I worried about another obvious thing: *Is Chuck going to tell people at school about this?*   Part   of   me thought I should call him. Part of me thought it was stupid to call and give him a chance to yell at me.

I *didn't* think much about the man with the knife. That still felt too scary and immediate. I wrapped it in my mind and packed it away to deal with later. There was already enough to worry about. I lay awake late that night with anxiety gnawing in my stomach.

The next morning I rode my bike back to the tracks where we'd been ambushed. I thought I found the exact spot because a lot of dirt was kicked up and some branches had been snapped off on either side, but another minute's walk and everything looked the same. I wondered if there were a lot of fights like that along those tracks. Greeks and Cretans massing up against each other once or twice a week, kicking ruts on and on forever. Hundreds of love triangles leading to thousands for feuds, blades, guns, slugs, ropes. I felt nervous, like someone was watching me, but of course nobody else was there. I walked back home.

It was time to go to Michael's.

31

My street was just part of a bunch of blocks lumped together as the "South Side," bordered by South Street on the west and Aurelius Road on the east. It was a hood, but not a uniquely bad one. At least not for Akawe. There was still enough arson and demolition to make some blocks look like a pirate's patchy grin.

Across South Street, past the cemetery, Ashburn Heights did a bit better. The Zibi carved a gorge separating Ashburn from XAI and the blue-collar bungalows of the South Village, and even they were pretty nice for Akawe. But Ashburn Heights was built for more of a middle-class crowd, and through '93 it had stayed that way. Brick split-levels rose over stone retaining walls while honeylocusts shed their middlebrow leaves on the knobby knees of white pines. This was where Aunt Mabel had bought her house when she had gotten her full-time teaching job at XAI.

My father wondered why she stayed in Akawe at all, but her little street, poised under the literal shadow of Temple Medical Center, felt more suburban than the gravel-paved sidewalk-free inner-ring 'burbs did. Her house was a Cape Cod. A large one. Still pretty modest for an tenured engineering prof for one of the First Four automakers. Something pretty impressive for this desperate little town. Kinda like Mabel herself who, eschewing my father's untucked fuckitness and my

Aunt Ellie's easy grace, had inscribed a kind of severe majesty in her tight-bunned hair and professionally tailored suits. If the middle child is supposed to be the one who rebels, this driven, austere, affluent Reaganite played that role to the hilt.

But what do I know about it? I'm an only child. Just like Michael.

He seemed about as happy to see me as I was to see him. I realized that my aunt had probably called my father and they took things from there.

"You don't remember," Mabel said, my father hovering over her shoulder, keys in his hand. "But we used to have you over here all of the time. You and Michael and Ellie's kids back before she passed."

"It's almost been ten years," my father said. "I still think about her every day. Every day."

"I do too, Mark."

My father waved and went back down the driveway.

Michael and I didn't talk much as we sat with Mabel at the glass table, eating manicotti and sipping quarter-full glasses of dark wine, looking out over twilight on the miniature French garden in the back. It all seemed quaint enough, but I knew that the Temple dumpsters were right on the other side of the brick wall. Michael and I didn't talk as we went down into the basement, lounged in the leather sectionals, crunched popcorn while watching *Terminator 2*.

"Hasta la vista," Michael said once, for a laugh.

I didn't laugh.

But eventually, we had to go up to his room, with a bunk bed set up so that the friends he didn't have could sleep over. The room was sparse, clean, with a dark blue carpet and some framed baseball cards on the wall. It occurred to me that obsessive neatness might be the only thing I had in common with my cousin.

"Do you want the top bunk?" Michael asked.

I shrugged, but he kept looking at me, so I said, "You take it."

He huffed as he climbed the rungs and I told myself that this was probably the only exercise he got most days. *Phys Ed is going to suck for him.*

"Can you get the light?" he asked.

I flipped the light switch, and immediately the phosphorescent light of stickers – stars, planets, comets – glowed out at me.

"That's cute," I said.

"What?" he asked in the dark.

"Nothing," I said, and stripped down to my boxers. I crawled under the covers.

The silence was heavy. For a minute I thought it was just hot in there, but it wasn't. They had central cooling and the temperature was perfect all throughout the house. Something else was making me twitchy. *Am I am a coward? Am I a chicken shit? Who is Chuck going to tell about the fight? What does Patricia Perez think of me? Who was the man with the knife?*

"John!" Michael said.

It was meant as a question, but it almost came out as a shout. My cousin didn't really want to talk to me. He didn't want me in his house at all. But I was the best he had, so he was going to screw up his courage and say something daring.

"What?" I asked, making my voice as acid as I could.

"It's just." He stopped on a dime. Took a deep breath and plowed right on: "Thanks for doing...what you did...last week."

"What?" I said. "What did I *do?*"

I heard him breathless in the black.

"You know," he murmured. "When you told Jay to...to leave me alone."

I let his voice peter out. Just dissolve into the darkness along with his confidence. I waited for several moments before I answered him.

"I didn't tell him to leave you alone," I said. "I told him he was a fucking dick sucking faggot, which is what he is. And if Chuck hadn't jumped in, I would've kicked his ass myself."

I heard the springs above me squeaking again, and in the sound I heard his awe radiating down upon me. *He's actually buying this shit!* To drive the point home: "You gotta stick up for yourself, cuz."

Somehow, this reassured him. He thought I was encouraging him, not dismissing him. He said, "Wanna hear some music?"

"What?"

"I got a new CD at the mall last week. My mom doesn't know. She wouldn't like it. But I love it. It's... it's... when I listen to it, I do think I could stick up for myself. Like you said."

"I don't want to hear no Genesis or nothing, Michael."

"Oh no," he said, a half-whisper. "It's nothing like that."

I heard him clambering down the side of his bed. Reaching under me – too close – and fishing out a jewel case. He did it instantaneously, with no light. He'd memorized where it was.

"It's called Nine Inch Nails," he said. "They're a band. I mean, they're just this one guy. And this is their first album."

"Fine," I muttered, but he'd already put the music in the CD player and turned it on.

"If I play it soft," he said, "my mom won't hear it."

I already heard his feet clambering up the rungs again, much quicker than before, when the music first erupted in a soft series of clicks, ticks, and whirs.

"What do you think?" Michael asked.

"Shut up so I can hear it," I said.

The song played on, guitars and electronics and wails and screams and servants and punishments. Excited as he was,

Michael must have been tired because soon I heard his breathing settle down into a quiet, regular rhythm. The glow-in-the-dark stars had dimmed to nothing.

Then the first song clipped into the next. Clanking pipes. Moaning about lies. Shouting about them. The sound was alright, I guessed – not really my thing – but it was all pretty melodramatic. I replayed the week to myself in the dark. That first awful night before school had started, when I dreamed of the falling boy. Adam's Plan: power and pleasure. The afternoon sun beaming into classes reawakened by motion after summer slumber. Jay Flighting's tragic life and murder instincts. It was all easy to recall; my room never got as dark as Michael's did. He had blackout curtains while mine were translucent, letting in the light from the street. Compared to that, this was like a sensory deprivation chamber. I remembered the sweltering underpass and my blue bottle teashades. I remembered the battle on the train tracks. My sudden panic – *got to get out of here!* – through weeds and rushes, over chain-link-fences, stockade fences, shadowbox fences, past multiplying dogs, blanket haze, and at the end of the road, standing in the bloody sun, the man. His knife. *Am I a coward? Will Chuck tell what happened?* Those were abstract, daylight fears. Now, in the darkness of Michael's room, with synthetic beats raining down around me, the starker, sharper, simpler fears finally had room to stretch.

"Where did you get those sunglasses?" the man had asked.

Why did he care about my sunglasses? He had chased me, and we were all alone with the dogs. *What would he have done if he had caught me?* He hadn't said, but he had drawn a knife and run at me. For a moment – involuntarily – I imagined if I had tripped, or turned a wrong corner. Hit a dead end. Froze in fear. I imagined that slight blade slipping between my ribs, a silver sort of pain that hurt like cutting, like silver blood pouring, painful, but still not as painful as the knowledge of the damage it caused. I imagined the man taking my sunglasses and telling me they were his. That *he* had been sleeping in the corner of the underpass. That he'd finally caught me: the thief. That he'd been perched up on my roof each night, looking in through my window and watching me while I slept. That his sunglasses chased away evil, and now that he had taken them back – now that I was bleeding and weak – the hungry ghosts would smell the stench of my blood and rush in upon me.

Michael gave a sleepy snort above me, and rolled onto his side.

That's ridiculous, I told myself. *Mostly.* One of my concerns was more immediate. Less abstract. "What's your name?" the man had asked. "I'll find out," he had said. "I'm always able to find out."

The songs had pitched up and down, angry and haunted, and always full, too full, of fierce emotion.

But now the music took a plunge downward, like the continental shelf finally sinks toward the true depths. When the feedback finally dissolved into a piano's aphotic undulations – mutterings about loves lost and pains numbed by cold water – I felt myself falling farther. At last, I thought, I came within sight of the unbounded bottom. Beaming lines radiated out in all directions. They were so long, so extensive, that if I cut out a point or segment, what remained on either side was every bit as long and limitless as it had been before. These lines seemed grand to me. Too huge to fully visualize. Roads you could spend your whole life following. And then those lines, which had been length without width, suddenly widened, endlessly, beyond the extent of Michael's midnight blue carpet made black from lack of light. The carpet colors projected themselves upward and downward and became all visible space invisible, and space stretched and flexed and saddled itself out into infinite infinities. As space, as coldness, it was terrible. My brain was too small to take in the extent of this terror, and so terror coupled with terror; proliferating fear. A fear of fading blues and illogical, impossible motion.

And then I had a premonition of an empty room on the darkest road of the dying city. It was a bleak place. Blank and unilluminated. Its last light long lost. Unseen. Unknown. Functionally invisible yet there. There.

That's when Michael's awful song wrapped up on a major key and clipped out with a bird chirp. Then the music ramped back into squeaky syncopation. The next song was just a song, the carpet was just a carpet, the bleak house had vanished, and now Michael was snoring up above me. *Nothing going on here.* I was still able to shut out my fear. I was still able to focus on the next day's opportunities: the Plan, the Plan, the Plan.

"You'll have plans one day," my Aunt Ellie had told me, ages ago. I could still hear her voice, grainy and warm, even though I couldn't picture her face. "Wash your hands and pull up your pants, because someday you're going places!"

"I will, Aunt Ellie," I murmured to myself.

I rolled onto my side and fell asleep.

32

There's a small cuckoo clock,
on our bookshelf it stands,
and it points to the time
with its two little hands.

And may I, like the clock,
have my face clean and bright,
and a bird in my breast
keeping watch through the night.

When I was three, almost four, my Aunt Ellie went into the hospital for the last time. The cancer had spread throughout her body by then. "From the tips of my fingers to the nubs of my toes!" she'd said with a merry laugh.

Things had changed around my house. My mother smoked cigarette after cigarette, fidgeting as she lit up. Whenever she spoke to me, she sounded annoyed like when I was climbing onto the piano or standing on the coffee table. My father was worse. He sneezed all day long, red faced, then stayed up all night watching boxing on TV. The next morning, he'd be up again, sneezing and pouring water into his coffee from a big glass bottle.

"What's wrong with Mark?" I had asked my mother.

"What's wrong with your dad, you mean," my mother said.

"With dad."

"He's sad."

"What's he sad for?"

"He's sad... he's sad because he thinks his sister is going to die. Aunt Ellie. They love each other very much, and he's sad because she is very sick."

"Sick with a cold?"

"She's... it's like..." and her voice trailed off.

Ah, I thought. *I see. Sick like Timothy Brisby. An accident like Wile E. Coyote's. A death like Casper's. Not much to worry about because "it's going to be okay."* She'd told me so herself.

She'd told me so many times.

I couldn't imagine death. All *I* could think of was the pleasure of the present and the exciting future. Climbing on the playground with my friends, getting to stay up and watch a movie, and opening presents on my birthday. Every day was a chance to become something new – an astronaut, a dinosaur hunter, an autoworker like my dad – and I would never run out of days or becomings.

On the beautiful, *wonderful* night when my Aunt Ellie was finally going to die, my Grandmother Richter came over to pick me up. My parents were leaving for the hospital, but I had my jams and my pillow and my toy airplane ready to take the ride out into the suburbs.

An overnight visit!

I had climbed into my grandmother's car, into the booster seat, and my mother fastened the seatbelt across my lap. Grandmother Richter drove out past the Temple Medical Center, an alabaster tower ringed with blue neon bands at the top. In one of its higher rooms, I later heard, Ellie had turned her eyes out the window and mistook the glowing neon for the lambent aurora that had danced over Alaska on her honeymoon sixteen years before.

One-hundred feet below, my grandmother and I hurried out into Arcadia where the sweet and bitter scent of coffee and hot donuts for the third-shift factory workers, the rolling hills with their hundreds of porch lights shining off brick tiles on terraced lots, the dull red beacons winking from the top of radio towers on the hazy horizon, the river riding black and fast with mane of foam, the festooned constellations, the enemy stars, the waving trees, and a gospel song rattling through the dashboard radio – "This World is Not My Home" – all merged into a promise: *This is a world without end. This is a life full of joy. This city is alive, and it goes on forever.*

Even after we had arrived at my grandparents' tiny house, and I had brushed my teeth and lay down on the pull-out couch in the living room with my little airplane and the amber-colored night light, I thrilled with it all. I trembled at that unfolding. I marveled at the splendor and the luminescence of the universe even as one of my father's bright stars went out forever.

33

When I woke in the morning, Michael's bed was empty. A sere white light seeped in through the cracks in the curtains.

"Happy Birthday!" Michael said when I'd made my way downstairs. "You're a teenager for real now!"

My father picked us up and then got Adam from his sister's apartment. Adam slid into the back seat next to Michael and said, "Wow, you guys are still driving this piece of –?"

"You can walk, Adam," said my father.

"Just kidding," he said. "You know what car my dad drives? The soapmobile! 'Cause he's in jail! I just found out yesterday."

Michael laughed, too loud.

"Your friend lives down by Starr Highway?" asked my father.

"Yeah," said Michael.

"Friend?" asked Adam. "So this is a party after all."

Michael's "friend" lived in a small but tidy South Side bungalow. If you haven't guessed this plot-twist already, she was a girl: a cute redhead named Cora. Okay, so she was little and young looking. Prepubescent, almost, with a porcelain doll's face and cupcake cheeks. Where Patricia's hair was sharp red, Cora's was soft strawberries. "Hello!" she chirped, and I shivered in annoyance. *How the hell did he get a girl before*

Adam and me, anyway? What the fuck?

Michael started to take his seatbelt off to slide to the middle for her, but Cora opened Adam's door instead.

"Huh?" said Adam, then flashed his smile, and since he had never fastened his seatbelt in the first place it was easy for him to move to center. Cora laughed and climbed into the car. Michael frowned at the floor. My father turned the car toward Arcadia.

Arcadia and her ugly sister Acheron had been two charter townships that incorporated in the 70s to escape annexation by Akawe. They both suffered, more-or-less, the fate of most inner-ring suburbs: slightly less crime and slightly better housing paid for in soulless sprawl, dirt roads, and shitty services. But Arcadia, at least, had a sort of identity: It's where Basadina County came to shop and play. Aurelius Road widened to five lanes south of city limits and took in all of the obvious chain restaurants and big box stores before climaxing at the Basadina Mall two miles out of town. To junior high kids, this was the promised land. Don Pablo's sat near the midpoint of this strip on a scrubby hill looking out over I-92. Inside, high windows filtered midday sunlight onto a brick-tiled courtyard studded with potted palms. "Where do you want to sit?" my father asked.

"We're going to sit over there," I said, pointing to a table for four. "If you don't mind."

"Fine," he said. "I'll be at the bar. I mean, with a coke."

Once we'd been seated with a basket of tortilla chips, Adam said, "We've got to let them know it's your birthday. Maybe they'll bring you a slice of cake and some fried ice cream."

"Don't," I said. "This isn't a party. I just wanted to get some lunch."

"Why you look so mad?"

"I ain't mad."

"So what is it?"

"You know what it is."

"That thing Friday?"

"Yeah."

"It's fine, dude."

"You think Chuck ain't pissed off?"

"Oh, most def, Chuck's mad as hell. But what's he gonna do? He's our friend. It was his fault."

"It was kind of your fault."

"It was Sara's fault."

"What are you talking about?" asked Cora.

"Fight we got in," said Adam, crunching on a chip. "You know, on the tracks by the cemetery? Last Friday."

Her eyes went wide. "With who?"

"Just some kids messin' with my bro'. They ran off. It was over pretty quick."

Adam took a long pull of coke and stared her in the eyes. "So, Coral –" he started.

"It's Cora," she said.

"How you know our boy Mikey?"

"Mikey?!" said Michael and I.

"Yeah, that's what all his friends call him, right Mikey?" Michael smiled weakly.

"Mi-key is in my math class —" Cora said.

"Advanced Math class," corrected Michael.

"Well," she laughed, "it is for you."

"What do you mean?" asked Adam.

"It's Math 8," said Michael, and seemed to puff his chest out a little.

"Oh, so you're an eighth grader?" Adam asked Cora.

Holy shit, he's making a play right now!

"Yeah," she said. "Hey, didn't you ask out Sara Lupu? Not the tall, you know, black guy, but weren't you the one who gave her the note and she thought it was from him?"

"Yeah," sighed Adam. "I used to like Sara."

"Used to?" asked Michael.

"I'm a romantic soul," said Adam. "Sara's into thug life, right? She got us into that fight I was talking about. I'll throw down when I need to, but I don't like to. John and me, we're all about peace. Right, John?"

I made a peace sign.

"Well, I never got into a fight," said Michael.

"That's not quite true, Mikey," said Adam.

Michael looked at him, puzzled.

"Way back, we were all in nursery school at Truman, and Mikey had these... these plastic African animals. Lions and gazelles and giraffes and shit, and if any other kid touched them, Mikey would drag 'em out and beat their head on the ground."

"No I didn't," mumbled Michael.

"You were a monster, Mikey!"

Adam's eyes went wide like a wild animal's and he throttled the air. Cora and I laughed. Michael looked at the floor.

"Okay, okay!" he muttered.

"See, I don't think a boy can be a good man to his woman if he's always looking to start shit like Chuck and Mikey do. A man has to fix all his attention on his woman. A man has got to be romantic."

"But what about Sara?" I asked.

"A woman who tries to get her man to brawl? That ain't good."

I snorted. Cora laughed. Adam expounded: "Woe unto the woman who makes her man throw a blow, and woe unto the man who hurts a bro for a dirty ho. I think that's from the Bible."

Michael wasn't laughing.

"What's wrong, Mikey?" Adam asked.

"Nothing?" said Michael. His eyes were wet. He stood up. "Be right back. Goin' to the bathroom."

"The waitress comes back, should we order you the grande grande grande?" called Adam after him.

"What's wrong with him?" asked Cora.

"A bro is a lonely soul." mused Adam. "If he'd rather lick a dick than kiss a ho."

Cora looked at Adam for a moment; she wore a strange expression. Her eyes darted across his face, as if deciding whether to take up some challenge of translation. Adam answered her by miming a blowjob: tongue-in-cheek and hand-as-tube.

"I'm kidding you know," said Adam, seriously. "I mean, not about Mikey's licking dicks. That's all true. I'm kidding about kissing a ho. I only ever kiss ladies. Women. You know, sometimes people look at me like I'm just a little kid, because I'm small and skinny and shit. But I've lived through too much already to be a little kid. My dad's a junkie. He's left me alone for days without nothing to eat or drink. Shit, without electricity in the winter. You can't tell what someone's been through just by the way they look, you know? I know not to take it for granted. I don't kiss hos, and I don't kiss little girls. Just ladies and women, and that's just where it starts."

34

On Labor Day, I finally screwed up my courage and called Chuck. Nobody picked up. I waited five minutes and tried again. Nobody was home.

Even though it was pointless, I felt myself calm a bit as I put the phone back in its cradle. A whole weekend of worry couldn't fix the five minutes I'd fucked up on Friday, but I'd done what I could.

"John," called my mother. "Angel Demnescu has some crabapples for us. Will you ride your bike down to get them?"

"No," I said. "Get father to get them."

"He's sleeping," she said, her brow creased. "He's got to go into the shop tonight. So let me say it a bit differently: Ride your bike down and get them."

Moving north, as the South Side narrows toward Downtown Akawe, a different set of neighborhoods slope toward the river, utterly different from Ashburn Heights. The oldest factories in the city had been sawmills and carriage factories built on the opposite banks of the river. Then, torn down and rebuilt in fits of automotive fecundity, the riverbanks gave way to the great brick and metal slag of the Old Benedict complex: A, B, C, D, E, F, and G.

On the west bank, between the factories and Downtown, the carriage barons had erected fancy Victorian and Queen Anne mansions on postage stamp-sized lots. With

Akawe's decay, this neighborhood – the Old River District – had festered and partially dissolved.

The east bank had never known a golden age. The closest it ever came were the sweaty dances on the beer-stained tables at joints like the Butt Hut where my father's coworkers stopped for drink and company on the company, Sunday to Sunday. This neighborhood was called the Cellarway, a swampy area between the river and Sellers Creek, where willow trees grew wild between yellow block garages and the grass glowed fluorescent green. And at the very bottom of *this* mess lay the the four square blocks of Cartierul, levied against the creek and wedged between Adams Street and the South Street viaduct. There were only two ways in: off Adams Street as it rose one-way toward Downtown and by a set of crumbling concrete stairs that descended from the viaduct.

I rode my bike down South. When I turned onto Jordan Street, the last of the houses fell away, and at Adams Street the cottonwoods began. The sound of insects overwhelmed the hush of traffic. I breathed in the perpetual fog that hung over Sellers Creek and steered around the manhole-sized holes on the bridge, a twenty-foot drop to the rushing brown water. Then I turned onto the top of the grassy levy that had finally put an end to decades of flooding. Two stories up, I could see the carefully-tended rows of berry bushes and pear trees behind houses that hadn't seen a fresh coat of paint in fifty years. The occasional trampoline or wading pool. All the air hung thick with the pungent smell of crushed and rotting apples.

I turned off the levy and pedaled the last block to Selby's house at the corner of Prahova and Poteca Streets. The house sat on a double lot with a huge oak looming up on the corner. The house itself was a hulky bungalow covered with soot-stained gray shake siding and oddly spaced and shaped windows, but the wood picket fence around it was painted bright red. When George Senior had died, he'd probably left Angel enough money to put the family somewhere nicer, but the Demnescus had stayed in Cartierul, where Romanian was still spoken in backyards on summer evenings. Where eggplants and peppered steaks smoked on charcoal grills throughout the neighborhood. Angel still had her garden and her oak and her wind chimes. She still had her apple tree.

Selby's younger sisters played at the edge of the road. Aria, the youngest, was playing in a mud puddle, while Celesta sat on the curb and sneered at her sister over the top of some Beverly Cleary. Selby's older brothers, George and Demetrius, were nowhere to be seen, but Selby stood a few feet away, raking apples from underneath an apple tree.

"Hi Selby," I said, leaving my bike at the curb.

"Hey John," she rasped. "How's your plan going?"

"Good for Adam," I said.

"It's working?" she said. "With Sara?!"

"No. Some other girl."

"That girl's a fool if she decides to get with him."

"A lot of people are dumb."

"Get a rake and help me out."

"I'm here for apples."

"I know. Get a rake."

I got a rake and started dropping and pulling it, picking up giant clumps of grass along with the fallen apples.

"Just get the apples, John!"

"I'm trying!" It was hard work. "These look pretty bad."

"Those are the rotted ones. We'll use them for vinegar. We're going to shake some of the ripe ones off once we get these all picked up."

After a half hour we had finished raking up the rotten apples, and I was sweaty again. I didn't like it. Now Selby lifted her rake overhead and used it to shake a branch until all the ripe apples fell off. We dumped them into large white buckets. Aria screamed. Celesta had thrown her little doll into the puddle. Now Aria was crawling around, looking for it.

I couldn't remember any time in my life when I hadn't known the Demnescus. They felt completely familiar to me, which was strange because their family was so different from my own. The number of kids and the tragedies that chased them through their lives. The color of their skin and the dancelike language they spoke at home. My shitty house up on a hill and their shitty house down in the valley... though we had both started out in the valley. Selby's glass-on-chalkboard voice. It seemed like there should have been a great distance between us, but I thought I could hear her. What does that even mean? It's the only way I can describe it: I could *hear* her. *Do I want to be heard?*

"You know," I said. "I don't *have* to do Adam's plan. I mean... maybe *we* should go out. Maybe *you* should be my girlfriend."

"You don't want me, John," Selby said, wiping her brow. "I'm damaged goods. I was sexually molested as a little kid. Why you think my voice is like this, huh? It was the worst thing ever. I cried and cried."

She was funny, but it turned me off.

"Don't even joke about shit like that," I said.

Aria laughed.

She'd found her doll.

35

We were all damaged goods. At least *we* thought so. Some of us were more right than others. I didn't know many of Selby's stories, but I knew plenty of Adam's. Sure, I thought my life was hard because I had to carry pepper spray and get away from dogs sometimes and cross the street when some fiend stuck his head from a doorless doorway. I had known I was really out of my depth, though, when I was nine and went over to Adam's house for New Year's Eve. He wasn't staying with his mom or dad then, or his grandparents, or his sister. He was staying with his Uncle Mickey. At midnight, Mickey handed us his Glock 9mm and sent us out on the back porch to celebrate.

Neither Adam nor I had ever held a gun before, so we didn't know what we were doing. When I pointed the thing in the air, I held it so close to my face that the kickback drove the grip into my nose and I started bleeding all over. Adam was laughing at me all night, while I sat up worrying that my parents wouldn't buy my story. I told them I'd fallen out of his bed. They bought it.

While Adam still lived with his dad, we had to share a bed whenever I spent the night. There were only two beds and one couch in their various tiny houses, and the revolving door of friends and family – anywhere from two to ten people living there at any one time – meant that everyone was lying down with someone. Sometimes, the rough acrylic blankets smelled faintly of grease. Sometimes they smelled like pee. Once, they smelled like rotting potatoes. The kitchen always stank sweet of fermentation, and the living room stank of pot and tobacco. Often, the hallways smelled like shit. Kris Miller had gotten a dog, and it shit in the hallway and nobody cleaned it up for days. Their houses were close and claustrophobic. Kris kept the curtains closed all day long. I'd always take a shower as soon as I got home.

Chuck and Elizabeth both lived on blocks where most of the houses were boarded up. Chuck's sisters were always getting in trouble, but at least his mom kept her shit together. I got the sense that Elizabeth's life was more chaotic, but it was hard to say for sure because she never talked about it with us. On the one hand, Michael's house in Ashburn Heights was probably worth as much as all the houses on Chuck's or Elizabeth's blocks put together. On the other hand, Michael didn't have any friends, and you needed friends in a free-for-all like Akawe. Quanla's neighborhood was struggling, too, but her dad still made those X Auto wages. Her parents sent her to church camp in Muskegon each summer while Selby raked up rotting apples to press for vinegar and helped Angel knit quilts to sell to pay the mortgage. And that brings it all full circle to Selby.

School, at least, seemed to mix us all together. Hundreds of kids, shades of black and white, brown and shy, each with their own walk, words, promises, secrets, laughing at each other, some of them really confident and some just faking it. Tough boys and pretty girls and everyone all confused, noisy, tricky, and weird. Adam was right; this would be a strange and exciting kingdom to rule over. And not just because of the kids, either. I felt like I was starting to get sucked in by some of the teachers and the things they were teaching. I thrilled at the runes in the later chapters of Mrs. Norman's textbook... I'd heard of *x*es and *y*s but what were the triangles all about? How did junior high math partake of earthly sin? It was right there in the book. I felt the desert-hot and ocean-cool posters in Ms. Ropoli's room. I read about the Usher house and the monkey's paw with Mrs. Anders. I discovered the whole world all over again, as if it was all brand new: each morning, a perfect number of perfect diamonds hung from spears of grass and shot out their sun-bright reflections. A pollen foam settled over the steaming city and braced me against the bitter dark of future experience.

So damaged goods, cracked glass, yes. But fuck it. We saw sunlight reflected. We puzzled out its angles. Each morning began with a mystery that only we could solve.

36

The next morning, I met Adam in front of the school.

"We ought to meet at the back," he said. "More places to talk, and that's where the buses stop. We can catch the girls as they walk in that way."

"You gonna make a move on Cora?" I asked.

"Yeah, I think so. Your faggot cousin gave me a great birthday present on your birthday, John. I'ma hit her gut this week, I promise!"

"So you're giving up on Sara."

"Yeah, Chuck wants her."

"He said he didn't."

"You believed him? I didn't believe him."

Adam kicked some grass, exploding dew.

"What about you?" he asked.

I laughed. "You know," I said. "I asked out Selby yesterday."

"What?!"

"It was just a joke... I knew she'd say no."

"No, no, no, John. That's not the Plan at all. Selby's our friend, and she's in seventh grade like us. You have to ask out an eighth grader, and it has to be someone you don't care about so you don't feel bad about it. So you can dump her right away. Like Cora."

"Hold up," I said. "'Cause I'm wondering about that. I get the Plan and all, but what if we end up liking the girl we ask out... I mean, we gonna dump them anyway?"

"Yeah," he said. "We are. It ain't about getting with someone you *like*, John! We're looking at the next few years here. We set ourselves up as playaz now, we can see whoever we want later on. You wanna dump some hot trick and go out with Selby, that's fine... *after* we got our reps. You got it? We gotta be smart about this. We gotta turn on our brains!"

"Okay, fine," I said. "Anyways, I keep thinking about Patricia Perez. Sara's friend. *She's* an eighth grader. And maybe —"

"No," said Adam. "I told you. She's too fat."

37

When I got to Science Class, I found Chuck standing by Elizabeth's desk, talking to her in a low voice. She shot me a dirty look.

"Chuck," I said. "Can I talk to you in the hall?" I could hear my voice shaking.

"Sure," he said. His face was blank.

The hall was dark. The last fluorescent light had finally died.

"I tried calling you, but you weren't at home."

"No, I was dodging Kerm all weekend."

"Shit, is he still after you?"

"Yeah."

"Shit, shit. Okay, look, I'm sorry... about... I mean, I'm sorry... that I —"

"I'm not mad, John," he said.

"Yeah, you're mad!"

"No," he said. "I knew you two would run away. It's okay."

I shook my head, perplexed, but Chuck laughed.

"Come on, right? You're too short, you don't do sports. I like you, John, but it's not like you could even win a fight with many kids in our class. Adam neither. Running was the smart thing for you to do. I *was* able to take Kerm, you know?

If his friends hadn't been there — if the cops hadn't shown up — it woulda turned out a lot different."

"So Adam thinks you're still going after Sara Lupu."

"Yeah... I am. Yo, she seemed pretty interested in me, don't you think?"

"I guess so."

"People say all sorts of shit, but watch me this week, John."

"Chuck," I said, and my voice was shaking. "I shouldn't have run away. Even if you say it's okay, it isn't. I'm not like that. I'm not that kind of person."

"You got freaked out, John. I'll bet it doesn't happen next time. Your hood ain't rough like mine."

"I don't know. Do you remember an older white guy? Like older than high school, with Kerm's friends?"

"I think so. What about him?"

"Who was he?"

"I don't know who any of them were. I don't hang with Kerm a lot, you know?"

"He chased me. He pulled a fucking knife on me."

Chuck didn't answer, but a voice did come out of the darkness behind us: "Time for class."   It was a thin voice, feeble but annoyed. Mr. Kolin.

Chuck and I returned to the classroom and took our seats. Mr. Kolin followed. He was white, tall, skinny, balding. He wore pleated khakis and a button-down flannel shirt.

Glasses and thinning black hair that curled tightly around his head.

"I must apologize," he drawled. "You were here last week, and I was not. I had come to all the prep sessions – they have prep sessions for the teachers during the summer, you know – but I didn't understand that we were starting the week before Labor Day. It was an honest mistake, but I am sorry."

He wrote his name on the chalkboard:

MR. KOLIN

"We," he began, "are going to have the opportunity to talk about many things this year. They will be beautiful: Hydrothermal vents that are a source of life – very early life – perhaps five thousand years old, or maybe five billion. They will be awful: Children from Liberia with gangrene in their faces. Science can be lovely and awful. We'll talk about you. This is a very important time for you, my students. You aren't children any more. You're becoming adults. Adults in a very exciting and a very scary world."

He filled the chalkboard with some of the words he had spoken:

HYDROTHERMAL VENTS
GANGRENE
THE WORLD EARTH

"You know," he said, "statistically speaking, ten percent of American seventh graders have had sex. That means that three of you in this classroom have had sex already. Usually, you can guess who it is. It isn't good. You'll worry about pregnancy, but not diseases. There are lots of diseases you should be worrying about."

He turned to the chalkboard again, stabbing in words with broad, forceful jabs that sent shards of chalk flying off into the air:

GONORRHEA (THE CLAP)

CHLAMYDIA

SYPHILIS

GENITAL WARTS

A.I.D.S.

I looked around the classroom. Elizabeth was taking notes, but Adam was biting his index finger, trying hard not to laugh. Chuck smiled a little. Most of the students watched Mr. Kolin with expressions of amazement.

"This year," he said, "we will talk about how you can measure the speed of light with a rainbow. How the water you drink might be poison. How the universe might be, a bit, like a ball of... yarn. You hold one end of the string in your hand, and the rest unravels. It just rolls along the floor until there isn't any more. What do you have then?" He waited for an answer that wasn't coming. "You have a mess."

The kid sitting next to me handed me a note:

"Watsh news tonite. Big gang war West End. Satan's Master's vs Demonik Mafia. 1 of them gong down. My cuz scared. Reepers and SM hang. Thats why he'll leave me alone. + the Os. Not sure wuts going on there. - Chuck"

38

We ran laps through gym but the rumors ran faster. When I got to lunch, Michael was already sitting alone at his table taking shit from three boys.

"You fucking Jay Flighting?" they asked.

Then I knew that Cora had brought Adam's stories back to school and they had put my cousin in bed with his bully. It sucked for Michael, but it was funny, too, because of Jay. He'd come to Radcliffe ready to tear down walls, but he'd gotten torn down instead. Nobody had seen him in days; he was gone, and nobody was surprised. As for Michael, the sooner he got a clue, the sooner he'd get left alone. He *didn't* have any friends here, and it would be better if he ate his lunch in the office or the library. Anyway, Cora wasn't for him. I was surprised she'd even go for Adam.

Michael must have figured out the same thing, because he finally got up and left.

Selby and Quanla sat down at the end of the table.

"You sitting here again?" I asked.

"It was too loud over there," said Selby.

"You forgive us then?"

Quanla snorted.

Between bites of pizza and fries, they picked up an argument they'd been having during Lit class.

"No," Quanla was saying. "It doesn't matter who you know or what your priest says about it. Gay is gay, and wrong is wrong, and it's right there in the Bible, and God gave all the words in the Bible!"

"Giving Mrs. Anders shit, huh?" I asked.

"Not me," said Selby. "I like her. She's cool."

"She's a hardass," I said.

"Well I think she's cool, too," said Quanla. "And I think she's a good teacher, but that doesn't mean I think every *thing* about her is cool if you know what I'm sayin'."

"What *I'm* sayin'," said Selby, "is just because you've read some of the Bible doesn't mean you understand it all... what it's trying to tell you. My priest has known thousands of people from our church. And a lot of them – good people who have been in our church for years and years – are gay. And he knows more about that than we do!"

"Why do I need a priest, Selby? Why do I need an old man to tell me what God is saying when I can read what God is saying for myself? Really, y'all just need to pray. You think He's missing anything going on down here? He sees everything. All a priest can do is tell Him what He already knows."

"The priest ain't there for God," said Selby. "The priests are here for *us*. They spend their whole *lives* learning about God! I mean, you want to go to a dentist or fix your own damn teeth knowing what you know?"

"Jesus," I muttered under my breath. They both glared at me. I stood up and looked for Adam. Looked for Chuck. They were somewhere up ahead in line. *Anyone?* I sat down again.

"Why we gotta argue about this?" Quanla asked. "We always fight about it. We never get anywhere."

"Because there's people *different* from you, Quanla, and they ain't *all* bad."

"Like me," I said. "I don't even believe in God."

They both went silent and stared at me. I hadn't decided to say it, exactly. It wasn't something I'd thought about a lot at that point. I wanted to end their unending argument. And, maybe, there was something a little thrilling about being something different than what I had always been.

"See?!" said Quanla, "John's Catholic! He's got priests too. How you say a priest helped him understand things?"

"Well," said Selby, "it doesn't do no good if you don't listen to the priest, and anyway, Catholic priests are bullshit."

I smiled.

"Too much money," Selby said. She was trying to get me going.

"I'm not joking," I said.

"Shut up, John," said Quanla.

"He's full of shit," said Selby.

"No, I'm not!" I almost shouted. I wasn't thinking, but my face was hot. It felt like I meant it.

"So you changed your mind?"

"No."

"You're gonna change it back tomorrow," she said, smugly. *Oh, she think she's got it all figured out.*

"Maybe? Maybe not. It don't matter."

"It does matter."

"That's not faith," said Quanla in a disgusted voice.

"Why would it matter?" I asked. "You think about that stuff, you just believe it 'cause they tell you over and over. Think about it. It doesn't even make any sense. It's obvious it doesn't make sense. If there's a God out there, he's gonna be out there whether I believe in him or not. And I don't think, if he is out there, he really gives a shit whether I believe in him or not. If he's so powerful, what difference does my believing in him make?"

I was talking fast, but the words I heard myself saying sounded perfect to me. Obvious things, answers to lies you would swipe away as easily as a spider on your arm or a fly on your face. "Can't you see it?" I asked. "Can't you see the shit they're selling you?"

"Why you saying this?" rasped Selby.

"I'm saying it 'cause it's true!"

"I Am That I Am," said Quanla.

"'Don't be afraid, it's me,' he says," said Selby.

"'It's me,'" I quoted. "'It's me me me!' Funny, right, when you hear a kid talking like that you know he's spoiled!"

"I don't believe it," said Quanla.

"We knew John was an asshole," said Selby.

"John, you ain't never gonna be happy until you look deep inside your soul and learn to be humble in your life, and turn your greed into gratitude."

"No, he's just an asshole."

"No, he cares. I know John. He likes to act cheap, but you ain't cheap John."

"No, I ain't cheap," I said. "If I had more money I'd wear nicer clothes, but that don't mean I buy this God bullshit."

"You mean you really don't believe in God?"

"It's better if there ain't no god, because if there is, he's evil."

"That's the devil talking."

"He does evil things."

"No he doesn't!"

"He lets evil things happen. You hear about those kids jumped off that hospital last week? They all, like, died? Tell me that shit ain't evil!"

"They did that to they own selves!"

"Bullshit!"

"Jesus, John," said Selby. "Don't you notice, they talk about evil all the time in church. It's, like, all they ever talk about."

"Yeah!" I said, loud again. "That's right. They talk about it all the damn time. Have they ever given a good answer? Have they ever? Hey, hey, your dad died. He died on a construction site, right? Well, why did that happen? If there's a God who can make things happen, you ever get a good answer for why your dad died like that? No! It's just trust. Just trust, all the time, and if you die, and you're good, oh, *then* it'll all make sense. Yeah, just give me all your money, and *trust* me, I'll give you back ten times as much. Would you listen to anyone who said shit like that? Oh, hey, I'm just going to borrow your car, but I'll give you two, three cars tomorrow. It ever occur to you that with God it's just the same thing?! That if they're wrong, and you die, you won't understand shit? You'll just be dead. You'll never know more than you do right now. Kind of seems a waste to waste right now, when you are alive and have a chance to understand something."

Selby looked pale and silent now. I saw her jaw clenching.

"John," Quanla said, "what you're saying is unholy, and it's like, like, it's like a self-fulfilling prophecy. You say that, when you die, it *will* be death. You won't have any friends around anymore. You sure won't see me or Selby. We'll be in heaven. I think your parents will be too, and your priest too! It'll just be you and your best friend death... your only friend! You say you're going to death when you die, well you're going right ahead! You say, 'oh, there's evil in the world, there's bad, life sucks, when I die I'm just dead. I don't have a soul, I just have a mind... a mind is all, right now, because my heart is beating blood.'" She thumped her fist against her chest. "You think I don't know what you're thinking? I've heard it before. I've heard it. And you think, 'when I die, my body's gonna rot, and everyone will forget who I am, and everyone will forget what I did, and I'll fall apart just like... just like a cloud!' Well it ain't raining, John! And people like you, like you, they think, 'we're gonna die anyway, so let's live our life right now and just... burn through life like you're some bug crawling up a candle. You know what happens to those bugs, right? And that's when you people become drunks and robbers and pimps and prostitutes, and you buy fancy cars and lay down with dirty people too. Because, I mean, because, I mean, if they're just going to die too, they won't be around long to remember the wrong you did by them, right? So you rob and beat up people, even if it's little kids or old ladies. And you see someone who does know God – because there ain't any belief about it, John. We don't believe, we know. We *know* – and you think you're so much better and you know so much more, and you say, 'what a freak!' And you say – you people say – 'Hey, I have an idea, let's beat him up and rob him, because he believes in God, and if there's a God, God'll save him.' And that's why you kick in his teeth! And you say, 'Hey, I have an idea, let's kill him! Because he thinks he'll go to heaven, let's get him there a little quicker!'"

Her face was flushed, her breath fast, and there was an animation about her that I hadn't seen in a couple years, not since we'd ridden bikes together through the South Branch, trying to pull away from the cars.

"Jesus, Quanla," I said.

"That's right, John," she said quietly. "Jesus. That's exactly right."

That was when Adam and Chuck arrived with their hot lunches.

"Hi!" said Adam, "You're back at our table."

"John doesn't believe in God," said Quanla.

"Oooookay," said Adam, and he sat down and started eating.

But Chuck glared at me long and hard before he sat down.

Several minutes passed. We concentrated on our food. Then Selby stood.

"Fuck you, John," she said. She threw her tray in the trash and left the cafeteria.

"Way to go, jerkface!" said Quanla.

"I don't have anything to say to her," I said.

"You said a whole lot. All you said was wrong."

"Look, sorry. I shouldn't have said nothin'. I won't next time."

"Well, I'll keep saying things. Someone's got to get through to you."

"It's just a story. It's not even a good one."

Chuck banged his fist down on the table.

"That's the devil talking," Quanla said. "The serpent."

"Come on!" I shouted. "A snake's an animal! You see them at the zoo!"

"Yeah, well that serpent ate his own tail and kept eating till he was gone, so you just think about who your friends are and think about what evil things do to themselves!"

"I'm not telling you or Selby or anyone what to believe, okay? It's me. Don't blame some dumb snake that probably never existed. Blame me."

"I'll blame you," said Chuck.

"Thank you! Thank you, Chuck!" I snapped. "You can all try to make me feel shitty, but it ain't gonna change nothing. You ain't change me 'cause I know I'm right. And I think you're all a bunch of assholes!"

"Hello?" came an amused, slightly confused voice from the head of the table.

Sara was standing there. Patricia stood right behind her. *Patricia Perez!* I'd been so caught up in the argument that I hadn't seen them approach.

"Hey," said Chuck.

"What's, uh, what's going on here?"

Adam and I stared.

"Nothin'," said Chuck. "What about you?"

"Yeah, my church is throwing this really lame dance on Friday, and I thought you all might like to come."

"What, us?" I asked.

"Yeah."

"Liven' things up a bit," said Patricia. Her voice was rich and eager, so I gave her a smile, spread my legs, and leaned back.

"A church party?" said Quanla. "Well don't invite John because he'll just desecrate everything."

"He'll what?" asked Sara.

"They're mad at me because I told them I don't believe in God."

Sara shrugged.

"My dad says religion is the opiate of the masses," said Patricia.

"Well, anyway," said Sara, "you're all invited. John's invited. Just tell them I said you could come. They won't mind. It's pretty lame. St. Francis on the North Side."

"You go to St. Francis?" I asked.

"Used to."

"In the Os, right?"

"Yeah." Sara gave Chuck a piece of paper. "Give me a call if you're coming."

They left.

I leaned over the table.

"Just so you know, St. Francis is ghetto," I said. "They got rats in their cafeteria."

"Shut up," said Quanla, and stood up. "I'm gonna go find my best friend."

She left.

Chuck watched me for several moments, then cracked his knuckles in an exaggerated way.

"You wanna go to this dance?" he asked.

"You know I do," I said. "Adam's got this girl Cora. Maybe I can get with Patricia. You get with Sara. You want in on our plan?"

"I don't want in on your shitty plan," said Chuck. He thought for another moment. "You're going to apologize to her," he said, nodding in the direction of the doors out.

"To Selby?" I asked.

He shook his head.

"To Quanla?!" I asked.

"How else you think we're gonna get there, John? Her brother's the only one we know with a car who's gonna drop us off in that neighborhood."

39

When I got home, my mother was washing dishes alone at the sink.

"Where'd father go?" I asked.

"He's picking up some pipes for the basement."

"Something wrong?"

"Oh, you know. It's a wreck. It's always a wreck down there."

"Do you think God is real?" I asked. I didn't like the way the question burst out, so I tried to make it sound sarcastic.

"Oh, Jesus, John," my mother said. "It's been a really hard day, do you have to ask me stuff like that?"

"Sorry."

"Here, don't just stand there. Dry some dishes. Make yourself useful like your father."

My mother always washed the dishes and my father always dried. He figured he owed her this because she had always wanted a dishwasher and he had never bought her one. It had always struck him as an unnecessary luxury, even though there had been a time – before the property values fell, before the layoffs and cutbacks, before the moss on the roof – when they certainly could have afforded it. This nightly ritual was often the only time they spent alone together... especially when my father was working third shift. The silence between them.

The occasional muttered joke, muffled laughter. Steam clouding the window. The clink of glass and porcelain. My father would walk out of the kitchen with a wet towel in his hand. My mother would follow with her arms red from the heat.

They had met in college. At Michigan State. 1972.

As a kid, my father had always heard about the security of the shoprat's life. It was a boring life, yeah – the hypnotic churning of conveyor belts, cycling chains overhead, a constant beat in the pulsing of pneumatic veins. But it was secure. To my father, those factories printed fresh money as surely as they assembled cars. Or, that's what he'd say whenever he told the tale. It was one of his favorite lines.

When my father's dad had died playing a drunken game of chicken with a train – my father was ten when it happened – my Aunt Ellie had gotten a job at the new Meijer's on Arlington Road. She bought the family's food while my Grandmother Bridge worked to pay the rent. After work, my grandmother holed up in her room and slept and read and cried and watched television. Ellie raised her brother and sister in poverty, and Mark knew – he *knew* – that he had to make a clean break – a clean shave to swipe away the spears and the grit on his face. Money was the skeleton key that would open the door to his future.

And so, the same year that he went off to college, he also applied to work at X Auto, building Aubreys in the Old

Benedict. He had to skip a lot of classes to make his shifts: X didn't hire part time. X only offered overtime and a lot of it. As his paychecks went up, his GPA went down.

My father didn't know what he wanted to do with his life, really. He just knew it involved traveling far and wide over the world. Siberia, Mexico, Indonesia, Argentina – as long as it wasn't Akawe. But X Automotives was in Akawe. His skeleton key was fixed to a short chain. He was accidentally aping George Bailey. One day we were watching *It's a Wonderful Life*, and I realized that if Jimmy Stewart's character was a short, stubbly redhead with a beer belly who worked in an auto factory, he'd basically be my father.

Theresa had been raised with more choreographed goals. Her father proudly traced his roots back to the owners of a Mississippi cotton plantation – *what if my great great great grandparents had owned Chuck or Quanla's great great great grandparents?* – but their family had made the journey north with millions of others and found work in the X factories after World War II. They settled in the little suburb of Elmwood and my mother had gone to white suburban schools with as many doctors' kids as shoprat brats, as many Indians (Asians) as blacks. "That house had felt like an upholstered prison," she'd told me. After years of private piano lessons, swim meets, and cheerleading, she had plans that were more defined by the kinds of halos she would wear than the miles the journey would put between herself and home.

My parents sparked together one winter. They met at a dance. He was wearing a powder-blue suit and impressive sideburns. She was dressed a bit too much like a Southern Belle. They've never told me about it in more detail than that.

Then Mark dropped out and moved home. Theresa started an internship with WUOM but commuting to Ann Arbor to work, to Akawe to see my father and her family... It all wore her out. She had dropped out by the end of her sophomore year. She thought a job was on the horizon, but without a degree, the station wasn't going to offer her any sort of full-time work. Meanwhile, Mark was bringing home $400 paychecks, and Theresa realized that her own chain was shorter than she had thought. She moved back in with her parents. A month later, she moved in with Mark. A year later, they got married.

I've heard people – my Grandfather Richter, mostly – say from time to time that they wondered how it happened. How this tall, cool, graceful woman chose to marry the short, loud autoworker.

They weren't looking closely.

When I said that they sparked together, I meant it. The sparks were real. When my father used his Calculus exam to roll a joint and stalked out of class, smoking and smiling, the ties that held the two together were already strong. They had locked themselves knowingly together. They bought a house in Akawe and had a single child – me – and defied the world to give them any shit over the life they had decided to build together.

It sure made Adam's Plan seem petty and selfish and small by comparison, but I wasn't growing up in the shadow of Vietnam and Kent State and Watergate. I didn't have to worry about my country and family coming apart at the seams. My worries were that my friends' families and homes would disintegrate into ragged shreds of drugs and bullets and pillars of dark smoke. Stacks of unpaid bills. Mattresses and underclothes thrown out onto some dirty curb. All the kids misplaced and neglected amid the blocks of empty houses. So my parents' moment couldn't be my moment. I had to make my own moment on my own terms. Besides, I didn't think I could just *will* myself into sacramental fusion with another human being. I figured it had to happen on its own or not happen at all. Which was why the Plan seemed like the best I could do in seventh grade.

We'd finished washing the plates and bowls, but not the glasses or utensils. I dried my hands.

"We done now?" I asked.

"No," she said. "Not really."

"I want to go," I said.

"Fine," she said. "Go."

40

I wanted my bike to take me somewhere I could think, but it needed me to push and guide it, so I started off in the easy direction. Turning out my driveway, South Street was downhill. South Street it was. When I got there, I turned right, because nothing was to the left except the weeds and the cemetery. I wanted to stop at the Mexican restaurant where South met Whitmore, but I didn't have any money. The only other things there were a few ratty houses, a parking lot, a party store, and a florist. But it was one of the best views of the city. Through vacant lots, I had a clear view of the hazy skyline, all dust-colored. Behind the restaurant, a steep hill fell off toward the Zibi River. On the far side I saw the brick-and-steel buildings of the XAI and, beyond it, South Village. I saw the spire of St. Brendan the Navigator Catholic Church – *my* church – maybe a mile away.

Okay, then, I thought, and continued on down South Street.

I turned off onto Jordan, which plunged on into the Cellarway, but then took a left onto Aubrey Street, which brought me right down between the Benedicts B and C. They had both been idle for almost a year now, and a stalled conveyor straddled Aubrey with its oily chains frozen in place thirty feet up. Past that, the bridge spanned the river, and this was the exact spot where the Benedict March of Hunger – a union drive that had turned violent when the cops showed up – had happened more than fifty years before. Off to my right, the river bed, concrete-lined for flood control, swept upriver toward its confluence with Sellers Creek, then vanished between the dozen or so mid-rises left Downtown. The empty Ashburn Hotel to the west, the Two Rivers Bank to the east. Slightly shorter, the Pyramid Bank Building was getting ready for a daily immolation.

The most recognizable feature of the Akawe skyline was this ten-story tower topped with a pyramid of burnished copper, parallel horizontal panels alternating with narrow slats and tapering toward a point. Each day, the sun cut through its perforations and cracks and fired out rays of light in every direction.

But really, this dramatic view from Aubrey Street was only possible because half of the Old Benedict had already been demolished. I was separated from Downtown by a long flat of concrete, with chicory and poplars sprouting up wherever water had split the cracks. The river funneled a breeze toward me, but it stank of decomposing weeds. It had been too long since it had rained.

Pushing on up the other side, I made it to the corner of Poplar Street, the heart of the XAI, and it must have been near the end of class because students were leaving the brown buildings and heading out to their overheated cars that glittered like stars in a black asphalt sky. Some of these students would spoke off south toward Ann Arbor or east into Metro Detroit. Maybe a few toward Lansing or Flint. Others crawled home to dilapidated frat houses, perfectly at home in their sighing neighborhoods. Some of the houses sat on Aubrey Street as it wound upward, away from the river, with damp couches nesting on their porches, torn screen doors, and loud laughter wafting out toward the street. The students weren't always good neighbors. Eventually, the frat houses gave way to steep bungalows rising up on small hills to warily watch over the boulevard.

I can't say that St. Brendan's Church and School loomed over the neighborhood; its look was too gentle and airy to impose magisterial gloom. Nor did it tower; the steeple was fifty feet tall, tops, and the rest of the church was, on its hill, roughly level with the second floors of the nearby houses. The church had been built in the sixties and radiated community and warmth instead of Gothic gloom. The church and parish school took up a whole block on a major road, and so seemed to spread its arms out to take in the whole neighborhood as its chaperone – maybe even its mother.

I stashed my bike behind one of the school dumpsters, crossed over to the church – its flat white stones, its thin, vertical windows – and went inside.

41

I crossed through the narthex and entered the nave. It was a large room with a high ceiling. Cylindrical white lamps hung from long gray cords. The stained-glass windows shot geometric cuts of kaleidoscopic color across the red carpet, the blonde pews. The light took on an earthy sheen as it reflected off large panels of green faux marble. Above the sanctuary hung an alabaster Christ, his features, his wounds, his cross commemorated as a field of focused brightness. My overall impression was that of standing in light shade on a sunny day. There was something luminescent and ethereal about the cast of shades that radiated through St. Brendan's Church and shifted as afternoon aged toward evening and night. This was where I had been baptized, where I had received my first communion at eight and another every so often after that. I smelled a faint ache of incense in the air. Crushed rosebuds, burnt and scattered.

A low voice came from one of the confessionals. Weekday mass would start in an hour. I had plenty of time. I found a pew, two-thirds of the way up, and sat, and closed my eyes so I could rest and concentrate.

I didn't think Quanla was really that pissed at me, but she did expect me to tell her that I was wrong. I wasn't going to, though, because I thought I was right. That meant that the only way I could get back on her good side – and get a chance to ask Darius for a ride to the dance – was to have Selby say something on my behalf.

In a way, that seemed even less likely. Selby couldn't give two shits about my immortal soul, but she was pissed that I'd brought up her dad's death. That made sense, but while I expected Quanla to at least take my call, I didn't think Selby would even talk to me. Unless Quanla talked to *her* first.

"The Lord hates a lying tongue," I muttered to a statue of Mary that stood in an alcove a ways up, her palms pressed together, surely agreeing with me. Still, I thought I'd better clarify for her, just to be on the safe side: "Quanla's a tightass and Selby's trouble."

Mary didn't answer. She prayed. Or didn't. I mean, it was just a statue.

I'd been raised Catholic, though my mother had been brought up in an evangelical church and had converted for my father; one more strike against Mark Bridge with the Richters. To be honest, I suspected that my mother didn't buy Christianity in any of its many costumes. Maybe religious skepticism was genetic, or maybe I'd caught it when I saw her rolling her eyes equally at the prayers for the unborn at each mass and at my Grandfather Richter's Biblical rants against welfare and food stamps: "It isn't charity if it's compulsory!"

My father seemed to buy Catholicism, though, even if he didn't buy into all of its political particulars.

When I was young, we went to mass each week and all of the holy days of obligation. As I got older, we went less often. My father would say a prayer for important occasions sometimes – a birthday, an anniversary – but the inertia of routine had dragged him down. My whole experience of religion – of God – was all twisted up in habits half-learned, prayers half-remembered, moments of clarity and grace which nevertheless felt too distant, too rare, to be an anchor or a mooring, much less a salvation. Hands too far away to grasp me by the wrists and pull me in out of the deep-yawning water.

Still, I felt something genuine, sometimes, in big places, in empty, silent places, like the nave of St. Brendan's that afternoon. The silence, I believed, whispered. The empty pews were noisy and crowded. I looked from pale lights to white walls, and shivered and imagined them taking on a thin film of blue light.

That part was all in my head. There was no blue light.

Instead, the walls were open, clear, waiting. Inviting me to pray.

I hated to pray.

If there *were* things out there, invisible things, listening things, then *they* would hear my words. If I made myself vulnerable, I believed, I was opening up to *them*. If I prayed, then *they* might learn my sins and fears and turn them against me.

Whatever they were, they weren't angels. They were predators. I knew they wanted to devour me, though I didn't know how or what this meant. Maybe they would visit me in blue-hued dreams. Maybe they would whisper my blue-tinged secrets to my unknown enemies. The man with the knife. Maybe they would make a home in some blue corner of my brain and tell me to just close my eyes and leap from some high-up place. Now that I was sitting alone at the church, I was feeling less sure of my skepticism, yet this didn't comfort me at all.

Still, I'd ridden my bike here, the whole way, and I was getting hungry and tired. After all that, I thought I should at least say a prayer. So I said:

"Soul of Christ, sanctify me.
Body of Christ, heal me.
Blood of Christ, drench me.
Water from the side of Christ, wash me.
Passion of Christ, strengthen me.

Good Jesus, hear me.
In your wounds shelter me.
From turning away keep me.
From the evil one protect me.

At the hour of my death call me.

Into your presence lead me,

To praise you with all your saints

For ever and ever.

Amen."

When I finished, a shiver ran through my body. I felt dizzy and sick in my stomach. But I said:

"Show me something incredible. Show me something that I can't believe. Show me that it's real."

The feeling of sickness left me.

Instead I felt foolish, asinine, naked.

The priest – it was Father Xavier, the younger one, with open eyes and a slight smile – was standing outside of the confessional now. He saw that I was the only person in the church.

"Are you here for reconciliation?" he asked.

"No," I said. "I'm all done here."

42

I was in a weird mood for the rest of the day, like I was wearing someone else's skin and it didn't quite fit right. I didn't sleep well that night. I woke up when it was still dark outside and opened my window. The wind felt cool on my skin. Summer was leaving. I cleaned my room and got to Radcliffe twenty minutes early. Adam and I met up at the back entrance, as we'd planned.

"Hi," I said to a black girl with long, braided hair. "I'll do your homework."

She gave me a wry smile for a moment before going inside.

"You got it today," said Adam.

"Nah, I ain't figured out what to do about Selby and Quanla," I told him.

"It feels like they're super pissed, don't it?" he said. "Sometime's people aren't half as pissed off as they say. You'll be cool. We'll all be cool." When we got to Mr. Kolin's class, the radiators clicked into life for the first time, and I could smell the cracked paint warming in the stale room. The sun shining in through the windows was redder than it had been before. Mr. Kolin squinted in the rising light and lectured us on Mitosis.

"My toeses are coldses," he said and giggled.

A note arrived from Adam:

"hey john, this class sucks donkey dick. did chuck tell you wat is happen with kerm?"

Adam had also drawn a family of stick figures and labeled them for me. He was groping Mrs. Kolin's huge breasts while I made out with Mr. Kolin's daughter. Mr. Kolin sat in a different room, cluelessly watching Jeopardy. I knew this because Adam has written "jeperdy" on the TV screen and a short stick man with a mustache who must have been Alex Trebek.

"No," I wrote, and passed the note back.

"Telophase," said Mr. Kolin, and I could see his brain working, trying to make a pun out of it.

The next note read: "kerm nows were going to dances on friday w sara L but chuck think it haroin." *What is he even talking about?*

Below this, a T. Rex took a shit in Mr. Kolin's mouth.

"What do you mean?" I wrote. "PS. That's sick."

Adam got the note, covered his mouth with his hands, laughing, and wrote an answer. Folded it and passed it back.

Mr. Kolin started on Meiosis, watched the note as it crossed the room, and suddenly lunged forward. The girl holding the note gave a little scream and stuffed it into her mouth.

"Give me that!" said Mr. Kolin.

The girl shook her head fast – her dark hair flew out – chewing furiously. Everyone watched her.

"Give me that note!"

But she kept chewing and finally swallowed it.

"It's not yours," she said, her voice catching. Her voice sounded diamondy and girlish, like indescribable things, like clear syrup flowing, like the river shaded by the lindens outside of town, like dry furnace heat on a dark night and the candle glow after Christmas. Her voice washed over me because the snow in that future had melted too quickly. Her face flushed.

"I'll give you detention," said Mr. Kolin, testily.

"Sorry," the girl said. "I already swallowed it."

Who is she? I wondered. And since the school year had started out with Adam and me scoping out every female in our vicinity, I wondered how I had never noticed her before.

It had happened like this: On the first day of school, when I had given each girl in the class a good look, yeah, I had noticed her. *She's kinda cute,* I'd thought, and then my eyes had moved on to the next girl. She could have even been a second-tier popular girl who gets some attention from the boys, except she didn't do any sports so she was shut out of the jock tribe. She didn't talk much, so the gossip – even little gossip like Adam and I traded with Chuck and Elizabeth – radiated away from her. She didn't click with the geek cliques either; they were helpless and cynical. They bit down against the jox and gainstaz. This girl didn't resent anyone. She rejected most of the social compacts the rest of us assumed without thought. She wrapped herself in self-conscious privacy.

Without allies, without enemies, despite casual poise, she separated herself from the rest of us. She became invisible in plain sight.

But nobody can stay invisible when they eat and swallow a folded piece of paper with the teacher yelling at them and the whole class watching. So I took a second look, along with everyone else: She was a white girl, short, flat-chested, almost a suburban Caucasian, like she wouldn't have any idea what to do with slack jeans, weaved hair, rap, or collard greens. She had shoulder-length dark hair, just a bit full, just a bit wavy, and way too black. A sloppy black dye job, but she wasn't a goth either: she carried a pink and white backpack. She wore little earrings. Shiny studs. She wore pink tennis shoes and a white wool sweater. Her long eyelashes hung over slate gray eyes.

She didn't have much of a chin. It dissolved into her neck.

She had big hips, a narrow waist, and straightforward fingers.

Like I said, she was beautiful.

"I want that note!" Mr. Kolin screamed.

She held up her hands as if to say, *what do you want me to do?*

"No kinky notes in my class!" he shrieked. "No kinky notes here!"

We all laughed at him. He was funny. His fury seemed flustered and impotent. He reminded me a bit of a garden gnome.

"You two are going to detention!" He pointed at Adam and the girl. "You are! And for the rest of you... a test on Mitosis right now!"

We took the test. I failed. I hadn't been doing the reading and I couldn't stop thinking about the girl and what she had done. Paper and food. Two different things. But this girl had forced them into one space. She had saved Adam and me by making our thoughts into food. By mixing the ink and paper with spit and acid and cycling it through her body. I'd escaped punishment. She was punished. And the words I had written had become part of her.

Although I was still shaken, I went up to her after class.

"Thanks for saving my ass," I said.

"That's okay," she said. "It's not a big deal."

"My name is John," I said.

"I'm Lucy."

43

When I got home that day, I found my mother reading on the front porch with her bare feet kicked up, the dirty soles facing me.

"Put on some shoes!" I said. "It's gross out."

She laughed and stood up. "I was waiting for you," she said. "There's something I think you might like."

I followed her inside. She didn't even stop to scrape the dirt off her feet. She opened the record cabinet and thumbed through my father's well-worn jazz collection, neatly stacked in alphabetical order. At the back of the stack, she came to another, slimmer pile of records that didn't seem to be arranged any which way. She found the album she was looking for and pulled it out. A black-and-white photo of a white woman dressed in a black-and-white suit, her black hair wild, the black jacket slung over her back. The woman's eyes confronted me. They told me that she was one of the cool kids, and she might not have time for me at all.

"Patti Smith," my mother said. "Any of your friends listen to this?"

"I've never heard of her," I said.

"Well, I thought you might like it. Especially the first song."

She dropped the needle and the album crackled into life. Low piano notes, a hiss in the background, and then the sullen drone of the woman's voice: "Jesus..."

My mother smiled and left for the kitchen. I sat down on the couch and took in the bending guitars, the jangles, the feverish cat scratch voice. The sound built and built, as loud as a train or a jet engine – all our neighbors were listening to Patti now – but I also saw its contrast with the cool currents of mote floating through the silver afternoon light. I must have caught a glorious code in their lazy constellations, in Patti's frenzied declarations, because I knew then what I had to do. It wasn't that I was missing the solution. It was that I had misunderstood the problem.

As soon as the song ended, I looked up Quanla's number in the phone book and gave her a call.

"Oh, John Bridge!" her mother said. Kimmy Adams had always liked me. More than my own parents, it seemed. She handed the phone off to Quanla.

"What do *you* want?" she asked.

"I want you to listen to me," I said, "because you know Selby's not going to. And if you're mad at me after that... I guess there's nothing I can do."

"Uh huh," she said.

"I can't apologize for most of what I said, because I don't think lying is right. I go to church when my parents go,

201

and I listen. I *like* the priests, but I don't believe everything I see and hear. You know what I mean?"

I could hear the hesitation in her voice. "Yeah," she said. "I mean, sometimes. But you got it wrong, John. The pastor should be truthful and wise, but you don't have to believe the pastor. It's Jesus you have to trust. It's God you have to trust."

"I hear you," I said, "and that's why I keep listening. And I will keep listening. I know how you feel, but I don't think you can ask me to do nothing else. I mean, anything more than I'm doing right now."

"John, it's almost dinner here —"

"Just tell me you aren't mad at me any more."

There was a long silence. Then, I heard Quanla sigh.

"You say you'll listen," she said, "but will you pray too?"

"I'm a Catholic," I said. "They tell us that listening is a way to pray. Do you buy that?"

"But only if you listen for God..." she said.

"Who else would I be listening for?" I asked.

"Okay, fine," she said. "I don't want to be mad at you, John. I don't want you to go to hell, either. So you keep listening, and praying, and talk respectfully to the rest of us who... who aren't as doubtful as you are, okay?"

"Right, right," I said. "Of course I will."

"Is that all? I've gotta go..."

"That isn't all."

"What else then."

"See, I knew I wanted to talk to you because I can be up front with you. Selby's mad at me too, but she's mad at me because...because of what I said about her dad."

"That was pretty mean."

"It wasn't mean. I thought it made my point, but I swear I wasn't trying to be mean. It's like, you mention her dad, and she just totally flips out."

"Yeah, well, that's why we don't mention him. What do you want me to do about it?"

"Could you say something to her for me, Quanla? You don't have to say a lot... just let her know... let her know I wasn't trying to make her feel bad? I honestly wasn't."

"Well..." she said.

"I know you gotta go," I said. "But just... mention that to Selby for me, okay?"

She sighed again. "Okay, fine."

44

I could accept what Jesus meant to Quanla without changing what he didn't mean to me. The fight was so easy to fix I couldn't believe how much I had worried about it. And now that the trumpet call of mutual respect had brought down the walls of Quanla's anger, I thought I saw an empty stage beyond, at St. Francis School, enticingly lit, a hint of background static, where Adam could act out his plan upon Cora while I might bring it to life in Patricia.

Adam was wrong, I'd decided, about her weight wrecking her for the Plan. "Liven' things up a bit," she had said. "You got a trashy mouth and mom." "My dad says religion is the opiate of the masses." Patricia walked into every room like she owned it, and if she wasn't skinny like Sara or delicate like Cora, she still had more swagger than the two of them combined. And that made me think of something else: Adam could dump Cora if he wanted, but I was starting to feel like I could learn more from Patricia than I could from other girls. That she'd be much better to have a girlfriend than an enemy ex. I just had to seize the moment. To step into the woozy lights and the bumping bass and make her want me.

It was just three days away.

The next morning, I told Chuck and Adam about my talk with Quanla and we came up with a plan of attack. Quanla talked to Selby during Lit class, and I caught her just afterwards and apologized for bringing up her dad's death. Then, I came to lunch late so that I was away from the table when Chuck and Adam asked Quanla if her brother Darius could give us a ride to St. Francis. Chuck gave the smallest nod when I finally arrived with my tray of pizza.

"And John too?" asked Adam.

"But Selby gets to come, right?" said Quanla.

"Oh yeah," said Chuck. "They'll let me invite whoever I want."

"So you, me, Selby, this Cora girl, and these two crackers." Quanla gestured to Adam and me. "It'll be crowded."

Chuck arched his eyebrow. "Come on," he said. "Darius is going to have a problem with that? I don't think so."

"Yeah, I'll ask him."

"Ask him what?" I asked.

Selby gave me a long look and I couldn't read her face. "You always wear sunglasses to school, John," she said. "You even wear them inside. You gonna wear them to this dance, too?"

"Probably," I said and grinned.

September marched on, another week of school died, and on Friday, Darius Adams swung by my house with a bunch of kids packed into his back seat. I got in quick, before my parents could see that there were more kids than seatbelts.

45

Selby and Quanla shared the front passenger seat, while Chuck, Cora, Adam, and me – "Chuck and the Crackers" as Quanla called us – shared the back of the cream-colored Starr Daphne, one of the most subcompact of X's awful subcompacts.

Heading north, South Street converged with Whitmore and picked up a couple extra lanes before sweeping past the derelict Basadina County Lunatic Asylum. It was a huge brick building, ninety feet high and the size of a city block. Broad stone stairs climbed past tree trunk-sized columns to massive wooden doors surrounded by oaken frames filagreed with laurels and hemlock fronds. It was all empty and rotting now, surrounded by a stately circle of attending beeches and sycamores and a huge bank of dark trees behind it.

After passing that, the ground fell away under the South Street viaduct, and if I had looked out the window at the right moment, I would've seen the very top of Selby's house between the young poplars clinging to the side of the earthworks, their leaves coalescing in the wind. This was where Adam and I had met on our bikes before the first day of school. Before the Plan, before the sunglasses, before the fight, before tonight. I felt like my life was racing faster than Darius' car.

The north end of the viaduct marked the beginning of Downtown. Still plenty of wood-frame houses here, but some taverns and party stores, too. Bitternut hickories and American elders. We passed old Victorian houses that had been subdivided and bought on the cheap, then converted into lawyers' offices, bail bondsmen, and notaries public. Afterward, a couple restaurants and then a giant white rectangle flanked with classical columns: the county courthouse.

Darius turned left onto East Street and made his way down the main drag. East Street actually looks like it belongs in a larger city than Akawe. The monolithic Arcade Vecchio, the Presbyterian and Lutheran Churches, the various government buildings and businesses, shuttered boutiques and bars, and above all, the stone stalwarts: the Two Rivers, the Pyramid, and the Olan Foundation Building. Arthur Olan hadn't been a founding father of Akawe, but he might as well have *been* Akawe when it was a wealthy city. He had owned and steered both Akawe and X Automotives from behind the scenes, and these three towers could only have been built in a place with a lot of people and a lot of money. The buildings had outlasted both people and money.

In '93, Downtown Akawe wasn't quite dead. As the outer neighborhoods lost jobs and people, a lot of public and private money flowed into the seven blocks of East Street between South Street and the river. Southern Michigan U had finally built a dorm here, and coffee shops and sidewalk cafes had followed. As we rolled down the pavement toward the river, a breeze stirred through our hair and the sun set the scene on fire. In Downtown Akawe, red brick was everywhere, covering the streets, the sidewalks, and the buildings. A giant multicolored brick mosaic inlaid in the center of the street projected a vision of four great wheels – a chariot wheel, a wagon wheel, a locomotive wheel, and an automobile wheel – up into space. This message to the extraterrestrials was unmistakable: this place had bet its life on motion, and if it didn't keep people moving, it would die.

When we crossed the Zibi River, East Street became West Street, and the tallest buildings receded behind us. To our right, a vast green field dotted with willows spread out in a broad triangle between West, Reuther Avenue, and the curve of the river. This hadn't been any intentional park. In the early 80s, Hand-in-Hand Workerland, a theme park paid for by both the city and the Olan Foundation, had tried to fix Akawe's slumping economy with tourism. Ten years and $200 million in the hole later, the theme park was demolished. All that was left now was a view, and while it was a nice view, I had heard my father talk about the bookstores, bars, schools, and houses that had been torn down for the massive project. It had all added up to a big fat zero.

Dusk had fallen by now. The sun had sunk. Lights clicked on within the Pyramid's triangle, and the bulbs made a tetractys, a harmony of light, a unity of dividends, limited fiduciaries with unlimited interests. The tetrad began its pale yellow vigil over the rowdy-poor city. Someone gunned an engine on a drag strip far to the west. We turned onto Reuther Avenue and resumed our trip north.

The skyline vanished behind us after we crossed the river again and we passed the Farmers' Market with its green shutters, the dull HoJo squatting on a geographic anomaly — no neighborhood, no business here, really, just an urban renewed patch of post-industrial concrete. Then we crossed I-292 into the North Side proper.

Reuther Avenue became Suarez Boulevard, a dividing line everyone knew about.

To our right — to the east — was the Anderson Park neighborhood: Campus Akawe with its planetarium and museums and auditoriums, Akawe Community College, and the quaint Cape Cods and Tudors beyond. It was one of the only really middle-class neighborhoods left in the city. School teachers lived here. So did police, nurses, doctors, lawyers, and half of the city's politicians. People whispered that some city council members actually commuted to their "resident" wards from their second homes in Anderson Park. Red and silver maples ranged away along the flat streets before dropping off toward Hunter Creek.

To our left lay the Pineway, a bank of spruce trees that walled off another neighborhood — the Os — from Suarez and Anderson Park.

We reached Orion Avenue and turned left into the Os. The home of the Crazy Chalks. The home of the Mexican Deadly Undertakers.

But, hey, homey gs, I'm exaggerating the vibe, yo. I was a South Sider. I'd been told to steer clear of the West End, and the North Side, and the East Side projects, and the rattier parts of the East Side, and the rattier parts of the South Side too, and everywhere industrial. Gangs ruled some of these streets, threw colors (they still did that in '93), drew their own invisible lines, and fought over them. Adam had lived over here once, and so did Bill Chapman. The Os didn't bother Selby much. This was a busy and half-empty place. A noisy, cluttered, hollowing-out, diverse place full of tiny wood-frame cottage-houses that were now mostly empty, burnt out, or torn down. Between the abandoned houses, the Os wore bright colors, and these shone when Darius' headlights reflected off the stoops, porches, doors, and walls. There were plenty of trees in the Os, tall trees that would give you privacy for some quiet conversation. Or a kiss. Or an arson. Or a robbery. Or a quick fuck in the shadows.

It was still warm enough out for the air to carry the thick stench of oil and ozone across the river from the Benedict Main. Laughing gas whites blasted Ted Nugent and ICP from their bedrooms and back porches. Blacks blew NWA across the speakers of their rusted Benedicts and full-sized Aubreys. A little French and a little Lingala. "O melaka likaya?" "Ée;

matóndo." Right before we crossed Owen Road, the neighborhood's main drag, we heard a canned mariachi band rattling out a frenetic tune from a taquería that was just now opening for the night. This was a strange sound for Akawe, where neighborhoods almost always tilted chocolate or vanilla. And through it all cycled the relentless sequence of O Streets: Ockeghem, Odette, Ogden, Ogema, Olivet, Olthoff, Omira, Ormond, Orr, and maybe a dozen others. We passed King Michael's Famous Coney Island and a Kroger's, but after Owen Road every last business was boarded up or burned down until we reached the church a half-mile later.

"That's it," I told Darius. "That's St. Francis."

"Right," he answered.

He dropped us off in front of the rec center.

46

St. Francis was an anomaly in the middle of the Os. Its roof was green, copper, circular, and still. The rest of the dilapidated neighborhood seemed to blur around it like the winds about the eye of a hurricane. To the south, across Orion, the heart of the Os fell in black shadows under un-illuminated trees. After the houses had burned down, they had been demolished, and when block after block had been reduced to flat lots and meadows, the city had cut the lights. On the north side of Orion, the gutted hulks of undemolished buildings hung out on either side, many of them blackened from flames, windows blown out, guts stuffed with rotting mattresses, plastic trash bags, and rancid carpet carcasses. St. Francis kept a calm vigil over it all.

"This a rough hood," said Chuck.

"Rednecks with shotguns?" I asked.

"KKK," said Quanla.

"And the Undertakers," I said.

"No," said Adam. "They're over there." He pointed into the shadows across Orion. "This here is Chalkland."

We went inside.

We entered a large room where the beige tiled walls reflected carouseling bars of slick, liquid light. A strobe flashed in one corner. Thirty or so kids stood around, and four or five of them were dancing. I strained to see Patricia, but she wasn't on the dance floor. I strained harder, looking for her in the crowd, and I didn't see her, and had a sudden panic that she was in some corner with a boy. What were they doing back there? The shifting lights were unable to overcome the darkness in the corners. This was my first dance, but I wasn't planning to let anyone know.

A nun in a habit stood at a small card table with a boom box playing a TLC CD.

"By the pricking of my thumbs, sumthin' wicked this way comes."

Until we had arrived, TLC's were the only black voices in the room. Thirty brown and white heads nodded sleepily up and down.

"Hey," I said, "looks like Chuck and the Crackers just got a lot bigger."

"Who dat?" someone called out.

"Chuck! John! Hi," said Sara, walking toward us. Behind her, I finally saw Patricia. She stood near the limit of the light, dancing with a lanky white boy with straw colored hair and fake gold chains. They were dancing close. He looked older than the rest of us. Maybe even a high schooler.

"Who's that Trish is dancing with?" I asked.

"You just call her Trish?" sauced Sara. "That's Lark, the DJ."

"The DJ? Then who's that playing the music?"

"That's Sister Margaret."

Patricia made knots of her arms around the boy. Their shadows flew wild, and I accidentally bit my tongue. Hard.

"So Chuck," Sara said. "You do karate?"

Adam nudged me.

"Let's go dance," he said.

"You and Cora?"

He grinned. Cora was already swaying out on the dance floor.

"Who'm I gonna dance with?" I asked.

"We'll make a Cora sandwich!"

The song ended and Lark, the "DJ," ran over to the table and gave the nun a new CD, and so Madonna clicked in and told us to bump and grind. We did our best. A few more of the kids were dancing now, happy to strike a pose, and I realized I was at the whitest party in Akawe. Cora was cute, in a creepy little girl sort of way, but she had no ass and no sense of rhythm.

Patricia, on the other hand, seemed to be having the time of her life.

I left the dance floor and got a cup of punch.

Patricia came over with Sara and a tiny girl with dark eyes, brown skin, and straight hair that bobbed at her shoulders.

"Sara told me you were here!" Patricia said. "She said you called me Trish!"

"Ain't that what you're called?" I asked.

"No, just Patricia." She was shouting over the voguing.

"That takes a long time to say." It seemed clever in my mind but sounded salty when I actually said it. The girls laughed, and I felt like they were laughing at me.

"I think your DJ's got another date," I added.

Lark was talking excitedly at the nun, who nodded with a beatified smile.

Patricia grinned at me. "Lark's not my date. Oh, he thinks he is. He was telling me that he was writing our initials in his driveway with his bike. "

I didn't say anything.

"It's a gravel driveway," she explained.

"His bike?" I asked. "You mean with his motorcycle gang?"

"You're funny!" said the Latina girl.

"Lark is in ninth grade," said Patricia. "He's not much older than you are. He's my neighbor too. We live on the West End."

"He don't look too West End," I said. "He's whiter than I am."

"And he's got a white ass too!" said Sara, and she squealed and ran off.

"Sara's loco," said Patricia. "She likes your friend Chuck, I think."

"Good for her," I said.

"Do you like Smashing Pumpkins?"

"What, like on peoples' porches?"

My question hung in the air for a moment. I stared at the two girls, and they stared right back. By the time I figured out that they were trying to decide if I was joking, they'd realized that I wasn't.

"They're a band," Patricia said. "Alternative."

"Sure they are," I said.

"So," she went on. "This is Juanita. You guys have, like, the same name, right? I mean, hers is Spanish. Yours is English. So I think you two should dance together."

Juanita smiled. She looked like a child. Even more like a child than Cora. She didn't exactly thrill me.

"I'll be back," Patricia said, wandering back toward Lark and the nun.

Juanita waited.

"How old are you?" I asked.

"I'm in seventh grade," she said.

"Yeah, but how old are you?"

"I'll be thirteen next summer, but..."

The song was over.

More shuffling of CDs.

The new song came on. *Girl You Know It's True* that John made up with Quanla just so he could come here tonight. *Girl You Know It's True* that Lark's a tool. *Girl You Know It's True* that Milli Vanilli sucks!

"I don't think I can dance to this," I said.

"But you haven't gotten me anything to drink," said Juanita.

I gave her my cup and left the room.

I left the rec center and stood on the edge of the parking lot.

Selby found me there.

"What up?" she asked.

"This is not what I expected."

"Want to go for a walk?"

"Can't hurt," I said.

47

White spray paint jagged along the side of a broken gray house whose own paint had been scraped off by many years of rough weather. The new tag said:

Welcome to the ghettOs

Selby and I turned our backs on the forbidding vacancies across Orion and headed down Octavius, where lights twinkled in the windows of the ragged little houses.

We crossed Pasadena Avenue.

We crossed Oakdale Street.

My hands were clenched into fists in my pockets.

"You want to get with Patricia, don't you?" Selby asked.

"Yeah, I thought so. But it looks like the DJ is more her deal."

"But you want to get with her, like, with your plan right? I mean, you want to get with her and then dump her?"

"I mean, it's Adam's plan, you know? I know I want to get with her. I'm not sure I'm down with the dumping part. I mean, why does it even have to be Patricia? I mean, who the hell is she?"

"Is Adam going to dump that Cora girl?"

"How the hell do I know?"

"He says he will though."

"Yeah..."

"He won't dump her. Who else he gonna go out with?"

"Whoever he wants. He's good at this."

"And you're not?"

"Well, there's always Juanita."

Selby laughed.

"She's not my type," I said. "Too... little kiddish."

"John, anyone that's female ought to be your type."

"Oh, ow Selby. Ow, you really got me there."

"Even female dogs... even bitches."

"Oh, Selby, you're really hurting me."

I couldn't tell if I thought she was funny or if she was just pissing me off. It seemed like it ought to be obvious, but it wasn't.

Far away, tires squealed.

Further off, the train.

Welcome to the GhettOs.

There were lots of ghettos in Akawe. Two of them were a bigger deal than the others: the West End and the Os.

The West End wasn't completely a ghetto, but a lot of it was. It followed the sprawl of the Benedict Main and the Benedict West, carrying the warehouses, rail lines, houses, and parks farther and farther from the old river crossing. The neighborhoods there had risen quickly and had fallen faster. When courts overturned the racist housing compacts, black Akaweans, who had been crowded into a few polluted hoods near the factories, spread out across the city. Just as fast, the whites booked it for the suburbs, causing housing values to crash. A decade later, the factories started closing, and they took the supermarkets, the restaurants, the little tailor shops and shoe-shine stops, the bars and blues clubs with them. The West End had been a city within the city. Now it was a desolation within the city. And most of the time, Akawe's ruling class, its fresh-scrubbed officials in Anderson Park and the X elite down in Bellwood, did its best to pretend that the West End didn't exist. But this was difficult, because half of Akawe lived there.

The Os, on the other hand, was an older neighborhood, but even maps gave the unsettling impression that Akawe didn't want this area. The city had sequestered the neighborhood on every side. The barriers to the south: the Benedict Main, the Zibi River, and I-292, pushed through in the 70s. Then the Pineway walled it off on the east and more factories lined the northern boundary of Ash Highway. But while the factories separated the Os from the rest of the city, their proximity gave the neighborhood a reason to exist. Wood-frame houses sprang up during the 20s and 30s, and plenty of white autoworkers made their homes here, where it snowed soot on chilly winter nights, and the industrial stink steeped thick across the opened-vowel streets. Of course, those factories closed too. By the 1990s, the remaining houses were almost entirely rentals held by dozens of unseen landlords. If the autoworkers had moved on, their immigrant neighbors had not. Mexicans lived along Pacific Street, Chinese along Owen Road, and Appalachians lived the length of Orion, Pasadena, and Olympia Streets. Neighborhoods within neighborhoods in another city within the city. Like the West End, the Os had fallen far. Unlike the West End – unlike its own name – the Os were closed off.

As we walked, every second or third house had been boarded up, scrapped, or burned down. Some houses were houses, and some were clapboard shacks, but it was hard to say for sure because the box elder leaves were thick in the air and all around us. When some streetlight managed to make its way all the way down to the pavement, it was a sere yellow light that lit up the pits and crags in the sidewalk.

I didn't like walking in the Os, but I didn't want to go back to the dance, either. Getting mugged or shot would be less embarrassing than another conversation with Patricia.

We reached a street corner. Some wind tousled the leaves overhead. A cricket chirped, and all went silent.

A glassy, sad hulk of a house sat to our right, and its porch was graffitied with a pink X surrounded by a blue O. I thought it was one of the tags put up by the power company saying that the gas had been shut off. The house seemed to stare at us through its open windows. Most of them were broken, but a few were not.

"Make a wish," said Selby, and she picked up a rock and hurled it through a window.

Immediately, the night came alive. The crickets resumed, the wind picked up, and I heard a voice from deep within the house growl. "Why'd you do that?"

Selby grabbed my wrist and squeezed. I wanted to run, but she remained rooted where she was. So we waited as the faint glow of a cigarette sparked in the dark, lifted itself to invisible lips, and swayed its way toward the window.

"Here I lie, resting my eyes, but not my mind," came the muffled voice. "It is traveled by thick-coming fancies that keep me from my rest. Do I see two Caucasian Tribesmen carrying the dark mark of the burning coffin on their brows?" He stopped just within the broken window, an indistinct shape. "No," he went on. "I don't think so. I don't see the mark of the beast on you. Who are you?"

"I'm Selby Demnescu," said Selby, "and this is John –"

"Shut up!" I said.

The shadow took a pull on his cigarette.

"You should listen to your friend, Selby Damnbooboo. He sounds smart." He flicked ash. "Woman was sin's beginning, and because of her we all die." He coughed. "If she walks not by your side, cut her away from you."

"Well...who are you?" I asked.

The figure appeared to think about this.

"You can call me Chalky," he said. "I been a Chalk a long time. I was a Chalk when the Christian decided to invite the niggers and spics and chinks into our gang. My daddy was a Chalk when Ernie Pops started the gang to keep 'em out of the Os. I'm a kind soul. Unless you're with the Undertakers. Then I'm a beast with ten horns and seven heads. Are you with the Undertakers?"

We didn't answer.

He went on: "Don't be afraid to speak. Our law does not judge people without first giving them a hearing to find out what they are doing, does it?"

"We're not Undertakers," Selby said.

"Well, I'm glad to hear that, Selby Damnbooboo, because the Undertakers are devils. But I think they'll be ringing up zero in the Os before too long."

"What?"

"Where do you live, John? You don't look like an O creature to me."

"I ain't!" I said.

"In the city?" he asked. I didn't answer. "In the burbs?" I waited. "Ah, he's smart here. He knows you don't say a lot of shit to strange men living in abandoned houses. Fine, John. I think I can guess where you live, but I can't say for sure. But Selby, you aren't so lucky. Damnbooboo. That's a Romanian name, isn't it? You live over by Downtown, down under that bridge, with the other gypsies and niggers."

"Watch it," I said, although my voice shook as I said it. I wasn't feeling brave but I knew it was better if Chalky thought I was.

The man lifted his arms defensively. "I ain't got no trouble with niggers," he said. "Didn't I tell you that the Christian decided they could be Chalks, too? Who am I to contradict the interdiction of Dear Leader?" He paused. "I might think he was wrong, but I abide, I abide."

"Aren't you afraid he's gonna hear you talking like this and come after you?"

Chalky coughed. "I don't think so," he said. "He's in prison a long time, but even if he heard, Dear Leader must abide the opinions of his favorite agitators and loyal retainers. Ash abides. EZ abides. I abide. Even God abides. But you think we're all racists and criminals, don't you?"

We barely breathed.

"You're terrified of me, aren't you?" Chalky laughed. It was an awful, wheezing sound. "You don't have to be scared. I'm not going to hurt you. In fact, I'm going to help you. You see, you could have said 'yes,' because we are all racists, and criminals. Almost all of us. We were born poor and hungry in the Os – crack babies born addicted to rock, rock children ground underfoot by the sturdy heels of steely police boots, those big cars that bum badum bump through this shitty town. Our lives made us monsters, but that is why we are divine and to be trusted. God chose what is low and despised in the world

– things that are not, to reduce to nothing things that are, so that no one might boast in the presence of God. Don't you trust me?"

"No," I said.

"Good, you shouldn't. But John, you can't hide everything. I'm guessing you're a nice white boy from the South Side. Is that right? South Village? Ashburn? Or maybe closer. Anderson Park? But Selby, how exotic. Right now I see a Blaromanian who lives down in the mud, and we don't see many of you around here. You remember Master Manole? He hangs around here these days. His spirit haunts the Os."

Selby squeezed my hand so hard that I almost cried out, but this must have been a rhetorical question, because Chalky went on.

"No, we aren't evil. We're gentle monsters trying to make the world a happier place for ourselves, our children, our brothers in arms, our neighbors. Everything good that's ever happened in the Os has happened because of the Chalks. The cops'll lie. Politicians lie. They say we're thugs. We're really totalitarians. We were children once. As children, we played in the mud – just like you, Selby – and we fought each other, house to house, block to block, street to street, all across the Os. Even in the good old days – it was a lot nicer back then – we fought each other as the Counts and the Tomahawks. But then the spics and niggers and chinks started in. Ernie Pops knew that, to quote the Bible, 'he who rests—rusts,' and so he

225

brought us all together, and that's when the Chalks were born. 1955. I grew up in this house right here, behind me. I grew up with the salt of the earth. What color is salt? Salt is white. You know that. But if the salt loses its saltiness, how can it be made salty again? Do you see what I'm saying? Look, I have no problem with niggers on the West End, the East Side. They can take over there as far as I care. I don't mind if the spics open some Taco Bell over on the South Side. I eat Chinese food time-to-time, when I want, where they are. But these here are the Os. They outnumbered us. They were crushing us on all sides. Zero and his Undertakers. Ernie was a good man, but he didn't know how the real world worked. He woke up dead in a trunk one day." Chalky made a gun with his hands, pointed it sideways at me, cigarette still between his fingers, and said "pew pew." "That's when Christian Compton took over. That's when we let the others start joining up. Kids from Brighton, even. It worked. We pushed the Undertakers back. We started taking the neighborhood back. You see, all that shit we do, it's for the good of the community. You hear someone gets shot, you realize it's someone evil? Someone who could go creeping into your house. Into your room. Rob you blind. Shoot you in the head, John. Rape you up, Selby. When we have to kill, that's who we kill. The drugs? Who do you think pays to give these poor people food when Uncle Sam closes his wallet, because you know *he's* decided to let us all rot in hell. We are criminals because we were born low into an evil world, my friends. But we do the best we can, to survive, and to thrive. To lift our neighbors high. I do not think that we have lost our salt yet."

Chalky had reached the end of his speech and his cigarette at the same time. He flicked the stub onto the ground and reached into his coat pocket. I started away from him, but he put up his left hand to calm me.

"Relax," he soothed. "Relax..." He pulled a baggie out of this pocket. "You don't trust me yet. That's smart. You shouldn't. Someone should give you many examples, many opportunities before he deserves your trust. But I'll start earning your trust right now. You don't look like crackheads, and I want to give you something."

"I'm not a crackhead," said Selby.

"No, I didn't think so. Crack will kill you quickly; I know, because I've seen it killing my brother. And hell, those cigarettes I have all day... they'll kill you slowly. So many things kill you fast or slow. But this thing won't kill you at all. This thing isn't a killing thing." He held up a bag with several pale white pills inside.

"What's that?" I asked.

"It's new. The Chalks make it. Only the Chalks make it. You can't get it from nobody else in this world without end. We call it O-Sugar, and it won't make you short of breath, or crazy, or unhappy. It will make you very happy. Make you see things. Beautiful things. Not ugly things like you find in the

Os. Beautiful blue things that sparkle and speak to you. True things you don't usually get to see with your little human eyes. This is a gift from me to you, on behalf of Christian Compton and the whole Crazy Chalk Nation."

"We don't want it," I said. "That's the stuff that made those kids jump off that hospital."

"Who, Drake?" Chalky said. "No. No, O-Sugar didn't have anything to do with that. We gave him some of that stuff, yeah, but he and his friends had a suicide pact already. They got up there on that roof and decided this world was too big and lonely for them to hang their hats. They decided to jump. Why else you think they went up there, seven stories up, in a building filled with dead ghosts like that?"

"I think your house is filled with dead ghosts," I said.

"I think it is," Selby said suddenly. "I think it's filled with blue ghosts."

Chalky looked at her for a long time before he spoke.

"Are you sure you don't want the O-Sugar? You could take it now, start feeling it in an hour or two, have a great night. Don't worry about your parents. They won't know."

"No thanks," Selby said.

Chalky nodded. "Fine. Wise girl," he said. "Now you know where I live. Someone's always here. Stop by any time."

The man must have stepped back and walked into the house because the window seemed emptier than it had before.

Selby and I walked quickly back toward the church. We were halfway there when I noticed how violently she was shaking.

"That was..." I began, "really fucked up."

She didn't answer. Her breath came ragged and fast. I realized I was breathing fast too, but I wasn't shaking as hard as Selby.

"Are you okay?" I asked.

"No," she said. "Let's just get back to the church, okay?"

48

When we got back, Quanla was hanging halfway out of the door, peering into the dark.

"There you are!" she said. "Hurry up, there's gonna be a fight."

"What?!" I said, and started running.

"It's Chuck and one of the St. Francis kids."

Inside the rec hall, the music was louder and the light brighter, or maybe my eyes were just adjusting. The nun was gone, and now Lark stood alone by the boom box, squinting at the labels on some cassette tapes.

All the other kids had gathered in a tight circle a few feet away. I stood on my toes and was just tall enough to see Chuck facing-off against a white kid with neat black hair, fit enough to be in football. Just barely.

"What do you see, John?" asked Selby.

"Chuck and some kid," I said. I realized my voice was trembling. My mind had made it back to the rec hall with the other kids, but my body thought it was still standing in front of Chalky's house, wondering what he was going to do to us.

"John?" someone asked. The voice had a tighter, more pinched sound than I had remembered, but I saw the one eye staring off into nowhere and recognized him right away.

"Bill," I said. I'd seen him last spring, but he was taller now. Still a skinny white kid with a lazy eye, curly hair, and glasses.

"What are you doing up here?" he asked.

"We got invited," I said. "By Sara Lupu and Patricia Perez. You know what's going on?"

"Yeah, James wants to get with Sara, and I think he thinks that, uh, that other dude wants the same thing."

"Yeah, that's my friend, Chuck."

"I thought so. Is he in sixth grade or junior high?"

"Junior high."

"You think Chuck can take James?"

"Yeah. Chuck's a red belt."

"In what?"

"Karate."

While we were talking, the two boys spoke quiet and deadly into each other's faces from an inch or two away. Whatever they said, they both got to save face. James went back to the wall where he talked and laughed with his friends, and Chuck went over to the table with Sara and got some punch.

"Where did the nun go?" I asked.

"She got a call from her sister," Bill said. "I mean, her real sister. She thought Lark was okay to look after things while she was gone."

"Yeah, he's doin' a real great job. You know Lark?"

"Not real well. He doesn't live over here. Sara goes to church here, though. Sometimes Patricia comes with her. Like, to events and stuff. Once they showed us all how to get up on the roof."

"Oh. So that's where the rumor started."

"What rumor?"

"Nevermind. Hey, man, you think I could take Lark?"

"What, like in a fight?"

"Yeah."

"No. No, man. No way. He'd kick your ass."

"Thanks."

I watched Lark. He must have figured the nun was gone for good, because the next song was louder and fatter than any we'd heard that night. "Motherfuckers," rapped a deep voice.

"What's this?" I asked.

"Biggie!" chimed Adam and Sara.

Windows were locked. Doors were closed.

"This your first dance?" asked Bill.

"Maybe not," I said. I felt in my pockets and found my new blue shades.

"Mine too," he said.

I put the sunglasses on. Now it was thick dark; I could only see where people were standing because of their vague shadows and outlines. Doors, walls, ceiling, and floor were all swept into a blank gray smudge. I still felt like a badass, though. *I should've worn these when we were talking to*

Chalky. I'd tell that motherfucker how to take his pills. I wondered if Bill was right about Lark being able to kick my ass.

The loot was taken from the slave ships.

"Cool shades," said Bill.

"Thanks," I said. "I'm gonna see if Patricia wants to dance."

"Nice. Yeah, give me a call. You should come spend the night. I got all the new AD&D 2nd Edition books. I mean, I mean all the supplements!"

I nodded and moved toward where Patricia was standing, halfway between the punch table and Lark's station. I peeked over the top of my shades to make sure it was Patricia; she seemed to be looking at me. She was smiling. Most of the other kids were standing around talking, but Adam was dancing with Cora and Juanita.

"Wanna dance?" I said.

"Sure," said Patricia.

I'd seen bumping and grinding on TV plenty of times, and once or twice in person. I didn't really know what I was doing, but I was either good at it, or Patricia didn't want to tell me I wasn't. Or she didn't know what she was doing either and was worried about the same thing. I kind of doubted that, though. It seemed to work fine, and I thought I saw envy contort the gloomy faces of those North Side Catholic kids. Then I caught Lark glaring at me, and I flashed my brightest smile. The Biggie song ended, and Lark swapped one cassette for another.

The new beat was just as drunk as the last, but more ragged, and this new acid rapper announced that he was an atheist.

"I'm thirsty," Patricia said.

"Oh," I said. Then, "would you like me to get you a drink?"

I got us some punch. *This is like a sitcom.*

"Lark's a pretty good DJ," she said. "Doncha think?"

"He's okay."

"What sort of music do you like, John?" she asked.

"I don't know. I listen to jazz, mostly. But um... NWA. Michael Jackson." Patricia winced. I ran band names through my brain. "Nine Inch Nails?"

Patricia's face lit up. "Yeah, I love Trent! What do you think of Broken?"

"I like it."

"Pretty twisted, right? Sara likes Pretty Hate Machine more, but I think Broken just... burns it all down."

"Yeah..."

"Do you write poetry?"

"What?"

"I write poetry, and I think it sounds a lot like Trent's lyrics. I'll show you sometime. Do you do anything creative?"

I thought. I wasn't coming up with much. I did remember one assignment I'd done for Ms. Ropoli's class. She'd asked us to draw "a map of the planet with a twist." I had the idea of using the photo-negative colors of each ocean and landmass. My father had helped me figure out the color scheme and then picked me up a bunch of old magazines for cutouts. I'd gotten a 100% A on that one. I told Patricia about it, but cutting my father out of the story.

"That's pretty cool," Patricia said, "but poetry's really important and hard."

Now a new song came on, even louder, a rock song. Many guitars, together. A stubbled voice rolled up a long throat like polyurethane wheels down a cement pipe and sang about a homeless man's hard life. Lark nodded over at us with a grin of victory.

"Oh!" said Patricia. "This is one of my favorite songs!" She ran over toward Lark's table, and they started jumping up against each other. After a couple minutes, a few St. Francis kids joined the mash, but Lark was too big. Whenever he jumped into someone, they'd fall on their ass.

I found Adam.

"Is that Smashing Pumpkins?" I asked.

"Smashing what?" he said. "I don't know."

"It's Pearl Jam," said Juanita.

Cora rolled her eyes.

Selby joined us.

"Hey John," she said, "looks like you were right about the DJ. Looks like Patricia was playin' you to get with him."

We watched the crowd for a few minutes.

"John, want to dance?" asked Juanita.

"A'ight," I said.

We danced through an ever louder, ever more discordant string of songs. When one song ended, Lark ran back to the table and swapped one tape for another, then rejoined the mob. The St. Francis kids had been nervous about the bump-and-grind of the earlier music, but this was just jumping around. Jumping into each other. Violent but mostly asexual. It was easy for them. Then, Lark put on a mix-tape he had made off of the radio, and he and Patricia vanished into the shadows.

That was when I noticed that Juanita seemed to be steering me, too, past the spinning carousel of light, past the black boombox shuddering with static and exertion, crackling with its last life like a September storm might scrape oak leaves across the stained glass windows of St. Francis Church on their way toward the grainy pavement. We'd left the wide open space in the center of the rec hall. We were drifting toward a dusky corner, where the air tinged autumn, auburn, like Patricia's fire hair.

I imagined that hair, bright and bloody, when Juanita pushed her lips into mine. Then she said, "Not right here," and took me by the hand. She led me outside to the church dumpster. The air mingled the russet scent of burning leaves with that of bruised apples, spilled beer, piss, and vinegar. And we kissed for a long time. The kissing was nice, but then again, I couldn't stop my mind from racing. *This isn't the Plan. The Plan is about eighth graders, not twelve-year olds!* More than that, the plan called for vision and daring and power and control. *Why be a prince when you could be a king?!* Who was this girl, even, and why was I with her instead of Patricia? Or at least, Cora? Or even Selby or Quanla? Somebody my age. Somebody from my school. *Will Patricia figure out I like her? Will this affect my reputation? What will my friends figure out? What if Juanita wants to go out with me? Will Patricia hear about it? How will I talk to Patricia? What will Quanla think? What about Selby? What about Lucy?*

The last thought surprised me. I had talked to Lucy once for about ten whole seconds. Who was she, anyways? She was an invisible girl I had met once. She had eaten a note, and that had caused me to notice her. She wouldn't think anything at all about my hooking up with Juanita, because she didn't even know me. *It's not like I know her either*, and that was when I realized that one of Juanita's hands had found the zipper on my pants.

"The fuck?!" I said.

The music stopped, suddenly.

We heard an angry adult voice from inside the church.

Juanita stopped. We made our way back inside and found an ancient priest in pajamas screeching at the confused kids. The confused priest. All of the lights were suddenly on and everyone blinked their eyes. The party was over. It was over all at once. The neighborhood kids walked home from there, while others called their parents. Before Darius arrived, Juanita tried to catch my eyes and mimed holding a phone to her lips. But I put my hands in my pockets and walked outside to wait.

49

I slept in until ten the next morning. My father woke me up.

"John," he said. "Phone call."

"What?" I asked.

"Bill Chapman."

Bill told me that his Tarot cards had revealed that he would have a fateful meeting at the dance. He had thought that that meant a girl. It didn't occur to him until later that old friends counted too.

"Want to come over and spend the night?" he asked. "I've got the *Book of Artifacts* and I played this game where this guy found the Eye of Vecna, and he gouged his own eye out under the power of the relic, and put it in instead, and it was twisted. He ran out and killed everyone after that!"

My parents said that I couldn't spend the night, but they agreed to take me over for the day. We drove up to a slanted, shabby neighborhood on the far North Side. My father called it the Bargain Bin. The houses were mostly split-levels, and their broad yards opened up onto a fierce blue sky. This zone had been annexed in the 70s to provide Akawe with extra revenue even as its core neighborhoods emptied out. It didn't work for very long.

"We're renting now," Bill told me. "We don't know the landlord, though. He owns like a thousand houses all around the city."

Bill's mom fixed us a lunch of macaroni and cheese with cut up hot dogs mixed in. It was a favorite of theirs. We sat at the Formica table in his breakfast nook, ate from red plastic bowls, and drank apple juice from red plastic cups. It took me back years.

When I was five, six, seven, eight, Agit Street had looked very different. Or, I don't know. Maybe it didn't. Maybe I'm just confusing the lifefullness of being a kid with the fulloflifeness of a city street. Back then, I imagined, the sun usually beat the clouds and the summer was longer and stronger than the winter. Back then, there weren't any abandoned houses on Agit Street. Yeah, some of them looked run down, and this guy named Maxwell Pulaski drove a semi and parked it so far out into the street that my father had drive up onto the opposite curb to get around it, but this was all worth it for the lived-in houses, the mowed lawns, the smell of lighter fluid and smoking charcoal on a golden summer afternoon. The city hadn't been dying for long yet.

Back then, there were four kids on Agit Street: Bill Chapman, Adam Miller, Adam's sister Carla, and me. We rode our Big Wheels and then our bikes back and forth across Agit, leaving balls and baseball bats and toy cars and plastic soldiers littered in the dirt and the grass. We'd leap and wrap our arms around the maple in my front yard and slide down, always, because the lowest branches were still too high for us to reach. Then I'd received my first communion. Adam's dad got evicted from his house and they left Agit Street. A couple months later, Bill's parents got divorced, and he moved over to the Bargain Bin with his mom. By the end of the summer, I was the only kid left of the block.

Bill and I still met up sometimes. Sleepovers at his house. At my house. We played video games. Played *Dungeons & Dragons*. Talked a bit about girls. Bill talked about a waitress he liked at a Chinese restaurant in the Os... it was a big detail because his grandpa had been wounded at Okinawa, and the Chapmans never differentiated among Asians or their generations or attitudes.

"I would become a samurai," Bill would whisper after he had carefully closed his bedroom door. "I'd cut the heads off all the gangsters!"

"I don't think you can be a samurai with a lazy eye," I told him.

"I'm working on that, you know," he'd say. "I do these exercises with a prism. Sometimes I wear the eye patch, like a pirate. And that's badass too."

The more time passed, the less I saw Bill, and the less I cared about not seeing him. By the time I was in seventh grade, he wasn't on my mind at all. I thought about Adam, and Chuck, and Elizabeth and Quanla and Selby. I thought about Patricia and Sara. Bill was less than an afterthought.

"We've got to go to Lewis," Bill said as he wiped a bit of melted cheese from his chin.

"Lewis?"

"Yeah! Lewis Junior High School!" he said. "For my Quiz Bowl practice."

"What's that?"

It's basically Jeopardy for kids.

Lewis was the newest and dullest junior high school in Akawe, built on the edge of the city as small and cheaply as possible, with dun colored walls and vinyl faux window shutters. It wasn't as brick-and-rough as Poe or Reeve, or even Radcliffe, but was simply a "good enough" school for working-class white people. Radcliffe, with all its fights and its grime, was noisy with life and activity. Did Lewis have a high dropout rate? I didn't know, but I would've dropped out if I'd had to go to school in such a boring place. We went inside and started making our way down a broad beige hall.

"I don't think Radcliffe has Quiz Bowl," I said.

"It doesn't," Bill said. "A few years back one of the Radcliffe Quiz Bowl kids got beat up after practice. So Radcliffe suspended the kids for beating him up, and they canceled Quiz Bowl." Bill sniffed. "It wasn't Quiz Bowl's fault."

"What were you doing at St. Francis?"

"I wanted to ask you that. My mom started taking me to church there when we moved to the Os. You remember that, don't you? Anyway, I know most of the kids that go to school there, and my parents thought I could make some friends there. How do you like Radcliffe?"

"It's a lot better than this."

Bill had red rings under both his eyes, and he slouched while walking. Whatever he was doing with the prism and the eyepatch, his lazy eye hadn't gotten any better. It seemed to have gotten worse.

"I'm not surprised," he said. "Lewis sucks. What are the cool kids like there?"

"I don't know," I said. "I've only been there two weeks."

"The big story here is that a guy, Rob Masin, stole a bunch of CDs from the Acheron Mall, and ran across the street to Akawe so the police couldn't get him."

"What do you mean? They could go for him."

"They didn't though. They stopped at the city limit and yelled at him to come back. They said they'd call the Akawe police."

"The Akawe police won't do nothin'. They don't care about CDs took from the Acheron Mall."

"I know."

"So he got away?"

"Yeah, but he can't go back to the Acheron mall."

"I didn't even know it was still there."

"It is. It's the only thing to do over here. Go to the mall."

"I thought they tore it down."

"Nope."

I heard the sound of voices from a classroom up ahead.

"So, should I just sit and watch?" I asked.

"I kind of thought you could join in."

"That's okay. I'll just sit."

For the next two hours, I sat in a classroom and watched a row of nervous-looking kids raising their hands to answer questions about math and science and geography. During his break, Bill talked about Quiz Bowl, his new AD&D books, the 3DO he wanted for Christmas, and how much he hated Lewis. I told Bill about Adam, the Plan, Chuck's fight with Kerm, the man with the knife, Chalky, Patricia Perez, and Juanita.

"Adam, man," said Bill. "Jesus." As if that encompassed everything that had happened to me in the last few weeks.

In the end, I decided I was glad that my parents hadn't let me spend the night. I liked the things that Bill liked (well, except Quiz Bowl), but for him they were still *escapes* from the world. From his home, his parents, his school. I wanted to escape *into* the world. Radcliffe was my new center of gravity.

50

I sat next to Michael in church the next morning, but he wouldn't speak to me. When I shook his hand and said "peace be with you," his lips were shut and he seemed to stare past me, over my shoulder.

The next morning, I started the third week of seventh grade, and it had finally started to feel routine. You just had to deal with the week so you could get to the weekend. In Mrs. Norman's class, I found myself sketching out plans for the Friday ahead. Impersonal and cold-voiced extraterrestrials would offer to take my friends and I away from the earth. We'd steal the best boots and pants and leather jackets from the Basadina Mall. We'd take flight into a lens flare portal, a haloed rainbow, a kaleidoscope shining, burning like waxy plastic, and never return to Akawe or Earth again.

I failed Mrs. Norman's pop quiz.

Adam officially started dating Cora. He told me on the phone that he would dump her after a week but I didn't believe him. It was starting to piss me off that Adam would get to hook up when he didn't even care about unhooking. Chuck asked Sara to go out with him, and she also said "yes." Kerm's dad had gone into rehab, and now Kerm was staying with his mom out in Ecorse. With his cousin an hour away, Chuck started eating at Sara's table, and it was starting to piss me off that Chuck got everything *he* wanted. Selby and Quanla moved away from our lunch table too, but this time they never bothered to let us know if or how we'd pissed them off. I ate with Adam and Cora. Nobody messed with us.

I didn't hear a thing from Juanita. I hoped she'd forgotten my name, but I knew she could track me down if she wanted. I started to think that maybe my only option was to lay it all on the line and ask Patricia out. Or maybe I should just show up at Lark's house and punch that fucker in the stomach. Then I could write my initials next to Patricia's in his gravel driveway.

On Wednesday, Chuck, Patricia, and Sara approached our table.

"Patricia's really excited about Laserpalooza on Friday," Chuck said. "At Campus Akawe. The planetarium. You guys want to come with us?"

He was holding Sara's hand.

"Sure," I said. I was sick of looking like I didn't know about songs and bands. I waited for someone else to take the fall.

"What's Laserpalooza?" asked Adam.

"It's a laser show for the music of Lollapalooza. They'll play Nirvana, Smashing Pumpkins, Stone Temple Pilots, other alternative."

"I want to go," said Cora.

"Me too," said Adam. "I'll tell Elizabeth, too. She'll like it."

"Okay," said Sara. Then, to Chuck: "Ask them."

Chuck licked his lips. "Do, um, do you think you could ask Quanla if Darius could give us a ride?"

"Why don't you ask her yourself?" I asked.

"She's mad at me about something."

"What's she mad about?"

"I don't know. She just stopped talking to me."

"Maybe you should apologize to her," I said. Chuck bit his lip. "That's okay," I said, magnanimously. "I'll talk to her."

It worked out for everyone. Quanla denied even being angry at Chuck, and Darius still liked to drive every chance he got, so he said yes. We all got ready for another brave weekend of driving and dancing, fires and rage, guns and love, and killing bitches. Of jumping around. Of getting down after having gotten up twice.

"Take your jacket!" called my mother as I swung out toward the door.

She was right; it had started getting cool at night.

51

"He better get his ass out here now," I heard Darius saying as I hurried onto the porch.

"John!" called Quanla. "Hurry up!"

I stopped short of the car. I think my mouth actually fell open. The Daphne wasn't just full; it was brimming over with my friends' arms and legs wedged haphazardly against the windows and doors. Darius hunched over the steering wheel with the drivers' seat as far forward as it would go. Quanla rode shotgun with Selby sitting on her lap. Patricia straddled the stick shift with her back to the radio console. Elizabeth sat behind Darius, probably more comfortable than anyone else in the car. Adam and Cora sat bitch, and Chuck and Sara sat behind Quanla.

"You're gonna get pulled over," I said.

"Shut up, if you don't want me to leave you behind!" snapped Darius. "Just get in, get in."

"Where am I going to get in?!" I looked over my shoulder. If my parents saw this, it was all over.

"Just climb in the back!"

I found myself crawling sideways behind the seat in so that I lay across the back, my feet on Elizabeth and my head on Sara's lap. People laughed. People complained.

"Shut up!" snapped Darius, and he rolled back down the driveway, carried as much by our massed weight as the

Daphne's sputtering engine. I wondered if the brakes were going to give out.

Once again we were heading toward the North Side. I couldn't really look out the window, so I didn't know which way we were going. I did glimpse a couple of empty eye-socket windows and jagged tree branches as we hurried past them, but there was light, too; a humid, sulfur haze that hung heavy in the tattered air. I felt a dark breeze across my brow. It cut between my eyes and I teared up. It smelled like smoke.

"What's that smell?" I asked.

"Fire in the Os," said Sara.

It's hard not to think with your senses – your palms and your pores – when lying across the laps of three girls. It woke me up all over, no matter how platonic the whole thing was supposed to be.

"John," asked Patricia. "You called Juanita yet?"

"No," I said.

"She was asking my friend Jimmy about you. She wants you to give her a call."

"I don't have her number."

"I can get you her number."

"She's a sixth grader," I said, trying to end it.

"A girl can date an older boy. I'm seeing Lark and he's a year older than me."

I twisted to look out the window again.

Lark isn't going to stop me from asking you out. Anyway, I could write poetry too, if I wanted. I could write better poetry than Trent Reznor.

I could tell from the tall lightposts that we were crossing 292. I saw the upper stories of the senior public-housing tower and then the massive brick turrets of the Olan Academy. Akawe's honors high school. We'd arrived at Campus Akawe.

In the 1950s, when the city was rich and X was still expanding, Arthur Olan had divided most of his sprawling property between the community college and Campus Akawe. On either side of Jordan Street, under spreading oaks and elms, on lush lawns, in neat stone buildings, the Campus was different from anywhere else in the city. The Bonbright Theater, the Simcoe Museum, and Suarez Planetarium and Observatory crowded around a reflecting pool. Its rainbow lights shone out onto the unrippled surface. In the summer, little kids ignored the DANGER signs and went swimming in the shallow water, their fingertips brushing against the electrical cables at the bottom. Further down: the Whittier Auditorium, the Benedict Gallery, the Music and Art Institutes, the Akawe Public Library, and the school administration building. To most of us, this all looked like it belonged in a completely different city. One block west was Suarez Boulevard, and then the Os, but the Planetarium had been painted in vertical bands of purple and gray inset with steely chips of rough stone. At a distance, its huge, windowless dome suggested a rising crescent moon.

Darius slammed on the brakes, and the car slowly rolled to a stop. I slid against the seat and Sara slid off Chuck's lap.

"Out, now!" shouted Darius, and we crawled out from the Daphne.

"I'll be here in two hours," Darius said.

"Don't be late," said Quanla.

"This is some bullshit. You crazy, Quanla, and if I tell mom about this –"

"You tell mom about this, you ain't driving no more!"

"Bullshit," Darius said.

52

It was still fifteen minutes before the show started, but a line ran halfway down the sidewalk toward the parking lot. Most of the kids were older than us: tenth grade, eleventh grade, twelfth grade. They were suburban white kids, scruffy looking "nice kids," wearing band T-shirts. One kid had a nose piercing. Another had gauge earrings. I'm sure there were a few tattoos out there. After five minutes, we made it up to the dusty, faux-marble counter and bought our tickets from a balding man with a pencil-thin mustache.

"Thanks," said Sara, and smiled.

Further in, a small gift shop sold glow-in-the-dark stars, astronaut ice cream, and giant sky maps. The dome itself was ringed by a narrow corridor painted with constellations, nebulae and galaxies, and a background blacklight glow. Chuck and Patricia laughed, and their teeth shone bright white. My shoelaces popped white beneath me. Socks and t-shirts. The acid stench of stage fog. Everyone was talking. Everyone was friendly. The crowd moved down the passage in a broad sweep, past a display of phosphorescent rocks and into the auditorium.

The central dome had a hundred and change seats arrayed in concentric circles around an elongated spider of a machine made of black metal and fitted with portholes and lenses: the optomechanical projector. The ceiling rose above, softly lit, the color of a brown egg and criscrossed by faint seams.

So many people had shown up that there weren't enough seats for all of us to sit together. I tried to wedge my way past Sara so I could sit on Patricia's other side, but she grabbed a seat on the aisle instead. I had to find a place in the front row, between Selby and Elizabeth. Quanla sat next to Selby while Chuck and Adam ended up behind us. The doors hadn't closed yet. The seats had all filled, but people were still filing into the auditorium. They orbited in toward any empty patch of carpet and squeezed together. The concentric circle filled in around the projector and then spread back until there was nowhere else to sit. Ushers were turning kids away at the doors. A slender girl, my age maybe or a little bit older, sat at my feet. She learned against the armrest, her back grazing my leg.

Suddenly, she turned around and looked right at me, her face alight with startled joy. She was pretty, but her prettiness was more a projection of warmth than anything specific about her features. She had a straight bob with big bangs, brown eyes, and no tension in her expression.

"I've never been to a planetarium before!" she chirped.

I wasn't sure what to say.

"I have," I said.

Selby snickered.

"But I've been wanting to go for a long time," said the girl. She smiled and turned back to face the projector.

I looked back up at the ceiling.

The lights dimmed.

53

The music came, and with it, light.

Red ribbon quatrefoils beat like a heart and bloomed out into bright blossoms while the sound ran the seams with rays and song and bound us together like we were one flesh. One tribe. One actor. It was – wait for it – a weight that filled our chests. We had mostly come as critics, amateurs, poseurs, play juries and judges, to energize injuries psychic and physical, to pledge our urine as proof of the relevance of our thoughts and actions, to co-opt the plague of rhythm to give our own lives meaning because we didn't want to settle for a sex pack of neutered allusion. That's what the beat said, and we bought it at the mall and on the radio and in the planetarium dome.

But *I* grew up in a jazz house. *This* was the big outdoors for me. I hadn't seen how it had all fit together, but finally thought I was figuring it out.

The first song came out as a wail that rang up to the knit panels of whatever fine fibers make up the smooth surface suited for optomechanical projection. It was the same voice that called Patricia away from me to that asshole Lark, leaving me with the sixth-graders. He was singing so fast and throaty that I couldn't understand his words, but there was no mistaking that hollow halfpipe voice or the maudlin guitars that wove weaves with guttural speed. I could almost see the spit and the spark in the twining kites and crescents overhead as they downshifted from red to bruised violet. I got lost in it. Laser habits – not nuns but Klan – bled witch black and filled pools with blood. It was the lasers telling the story. It was a story of a child and a Jesus, eyed and knifed and locked inside a cheap valentine. Meanwhile, the planetarium telling this tale was one of the most expensive things in Akawe.

The priceless device upon which the whole act hinged was the Zeiss-Jena Universal Projection Planetarium Type 23/6 built by comrades whose far-sighted lenses were tolerated in Akawe even if their folks' wagons were not, moving with a smooth curl, shooting stars, while rays mounted above the doors steamed fake fog out on us, shooting beams across the illusory abyss and pouring into the porous panels.

Impressive. Even Adler impressive when Campus Akawe turned on for the night. The spotlights shot white beams against Suarez's Carborundum chips and reflected celestial diamonds out into the night – an inside, an outside, mutual mirrors making hyperbolas and stars for everyone.

Jagged laser, black-and-white, fuck you fuck you, blah blah, parental advisory, explicit prose, implicit pose, and another song began. This one was an angry march, a pulse, blood beating, youth on the move, like we could march out, never return to school, and show the unions – the guys who made the Terraplanes and the Aubrey 7Ts, the Rolls Royces and the Valentine Deca 149 – how to do it right, voices strong, raindrops falling down our brows.

It was Nine Inch Nails. That band that Patricia liked and Michael worshiped. This song was more militaristic, harder sounding, harder to listen to than the songs Michael had played to me before. But I still heard something familiar here. Something kindred, a son maybe, of the song my mother had played me a week earlier. That song had been a permissive mother; she had breathed an atmosphere where it all was allowed. Yet she, too, was kindred to that which my father played all the time. Sad songs, blue songs, blue notes, blue beats, the stresses and struggles of men and women, blacks and sharecroppers, that beat the hot earth with shovels and fists and packed their way north once upon a time, and that almost, almost, almost brings us back to the – *Glorious!* – the man with the hollow voice and the hollower man who made such a voice heard.

I didn't know all this in words, but it was resonant in my cells. I'd heard enough to draw connections even when I didn't know most of the names of the streets and stretches, the neighborhoods and intersections of my own dying city. I just knew that all this glamour and destruction had begun with the sound of men working on a pain slang. Songs sung in turbulence to keep others close, to link the locked bonds of a people struggling to stay on their feet, to drop hammers, lift voices, to see the sun set and rise again. It was a hideous, violent, awful world, but what a wonderful world to give birth to such treasure and riches, green trees and roses of red, catharsis and annihilation.

I wondered, momentarily, if Michael only going to hate me for the rest of seventh grade, or if I really was his big line hard time bad fist luck fuck?

We rotated, sidereally, into the next song. The beat dropped and copped to a calm shot hot palm spot. The gentle strumming of handsome men carrying tattoos upon their fingers and, I guessed, some STDs. His mellow voice about his home. His city. His only friend. His city of angels.

I lived in Tenth Town, Akawe, and it wasn't anyone's friend. It tried to devour us. It was always hungry. It was never full. I felt empty, felt a vast hunger had opened up inside me, like Adam and I had only been lying to ourselves when we had promised to enact his Plan. Were we trying to save face with ourselves while asking someone to simply cling to us? To hold us close? To let us know that we weren't forgotten?

I found myself thinking, *What a faggot,* as I saw in my mind's eye the laser-drawn green-haired shirtless sonic rock god jogging out of the green dome and lunging into the audience.

I turned my attention to the girl sitting at my feet. I couldn't see her – my eyes were swimming with lights from the show overhead – but I could feel the weight of her back against my leg and, what's more, I could smell her. She carried a trace of cherry balm, of sandalwood and something else, something musty, and I felt, Sherlock-like, that she must live in a dank, damp place, but that she had standards and good hygiene. She kept herself as clean as she could, even though she did seem pretty dumb. That vacant smile. Those vacuous words: "I've never been to a planetarium before!" She would have been *perfect* for the Plan. *Is she in eighth grade?* I wondered.

I waited impatiently for the next song to begin.

Again, the music came. Akawe was like a jungle, always. In the dark, everyone's skin was dark. But we carry our souls, the sins we carry, and every forgotten history, whether we're born ivory or ebony, tanned or burnt, bleached or Chalk crude, whether push or pimpers, money or prostitute-makers. I knew this song. I knew Ice Cube's voice from Adam's NWA cassettes just like I knew Trane and Miles from my father's records. *Why do I know black music through my white friends and family? Why don't I ask Chuck what he listens to? Quanla sings in church; why don't I ask her about that? Why is it always Adam telling me about rap? Why is it always my father teaching me about jazz and the blues?*

And then, another thought: *Africa is broad and deep and busy and crowded, fecund and fertile. But Europe sits on top, and Europe is heavy. Europe wears metal and oceans, and it's hard for Africa to hold itself up with all that weight pressing down from the north.*

Akawe is kind of like that. The West End goes out, mile after mile, block after block, and the city, the county, the state, the world, they take and take, they pull and pull til it's all gonna fly apart at the seams.

Ice Cube played through Laserpalooza to a crowd with maybe a dozen black kids (*and Chuck, Quanla, and Selby are three of them*).

One of these songs is not like the others...

But all I could do was boink a boink boom my boom a dank dick dank. Another song. Jicha jocka jicka jocka jicka jocka jicka jocka jicka jocka jicka jocka jicka jocka jicka jocka. The laser spasmed like the kid tweaking in the aisle off to our right. I refocused. Looked at the rays beaming above. Felt, again, that feminine weight against my leg. Breathed that cherry balm.

I don't want to die just like Jesus Christ.

I would much rather walk on water than wear a crown of thorns.

I would much rather die rich than poor even if I have to soul-thread the eye of a needle.

I don't want to die at all. Ever.

But if I have to die, I want to go peacefully in my sleep on the night after I've solved all the problems of my life. I want to pass my essence into the world, my signature written on it in ways that will never be erased. I want to feel the peace and comfort of sure knowledge. Then, if I close my eyes and go then... that would be okay.

Green guns flickered on the dome overhead. Green soldiers stalked under green-soaring clouds, and the guitars phased into wind chiming lyres, like their notes had been sculpted from the grassy cones of early mandalas before ringing out like shovels striking dulled bones. Everything was dark in this music; it reminded me how we had been raised to mourn our bruises and black eyes while those we had blinded forgave and forgot because they'd been blinded by many, not a few. Three black-sounding women – at least three – threw out a "whoooo" that I could have heard in Quanla's church, though this song wasn't praising God.

I risked a look at Quanla; the light flickering off her lips and nose made her eyes glassy in the atmosphere, but she was listening, watching closely. One of the best listeners, the best watchers I'd ever known. She caught me looking at her. Buried me up to my neck with her contradicting eyes. I turned back. Looked up. Focused on the girl at my feet, who was oblivious to my attention. Focused on the colors swirling overhead.

What happened to that rooster? Was he extinguished in the end?

The lasers collided like stones, built a brick wall, blew it down, and started from scratch. Their rectangles were hard, rough, sloppy. They preferred to draw curves and arcs, spritish dancers, while the cob nobblers sat bound-and-hagged, bloated on their own fermenty piss, my kin and tribe swung on the flippity-flop, warm in fuzz, svelte in plats, loose in wack slacks, and furious at everyone on the outside. Akawe wasn't Seattle; too cold, too small, too damn flat, too fucking dry.

Flowers on the wall. Twirling like clover between a girl's thumb and forefinger. Green brick now blue. I tried to pour my total senses into my leg, to feel the essence of the girl leaning there. She felt like a hyphen, a sugar still, a raspberry moment, a lip balm, perfect helixes, perfect rotation, so someone shrilled what Jane had said, and I was grateful that nature had built us this way.

That's when someone across the room blurred and stood up. Or did he? Did he stand up and blur, or blur and sit? Whatever, he rammed himself into the super-rare, super-expensive Zeiss-Jena Universal Projection Planetarium Type 23/6 imported from East Germany. And again and again. Then stopped.

The music stopped.

The lights came on.

We all blinked in the glare.

We saw a tall, skinny, white teenager with blood running down his face, while several lenses on the projector were askew.

"I, I, I," the guy said. "I'm really sorry." He grinned. "All in all is..."

54

A few minutes later an ambulance had arrived and taken the boy away, with a cop following behind. The boy's friends were questioned out in front of the planetarium. The show was over early and nobody knew if there'd be another. We'd seen almost the whole thing, so no refunds.

Since Darius hadn't shown up yet, we hung out in the lobby with some of the high school kids waiting for their rides. They were all bigger than us, and they knew we were younger than them. They ignored us. Chuck chatted with Sara and Patricia while I sat with the others. I looked up just in time to catch a glimpse of the girl who'd sat at my feet. She was making her way toward the exit, her face puzzled and sad. She caught my eye, smiled, brushed her short hair from her face, and left. *But where is Patricia?*

"Dude was trippin'," someone said.

"Acid?" someone answered. Boys.

"Yeah."

"No, that ain't acid."

"Then what?"

"That's O-Sugar."

"O-Sugar? I've done O-Sugar."

"No you ain't. It ain't even been out long."

"Since when?"

"Don't know. Not since this summer."

"Sounds familiar."

"No it don't."

"Yeah. Wasn't that in the news?"

"Oh yeah, my bad, it was. That was what made those kids jump off that hospital a few weeks back."

"No it din't," said someone else, halfway across the room. This was a boy with either the beginning of an intentional goatee or the end of a week without shaving. He had a spiky, triangular face and tired eyes, but he was clearly older than most of the kids stuck here. He was a bit annoyed with them. I wondered why he hadn't driven himself; most of the suburban kids borrowed their parents' cars. So did some of the Akawe kids.

"What do you know about it?" retorted one of the other boys.

"I know it 'cause I'm on O-Sugar now, and it din't make nobody jump."

This changed their attitude. I was curious too.

"You're on O-Sugar now? Where you get it?"

The older boy shrugged, but lowered his voice. "A guy was giving out some in the parking lot earlier, but this ain't my first time."

"You like it?"

"Like it? Fuck. It's... fuck. You ever stare into the eye of God?"

The younger boys smirked at this. "Oh yeah, he got the good stuff," one of them muttered.

"Where you go to school?"

"Owen High."

"I go to Parc Pierre. We got it out there. You can get some soon enough you want to."

They were curious again. "What's it *really* like?"

"Words won't tell," said the older boy. "You travel through time on O-Sugar. You touch space, you know? I'm still watching that laser show right now, even while we're talking. I can hear the music, and it all glows blue. I've tried everything in the book, but I never tried nothing like that."

"So why did those kids jump off the roof?" asked one of the younger boys.

"How the fuck do I know?" the older boy answered. "Do I know him? This shit makes me feel better than I ever have before. It makes you want to live, not die. It doesn't make you clumsy, neither. I know exactly where my hands and feet are going... I can almost see where they're going before they move. If those kids jumped, it wasn't 'cause of O-Sugar."

Maybe it was a suicide pact, I thought. I couldn't believe it, but...

I looked out into the parking lot to see if there was a dealer lurking about. I didn't expect to see anything other than a few kids talking and smoking... but I *did* see something. Someone. And I knew who it was, because he was wearing the same clothes he had worn on the day he'd chased me and pulled a knife on me in my own neighborhood. He was talking with a few kids out there, then looked over my way. He looked me right in the eye. He winked.

"I want to get out of here, now," I told Adam.

55

"I'm gonna ask to use their phone," I said.

"Why?" Adam said. "Darius'll be here soon."

"No, I don't want to go out there."

"Why not?!"

"Because... because his car was too damn crowded."

"But I was gonna ask if you and Chuck wanted to spend the night at my sister's."

I thought.

"Sure," I said. "Yeah, that sounds great. My parents can give us a ride."

"But... who's going to give Cora a ride?"

"My parents can give Cora a ride home!" I was surprised he didn't catch the urgency I was trying to put into my voice.

"What about Selby and Quanla?"

"Who the fuck do *you* think is going to give Quanla a ride home? Darius'll get them. Come on!"

"Okay, okay, fine. What's the deal?"

"I'll tell you later. You just ask Chuck, and I'll call my parents."

When I asked the box office to use the phone, they curtly informed that there was a pay phone in the parking lot. When I told them that I didn't have a ride, and they'd be stuck with me if I couldn't call, they relented. My father was puzzled by the request at first, but then got pissed-off when I told him that some stoner had broken the projector.

"Can I spend the night with Adam?" I asked.

"Sure, whatever," he said, not even catching it. "I'll be there in a few minutes."

"Wait, father," I paused. "Stop on Jordan, in front the Planetarium. We'll come out the side doors. It's way too crowded in the parking lot." It wasn't. There were only a dozen cars.

After he hung up, Adam walked over with Cora at his side.

"Your dad gonna give Cora a ride home?"

"I'm sure. Chuck's spending the night?"

"Yeah, he can."

"Great, Quanla and Selby okay?"

"I didn't ask, but you're right, Darius has them all set. Elizabeth too. I guess Lark is picking up Patricia and Sara."

"Awesome."

"Where did Selby go?"

"I don't know, the bathroom?"

Over the next fifteen minutes, kids drifted out of the lobby toward the parking lot, and it emptied as well. The man moved about, sometimes retreating to a rusty blue Starr where someone else was sitting. I was terrified that the man was going to come inside, ask me my name again, pull his knife out, but he didn't. In fact, after that first, brief moment of contact –

that quick wink – he didn't even seem to look over in my direction.

But the night had gotten weird, and I wasn't in the mood to take chances.

When I saw my father's Benedict pull up on the street outside, I strode to the side doors and pushed them open. They squealed fiercely, unused for weeks at a time. Chuck, Adam, and Cora followed, a bit more slowly, annoyed at my hurry.

I got into the front passenger's seat.

"Can't believe someone broke that thing," my father was saying. "Those projectors cost tens of thousands of dollars. At least."

He shifted into gear.

"Wait!" I said. "Can you give Chuck and me a ride to Adam's sister's to spend the night, and can you give Cora a ride home?"

He briefly clenched his fists. I saw his teeth clench, too. But my friends were already getting into the car.

"Thanks for the ride, Mr. Bridge," said Cora with a cheerful lilt.

"My pleasure," muttered my father as he pulled away.

I glanced out the window, half expecting to see the man watching us leave. He didn't look up. He was fully absorbed in his wandering path between the car and the planetarium. It didn't comfort me. It made him seem even more godlike. Like I was a fly beneath his consideration. However, as we left

Campus Akawe and crossed 292 again, I breathed a sigh of relief. I had gotten away without speaking to the man. He still didn't know my name. He still didn't know where I lived.

56

My father dropped us off without following us into Carla Miller's Downtown apartment complex, which was good, because if he had, I wouldn't have been spending the night. We went down the white cinder-block hall, up two flights of stairs and down another carpeted hall to a door that shook with the sound of bass and laughter from the other side.

It took a good minute for Carla to hear us knocking and when we went inside, we found a dozen of her friends, all in their 20s and 30s, drinking beers and 40s, and some of them jumping on her couch.

"What are you doing here?" Carla asked.

Everyone in the Miller family had the same Nordic good looks, the same innocent expression, which still surprised me when I caught any of them in a scene like this.

"It's my night to stay here," Adam said, "remember?"

"And John and Chuck?"

"You said they could spend the night."

"When?"

"When we talked last week."

She chewed this over in her mind for a minute. Someone threw a bottle of beer across the room; it missed an outstretched hand by several feet and shattered against the wall.

"Aw, fuck!" someone yelled.

"You'll have to stay in my room," said Carla. "I have company."

"Where are you going to sleep?" Adam asked.

"It's okay," she said. "I'll sleep on the couch."

57

That's how we ended up in the single bedroom, with noise spilling through the crack under the door and a cold white light angling through the blinds. Chuck and I put sleeping bags out on the floor, while Adam took the bed for himself. He'd smuggled a Bud from the other room and took big gulps before passing it to Chuck and me. We didn't like the taste. Our minds were on other things. We took small sips. Adam finished the bottle off on the next pass, and after another few minutes joking about laser-show stoners, he fell asleep.

"That was fast," I said.

"You ever drink before?" Chuck asked.

"No. I mean I've had some wine with my parents, but nothing real. You?"

"Once or twice. Sure don't feel like it now."

I laughed.

"What happened back there?" Chuck asked. "Why'd you want to get out so fast?"

"You remember I told you a guy pulled a knife on me the day we all got jumped?"

"Yeah."

"He was in the parking lot."

"The same guy?"

"I know it was him. He saw me too; he winked at me."

"What a fag."

"No, it was like he wanted me to know he knew I was there."

"Tell me again why he pulled a knife on you? I don't remember."

"I don't think I ever told you. He was acting crazy. He kept chasing me, but he never said what he wanted. He asked me where I got my sunglasses."

"The blue ones?"

"You don't understand. Those shades are weird."

I told Chuck how I had found the sunglasses under the overpass. How I'd wondered if the man with the knife was the homeless person who I'd thought – I'd assumed – was sleeping in all that blazing heat.

"You said the homeless guy smelled pretty bad, right?" asked Chuck.

"Yeah, he smelled awful. Though I didn't really get a good look, but it was a person in there."

"The guy with the knife. Did he smell bad? Did he look like he was homeless? Homeless people usually got a stink about 'em."

"He looked like he'd had a bad day." I thought about it. "But no, he didn't look that bad. I don't think he smelled, either."

"Huh. So what's the deal with the sunglasses?"

"They're really thick and dark. They're handmade. I think that the lenses come from beer bottles or something. They're mostly blue but parts are green and purple."

Adam snored. Chuck and I laughed and then were quiet for a minute. I weighed out my next question carefully before asking.

"Do you think the guy – the guy with the knife – was there for anything to do with me tonight?"

"I really don't know," Chuck said. "It doesn't sound like it, though. If he knew so much about you that he knew you were going to go to the planetarium, don't you think he would've gone after you somewhere else? Like on your way home from school or something? Where there wouldn't be a ton of people around?"

This made sense.

"What I *do* think," Chuck said, "is that maybe he was there dealing O-Sugar. If this guy was a dealer, he coulda been with the Reapers. Kerm brought him along for the fight, and that's why I wouldn't have known him when we saw him on the tracks. Plus, you said that stoner at the planetarium said he got the O out in the parking lot."

"But I heard the O-Sugar all comes from the Chalks. Are the Chalks and the Reapers, like, allies?"

"I dunno. They're both white gangs but that doesn't mean they're allies."

"And anyway, doesn't it seem... kind of, like... I don't know... a pretty crazy coincidence that he would be in the same place as me? I mean, if he *didn't* know I was going to be there?"

Chuck paused. "No," he said. "I don't think so. Sometimes, you know, sometimes Akawe seems smaller than it really is, but sometimes it seems bigger. Know what I'm sayin'?"

"No... what do you mean?"

"You don't know everyone here. I don't either. Nobody does. But I bet I know just about everyone through someone, right? I could... I don't know, connect with anyone in Akawe just by asking the right people I do know. I would just have to know who they were. And who to ask."

"This guy wanted me to tell him my name. I didn't. I'm glad I didn't."

"I'm glad you didn't, too. I really think he was just there tonight to sell drugs, and happened to notice you were there too. It looks like he hasn't forgotten you. But think about this: He already has a good idea how he knows you. Through my cousin. My cousin was going after me on that day. And I go to Radcliffe. So this guy probably guesses that you go to Radcliffe too, and if he asks the right person the right questions, he can probably find out your name."

"And then he can find out where I live."

"Right," Chuck said. "That's a bit what I meant back when I told you that you don't know what it's like out West. When you get drugs, when you get gangs, you piss the wrong person off, you can never get away from it, unless you move away completely. It ain't fun. It's happened to my cousin... it's happened to just about everyone I know from the hood. Now you gotta worry about it too."

"And if I would have just stayed with you and Elizabeth... if I hadn't run away, none of that would have happened."

"I told you, I ain't mad about that."

"No, but I am mad about it. I'm mad at myself. If I was a good friend, I would have stayed."

Chuck thought about this for a moment. "No. Everyone makes mistakes. A good friend feels bad about their mistakes. So you do feel bad. And I'm glad. I take back what I said about knowing you would run away because, next time, I don't think you will. A'ight?"

"Thanks," I said. "I can't figure out if I like Radcliffe more than Truman or not."

"What do you mean?"

"Junior high is way different than sixth grade was. But it isn't just the different teachers and classes and all that. That's the easy part. Everything's a lot more serious now, ain't it?"

"Yeah. I'd say."

"I didn't think everything would get so serious so fast."

Again, Chuck laughed. He wasn't laughing at me, but it sounded like he had figured all this out a long time ago. "How is Adam's plan going?"

"Yeah, the Plan," I said. "The Plan is dead. Dead for good. I was gonna ask Patricia out tonight. That didn't happen."

"You know she's a year older than you and way more experienced, right? You know she's going out with Lark now, too."

"I know. I know. I thought if I just asked her out, I don't know, she might change her mind."

"I think you should thank that man with the knife for keeping you from doing that tonight."

"Ha," I said. It was funny. And probably true.

"So John," Chuck went on. "Why was it you wanted to do Adam's plan in the first place? I mean, he didn't surprise me with it. That's just the sort of stupid shit he always tries. But what about you? You didn't want to date and dump nobody."

"Shit, Chuck, I don't know. It was a feeling, you know? It went back to the whole thing with Kiara —"

"You still got a thing for her?"

"No. No way! No, but that whole thing with her moving away made me feel like such an asshole. And then we were all going to Radcliffe and it just seemed like it all might, like, open up or something. I don't know. I wanted something new and different to happen. To feel like I was bigger than myself in some way. But I didn't want it to happen *to* me. I wanted it to happen *because* of me, you know?"

"Uh huh. Sure. I wanted the same thing. I get it. But let me ask: don't you think they want the same thing?"

"Who?"

"All these girls you and Adam been planning around? Sara and Patricia and even that Juanita girl from the dance. Cora. Hell, Selby and Quanla. We wanna get some ass, we want people to like us, we want new shit to happen. You don't think they want the same shit?"

I thought about it. "I don't think Quanla wants to get ass from nobody," I said. Chuck laughed. "But yeah, I get you."

"And you got some plan that's gonna make them look dumb. You don't think they're gonna figure that shit out? Turn that shit around on you? Especially someone like Patricia who's probably smarter than the rest of us put together?"

So you're saying I'm an idiot, I thought. Then I took a look at the premise of the Plan again: We date a cool eighth grader. We dump a cool eighth grader. We're kings of the school. *I am an idiot.*

"But Cora ain't smart like Patricia. And Adam pulled it off with Cora."

"Adam ain't gonna dump Cora!" Chuck said. "But even if he did, what you think happens? I bet she gets another boyfriend sooner than he gets another girlfriend. Radcliffe ain't

Truman. Adam's over his head there. He just hasn't figured it out yet."

"No, you're right," I said. "About all that shit. I mean, hey, if anyone made it work, it was you. Look, you got with Sara Lupu. She's older than you. She's hot. She obviously likes you. You're not going to dump her, are you?"

"No way."

"Her friends will be your friends. You'll do your karate. You'll go to dances. Everyone thinks you're cool." And I chewed the next words with some bitterness: "And it all started when you kept me from getting my ass kicked by Jay Flighting."

Chuck's laugh was a bit nervous this time.

"If you like," he said, "I can just let him kick your ass next time."

"No," I said. "I didn't have enough courage. With Jay. Or with Kerm. Or even with Patricia. If I just liked her and was up-front and all that, maybe it would've..."

I thought again about those five kids up on the hospital roof, the drug coursing through their blood, their lives and bodies spiraling out of their control, separated from death by open air and several seconds. About how they had surrendered their lives to the drug.

"Don't sweat it, John. It ain't over," Chuck said. "We're only three weeks into the school year. There's plenty of time for shit to happen."

He's right, I thought. *I have to stop thinking about them. I'm not like them. Their problems aren't like my problems. I have to let them go.*

"What kind of music do you listen to?" I asked.

"I don't know. I don't listen to music, much. Pretty much whatever you guys listen to, I guess. I liked some of the shit we heard tonight."

58

I had nightmares that night.

Maybe it was Carla's party banging through the shut door or the cold unfamiliar light of the white street lamps shining in without any trees to calm their cutting. Whatever it was, I dreamt of green ladders rising toward blue platforms. I climbed them, swung down hazy slides, and chased dozens of girls, all beautiful, all hideous, with makeup and masks covering their faces. They laughed at me. Harsh, donkey laughs. Each time they laughed, I jumped up, jumped forward, so that invisible hands, groping for me, hunting in the vast empty, behind, below, couldn't wrap themselves around my ankles and drag me back toward shackles, mouths, vacancies. Batlike ghosts. An abyss of blue.

59

There were three investors from Michigan
who wished to escape and get rich again.
Went to sea in a trunk,
but then the car sunk.

When I was four, almost five – after my mother got her Associates – after my father got out of rehab – I went to a concert with my parents, along with Michael and Mabel and the Demnescus.

Somewhere on the East Side, among parks that grew wild until they became jungles, past deserted baseball diamonds, behind parking lots and ramps chipped like mountains and quarries, below yawning and broken windows, among the tiniest factories, there was a little valley lined with great old sycamores. It was a golden corridor of reflected sunlight, and there in the very middle stood a windowless octagonal concrete building attached to an old school. We parked on the dirt there. We went inside.

We passed through a small lobby, where cool blue and orange tiles had been arrayed into bright mosaics, into a concrete auditorium with red chairs and a red carpet spilling down to a small thrust stage. There were a hundred or so people, young and old, black and white. We all sat down. Michael laughed and waved at me.

"Hi, John!" he said. "Mama, look, it's John!"

Michael pulled at Mabel's sleeve and pointed our way. Mabel nodded impatiently. Further down, Angel and Big George flanked Selby. She looked down. She didn't look up. She was looking at her feet.

A man got up on the stage, and talked about the good work that the library had done for Akawe and how our contributions made a difference. He introduced the band – alto sax, trumpet, piano, bass, vocals, and drums – and they tuned up for their performance. I closed my eyes. I felt tired. I felt the pressure of my father sitting to my right and heard a slight creak from Michael kicking his legs. When I opened my eyes, I saw a blue-jawed monster, stringy haired, with long and hollow teeth and star-hard eyes. Vacant eyes. All the empty windows on our street. My mother alone in the bedroom watching the TV. My father crying and Aunt Ellie dead in her casket. It was all blue.

"Hey," my father whispered. "You okay?"

"One, two, three, four," dimly, dark, ahead.   The music began, and the blue thing flashed its fangs at me. It was moving toward me. Its eyes were alive with blue fire. It was going to eat me.

I stood up and went out into the aisle and up the stairs. I was moving through the lobby faster than I could run and the tiles blurred like they were turning through a kaleidoscope. It felt like I was flying through space. I went out of the building, driven into the wilderness. Everything out there was bright and blue, and I heard blue voices – fanged voices – behind me, and I knew that I had to go faster.

Ahead, I saw the dusty parking lot and the maze of streets beyond, but I didn't want to go there – there there was confusion, there there were monsters – so I shifted to my right, off the path, up the hill, crabgrass clawing at my calves, dry dirt, dry wind, but I still felt like the demons were right behind me. I was still moving too slow. I blurred and shifted as quickly as I could, my blue feet tumbling beneath me, and the sun overhead was a bright blue-tailed comet that poured like liquid down the throbbing sky and mixed in the rolling green and purple leaves, the tearing veil, a cascade of entropy, raising walls, building defenses, an automobile, a civilization. Fast and farther up the crest came the blue-skyling with its teeming teeming, the whole atmosphere blue-airplane-full, the expressway below choked with blue cars sucked backwards into Akawe. But people didn't come to Akawe. People left Akawe. Just not my family and friends. We were left behind with the blue things. The arriving blue things. The dead blue things. Because the arriving blue things were all dead. I had figured this out. I stopped to try to catch my breath, but my heart beat faster at the sight of death and its spirits.

"John!" I heard, far away but fierce. "Come back now!" It was my father. He was at the edge of the hill, hurrying in my direction. My mother and Mabel were behind him, Michael clutching Mabel's hand. My father, I knew, was one of the monsters. They were all the monsters. All of them.

I started shifting and moving again. Light on my feet, an airy garland in my hair, floating and flying at great speed. By now I was high on the hill, the nettles scratching my leg, and I was bleeding and stinking. The unseen cars became a chorus. The light was mounting. The clouds faded out. The blue grew, was growing, becoming metallic, but the top of the hill was in sight. It was impossible for me to stop now. I went higher and higher and I heard my father swear as he plowed into the brambles behind me, angry and afraid. I reached a bank of raspberry bushes and lowered my head, shifting on in. The thorns scraped my hands and arms and face and eyes, but I had to get away and the blue glow still blew through the grass beneath me and coated my feet a deeper ocean green sheen that shot up the sky and stained the lacy spider-stranded beams of sunlight into aging copper wires that then rusted into royal purple, sidereal violet, a crystalline cerulean chalice, a chime for a champion, a song for the sincere and doomed, the brightly bitter sincere, a truth-to-be-broken, truth to be told, a beat, a drum, a ladder to climb, but the pulse of the pressure and the temper followed, the tempter, the call of the trumpet, a clash of hammers striking strings somewhere up ahead, I had thought behind, where a bronzed voice sang out sharp words and stories deep and sad. I heard it. I broke through. I crested the hill.

I stood before a cut-open chain-link fence, and down a steep drop, almost a cliff, the cars shot forward and backward along the expressway. I reeled with the height.

"John!" yelled my father, his voice near and ragged.

So I turned aside from the cliff and kept on going, on my feet now, running like a normal little boy, toward the lovely song and away from my father. I came out on the far side of the hill, where short grass, green grass, mowed grass, fair shade, relief brought me behind the concrete building and I went in through an open door and on toward the sound and burst onto the stage, in new light, blinding light, loud music, and froze.

I saw myself reflected in a mirror at my feet. My hair was tangled with twigs and leaves, and my arms and legs were scratched and swollen. The singer and her band played on as if I didn't exist, although everyone in the audience was staring at me. To my left, the drummer. I looked at him at the same moment he looked at me. Tired, wiry, dark, and tangled, his movements casual, his playing almost haphazard. But there was nothing sloppy about the sounds that snapped from the snares and cymbals beneath his hands. They divided, by a beat, mad chaos from strict order. The drummer rode that blade with careless precision. He was looking at me. The singer sang. She said that everything was blue, and I believed her. The drummer bobbed his head slightly. His mouth moved as if in prayer. I couldn't see his eyes, but he saw mine. He was wearing sunglasses, two perfect blue circles that hid his anger. Or maybe his fear. Or his passion. I felt him pulling my soul through my mouth to get a closer look, but I didn't know him at all.

Then he grinned and his lips were cracked and his teeth were black and sharp. His face opened up, either friendly or deadly, but present and absolute. I took a step back.

"John?" said my father. He was standing at my side. He had a nasty gash across his right eye, and his face was flushed and red.

"Don't hit me!" I yelled.

60

After he promised not to spank me, my father took my hand and led me back to my seat without a word. The Demnescus hadn't moved at all... It was as if they hadn't even noticed. Mabel returned with Michael, and then my mother.

"Please take him to the bathroom and clean him up," she said when the set had finished.

So, again, my father took my hand, firmly but gently, and led me out of the auditorium and into the lobby. When we got to the bathroom door, I pulled my hand back, and said, "I want to go all on my own."

I still didn't trust him.

"You sure?" he asked.

"Yeah."

"Okay."

Inside, a slight black man with close-cropped hair stood at a urinal, his left hand leaning on the tile wall above him. He looked tired. I washed my face, my hands, my stinging calves and ankles. The man finished, and started for the door. It was the drummer. He was still wearing his sunglasses.

"Why you wear 'em inside?" I asked.

He stopped and looked at me.

"Your sunglasses?"

"You was in the wrong place, you know," he said. "They don't let kids up on that stage." His voice was cracked, and he had a strange accent.

"I was running," I said.

"Why?"

"I was chased."

"By your papa?"

"Yeah. And by dead things."

"Really. And what did the dead things look like?"

"They were blue dead things, and they were from before, and they went backwards, and everything was blue."

He looked at me for a long time but, with his eyes hidden behind the sunglasses, I didn't know what he was thinking.

"Dead things," he said. "Just dead people?"

"No. Other things, too."

"Dead buildings? Dead cars?"

I nodded. Outside, I heard the singer start up again: "There's a time for everything on Earth." A flute echoed dimly through the lobby. "A time to be born and to die. A time to plant and to harvest. A time to cry and to laugh. A time to lose and to find."

"What is your name, little man?"

"John Bridge."

"John, those ghosts want to go away from you, but you run up and catch them. That's how you see them. How, I don't know. They are moving ghosts and leaving ghosts. Sometimes I caught them too, a long time ago. A long way away. They fly fast. Jesus knew them. Once, he ran up and catched one that had the sights of an old man, and brought it back and put that sights back in that old man's eyes. That man was so grateful he defended Jesus. And once, Jesus found a dead man. He ran up and catched the moving ghosts with the life of that man, and he took it and brought that life back to him. And the dead man came alive again. But you can't do that. I can't do that. We can't do what Jesus did. We can only see the ghosts. That's special, too. Mostly, no one sees them anyway."

"They wanted to get me," I said. "To kill me like they killed my Aunt Ellie. That's why I had to fly away from them."

"No. They only go away from you. If you saw them it's because you catched them as they were going away."

"Did they saw me?"

"Of course they can see you. How else would they run away from you if they didn't see you?"

"I don't want them to see me." I felt like crying. "I don't want me to see them too."

Again, he stood still. That strange mirrored expression that shot my own face back at me.

Outside a Hammond organ buzzed with moral authority. "A time to demolish and to build." I heard taut and swollen sounds crescenting out of a steel drum. "A time to hold it and to let it go."

"John," the man said, "You asked why I wore my glasses inside. I wear my glasses inside so I don't see them. I know they see me, and I know they're there, but now I don't see them, and they don't bother me. You see, they're all blue, so any blue glasses can hide them from you."

"Oh."

"Now I will give you these glasses, and then you won't see them. But first you have to let me say two things."

"Okay."

"In the village where I am from – it's far away – everyone there saw moving ghosts. A long time ago, my sister met a Christian man, and they went away so they wouldn't see the ghosts anymore. Then my brother went to try and find them. My sister and the man of God. Then I followed them, too, but I can't find them either. I took the path through the garden. I went through city after city. The last city was this city. Akawe. Now that I'm here, I see the ghosts again. It is the first time I seen the ghosts since I left my village. So maybe, if you, if your family leave this city, then maybe you won't see the ghosts anymore."

"Okay."

"The other. Do you believe in God, John?"

"I go to church."

"Good. The Bible doesn't say anything about moving ghosts, and the priest doesn't know anything about them. But they do say: 'Care for orphans and widows in their affliction' and 'keep yourself unstained by the world.' If we do these things, then we get close to God, and he comes to us too. If we don't do it, then we grieve his Holy Spirit. His sadness is our fear. Our fear is the ghosts. And 'what doth it profit, my brethren, though a man say he hath faith, and have not works? Can faith save him?' And 'thou believest that there is one God; thou doest well: the devils also believe, and tremble.' And that's what I say. No jealousy. No selfishness. We all die, but if we're good, then it's all okay. No ghost can hurt a good man."

His face did not move as he spoke.

"A time to rip and to bind. A time for silence and sound," came from the auditorium. I heard the trill of a ukelele. "A time of longing and love. A time of war and seeking peace."

"John," said the man. "Wear the glasses so you don't get scared. But more important: Be a good man. Love your family. Keep yourself clean. Then the ghosts can't scare you or hurt you, even without blue glasses. Do you understand my meaning?"

I nodded.

He took off his sunglasses and put them in my hands. His eyes were dark and deep, warm with caring and cool with hurt. Cold with cataracts and tiredness. I had never seen anyone so exhausted looking. Not even my father. This man's eyes were eyes that had been worn down by long nights and long travels.

"Let's go now," he said.

We met my father outside.

"Your boy is a good little man," he said. "He likes my drumming so I gave him a gift."

"Oh?" said my father.

"They are just some sunglasses," the man said, and looked at me. "Any sunglasses will do, but this one has seen a lot."

"Thank you," said my father.

The man gave a brief smile and passed through an unmarked door.

"Can I see your sunglasses?" my father asked.

I handed them over. I saw a blue shadow standing where the drummer had been standing. The shadow seemed to lean toward me.

"Huh," my father said. "Blue teashades? Haven't seen these in a while. Janis Joplin used to wear these. John Lennon. Hey, I could probably use a bit of whatever that guy was on." He sighed. "Here you go."

He gave me back the shades.

I put them on. As the world went blue, the blue things vanished. I felt my father take my hand and lead me back into the auditorium.

61

After another hour, the concert ended. When we returned to the lobby, folding tables had been prepared with small plates of cookies and technicolor orange punch in white Styrofoam cups. I got a cookie, and my parents got a plate and started talking to Angel and George Demnescu. Selby sighed and walked over to me.

"Mom and dad are sick and tired," she said in a raspy voice. I wondered if she was sick.

"I know that!" I said. "Look, I got some sunglasses."

"If you hold 'em sideways they make a eight!" she said. "My dad told me that."

I took off the sunglasses and held them sideways so that they looked like a figure eight.

"See, you got the eight," she said. "That means you never have to die. It means you get to live forever. A sideways eight is forever! Can I have them?"

"Only if you get your own sunglasses. The drum guy gave me mine."

"Can I weard them?"

"No!" I said. "These are the most powerfullest. When I put them on I don't see ghosts no more."

"You see the ghosts? I see the ghosts too."

"I don't see spooky sheet ghosts," I said. "I see the kind that's the blue dead things that go backwards!"

Selby gasped.

"That kind is the worst," she said. "The most scary. I see them every all over the time!"

"Even right now?"

"Uh huh. Every all over."

Michael walked up. "My mom says I can't have a pop, but I can have a cookie." Crumbs covered the kangaroo on this shirt. I lifted the sunglasses, so I was looking at him unfiltered. The kangaroo turned blue.

"Michael is a ghost!" I yelled.

"Whooooooooooo!" said Michael, and Selby and I screamed and ran away from him. He followed us in spirals, weaving among the legs and bodies of the tables and adults all around us. We ended up against the tiled wall.

"I'm invisible!" I shouted.

"And Michael is the ghost," said Selby.

"Whooooooooooo!" said Michael.

Selby went on: "And I am the brand new baby. I got blood on me 'Cause when I my dad said to save me the bad boy had to die."

"I don't want the bad boy to die," said Michael, trembling.

"He deserved it," Selby said, angrily. "He was a bad boy. The baddest."

"I don't want anybody to die!" wailed Michael.

"Okay, okay," I said. "The other baby didn't die because he had an eight to make him invisible."

Selby looked unhappy at this.

"Okay, fine, I'll let you wear my sunglasses now," I said. "So you can wear the eight and hide and you can be the other baby didn't die."

"As long as I'm alife, that other bad boy baby is *dead*," said Selby. "My dad says he has to be."

Selby put on the sunglasses. They were too big for her and her whole face vanished behind the huge blue lenses.

"Wow!" she said. "No ghosts anywhere!"

"But what about me?" I demanded. I saw the blues emerging throughout the room, under the tables, from doors and alcoves. "Now I need a eight or the ghost is going to get me."

"Whooooooooooo!" said Michael. "I'm a killing blood ghost."

"No," said Selby. "The ghost don't get you. They can't get you. They go away. They are going-away-city ghosts. Yeran Phantoms."

"I want my sunglasses back," I shouted, ready to cry.

"Fine!" she said. "That other boy had to die anyway. I hate that bad boy!"

"Fine!" I said, putting the sunglasses on again.

"Now I see the blue ghosts." She pouted.

"No you don't."

"You're a lie to yourself, John. You think you know, but you so stupid, so you can really know. Really!"

Eventually, the crowd started to thin. Our parents found us and led us out between the massive trees overhead and into the parking lot. Twilight had faded completely, and I imagined a night that went on and on, unendingly curving out into new spaces. I caught the dark blue of twilight rapidly fading to purple and black, but I couldn't tell if this was the way the sky usually looked after a sunset, or if the heavens were also ghost-infested. A cloud of flies spiraled in a frenzy under a pale streetlamp. I heard the staccato two-note three-trilled beats of a mockingbird a block away, and then, farther off, the mournful cry of the train he was imitating. The train brought parts for cars and it made the trip each day. Then, from behind us, a voice – rough and grainy – shot out from regions already black, beneath the trees, between the lights.

"Bye, John! Bye, Michael!"

"Bye, Selby!" I shouted.

My parents strapped me into my car seat, and we rode home in deep shadow.

SPACE

62

"Two days second," my father was saying when my mother and I got home the next day. "Two nights third, then a day off, then a day on first, then I'm back to second. Who knows what to believe anymore?" He was sitting in the recliner and reading the paper. He set it down with a tired smile. "I want Alec Baldwin to play me in *Prelude to a Pink Slip.*"

My mother gave a little sigh and walked into the kitchen to start on lunch.

63

As the fourth week of school swept us toward autumn, my friends and I all leaned in toward a dance. It was Radcliffe's annual "Welcome / Welcome Back" Dance, and it was the first dance most of the seventh graders would attend. This wasn't going to be like the tiny thing at St. Francis with a bunch of little kids and a nun for a DJ; this was going to be almost all of the six hundred students at Radcliffe Junior High, and we all had an angle. If the Plan was dead now, maybe the Dance could replace it. Chuck was right that I couldn't scheme my way toward imagined power, but maybe if I put on my cool and lay down on my back, power would wash over *me*. Maybe if I made myself one with the tide, it would pull me away toward its hazy horizons. I didn't care where it took me.

But the dying city didn't care about my thirst for adventure and freedom. I knew this because Radcliffe canceled the dance.

On the last Wednesday of September, some kid smashed through the front of a vending machine and then pulled a fire alarm. I say "some kid" because they never caught him. Or her.

We stood outside for a half-hour in the rowdy September breeze, the sun warm on our backs, and we squinted in that bright light, looking for a flash of flame behind the gritty windows.

When we got back inside, Mr. Rolison, the principal, came on over the PA: "If you want a dance this week," he said, "I suggest someone better let me know who did this." Static off. That was that. No one spoke up. The dance was canceled.

At first, I thought, *If I knew who it was, I'd tell.* It was a fist that had shattered the front of the vending machine; they'd found blood crusted around the hole. You don't just walk in or out of an inner-city school with a bloody fist and nobody notices. So *someone* had to have known who did it. *I'd leave an anonymous note. I don't care. They don't have to know it was me. Who punishes six hundred kids because of one asshole?*

But as I thought about it more, my anger shifted from the supposed criminal to the administration. After all, *they* were the ones punishing six hundred of us for what one person had done. Hundreds of kids in my class showed up to school smelly and sticky, without clean clothes, or with clothes too big or too small. This was what our families had been unable to give us. Some of us stole notebook paper from the teachers so we could do our homework. In a few of our houses, there was little heat in the winter and practically nobody had air-conditioning in the summer. We dealt with beat downs and a few of us with shootings and drive-bys. Our cousins got their friends to try to track us down and beat us up, and some of us didn't even have a home we could go to... just a collection of scattered family members who felt too guilty to turn us away.

"Can I sleep here tonight?" Adam would ask Carla once or twice each week.

"I guess so," Carla would say.

We wanted a little power, and we wanted a little fun, and Mr. Rolison was going to take it all away because of *one kid.* "Fuck you," we said. That week we spoke up. We transgressed the routine. We threw paper airplanes openly in class. Even in Mrs. Norman's and Mrs. Anders' classes. We threw rolls of toilet paper down the hall. The school had run out of TP by the end of the week. The cigarette smoke was so thick in the bathrooms that you almost couldn't taste the rank weed underneath, and then there was the tubey steamy shit that some pissed-off kid had taken on the floor.

But what about me? I wondered. *What am I going to do?*

64

One day, when Cora missed the bus home, she showed up at my house with Adam, and they asked for a ride.

"My father's got the car," I said. "And my mother isn't even here."

"K," said Adam. "Walk me home?"

"Where we going?"

"Grandpa M's."

It was only a mile away.

"What about Cora?" I asked.

"My grandpa'll give her a ride later tonight."

It's not like I had anything better to do. No plans or dances to plot out. Just homework, homework, homework. I locked up, and we headed out.

"It's so cold!" Cora complained as we walked south on Whitmore.

"No it's not!" said Adam.

"It's windy."

Adam pivoted so that he was walking backwards, in front of us, and the wind whipped his face. His cheeks were red and his hair flew behind his head.

"You know that Friday is the 13th?" he asked.

"It is?" said Cora.

"Yeah. We gotta do something. You know – it's the whole witchy month, Halloween, and we got Friday the 13th."

"I don't understand. Why we gotta do something?"

"It's October!"

"I thought Friday the 13th was every October."

"No," I said. This conversation was slowly annoying me.

"Oh," she said.

Quickly, actually.

"It's boring, not doing nothing," said Adam. "So... let's do something!"

He jumped in the air, came down on the irregular joint of two sidewalk squares, pinwheeled his arms wildly, and almost fell over. Cora laughed. Adam steadied himself, glanced over his shoulder, then resumed walking backwards.

"Like what?" I asked.

"I think..." he said, lingering for dramatic effect, "we should break into an abandoned house and have a séance."

"That's a great idea," I said.

"You think so?"

"No! I was being sarcastic. That's a fucking stupid idea –"

"But –"

"Crackheads, squatters. I don't want to get thrown in jail over a... fucking séance."

"But we can –"

"If you want to do it, let's just do it at Chuck's house," I said. "You look out his window, you'll see plenty of abandoned houses. Hell, my house even. If it doesn't work, we can just play video games or watch a movie." Because I knew it wouldn't work.

"Your parents are too chaperoney. And Chuck won't want it," Adam said. "He's... he's probably too busy being kissy kissy with Sara."

Cora laughed.

"He's back at our lunch table, at least," I said. "You don't know. He might go for it."

"I like your idea, Adam," Cora said. "And I think I know someone who knows a place."

Wonderful.

65

"No way," said Selby at lunch the next day.

"But... Friday the 13th!" whined Adam. "Come on! It's... it's gonna be so much fun! Right, John?"

"What if someone recognizes us?" I said. "We live over here, remember?"

"No, I scouted out some places in other neighborhoods. No one will know it's us."

"Where?"

"Over by the hospital."

"St. Christopher's? In Anderson Park? There ain't no abandoned houses over there."

"No, I mean over by Proctor."

"Oh, hell no!" said Selby. "I ain't goin' over there, even if there wasn't no bad luck."

"It ain't that bad," said Adam. "Chuck lives over there."

"No I don't, and yes it is," said Chuck. "It's that bad."

Elizabeth nodded. She'd skipped her Math class to join us at lunch that day.

"Well, what about the other houses on your street, John?" Cora asked me. "Couldn't we get into one of those?"

"No way!" I said. "There's no way we wouldn't be seen. My parents would kill me!"

"What about your dad's place, Adam?" asked Elizabeth. "That was pretty trashed."

"I been in there," he said. "That's boring."

"I'm sure we can find an abandoned house," said Cora.

"Yeah," I said. "With spiders and rats."

"How you know it'll be like that?" asked Adam.

"How *don't* you know?" I asked. "You been evicted from plenty."

Adam stared at me. "That wasn't nice."

"It's true."

"It's a really bad idea," said Selby.

"No no no no no!" said Adam, banging his fists on the table. "Last time I was out with my dad, he took us past this place over by Proctor, and it looks like the *Evil Dead* house. We won't get caught because nobody lives on that street. That place is the best and I want to go there, and we're going to go there, and –"

"This is stupid, Adam!" said Selby. "You go into some ghettoey place and summon the ghost of some dead person –"

"Or find a crackhead's body," I added.

"– and what you gonna say when they come? Huh? 'Oh hi, we just wanted to see the ghost of a dead person!' They'll steal your soul because they wouldn't even be around here no more if they were any good. My bunic's ghost shows up in our house sometimes, and he wasn't a very good person when he was alive."

"How you know he shows up?" asked Quanla. "You seen him?"

"No," Selby said. "He used to like brandy, so my mom leaves him some by the fireplace, and it's gone the next day."

"Yeah," I said, "I'm sure your brothers don't have nothing to do with that."

"Shut up, John!"

We were quiet a moment.

"Where is it, Adam?" asked Cora.

"I don't remember the address," said Adam. "It's behind the hospital."

"See?" I said. "We can't go! He doesn't even know where he's talking about."

"I can find it again. It know what street it's on. Church Street."

"You think you can do better, John?" asked Cora.

"Yeah, I do," I said. "Let's just go over to Chuck's. We can watch a movie or play games after –"

"No," said Chuck. "No way."

"Why not?"

"I don't want you talking to the dead at my house."

"Nobody's talking to them!" I said. "That's because they're dead. Dead people can't talk."

"You can see them sometimes though," said Selby. "You never seen nothing so twisted."

"You only see them if you do something unholy," said Quanla. "If you don't, they're invisible."

"That's what you think!"

"Adam, if you want to do this so bad, just do it with Cora," I said. "I don't think anyone else wants to."

"I kinda want to," said Quanla. "*Evil Dead* house? Hell yeah."

Everyone stared at Quanla.

"Ain't you fear the devil, Quanla?" asked Selby.

"Devil can't hurt me."

"Hell yeah, girl!" said Adam.

"I believe in Jesus," Quanla went on. "I ain't scared of a dead person."

"But we do need a ride," said Adam.

"Ha!" said Quanla. "The truth comes out!"

"Oh, please Quanla!"

"My brother ain't a taxi driver. He's a crappy driver. And I'm starting to think his car is the only reason you invite Selby and me to go places."

"Why you all want to tempt fate?" asked Selby.

"Because it's just a game, Selby!" snapped Cora.

"Just come over to my place," Selby offered. "My moms can tell us ghost stories, instead of a séance."

"Your mama's got bad breath!" said Quanla.

"What?!"

"Lucy!" called Cora.

"Look –" I began. *Wait, did she just yell at Lucy?*

"What you say, Quanla?!" snapped Selby.

"Sorry, it's true," Quanla said.

"Lucy!" Cora repeated. She was standing now, looking across the cafeteria. Amid the kids standing and taking their lunch trays to the trash, I saw Lucy's flowy fake black hair bouncing in our direction

"What you say?!" asked Selby.

"I'm sorry," said Quanla.

"Lucy, c'mere!" said Cora. "Sit down with us."

Lucy took a seat. She smiled and gave a little wave and Adam fell forward onto the table.

"This girl is like my favorite person ever," he gushed. "She saved John and my asses in Mr. Kolin's when she ate a dirty note I wrote. It was wicked!"

"Yeah, well," said Cora, "she also knows a sweet abandoned place we can get into for the séance."

"Lucy, are you going to save me again?" Adam asked. "From my friends who doth not care one licketh about the dead spirits that doth give muche wisdome?"

"What about the *Evil Dead* house?" asked Quanla.

"The *Evil Dead* house is awesome," said Adam. "But if Lucy knows a place like this place Cora was telling me about, it's even awesomer."

"Yeah," said Cora. "It's that place. We can get in there, right Lucy?"

"Well," said Lucy. "I wasn't that serious. But yeah. I... I do think we could get in there. We have to be careful. I could get in so much trouble."

"We will be sooooo secret about it," said Adam.

"What's it like?" asked Quanla.

"It isn't a house. It's an old auditorium. My dad's been trying to sell it for years. I know the combination to get in."

"Like an old theater?" Quanla asked.

"Not *that* old... but yeah, sort of."

"That's cool."

Lucy's brow wrinkled. "Okay," she said. "But we'll need to get a ride."

"My brother can give us a ride," said Quanla, suddenly eager.

"Why you want to do this, Quanla?" asked Selby.

"I told you. I ain't scared," Quanla said. "Besides, I want to see the old abandoned theater."

"John? Don't *you* think this is a bad idea?" asked Selby.

I didn't want ghosts overhearing us. I *was* a little worried about that, even though I wasn't sure I really believed in them. But I *was* curious about this old theater building. Also, I didn't want to contradict Lucy. Also, I kind of wanted a reason to spend some more time with her.

"Actually, I think it'll be cool," I said.

66

Friday the 13th arrived, cold, windy, and gray.

"Five dollars," Darius said when I stepped out to his car.

"I don't have five dollars, faggot!" I said.

"Watch your lip!" he said. "How much you got?"

It's not like Darius had gotten sick of driving. He'd just figured out that he was more important to us than we were to him. I pulled out all the money I had; a dollar bill and a pile of change.

"Like two?"

"Gimme it."

I got in the car with Quanla, Cora, Adam, and Lucy. Quanla rode shotgun. Cora was sitting on Adam's lap in the back, as usual. Lucy sat in the middle, so I had to sit next to her. She was wearing a white sweater and blue jeans, and I was conscious of my leg pressing into hers.

"Chuck and Selby not coming?" I asked.

"Chuck's watching his sisters, and you knew Selby wouldn't," said Quanla.

"Hi John," said Lucy. "Okay, take South Street to East, then turn right."

Lucy guided us until we landed in an East Side neighborhood that hadn't known whether to go industrial or commercial or residential. It had tried all three, had failed at all three, and had been uniformly abandoned. Small brick buildings with parking lots full of rusted scrap backed up against grimy storefronts and houses wearing plywood eyepatches over their widows. We made a few turns. The expressways were out there somewhere, just out of sight. East Street was nearby, too, but we couldn't see it either.

Then we turned onto a block that seemed even more abandoned than the rest. Almost everything had been torn down, and the shrubs and trees had been growing for so long that the block looked more like a meadow than a patch of city. On the left, poplars sprang out of the sandy pits of buried foundations, oaks loomed over the cracked fragments of lost sidewalks, and a towering black walnut dropped its poisonous fruit onto the weedy grass. Only one building was left standing: a vacant-looking bar made out of green painted not-cinder-blocks with rounded corners and splintery wood siding. A rust-stained metal sign hung out front, and if you squinted your eyes, you could make out the words: "TREEMONISHA CLUB ~ MEMBERSHIP REQUIRED."

"That isn't the place," said Lucy, a little nervously.

"Where is the place?" asked Quanla.

"It's out there," gesturing to the right. What had once been a parking lot receded between two large hills toward a grove of sycamore trees. I could only tell that it was a parking lot because the grass and bushes were patchier there than on the hills. Inside the grove, I couldn't see anything at all.

"Quanla," said Darius, with an edge in his voice. "I don't know about this. Mom and dad would be pissed if they knew what you're doing. I don't know it's safe."

"I'll be fine, Darius!" Quanla snapped. "Lucy knows what she's about."

"I'm coming with you," Darius said.

We got out of the car and started walking through the waist-high grass.

67

"Won't someone see us?" I asked.

"Nobody lives over here." said Lucy. "Nobody works over here."

More than anyone else I knew at Radcliffe, Lucy looked and talked like a suburban kid. It surprised me that she'd be taking us to this part of the city so inner it had gone to seed.

"So what *does* your dad do?" I asked.

"He's sort of like a realtor," Lucy said. "I mean... he buys a bunch of properties all at once, and then if there are people from out-of-state who want to buy something, it's like he sells it to them. He doesn't just work in Akawe. He does it in Pontiac, Flint, Detroit... we even live in one of them. I mean, my mom and my brother and Steven and me. My dad rents it to us. It's big too, because the house is connected to an old business. 'The Tent and Tarp Shop.' It looks pretty crappy from the road."

I heard the low rush of cars coming from the taller hill, which loomed off to our left and was completely choked by shrubs and brambles.

"What's over there?"

"992," said Lucy. "It sounds weird up here. The cars do. It's like it's got something to do with the way that the sound goes between the hills."

We entered the sycamore grove and the drab gray light dimmed into pale greens and yellows through the fluttering leaves overhead. The mottled bark – brown and rust, black and ivory – had a stone-hard solidity to it. The place seemed old. The sycamores had been planted a long, long time ago.

"These trees always make me think of a church," Lucy said. "Not my own church, but where I went to school. The light goes through the leaves... like stained glass."

"Where did you go to school... before Radcliffe?" I asked.

"St. Brendan's."

"That's where I go to church!"

"We're not Catholic. But my mom sent me to school there because she didn't like the Akawe Schools. But it got too expensive, which is why I went to Radcliffe after sixth grade."

"Shit, you probably sat through more masses there than I have. My family's Catholic, but we never had the money for St. Brendan's, and I didn't get the scholarship, so I've always gone to the public schools."

"Well, you know, we're both in the same place now."

We truly were.

Finally, we saw the building at the center of the grove.

I'd been expecting something as old as the trees, a looming cathedral built out of brick or even stone. Instead, I was looking at an octagonal concrete mass that was wider at the top than at the bottom. It was thirty, maybe forty feet high. There weren't any windows except on the ground floor, which opened onto a sort of lobby. All the glass had been smashed, with seed pods and oak and sycamore leaves littering the red carpeted floor. Despite the broken windows, which we could have easily stepped through, Lucy walked up to a reinforced metal door and turned the combination on a padlock until a small key popped out of the back. She unlocked the doors and let us in.

68

"Where are we?" asked Darius once we were all standing inside the lobby.

"I don't know the whole story," Lucy admitted. "But it used to be an elementary school. The theater here was built as an add on, and when they demoed the school, they kept using the theater for a while. They'd do concerts and put on shows here or something."

"It got a name?"

"I don't remember the name of the school, but the theater is Sycamore Grove, I think. That's what they called it."

"Damn."

Paper and plaster and brittle paint covered the floor. Blues and oranges – the remnants of bright mosaics – wrapped around columns and up the walls, but many of the square tiles had fragmented and fallen. Elsewhere, shreds of the maroon moll carpet clung to the foundation and, where the rain had gotten in, grew fuzzy tufts of moss.

"Lucy," asked Quanla. "Should we not do things here? I mean, should we not touch things? Since your dad is trying to sell this place?"

Lucy laughed, nervous again. "He's not going to sell this place. It's a death trap. I mean, they could only buy it to demo it, and there are places in town you can get better land a lot cheaper. Just don't get hurt. If you get hurt on something, I'll get in a lot of trouble, and so will my dad."

Something in Lucy's tone told me there was more to it than that, but I didn't want to pester her.

Instead, I moved across the lobby toward the huge double doors that opened into the auditorium.

Adam and Cora had moved ahead of the rest of us, and I saw his flashlight beam moving wildly against the walls and ceiling. It had been a large auditorium, with seats for a few hundred people, but some of these had been ripped from the floor with crumbs of concrete scattered about like the place had been hit by an earthquake. Tattered crimson curtains hung over a stage at the front, and there were heaps of other curtains lying about in holey, moldy piles. The leaves hadn't blown this far inside, so we couldn't smell the damp anymore. The air was dry, stale, almost chemical. It felt still. Watchful. It wasn't a dark feeling, but unsettling... as if whatever ghosts had been left from the auditorium's living days might still be floating around. They weren't about to speak to us or hurt us, but they certainly watched us. They would see what we did, and if they disapproved, they would judge. If ghosts here disapproved of our presence and gave God their testimony, or if God really was omniscient, omnipotent, what would he think? What would he do?

Adam had reached the stage. I watched the flashlight beam against a pile of old books scattered at his feet.

"John! Check it out!" he said. "Someone left a Bible here."

"Great," I said.

"We can read from Revelations. That talks about the dead, doesn't it?"

"It sure does," said Quanla.

She kept surprising me.

Adam sat down on the edge of the stage, Cora at his side, the Bible open on his lap, the flashlight beaming downward. He read:

"Then I saw a great white throne and the one who sat on it; the earth and the heaven fled from his presence and no place was found for them...I saw the dead, great and small stand... before the throne... and books were opened."

Adam closed the Bible. He held it solemnly on his lap for a moment before speaking.

"Okay," he said. "I believe that there is a dead soul floating right behind me now, and if you ask it a question, it will whisper the answer in my ear. So I'm gonna pass this Bible and when it's your turn, you ask it a question."

He passed the book to Darius, who sneered at it for a moment. He opened it. Flipped through briefly, then snapped it shut and said, "Fine. Am I gonna end up with some phat trick, or am I gonna end up lonely?"

"Darius, you fag!" said Quanla, but Adam spoke in a low and creaky voice: "Nooo. Yooou willll hoook uuup with a straaange and exoootic woooman born in a dissstant laaand."

Darius grimaced and shook his head and passed the Bible to his sister.

"Jesus, protect me," she said. "But I have to ask. What am I gonna go to college for after high school's over?"

"Yooou willl gooo into cheeemissstreee."

"Huh," said Quanla. She scratched behind her ear and passed the book to Cora.

"Oh dead soul!" intoned Cora. "Am I, am I, am I going to get lucky before Christmas this year?"

"Soooner thaaan thaaat!"

Cora giggled and passed the book to Lucy.

Lucy didn't even glance at the Bible but she looked hard at Adam.

"I want you to tell me what I am thinking about right now," she said.

"Aiii telll the fyooochooor, not the preeesent."

"Then tell me what I'm going to be thinking about an hour from now."

"Yooou willl beee thiiinking about how you fiiinally haaave sooome frieeends youuu caaan trussst."

Lucy didn't say a thing, but handed the Bible, almost dismissively, to me.

The whole time, I'd been wracking my brain: *What am I going to ask?* Urgent question after question flashed through me: *Has Patricia been leading me on or did she not even know that I liked her? Does anyone at our school like me? Am I really a coward? Why did the man with the knife ask about my sunglasses? Why did those kids jump off that hospital roof? Who is Lucy?* But was I really going to ask any of these questions in front of my friends?

"Is Mrs. Anders really gay?" I finally asked.

69

Elizabeth's locker was one of just a dozen on a landing separating the second and third floors of Radcliffe. A girl named Camille took the locker three down from Elizabeth. Camille shared her locker with Melissa. They were both bitchy, sparkly, white girls with asshole jock boyfriends. Both girls stained their hair violent, vibrant shades and combed their locks back over their ears. They wore red and pink lipstick, their breath smelled like mint, and a thin dust of glitter clung to their skin. They'd smile and laugh gentle laughs and turn their fragile looking faces to the side. They wore shorts so short I could see the denim tucked in the folds of their asses.

It started out with insults:

"You're such a faggot," Camille would tell Elizabeth.

"Bitch," said Melissa.

"You fuck your mama."

"Your mama and your dad are probably related, why you're so inbred and retarded."

"Nasty snatch."

"You drink Juicy Juice? More like you drink pussy juice."

Elizabeth told us about this but did her best to ignore the two girls. They didn't like being ignored. So they stuck their wet gum to the outside of Elizabeth's locker, then kicked it shut when she was getting her shoes out.

"What a faggot!" Melissa said.

"Whore!"

Then, on the Monday after our trip to Sycamore Grove, Camille and Melissa waited for Elizabeth on the landing. Camille grabbed her lunch sack and threw it against the wall, scattering her food down the floor. Melissa knocked Elizabeth's folder out of her hands – papers flying – and gave her a rough shove toward the stairs.

That's when Elizabeth tried *not* ignoring them. She looked at the two girls and said, "You aren't pretty."

It was a simple, perfect diss that cut through the heartwood of Camille's and Melissa's deepest fears. So they slapped her, punched her, pulled on her hair, then banged her head into the lockers one, two, three times before taking off up the stairs, laughing and chatting. A purple bruise swelling above her eye. Blood in her hair. Hair on the floor.

When Elizabeth told us about it at Science class the next day, Chuck was livid. The rest of us weren't too happy either.

"What's their locker number?" I asked.

"221," Elizabeth said. "But don't do nothing about it. I don't want drama."

"Sounds like you already got drama," said Adam.

"I don't want more."

"I know Derrick," said Chuck. "Camille's boyfriend. He's not a total jerk. I'll talk to him. It won't happen again."

I was doubtful. "You can share my locker," I said.

"You sure?" asked Elizabeth.

"I don't care. I never use it anyway."

I carried my books in my backpack. I'd given up stuffing my backpack with tea and sunglasses, and I'd gotten sick of the crowded halls between classes.

"Thank you John."

"221," I said, and Adam winked at me.

70

After lunch, Elizabeth followed me back to my locker. I told her my combination, and cleared out a couple of my textbooks I hadn't touched in weeks.

"I can't believe they called you a faggot," I said. "I'll bet they're the faggots. Probably a bit touchy about eating pussy because they eat so much themselves."

Elizabeth flipped out so loud and suddenly, I couldn't catch the first several things she said. I took a step back, and when I saw her red face and wide eyes, I realized that she was shouting at *me*.

"—such a asshole sometimes!" she was saying, and "I don't want your help if you're going to be as bad as them!"

"Whoa, just a sec, what do you mean?"

"You're always saying 'faggot this,' 'faggot that.' Your parents know you talk like that?!"

"I don't talk that way in front of my parents. Is that what you mean?" I was getting pissed off too. Here I was helping her out, so why flip out at me?

"Uh huh! Why don't you?"

"Because you don't talk that way to your parents, or you get grounded. *My* parents at least. I don't swear in front of them neither. What the fuck's wrong with it?"

"It's not a very nice way to talk about someone, John. What, would you call someone a nigger?"

"That's not the same," I said.

"Uh huh," she said. "How's it different?"

"Well... skin color isn't something you choose. You can choose what you do."

"So you're saying it isn't fair to call Chuck that because he can't choose a better skin color than the one he has!"

"What?! No! I ain't sayin' that!"

"I don't see you calling Selby or Quanla a bitch!"

"That's 'cause they don't act bitchy!"

"So you just go around calling everyone a faggot –"

"It's just another word for asshole –"

"Why don't you just call them assholes, then? I like 'assholes' a lot better. And I got a feeling your parents – your mom – would be more pissed off if she heard you calling someone a 'faggot' than if she heard you calling them an 'asshole.'"

I felt a shadow of fear; I *had* called people "asshole" from time to time in front of my parents and never got more than a glare for it, but I'd probably be in serious trouble if they – if *either* of them – heard me calling anyone "faggot." They both had gay friends. From the shop and from the radio station... neither more or less fucked up than anyone else I'd met. I knew I wasn't gay, but it didn't bother me if my Lit teacher was. But Adam threw the word "fag" around a lot and sometimes so did Chuck, Quanla, and Selby. At the end of the day, I thought, a diss was a diss. It was an effective word. It

shut assholes up, put them on the defensive, and sometimes –
often – that was useful.

"It's just a diss," I said.

"Fuck that," said Elizabeth. "It hurts people, which is
why you say it. You say it so you can hurt them. Camille and
Melissa say it to make me feel shitty, and you say it to make
someone else feel shitty. Like Michael."

"What? Who's Michael?"

"Your cousin Michael!"

"I didn't say nothing about him!"

"You heard Adam say a bunch of rumors about him and
you didn't step in and stop it. Even though he *is* your own
cousin. Now he's got people picking on him just like Camille
and Elizabeth pick on me. All because Adam started calling
him faggot! Good fucking job, John! Great fucking job helping
your own cousin out!"

"Well, maybe he is one!" I said.

I wanted to slow down the conversation a little. The
accusations rang down the hall and kids were staring. I didn't
want to be getting such negative attention. It angered me that
Elizabeth was pissed at me and not any of our other friends. It
made me angry, too, because I had been called a fag plenty of
times myself. What was I supposed to do, shut up and take it?
Why not return the favor? But Elizabeth was relentless. She
kept arguing and arguing, and she just wouldn't stop.

Whenever I tried to interrupt or disagree she started shouting and gesturing wildly.

Suddenly, I put up my hands because I had Figured It Out.

"Wait, wait, wait, just a minute," I said. "So... don't get mad at me, but... are you gay, Elizabeth?"

"Ha!" she barked. "I can't believe you're such a clueless asshole!"

"No, shhh! Quiet. Look, I won't tell anyone!"

"I'm not gay!" Elizabeth shrieked.

"I'm sorry," I said, quickly. "I just thought... it's probably... it's probably a bit because I spend so much time hanging out with Adam... that I say it. He says it every chance he gets, haven't you noticed?"

"Yes! Yes, I have noticed that, John!"

"So why aren't you so pissed off at him?!"

"Get a fucking clue, John!" Elizabeth shouted.

She slammed the locker – my locker – shut so hard that the bang echoed up and down the hall. Now plenty of kids were watching me, but I tried to ignore them. Elizabeth turned and stalked away, and I waited for her to look back, for a chance to at least try to wrap things up.

"You can keep using my locker, Elizabeth!" I called after her. "It's okay."

She held up her middle finger at me as she kept walking.

"Your girlfriend mad at you John?" someone asked.

"She's not my girlfriend."

"'Course she ain't. What a faggot!"

71

After school that day, I met Adam back at Radcliffe, when the sun was setting and the school had emptied except for a few custodians and the Chess Club meeting near the cafeteria. When we made sure that the halls were empty, we found the landing and locker 221, and Adam picked the lock with a nail file and a paper clip. We found a mess inside: textbooks, notes and papers, a sparkly sweater, and a fluffy hat. We took turns peeing into the locker, then slammed it shut and left the school.

72

Autumn had settled in for good on the night my father sent me down to Cartierul to give the Demnescus some empty mason jars. As I rode my bike along the shadowy streets, I caught the earthy scent of a distant brushfire before it was suffocated by the egg smell farting from the smokestacks of the Benedict G. It was cold and I put my hands in my pockets whenever I had to stop. My ears throbbed with the beat of invisible drums. When I arrived, Angel welcomed me at the front door with a smile. Selby hung back a little. I went inside and started taking the mason jars from my backpack. They carried them, four at a time, into the kitchen. Then Angel went back to her skillet of Hamburger Helper while Selby and I sat in the incense-heavy living room with a photo of Bunica Demnescu smiling reluctantly out at us. Celesta sat in front of the TV watching *Count Duckula*. The fanged green duck was berating his butler who had surreptitiously replaced a jar of the vampire's beloved ketchup with blood.

"Catching up on life back in the old country?" I asked.

"Ha," said Celesta.

Selby glared at me.

On the coffee table sat a copy of the newspaper. The front-page story explained how prostitutes were moving to Akawe from Las Vegas because we didn't arrest them as often here. Instead, the police were busting annoyed johns as they drove through ATMs because twenty bucks didn't cut it with the new arrivals.

"Let's go for a walk," Selby said.

"I should probably get home..." I said.

"It won't take long."

I shrugged.

We put on our jackets, already soaked with spice from the closet where a bowl of old potpourri sat under several cobwebs.

We stepped out into the swollen twilight.

73

The wind rattled the chimes that Angel never took down. The porch light shot starlike rays out at us, flashlight bright, halo broad, rainbow circled, a will o' the wisp light filigreed with moth wings and daddy longleg legs.

We left the light, crossed the sidewalk, and started up the stony road. Invisible drumbeats throbbed up ahead.

"It's a pretty funny show, actually," Selby said. The rasp of her voice caught me off guard. I was never ready for it.

"What is?" I asked.

"Count Duckula. The other day they... they met these Egyptian priests. With a mummy. I think... hm... I think one was named Hoomite. And the other was named Yoobee. So they went back and forth, asking the count who he was. They'd say: 'Who might you be?' And he'd say, 'yeah yeah, I know you are.' And they'd say, 'We are! But who might you be?' And it went on for a long time. Hoomite, Yoobee! The show is funny like that."

"Like Who's on first?"

"What?"

"Um... it's a thing that Abbott and Costello did. They're two comedians that my parents like."

"Oh."

"It was a long time ago. I think they've been dead a long time."

"So... do you like Quanla?"

"What?"

"I'm just... I just thought that maybe you liked Quanla."

"Like... like what?"

"Like her like... like you might want her to go out with you."

I had no idea how to answer, partially because I wasn't sure I wanted to answer, and partly because I didn't know what the answer would be. I had to buy some time. "Did... did she ask you to ask me?"

Selby smiled. At least, I thought she smiled. In the purple dark it was hard to tell.

"Wouldn't you like to know!" she said.

And all sorts of thoughts I'd kept separate from each other for weeks suddenly came crashing together. Patricia had only just receded from my mind – *Did I ever really like Patricia?* – and my jealousy of Adam. But behind Patricia – behind Juanita and Cora – there had always been Quanla and her wide eyes, Selby and her cunning eyes, and Lucy with her searching gray eyes. *Why Lucy? What's the deal with Lucy?*

In terms of the actual question, I felt, yes, there was something about Quanla; her startling sincerity, her obvious intelligence, and her crystalline voice that had tugged at me for years. But anything more than friendship with Quanla felt like a serious thing, and seventh grade was already too serious. So I hadn't really hoped to have anything more than a friendship with Quanla. She was maybe always in the back of my mind... a possibility that I had kept in reserve for the distant future, when I had my own shit figured out better.

I realized now that Selby had to be either asking for Quanla or for herself. If she was asking for Quanla, I couldn't trust her to keep a secret. If she was asking for herself, almost any answer that I gave her would send her a signal. *I have to answer without sending a signal.* That *was* the answer!

"Wouldn't *you* like to know if I like Quanla?" I said.

"I would," she said.

We walked on in silence through a large vacant lot where a few housewives had lost their keys and a lot of winos had lost their bottles of Mad Dog. Gravel crunched underfoot.

"That Count Duckula really got me thinking," Selby said.

"What?"

"Who might you be? Their names are a question. Their question is who you are. Their names are the answer."

"I don't even know what you're talking about."

"You ever look in the mirror and say your name?"

"No."

"Try it, John. It's real weird. I'll stand there... not when anyone's home. They would never leave me alone about it. But I'll stand there and look in the mirror and say my name: 'Selby.' Selby. And I look at the shape of my eyes, my hair, the color of my skin, the way I smile, the way I frown, the way I'm sad. And everything I'm supposed to be is right there in those sounds they gave me. Sell. Bee. Selby."

"Yeah, that's weird." But I liked it. But I didn't want her to know that I liked it. I decided that I would whisper my name to myself in the mirror later that night.

"I wrote a poem about it," Selby said. "Do you want to hear it?"

"Sure."

"But you can't laugh at it."

"Okay."

"You promise?"

"I promise."

"You promise you won't laugh at it..."

"Yes! I promise I won't laugh."

"Okay."

She fished a piece of paper out of her pocket and read:

Meaning,
by Selby Demnescu.

How do you know what it means?
If people and places are what they seem.
Cleopatra on the seas
dying from the Egyptian disease.

How do you know what it means?
How do you know if you have the keys
if you learn about the birds and the bees
and the mosquitoes and the fleas.

I can't hold this inside me.
Even I don't know what it all means.
I just want to know what it means.
I just want to know what it means.

How do you know what it means?
There must be a meaning to everything.
Like Cleopatra on the seas,
when I find out, I'll tell thee!

We walked.
"What do you think?" she asked.
"I don't know," I said. "I don't read poetry."
"Yes you do. Your parents read poetry all the time."
"No they don't!"
"Your mama does!"
"But I don't!"
"You don't like it."
"What? No, I like it fine."
"No you don't."
"I do!"

"And the beauty is the truth, and the truth is the beauty, and when I find truth and beauty, then I will tell thee!"

"What's that?"

"Another ending I thought of!"

"Yeah?!"

"Yeah."

We walked, our fists deep in our pockets.

The invisible drums grew louder up ahead.

"Four years ago," Selby said. "This Christmas. That's when they killed the dictator. Nicolae Ceauşescu. The shot him right next to a toilet, you know. He deserved it. And you know, we could get in touch with our people over there now if we wanted to. The Romanians and the... others. They all lived by Ploieşti, which isn't that far from Transylvania. That's who they are. People from all over the world know about Count Dracula, but it's not like what my life has been about. My mother remembers Romania from when she was a kid. Do you know what she remembers? The sunflowers! Millions and billions of sunflowers growing all the way out to the sky. So I don't know. Does it matter what we say? What we do? What if we die? If we die does it matter? I know it sounds weird, but I think about these things all the time. I do. I think deep things."

"Okay..." I said. "Who are you, Selby?"

"Who am I?"

"Yeah," I said. "I'm just being honest right now. I'm just telling you so much... truth! Do you mind?"

"Tell me who I am!" she said. She laughed her rattle laugh. "I want to know!"

"People look at you the first time they meet you, they see a black girl. But you speak Romanian at them and that trips them up. But the Romanians here know you're part gypsy –"

"Not gypsy. Vlax Romani. And whatever else?"

"Yeah. And anything else about you probably isn't something they think of because of those other things come first in their minds."

"Like my voice?"

"Your voice is jacked up. But I didn't know you wrote no poetry."

"Yeah, I like jazz music like you do, too. I just don't talk about it as much. And I would keep on dancing forever – years and years – but we ran out of money and I didn't get the scholarship!"

"See what I mean? Who *are* you?"

"I don't know." She gave an elaborate shrug. "I'm a Selby Demnescu," she said. "I don't even know if there are any other Selby Demnescus on the planet earth."

"I'm pretty sure there are plenty of John Bridges."

She barked another laugh. "People look at you, they see a white boy. They see someone who can decide what he wants to be and just be it! I got it rougher, but you can't tell me who I am. I can tell you. I will tell you. But I got it rougher."

"You got friends."

"Quanla is my friend!" Her fierce eyes.

"I'm your friend."

"Are you?" she asked. "Are you my *friend?*"

"What do you think?"

We walked.

"I don't know," she said. "I don't know what I think."

We passed a single, desolate streetlight. We'd reached Adams Street. The edge of the neighborhood. Across the street, some thready pines, Sellers Creek, a broad parking lot, downward sloping, and then the three factories: the Benedicts C, F, and G. Brick in back, brown and white aluminum siding in front. Black soot-stained windows tilted up top to help circulate and cool the air inside.

"My father used to work there," I said.

"Tool and Die?"

"Yeah. I got to go and see it all with him once. I mean, it was a tour and they walked us through the whole factory. I thought it was crazy. I mean, I knew he didn't like his job, but I thought the whole place was amazing. It was so loud. Everything was loud. Banging and crashing and spinning and shit. Like... like a loud wind sound. There was tape on the floor so we'd know where it was safe to walk, and, like, glowing red stop signs so that forklifts wouldn't hit us. Then there were these huge machines that you just know weighed so much, that could crush a person like a bug. They were hanging from these giant chains that moved them along the ceiling."

"That was Tool and Die?"

"No. That's what we walked through to get to Tool and Die. It was a lot quieter when we got to the part where my father worked. He had this machine work-station thing. It almost made me think of, like, a sewing machine. But there was rat poop on it, too. He showed me."

"They don't do Tool and Die down here no more."

"No. They moved it all out. He's over at Starville now. And he's worried they're gonna shut it down there too. I don't know. They probably are."

"They still got foundries over here, you know."

"Yeah?"

"Yeah!"

"My father's told me about that. He said it looks like Hell. Like a painting of Hell. The lake of fire and all that. Sounds pretty crazy."

Selby breathed for a moment as we stood there.

"You want to see it?" she asked.

"Can we see it?"

"Yeah!"

"Then yeah!"

"Follow me!" she said. "I hope you don't mind getting your pants wet," she added.

74

Selby led us to the edge of the bridge where the guardrails ran up against a chain-link fence. Here, alone, X had been negligent about security. Thickets of ghetto palms grew between the fence and the stream, and Selby leapt easily over the guardrails and disappeared into the mess. I followed her. We wove our way through the shrubs and weeds along Adams Street and eventually peeled away toward the river. Then, she led me down toward the stream bank, where the muddy shore gave way to a string of stepping-stones, about a foot under the fast-flowing water. Just downstream, a flood-control barrier made a small waterfall, as Sellers Creek narrowed down a concrete channel toward the river. I wasn't a great swimmer. It would be dangerous to fall in here.

Selby had already taken off her shoes and was wading into the swift current, stepping lithely from stone to stone. *This is insane*, I thought, but something excited me about her shadow dancing ahead of me, almost keeping the beat of the invisible drums that surrounded us. I took off my shoes and socks, hiked up my pants, and waded after her. The water was as cold as claws. The drums were getting louder. By now they were a persistent song of regular and irregular rhythms. Before they had steeped in the atmosphere as a distant but constant presence, something felt rather than heard. Now, I knew: they came from the machines inside the factory.

Once we reached the other side, we were past security, past the parking lot, and less than a hundred feet from the foundry gates. It was a squat concrete building with mottled corrugated panels facing the parking lot and out-tilted black windows. The gate yawned open, just ten or twelve feet high and twice as wide; it was a tease of this huge structure. The outside was different from the inside. On the outside, from the stacks, old factories like the C, F, and G belched out towering pillars of water vapor and a reek of ozone, sulfur, and bitumen. It tumbled up from the smokestacks like a reverse tornado into heaven. Grimefog. But through the gates, we saw firefog. Like lava flowing from volcanoes – from Vesuvius or Etna – rivers of fire and molten stone poured down black channels into dark cauldrons where they glowed like miniature suns. Flames shot up from some basins while steam hissed out of others. Cranes swung across the gloomy space holding glowing rods of metal, picking them up from one basin and dropping them off at the other end. Dark men, dense and sweaty, with stick brooms and heavy gloves walked back and forth in their insulated gray uniforms, tending the castings and the molds. One man stood on a corrugated grate, holding a pump that resembled a jackhammer, pumping some liquid into the bowels of the factory while the vibrations made the long black power cord flop around like an spasming snake.

And the sound was huge.

It was a billowing rush, not of air lost, but hostile to air, a hot breath, a heat that tried to drive breath away, to empty a dark space, to hollow it out, but of course there was always more air to be pushed. Then, the hissing. The crashing. A metal crash, a machine crash, the invisible drums, pulsing, beating, almost beaming. The light seemed so dark and brash while the computers buzzed with bright screens and sterile precision, and, in there, obscure forms twisted and melted into shapes that would eventually be solid. It sounded like a train, and as twilight settled into night, the inside of the space seemed to reach outward to meet us. The factory would unfold and spread its guts into the world and infect us all with industry and motion. We heard the winds rush, whir, shriek, and scream down the open, concrete passages into us, and I felt a flash of pride, a moment of strength, of solidarity with my father and my grandparents who had started here in the C, F, G, in the foundry, who had sat by idle machines in winter cold and blazing machines in summer desert dark heat sunspots shining. I felt solidarity even though the jobs were gone and the union dwindling, and there'd be no work for me here. My parents were right: I *had* to go to college. But with each crash, I heard an Apollo rocket ignite. With each drumbeat, I heard an H-bomb pulse through Akawe and rain its glory upon the nations. We still bled automobiles onto American highways and homes. We still shuttled them out into the world, toward India and China, Mexico and Russia, Japan and Korea. *Fuck anyone who says we aren't important!* It was so damn loud. The throbbing sounded deep and strong under our feet. Even the earth knew that this was truth. I was grateful to Selby for bringing me here, for showing me this.

"John," said Selby.

All at once, without thinking, I turned and put my hands on her face.

Her bony face.

"You asked me – Labor Day weekend – if I would –" she said.

Our faces met. Our lips met. Our mouths opened to each other. Selby didn't kiss like Kiara or Juanita. She kissed like someone who knew how to kiss, who knew it a lot better than me. The scent of potpourri was in her hair, and my heart was banging hard in my chest. Our arms got tighter and tighter as we coiled our bodies and faces together. I let that moment take me there, in the dark, surrounded by dirt and concrete, with the drumming firefog and the rushing river and blue jumpsuited foundry workers striding between their posts, all of them unaware of Selby and me kissing and clinging to each other in the midst of their immensity.

75

After a while, Selby let go of me and pulled back. I couldn't see her face in the dark, but she lifted her arm to dab at her mouth.

"My mom will wonder..." she said, so we crossed back over the stones, almost invisible in the dark now, and put our shoes and socks back on. Then we made our way back through the weeds to Adams Street.

We walked quickly to her house, holding hands uneasily as we went.

"If Quanla asks..." she started, and I shook my head, violently.

We made it back.

"It isn't..." she said, and I looked at her without blinking. She backed into her house, and closed the screen door. "Bye, John," she said.

She shut the door.

76

My stomach was in knots at school the next day. Did I *like* Selby? Did I *want* to go out with her? It had been easy to speculate when I knew there was no way she'd say "yes," but our kissfest at the factory had turned my thinking upside down. I'd known her my whole life, and the whole thing felt weird. Her questions about Quanla felt just as weird.

When I got to Lit class, I tried not to look at Selby at all, but when I did sneak a glance, she was staring fixedly at the chalkboard with more interest than she had ever shown before. Meanwhile, Quanla whispered excitedly over Selby's shoulder, clueless about her friend's distraction.

That afternoon, when I got from home from school, I found my father in the living room.

"Selby's here to see you," he said.

"Where is she?" I asked.

"Beats me. I thought she was right here."

Selby came down the stairs.

"What were you up there for?" I asked.

"I just thought I'd wait for you in your room," she rasped.

My father frowned.

"Let's go talk outside," Selby said.

As soon the door shut behind us, she turned on me.

"I'm sorry about last night," she said. "That was a bad idea. It wasn't very good of me or you."

"Did you really think it was bad?" I asked.

"I can't go out with you," she said.

"But –"

"Fuck you and your plan, John," she said.

"What? No. We stopped doing that! I mean, I never even did it. And Adam was gonna dump Cora, but he never did. It was a stupid idea, that's why we never even did it!"

"I don't want to be your prop."

"But you weren't. I mean, aren't."

"Do you like me?"

"What?"

"Do you want to go out with me?"

What could I say? I didn't know. There were too many girls! And they each had too many boys to choose from! I had resolved not to be chicken-shit anymore, but how could I take a stand when everything was coming at me so quickly?

"I..." I gave up. "I don't know what's going on."

"Well," Selby said. "I ain't mad, but it ain't going on with me."

She started down the stairs, then turned back to face me.

"Do you still like Patricia?" she asked.

"Her?" I asked. "No. She's with Lark now."

"Quanla's a really good person," she said. "A lot better than Patricia. Probably better than me, too. And don't tell her about... tell Quanla about... you know."

"I won't," I said. "Will you?"

"No," Selby said. "I don't think I ever will."

77

I couldn't concentrate on anything that night.

At dinner, my father told me that Tool and Die would probably be idled for a few weeks after Thanksgiving. It was a pain to lose money right before the holidays, but it was even worse for what was coming down the line. "If they're shutting us down temporarily, it means they're thinking of shutting us down permanently," he said.

"Did they say that?" I asked.

"They never say what they're thinking," he said, chewing. "You can tell what they're thinking from the things that they do."

Some melted cheese fell from the corner of my tuna melt. I scraped the plate with the side of my fork. It bugged me that my plate was a mess of crumbs. It bugged me that everything everywhere was a mess.

78

The next day, Radcliffe decided to give a dance another chance.

HALLOWEEN DANCE!

Fri., Oct. 27

7-9

$3 Free pop/punch

School rules in effect

No costumes allowed!

"Friday night is gonna be *your* night, John," Adam told me over the phone. "You'll seal the deal just like I sealed the deal with Cora at St. Francis. We'll find you another Patricia. A better Patricia!"

I didn't see it quite the same way. I still wanted to hook up at the dance, but I was through trying to script out what was going to happen. I was still waiting for a tide of happening to rise up around me and draw me away. It had teased me when we summoned the spirit in the abandoned auditorium... and when I kissed Selby in the dark firelight of the foundry. But it had always left me on the shore. I wanted to be drawn out to sea, to be confronted by unexpected things: scaled monsters and sudden storms and unexpected lights on the horizon long after dusk had fallen. Uncharted waters. I wanted this dance to thrust me into the unknown. *I don't care*, I told myself. *I'm ready.*

    I've been ready.

79

Friday the 27th was a cold night. Colder than it had been since last winter. I did a bit of homework to humor my parents, then made myself an egg-salad sandwich.

"You got a date, John?" asked my father.

He was teasing me, but then he got into an argument with my mother about keeping the gas tank full, and I went upstairs to get ready. I didn't want to overdress or underdress. This was one time it would be okay to go a little preppy, like the Catholic kids at St. Brendan's. I went for tan khakis and a blue polo shirt. Then again, it was cold out, and the cafeteria might not be very warm. I didn't think goosebumps on my arms would look good. I put on a plaid, button down shirt. I caught myself in the mirror. "Jesus," I said. I didn't want to look like I was going to church. I went into my parents' room and put on my father's Red Wings sweatshirt. It was way too big for me. I changed into a black turtleneck. I heard strains of Ellington drifting up from below. "The East St. Louis Tootle-Oo." *I guess they're not fighting anymore.* I put on a pair of gray sunglasses.

"Hey John!" I heard Adam's voice coming up the stairs.

"Christ, Adam," I said. "What you doing here so soon?"

"Soon?! It's already seven! You're making us late!"

Adam stopped at the door to my room and looked at me. "Dude," he said. "You look like Dieter from Sprockets."

He started doing a robotic dance, then stopped. "You can't wear that."

"Dammit!" I said. "Is it the sunglasses?"

"The turtleneck."

"Shit," I said. I rummaged through my closet. Adam opened my chest of drawers.

"How about this?" he asked.

"That's a sweater!"

"It's a cardigan," he said. "Like Kurt Cobain wears."

"Not a real one."

"It don't matter. Girls'll love it. Put it on over a T-shirt."

"Which one?"

"Let's see." He rummaged through my drawer. "Dude, is this my Ice Cube shirt?"

"Sorry."

"No, it's fine. Put it on, then the sweater."

I took his advice. It worked. "I need something else," I said.

"Cologne."

"Yeah."

I pumped the cologne five or six times and walked through the mist.

"Hit me too?" Adam asked.

We must have smelled like a rolling Drakkar lab.

"You got to gel your hair."

I went into my parents' bathroom, slicked my hair back with gel, then sculpted it into an impressive breaker.

"You finally ready?" asked Adam.

"One more thing," I said.

He followed me back into my room. I went to my desk drawer where I kept all of my shades. I wanted something more colorful than the gray shades. A bit more dramatic. I flipped through the pile of sunglasses: they had gold lenses, black lenses, red lenses, yellow lenses. I was looking for *the* pair of sunglasses. The strange blue teashades. I hadn't worn them in over a month. I couldn't find them.

"What is it?" Adam asked.

"Um," I said. "A really cool pair of shades. But I can't find them. I don't get it... I keep them all here. I always put them away. I don't know what happened to them. I haven't done anything with them."

I felt a shadow of fear, then. *The man with the knife. What if he did find out where I lived? What if he came into my room and took his sunglasses back?*

"Sorry John, but it's like twenty after. We gotta go, or they'll run out of pizza."

That's stupid, I thought. *You just misplaced them. You can find them later.*

"Okay, fine," I said and slammed the drawer shut.

I left my bedroom without any sunglasses. Things didn't seem to be getting off to a great start. We stomped down the stairs. My parents were sitting in the living room.

"Off to the dance?" my father asked.

"Yes, we're going now," I said.

"Mrs. Bridge," said Adam. "Is it okay if some of us go to Taco Bell after the dance? If my sister can give us a ride? It'll be over by nine... the dance."

"Sounds fine with me," my father said.

My mother thought.

"John," she said, "I'd like you home by ten. So give me a call if you aren't going to get a ride, and I'll come pick you up."

"Sure," I said.

"Have fun!" my father said.

The night had begun.

80

The night was cold and bright and filled with fierce wind and the threat of snow. My ears stung from the cold. I felt my hair to see if it was still wet. Adam buried his hands in his pockets. Fallen leaves spidered down Agit toward South Street. Further downhill, across the river, the XAI rose, billowing steam from its many chimneys. We turned away and walked up toward Whitmore. We walked without speaking. The wind was loud enough.

On Whitmore, old Benedicts and Aubreys blew by like mechanical dragonflies, their eyes shining with yellow light. The streetlights beamed down their carbon glow. Far off to the east, Starville exhaled light up into the haze while the Old Benedict smoldered resentfully behind us. Its smoke hung overhead like a sooted aurora. *Anything can happen tonight*, I told myself. I wasn't sure I believed it. *Everything will happen*, I thought.

The school hulked along its single block, defiantly dark in the midst of the all the shining and shimmering. Its darkness seemed to throw a challenge out to us. There were plenty of secrets I hadn't discovered. I knew my way between classrooms and lockers now, but I hadn't discovered the attics or cellars, the catacombs or ladders. The caves. I was starting to wonder if they really existed, although that night the batwing sprawl of the building suggested all kinds of depths I had never noticed in the light.

Adam and I swung the brown doors open and went inside.

81

We went into the cafeteria where hundreds of kids stood around, talking and dancing to the sounds of spindled beeps and electric claps. More kids were standing than dancing, but the dancers were doing the best they could to make up the lost motion. They did the bump on the the floor and against each other while an asteroid light threw kaleidoscope colors onto their moving arms and legs. Not far away, a projector shot music videos against the wall, but the shifting images didn't quite sync with the music. The only other light came from the kitchen, where a couple cooks handed out plastic cups of punch and pop and some reheated slices of pizza. There couldn't have been more than five or six adults in the whole place. I couldn't help thinking that maybe the admins had felt bad about canceling the last dance and were trying to make up for it by letting us get away with as much as we could. Boys and girls danced close in the dark, folding out and in whenever the synths soared or dropped an octave. Breaths and spirits were moving across faces and deeps.

About halfway between the asteroid and the projector stood a card table with the DJ, stick tall and scrawny, stubbled and dripping jewelry, a feisty Aries and a mordant Monarchist named Tom, or at least that's what I'd heard. He had been hired, I'm sure, by the same idiot who thought it was a good idea to leave the lights out on a few hundred inner-city seventh and eighth graders. Tom's machines surrounded him, overwhelmed him, almost seemed to consume him. He called these machines "the Leviathan," and this was where the bass speakers throbbed out beats too resonant for anyone but Tom to handle. Even the dancers worked well back from the speakers, clearing a small island on the floor where red light puddled.

Tom switched records. He turned up the treble and launched into a grunge song. Some of the bump dancers wandered back toward the walls. Other kids leapt to their feet and began jumping and boiling across the floor.

"You see Cora?" Adam asked.

"I don't see her," I said.

"Let's go get some punch."

We made our way to the kitchen, pressing between dozens of kids on the way. The big oblivious eighth graders and the animated seventh graders. Everyone was loud, shouting to be heard over the music. Everyone was looking for someone. Relentless drumming. Resentful distortion. Squeaks and chants. A chorus of guitars phased overhead. Virulent fuzz magnified contact through atmosphere. Airborne kisses. Projected glares. Wilting wallflowers. I looked back to see if Tom was running fog machines, but he wasn't. He was accomplishing this strictly through sound. *But what have I accomplished?* I wondered. *I've arrived, but what am I going to do?*

82

Adam got a pop. I got punch. We got two of the last slices of pizza. By now, they were cold and rubbery, but we ate them anyway. Tom was angling down the face of the sonic wave, programming in the next swell of sound. The momentary pause before the break was the closest we'd come to silence that night. An emcee invited us to try a sex packet. Powerful stuff. Tom's taste was as eclectic as Lark's had been, but much better. The emcee promised us the safest safe sex. *Fucking Lark.*

"We got to find you someone, John!" yelled Adam.

"Not so loud," I snapped.

"Sorry!" He looked around. "Let's go this way."

As we dove through the room, parting the kids on either side, then rising up against the walled perimeter, we started to hear rumors. Not the light kind: Avante's fuckin' Ashley or Alex stole Mr. Denis' master test. These were heavy rumors. Things were changing on the street and what the street loosed sometimes bled into the schools. The South Side Reapers were here and so was the Latin Mafia, but the kids and rebels in Akawe's street gangs had been thrown off center in the last week. First, a sting by the feds had gutted the leadership of the Demonik Mafia's Arlington Hood, ending their decade-long rivalry with the Hastings Hood Satan's Masters. Then, that very day, Kid Zero, chief of the Mexican Deadly Undertakers, had been shot dead at a bus stop in the Os. His house had been torched an hour later. In one week, two of Akawe's largest criminal enterprises had been more-or-less deleted.

"They got him!" some eighth grader shouted at his friends. "He was Superman! He was Superman! And bullets was his Kryptonite!"

Alliances and rivalries were already shifting in response. Despite their fierce names and gunslinging ways, most Akawe gangs were small groups of kids selling dope off corners and cruising slow on Friday nights. They didn't have a lot of connections outside the city. They didn't control turf. They fought outside schools, burned down each others' houses, and took potshots at each other, sometimes on the way to a friend's funeral. The Masters, the Mafia, and the Undertakers had been the three exceptions, because each of them linked up to a national outfit. Now, with the Mafia out of commission, the Masters were free to take over the rest of the West End. On the other other hand, if the Undertakers fell apart now that Kid Zero had been killed, that gave the Chalks room to grow.

In elementary school, kids had asked sometimes, "You Master or Mafia?" "Hastings or Arlington?" "Kin or Tribe?" Now, the question would be "Master or Chalk?" "Hastings or Os?" Since Radcliffe was neither north nor west, it was open season here.

There were Masters at the dance; everyone knew it. Hastings wasn't *that* far west. "Act with Class in Breath and

Death." But there were Chalks here, too. "Xs, Os, Gangstas, Hos." *Maybe Chalky's gonna come up in here.* Shootings happened out where Chuck and Elizabeth lived. *Maybe the man with the knife runs with the Masters.* It was my classmates' brothers doing the shooting. One day soon it would be my classmates, too, doing the shooting and the getting shot.

Tom blasted Kenny Rogers' "Gambler." A fuse blew within the Leviathan and it poured an acrid cloud out over the dim crowd. Or maybe I imagined it, this stench exhaled by young anxiety, sweat and weal, fear of pain, fear of loss. Tom disappeared into the machine, pulling out wires by fistful, and bobbing his shaggy head to the beat, as if saying, "Yes yes yes yes yes yes yes."

But even this mystery wasn't easily solved. Other scents, a higher order of odor crept in through marginal spaces where chaperones feared to tread because they sensed, somehow, where they were not wanted and obeyed the most silent, most glaring of the kids. Sown red? Indian blue? Maybe. But I'm mostly talking about the clear-eyed bite of burnt plastic you'd only catch if you sought out the third-story bathroom at the north end of the hall, where some sensitive kid had opened the window to air out the stink but only succeeded in making the stink cold.

"Fuckers," snarled Adam, coming back from taking a piss. "Gonna end up like my dad."

Even this was only half of the story, we heard. Something new was making the rounds, and it was so rare that nobody knew where it came from. You couldn't smell it or smoke it or snort it, they said, though it did have a bone-white, ghost-blue kind of shade to it. You took it as a pill. I guessed what they were talking about before I heard anyone say it out loud: O-Sugar.

Maybe they bought it from Chalky himself.

They sang: *God made it here and gave it a name and since it arrived it's been desired and claimed. Cut from scraps of discard and trash, a taste of dust and ash to ash. It doesn't grant power but vision in motion, a balm to the futility of our emotion. For a kid in school, it's better than hope. For the homeless, it's an Eden to cope. For the successful, a telescope. For the despairing in gray, a kaleidoscope. If you try it you'll want it for the pain it brings, though this is like nettles and loss and wasp stings. It grants a vision of a heaven in the past, closely connected to the first and the last. It asks you to murder and demands suicide at points where life and death coincide. It makes its way to Japan were cars are made and Russia where the tanks are displayed, and whether you're black or white or brown, it dissolves your memories into its own – so when you're arrested your own name is unknown. You can't, you can't, you can't, you can't overthrow its call, its cord is tight around your neck. Even the police know the O won't be second guessed, and if you'll hate it – and you'll hate it – as you lie in that cell you'll want it, want it, want it, like the swell of cold currents that pull deep water nutrients to the shore. The heaven O sings is a song you want to hear forevermore, even if forever is a nothing, an absolute zero, and you cannot escape. So climb into that sweet saddle and press space.*

A James Brown sound bled out of the Leviathan.

You are from below. I am from above.

"Hey, someone's coming over to us!" chirped Adam.

"Who is it? Is it Cora?"

"No," he said. "It's your fucking faggot cousin."

83

Tom started "Smells Like Teen Spirit," which was appropriate, since the whole cafeteria did. The projector shot the music video against the wall, and I wondered how much time and money the DJ had sunk into perfecting the Leviathan. At the very least, it included a soundboard, two turntables, a four-track, a projector, a VCR, and the impressively huge speakers. The video quickly resolved into a foggy, yellow-lit picture of dozens of teenagers moshing over the shadowy reality of a hundred teenagers moshing.

"Hi Michael," said Adam. "Suck any dicks lately?"

Michael's shoulders were stiff.

"I know what you said about me," he said.

"What we say about you?"

"You said that I..." he paused. He didn't want to say it out loud. "You called me a faggot."

Adam mugged.

"You told everyone I was gay," Michael went on.

"You *aren't* gay?!" mocked Adam.

Michael ignored this.

"I know you don't like me, Adam, but John..." and he looked at me. "Okay, maybe you don't like me either, but my mom is your dad's sister."

"More shame for John's whole family," said Adam.

"I didn't think you would do this to me," Michael said.

I didn't know where to look. *It's his fault,* I thought. *For being so fat and... weird.* I didn't know where to look, but I certainly wasn't going to look at him.

"Look at me!" he said.

I did. Looked him right in the eyes. "We didn't mean nothing by it, Michael," I said. "We were just joking."

"That's right," said Adam with a bark. "Everyone knows you never got play, from a dude or a chick. You'll get play when rocks float in the river! Yeah, you'll get play when tigers and deer fuck each other and have baby deer-tigers! Yeah, you'll get play when, when, when doves really do cry!"

Michael was having a hard time ignoring Adam, but carried on. I knew he'd probably spent all day deciding what he was going to say: "You know I can't even eat lunch in the cafeteria anymore? People won't even let me eat my lunch! I have to eat in the library. I can't go to class, can't go to the bathroom, can't take the bus... without someone giving me... so much shit!"

He yelled the word "shit," turned on his heel, and stalked melodramatically back into the mass of kids.

"Hey Michael," called Adam. "Who broke the news to you the whole school thinks you're a fag?"

Michael stopped on this. He turned back toward us.

"It was Cora, actually," he said with a big smile. "She told me you told her that, and she told everyone else. She said she was 'very sorry' for saying such terrible things about me.

She said she judged me wrong and some other people, too. I wonder who she's talking about, *Adam.*"

Michael took off while he still had the last word, and Tom was on to Metallica now. "Nothing Else Matters." Adam gave an elflike cackle.

"Well, that was justh fabulouth," he said, flipping his wrist.

But his eyes were wide and worried.

84

We finally found some of our friends, hanging back in the corner near the fire exit. Chuck was there with Sara, Selby, and Quanla.

"Hi," I said.

"Hi John," said Quanla, and Selby looked at the floor.

"Anyone seen Cora?" asked Adam, shrilly.

Chuck shrugged. Quanla shook her head.

We talked for a few minutes, about teachers, about Halloween and trick-or-treating, but something hung in the air. We kept talking so it wouldn't seem like we didn't have anything to talk about – because if we didn't have anything to talk about, there must have been a reason. *What if the reason is Quanla guessed something happened between Selby and me?* Selby wasn't helping, staring at her shoes as she scuffed them along the floor. Sara was whispering something in Chuck's ear and kissing his neck. Chuck laughed, seemingly more comfortable than anyone else.

Tom took the microphone.

"Thiza mid-tempo one fer the people 'at's dancin' eight," he said in a voice that sounded like a broken lawnmower rotor. "May goo me hi ya shah beer Ra!" A delicate synth riff blasted into a fake horn section, followed by some delicate female singing.

Sara and Chuck moved off, dancing on their own.

"Cora would love this!" Adam gushed. "I've got to find her." And he sprinted off into the crowd.

The second Adam was gone, Quanla sprung into action.

"John," she said. "Have you heard anything since you got here?"

"I heard there's drugs going around," I said. "Heard about the gangs."

"Not that! Anything about Adam?"

"What do you mean?"

"People are saying Adam's gay, and Cora broke up with him because he's a fag, and now she's seeing someone else."

"I haven't seen Cora since we got here... but maybe she's mad at him? I guess she found out he was telling lies about Michael, and she spread them, so she apologized to Michael. Maybe that's why she's avoiding him. Adam..." I laughed. "But no way Adam's gay. I've known him my whole life. I mean, you have too. He's been out with Cora a whole month now. And you ever see anyone get with girls like Adam does?"

I was sure this would convince them, but Quanla still looked uncertain and a little disgusted.

"Come *on*!" I said. "It's *Adam*!"

"Okay, okay," she said. "I guess you're right. But the thing is, at least a bit of it's true, because I *did* see Cora and she was totally holding hands with another boy."

"She was? Who was it?"

"I don't know. An eighth grader, I think."

"We have to figure out what's going on."

85

The "Thuggish Ruggish Bone" had commenced.

Quanla and I left Selby and moved out in search of Adam and Cora.

The night had changed. I had thought that I was going out into a world that offered lips and swagger as long as I could keep my eyes and mind open, as long as I could just roll with it. But how was I going to roll with this? As Tom furnished a new beat aftermath to xylophone telephone tones, I realized that the night might roll me instead. Now Adam, my advocate, was missing. Cora, his chief prop, was off with another G. I was looking out for my best friend, not the other way around. Adam had always been, of all my friends, the most popular, but people were talking about him now. Saying bad things. Things I didn't think anyone could just bounce back from. The scene was slipping out of his control. What's bad for the buggish luggish goose is bad for the tuggish muggish gander, right? But a repeated and regular succession of blue movements and sounds got caught up in a new wave from the frostbitten Leviathan; Tom kept confusing these kids. The more competent ones – way ahead of Adam and me – had transmuted like Eucharist their boring confusion into bright carnality; they followed the music, groped each-other with taloned fingers, and busted slob all along the walls. The geometry of it all: incline heads at complementary angles, open mouths the same angle at the same moment, approach at the right speed. Close your eyes (or keep them open!); it was wild that kids so bad at math would ace this pop quiz unpracticed.

"Oh, Sheila!"

"Oh, Adam!"

"Adam Miller's a fag."

"Adam likes to suck dick."

"No he don't. I heard he gets sucked."

"He gets the milk sucked out his noodle like a straw."

The words made my stomach turn.

"John Bridge!" someone yelled. "You Adam Miller's butt buddy? Y'all do everything together, doncha? You fuck his asshole, too, doncha?"

"Fuck off!" I snarled.

"Hey, John," and someone I didn't know grabbed my shirt. "You want to stop time? You want to time travel?"

"One to three," sang the Leviathan, easily. "A bee sea."

"What? What?" I asked.

"O-Sugar, dog. You want some O-Sugar?"

"No thanks."

"But it's free!"

"No!"

"H?!"

"Annn... thizza Papa Wemba!" Tom yelled into his microphone. "Soo kos!"

"I heard he sleeps with his sister," someone said. "They live together. They got one bed!"

"Naw, it's got to be his brother. He's a fag, 'member?"

"He ain't got a brother."

"He does. He got a half-brother."

"Is it true his dad's in prison?"

"Yeah. He's a dealer. Slang rock, slang rock."

Barry, Robin, and Maurice belted out their defiance through the straining speakers of the Leviathan.

"Fuck, man."

"Some raggedy faggoty incest shit there."

"Fuck, man."

Their mothers and brothers survived.

"All fuckt!"

"I don't get it," said Quanla, shrilly. "It's one room! Why is it so hard to find them?!"

Tom took up the microphone once more. "Ah jizz god a thing azay, an azay it a you 'cuz you a young an nahd pluted pie diz shit. An daz a diz: a univerz belongz a dancer. Buh no, thaz nahd rite. It ain't 'bout you! It ain't 'bout you! Iz 'bout what you can do! You dance, you dance, an' to a universe blongz a dancer. You don' dance, you don' know shit."

He started up the next song.

The machine shouted about alcohol and females maintaining one's rectitude, so long as one is able arrive at one's nocturnal concert.

"What if they're not in this room?" I asked Quanla. "There were some people in the hallway."

"Yeah," said Quanla. "I guess so."

We waded through the jumping kids toward a rectangle of yellow light, the door into the hallway. When we got there, we found a tight circle of kids watching something.

According to the Leviathan, a dance consisting of humping was an opportunity to hump dance. *Bhrank!*

"You're a whore!" said a boy.

86

Quanla and I tried to stand on our toes, but the crowd was too thick to see anything. We shoved and elbowed our way to the front. The center of the circle had cleared out. Adam stood on one side, and on the other was Cora and a tall, skinny white boy with dark hair and perfect teeth.

"What is this?!" asked Adam.

"It's just what it looks like!" Cora snapped back, her cheeks pink with anger.

"You're cheating on me?!"

"Oh, no," she said. "I'm not cheating on you. I'm dumping you. I dumped you."

"You didn't bother to tell me!" Adam's face was pretty red, too.

Only the tall boy seemed calm, pale, and he looked at Cora, his hands in his pockets.

"Yes," said Cora, "I did dump you. You want to know when I dumped you? I dumped you at about three or so this afternoon, when I got a call from my friend Crystal who went to Olan Farm. You remember Crystal, Adam?"

Adam stopped. I could almost say he died right then, because I'm pretty sure he stopped breathing. He just stared at her. Then his mouth opened, but he didn't say anything, and I realized it was because he couldn't think of anything to say. It was the first time I'd ever seen him speechless.

Adam had spent a week at the Olan Farm Summer Camp that year on financial assistance. He'd bragged about it to me. It was where that girl Britney had given him a blowjob.

Cora waited for him to answer, but he didn't, so she went on.

"I know you remember Crystal, which is why you won't say nothing 'bout it. She told me why you got sent home early!"

I hadn't heard this.

"You got a blowjob!" Cora spat. "You got a blowjob from a guy."

"Don't say that!" Adam roared.

"Yeah, I'll say it," said Cora. "It's true. It's all true. You're a faggot. A fucking faggot. I kissed you, and here you've probably been sucking dicks! Jesus, I got dick breath from you! Why you want to go out with me in the first place, huh?"

Adam's voice trembled, as he answered: "You'll regret this."

But someone hooked his foot around Adam's ankle and tripped him. Adam fell forward onto his hands and knees. The kids were laughing. "Faggot." "No wonder he talked so much shit; he was trying to cover his own ass." "No, he wasn't covering his ass!" Big laughter at that.

I couldn't move.

I wasn't trying to answer any of the questions I had. I had dozens of them, all at once, and I couldn't sort them out.

They just crashed together, and all I felt was confusion, like I didn't know anything at all.

When Adam stood up, his eyes were wet, but this only made the kids laugh harder.

"Hey look, the faggot's a pussy, too!"

"Fuck you, bitch," Adam said with a ragged voice.

Cora spit at him and Adam recoiled, turned and pushed his way through the crowd – everyone backed up like they were afraid of his touch – and ran off up the hallway.

I heard myself talking. "Let's follow him, Quanla. Maybe we can help him out."

"Help him out?!" Quanla said. Her voice was incredulous. "You want to help him out?!"

"Um," I said. Since I wasn't able to keep track of all the questions I had myself, I couldn't begin to answer Quanla's. "Yeah."

"Don't you see how he *used* you, John?" she said. "You were part of his cover. Just like Cora. He *always* talked such a big game. He *lied* to you."

"You think it's true?"

"You think he woulda taken that if it wasn't?"

I couldn't argue with that; there *was* no way he would've run off if it hadn't been true. Adam would have stood his ground and called her out. He *never* came up short in the dozens or their multiples. So that meant that Adam hadn't just lied to me, but he'd lied a lot. He'd lied about who he liked. He'd lied about what he wanted. He'd probably been lying to me for years, and I'd believed those lies when we'd taken our dicks out to piss into Camille's locker.

My brain could easily assemble a logic of anger around these lies, but I realized that I wasn't angry. Usually I had the sharpest temper of any of my friends, but for some reason – shock or confusion? – I was processing this moment without a lot of emotion. I decided not to flip out until I had more time to sort things out in my mind.

Quanla was still talking: "Besides, it's fucking disgusting. See, he made me swear! But I had to, because it is... *fucking* disgusting."

"He's my best friend, Quanla," I said. "I don't know. I think I have to try to help him."

"Yeah," she said. "Good luck with that. I'll be with Selby."

She turned and walked away. The crowd was breaking up with the kids all wandering back to the dance. For a minute, I thought I might slip away after Adam without anyone noticing, but a couple of kids from my foreign language class spotted me as I went down the hall.

"Hey, there goes Adam's butt buddy," one said. "Don't drop the soap, man."

"What a couple of fags," the other said.

I took a quick look at them, memorizing their faces, filing the information away for the future. When I sorted out how I felt, I would also decide how I was going to get even with those motherfuckers. I already knew that I'd have to look out for myself after this. Adam couldn't protect my rep anymore. But he could still wreck it.

87

At the end of the hall, I turned left and saw a bright light shooting under the closed door of the teachers' lounge. I heard Adam speaking fast through the door and I went inside. The lounge was a sparely decorated room with a few couches, a couple round tables, and a small kitchen setup. One of the couches had been overturned, a glass had been smashed against the wall and, there were also several streaks of blood.

Adam held a phone to his ear. He took the quickest of quick looks at me, but didn't otherwise acknowledge my presence.

"Yeah," he was saying. "Radcliffe Junior High School. Right, just out front. How long? Yeah? Okay. Thanks. Bye."

He hung up the phone.

He looked at me.

I looked at him.

"What the fuck you looking at?" he said.

"I don't know yet," I answered.

"Ha," he said.

"You okay?" I asked.

"What, my hand?" He waved his bloody right hand in the air. "Yeah, looks like I hit the wall. Didn't move, though. Stupid wall."

He tore a couple sheets of paper towel and pressed it against his cut hand.

"Was that... was that..." Too many questions, so I asked the easiest one: "You just call for a ride?"

Adam thought a moment, and laughed again. "Yeah. Called for a ride. Yeah, that's exactly what I did."

"It's... a pretty stupid dance." I had no idea what I was saying. "I don't think I'm going to hook up with anyone tonight, after all."

"No? Well, that's too fucking bad, isn't it? I'm really fucking sorry for you."

He strode out of the room and turned left.

"Where you going?" I asked.

"I'm going to wait for my ride. Duh! I'm not going to go back past all those assholes."

He was gone.

Dissociated thoughts kept floating up toward the surface of my mind. *Why did he keep calling people "faggot" if he's gay himself? Why did he say it about Michael? That doesn't make any sense. Is it really "fucking disgusting," like Quanla said?* A shudder ran through me at the sudden image of two penises slapping together, but then it was such a ridiculous thought that I actually laughed at it. Like, out loud. And I thought about a few times when Adam had seen my dick – changing into our swimming suits, or pissing against a tree – and I shuddered again. Then I thought about what Elizabeth had told me. I thought about Mrs. Anders and my parents' friends. Their normal lives, except for the fears they had and the secrets they tried to keep. The secrets they felt they had to keep. I found myself picking the table back up, then the couch. I grabbed some more paper towels and threw away the larger chunks of broken glass, then dropped a washcloth over the rest. I took another cloth and wiped the blood off the wall, and threw it away. Maybe the whole school hated Adam now. Maybe I was pissed at him, too. I hadn't decided. In any case, the last thing he needed was to get suspended for trashing the teachers' lounge.

I went back down to the dance.

"No," someone said, not too close. "He hangs out with Elizabeth Furrier, too. Told you she was a fag hag. Ugly one, too." I memorized the face, got my coat and Adam's, and left the school. I skirted near the building by the trees, in case anyone was watching me, but nobody was paying attention. It didn't take long to get to the corner where Adam was waiting.

88

If the dance had transformed after we'd started to hear the rumors about Adam, then the change in the weather outside felt like the anger of God.

The old night had been cold and windy and bright.

This new night was even louder with the wind careening around the trees and houses to punch my face, rake my ears, spear my coat and clothes. I was shaking.

I gave Adam his coat.

"What's with you?" he asked.

"It's cold out," I said.

He didn't say anything. He put on the coat. He didn't look at me.

I was used to Adam's humor. It could be mean, or sharp, but it was always playful. Even when he had called Michael a fag, there was vicious joy in it. But there was nothing playful about this clenched-jaw bitterness.

Clouds blossomed overhead like yellow-green mounds of cotton candy. The howling wind stuck close to the earth, but the clouds didn't move. The misshapen sky hung as still as a painted stage set while the hurricane walked the earth on turning feet.

"Where you staying tonight?" I asked.

"I don't know."

"I thought you said you called for a ride."

"I did."

"So where you going?"

"I'm doing what you all were too scared to do. I'm going to that abandoned house I found over by Proctor. I'm going to do the séance just like I wanted, and I'm going to ask the spirits of the dead to help me figure out some... things I'm going through."

"Wait, you kidding?!"

"Yeah, I kept saying it was sweet and you should go, but nobody would. Quanla didn't even want to ask Darius about it. Where did Quanla go, anyway? I saw her in the... with you."

"She went back to find the others."

"Ha. Yeah, sure."

"This is a bad idea, Adam."

"I don't give a shit what you think." He looked me in the eye. "You hear me? I don't give a shit what you think. I should care about... whoever looks out for me, right? Like you care about your parents. Well, I care about who cares for me, and that's me. Nobody else does. So I don't give a shit what you think!"

"Oh, right, Adam! I don't care about you at all! That's why they're calling me your butt buddy in there and probably thinking *I'm* giving you blowjobs? You ever think about that... how your being gay makes *me* look?! Jesus, I don't even know what *I'm* gonna do about this. But still, here I am, standing around, like a retard, getting you your fucking coat so you don't freeze, telling you not to go hang out in crack houses like an idiot. But fuck that shit, because I *obviously* don't care!"

Adam laughed, and with that sound, the chill that ran between us thawed for a moment.

A cab pulled up to the curb.

"This is a really stupid idea, Adam," I said.

"Yeah, fuck off," he said, in a friendly tone.

"I'm not letting you do this."

"Try to fucking stop me."

"Maybe I can't stop you, but I will go with you."

"Don't be a jackass, John. Go home. Don't talk to me on Monday. You can act as surprised as everyone else; it'll blow over. I'm going now."

Adam opened the passenger door. The cabbie looked at him, this scrawny little kid, concerned.

"You going to West Church? You crazy?!" asked the cabbie.

"Wonderful," I muttered.

"Look," said Adam. "I give you my capital, and you take me where I've got to go. Which is just my dad's house anyway, so shut up."

The cabbie glared, but turned back toward the steering wheel.

Before Adam could climb in, we heard the sound of footsteps approaching, running. For a second, I thought someone was going to try and jump us, but it was just a single, slow, chubby kid. It was Michael.

When he caught up to us, he put his hands on his knees, breathing heavily.

"I heard what happened," he said as panted. "I've been looking all over for you fifteen minutes now!"

"Yeah, laugh it up, fatty," snapped Adam.

"Are we going or not?" asked the cabbie.

"Yes!"

"I don't care about you," Michael told Adam. "But John is my cousin, and I'm going to treat him like my cousin, even if he doesn't even like me."

Now it was Michael who didn't want to look me in the eye. *Works for me.*

"So, what's going on, John?" he asked.

"Adam says he's going to some empty house over by Proctor, and I'm saying it's a really bad idea, and he should go home," I said.

"I'm going," hissed Adam, holding the door mostly closed behind him. "You won't talk me out of it. I'm going to talk to the spirits of the dead, and the rest of you can fuck yourselves!"

"Nice attitude," said Michael.

"I told him if he's going, I'm going too," I said.

"Then I'll go too."

"What? Don't be a retard, Michael. I'll get into a ton of trouble if my parents find out, but it would be a lot worse for you."

"Yeah, I've got so much to lose. What's she gonna do, ground me? It's not like I have friends I hang out with or anything."

"And aren't you afraid they'll think you're a faggot if you hang out with me?" asked Adam.

"That's what they already think," said Michael. "Thanks to you."

"Get in or get out!" snapped the cabby.

89

I figured that if it was Church Street, we were actually going Downtown. That calmed me down a bit, both because I knew the neighborhood a little and because we wouldn't be too far from home.

The cab ran north along Whitmore to South Street, then jogged over to Jordan and afterward, turned west onto Aubrey Street. We coasted between the hulks of the Old Benedict and across the river. The Pyramid was a torch in the distance. Downtown glittered. The river glistened with cold. We swung up through the XAI campus and hung a slight right that took us along an overgrown boulevard through the rattiest part of the South Village. The street was lined with decrepit trees and boxy bungalows, a bit smaller than my own house but in worse shape. This was different from any route my parents had ever taken Downtown, but what did I know?

Nobody spoke.

The taxi buzzed and rattled gently, and Adam clenched his knees, his knuckles white and red. He stared fixedly at the back of the driver seat. Michael looked out his own window, and I couldn't see his expression.

We stopped at a red light, sat, and then kept on going straight. *Elmwood Road*, I thought, recognizing the street I took to see my grandparents on holidays. Across Elmwood Road was where the West End begins. Everyone knows that. A park flew by, its trees slashing up the naked luminosity of silver street lamps. As we moved further west, the condition of the houses didn't change but I saw more and more vacant lots. We passed a white church, a boarded up taco stand, a liquor store, and some utility building, all low and brick, windowless, behind a chain-link fence and concertina wire.

I thought this was maybe the edge of the Palisades neighborhood where Chuck lived. I also knew that Quanla lived somewhere over here. I wondered if her house was far away and how long she was staying at the dance. Maybe she was getting picked up at that same moment. If I only could remember what street she lived on, maybe we could drop in to see her. She could talk things through with Adam. Everything hadn't changed completely in one night, had it? What had happened to our friendships, our lunch tables, our weekends, our talks and smiles and laughter and confessions? I was trying to figure it out, but there was nothing I could compare it to in my experience. Everything was harsh and new tonight.

The cab made a right turn. By now I had completely lost my sense of direction and I didn't see any signs that we were anywhere near Downtown. For a moment, I thought that we had entered a better neighborhood... a lot nicer than the part of the South Side where I lived. Most of these houses were large, even magisterial, built with brick and stone and stucco, with crescent moon driveways and stone porches. Most were three stories high with large yards. But then I noticed that almost half were boarded up, their wild lawns glazed with dew and frost. Most of the houses that were still occupied had bars on their windows. A couple houses had even collapsed in on themselves. This was a neighborhood that had once been in a very lofty place, but had fallen far and fast.

After a few minutes, the cab turned right onto a side street and stopped in front of a tiny blue cottage, or at least that's what I guessed it was from what I could see between the tall grass and weed trees. A pile of wet mattresses and splintered Formica furniture rotted on the curb.

"Here you go. 1540 Church Street," said the cabbie.

"This is it?!" I said.

"Yeah, that's it," said Adam. "Thanks," he told the cabby. "How much?"

"Five forty," said the cabbie.

"Um," said Adam, rummaging through his pockets.

"If he doesn't have any money, you'll just have to take us back, right?" I said. "I mean, that's what you would have to do, isn't it."

The cabbie stared at me.

"I've got two dollars?" said Adam, as if it was a question and not a fact.

"Here, I've got four," said Michael.

The cabbie took our money and left us on the broken sidewalk. I was trying to get a look around, but it was hard to see anything clearly. None of the streetlamps here were working.

90

As the lights from the cab vanished back around the corner, Adam was already slinking toward the shack.

"Are you shitting me?!" I hissed after him. "Thousands of abandoned houses to choose from, and this is the one you pick?"

"Shut up, John!" he said. "I didn't ask you to come, remember?"

As Adam faded into the shadows ahead, Michael swayed uncertainly at my side.

"I really don't like this, John," he said.

"Yeah, well you didn't have to come neither."

I started after Adam and felt something crunch under my feet. Plastic and glass. I looked down at the black pavement and swept it with my foot, trying to kick the thing into the light.

"Careful, John," said Michael. "I think you stepped on a broken bottle."

"That ain't a bottle," I said. It was the smudged tube from a love rose. "Stay here." I looked Michael right in the face. "I mean it. Stay *right* here. Do not move." I hurried up the reedy walk toward the shack, but even in the dimness, I was able to see that there wasn't any way in through the front door. It had been completely choked with filth and garbage, bags heaped high with moldy paper and foam on top. I started around the house toward the side and almost crashed into Adam as he hurried back around toward me.

"John," he whispered. "Someone's smoking crack in there!"

"Of *course* someone's smoking crack, asshole! What do you think, faggot?"

"Don't call me –"

"Shut up! Let's go."

"You okay?" Michael called in a loud voice.

"You're too loud!" Adam hissed, waving his arms as he walked back toward Michael.

We hurried away from the house, back in the direction we had come, but things didn't get a whole lot better as we went. The next house was occupied, with a Starr sitting in the driveway and some very unfriendly looking dogs glaring and pacing behind a chain-link fence. The next house was abandoned. Across the street, there were no houses; they'd all been torn down.

"Where are we, Adam?" I asked. "Where are we really?"

"I don't know, exactly" he said. "Somewhere on the West End near Proctor? I found out the address, but I thought it was closer to the hospital. But I can't see that anywhere."

We finally made it back to the boulevard, where the cab had turned onto Church Street. The sign read:

S. HASTINGS BLVD.

None of us knew the neighborhoods very well. I almost never crossed Elmwood Road, and when I did it was just to go to Chuck's. Still, every kid in Akawe knew about two streets in town. Everyone knew someone whose sister turned tricks up on Ash, and everyone knew someone whose brother got shot over on Hastings. It was just a boulevard with some old houses and a lot of trees, but it was awful. The yellow-painted lines seemed to bleed into the black asphalt. The night above was howling and sharp. Orphaned there, in that noise, that brightness, the city felt like a stage that had been set for an audience to watch the infinite earth swallow us whole.

"Well, at least we know where we are now," I said. "The middle of the drug corridor, right after the Mafia got hit. Now the Satan's Masters are spreading out from right here. Great job, Adam."

Adam looked miserable.

"This... this is, like, the worst part of town, Adam!" Michael stammered. "All the drugs in Michigan go right here. And the Satanic Masters! You know... there's been tons of cocaine right where we're standing right now! What are we going to do? Other than die?!"

"I'm sorry, okay?" snapped Adam.

"You know you're not doing a séance tonight, Adam," I said.

"Maybe if we find another house –"

"We're *not* gonna find another house! We're lucky we didn't trip over someone back there. This is fucked up!"

"None of my plans work out," Adam mumbled.

"Yeah, well maybe your plans are fucking retarded!"

Adam looked at his feet.

"Can we, like, find a pay phone and call another cab?" I asked.

"You heard me. I don't have any capital."

"Yeah, but that's not going to keep us from getting jumped!"

"You think we might get jumped?" asked Michael. He was sweating in the cold wind. He started stepping from foot to foot as if he was about to sprint off in whatever direction.

"I dragged us all out here for nothing!" said Adam.

"No, at least now you know who the idiots are who'll follow you." I took a deep breath. "I don't know. Okay. I guess we'd better start walking."

"Which way should we go?" asked Michael.

"Hell if I know."

"Well, where are we going to go?!"

"I don't know! Shut up and let me think!"

If this was *South* Hastings, then the boulevard ran at least roughly north-south. And I knew we were on the West End. Downtown – and the South Side – were all to our east. We could figure out east pretty easily. In fact, this Church

Street probably *was* the same Church Street that ran Downtown. But I didn't want to walk who knows how far on a side street without working street lamps and packed with abandoned houses and pissed-off dogs. At least Hastings had light.

So which direction on Hastings, then?

North seemed more of a sure thing, even though it would be out of our way.

I knew that Hastings eventually had to intersect with West Street, the main drag out here, and there would be a bus route there. Maybe we could tell a bus driver that we'd gotten lost, and catch a ride Downtown. Then we could either walk home or call. I wasn't looking forward to explaining this to my parents. I couldn't think of any lie that would keep me out of trouble. It was probably already after nine, and they wanted me home by ten.

I remembered the huge houses we'd passed on Hastings in the cab, further south. Some of them were in good shape. If they were, someone was taking care of them. You didn't take care of a house that size without some money. Maybe Hastings got an unfair rap. Looking south, the banks and depths, the curb and median, were lined with healthy maples. Their remaining leaves leapt in the wind against the stars, so that it was hard to tell which was moving: the stars or the leaves? They all shivered in perfect harmony in that perfect cold. It still seemed a risky way to go, but I thought that I could probably trace our route back. If Hastings intersected with Aubrey Street, then we could make our way back across Elmwood Road and onto the South Side. If I could get as far as St. Brendan's, then I could easily find our way home from there. It would probably take more than an hour, I thought, but it might be our best shot.

Still, I hated not knowing for sure.

I looked off to the north again, in the direction of West Street. Wherever it was, the Benedict Main Assembly would have been just a few blocks further. I knew that I had this part of it right, because I could actually see where the factories were. I mean, I couldn't see the factories themselves... but the gold and silver shine from their huge floodlights opened the sky up like an airport runway would have. I saw that metallic light lace through the billowing clouds of vapor, their unnatural phosphorescence amplified by the lamps that rose up over I-292 even further north. I imagined blimps floating slowly through the dense, cold air. Then all those factory currents driving the vessel up and up; an Akawean square. Local weather conditions. The sulfur and ozone would keep the sky from falling, maintain the stars, hoist Winkin, Blinkin, and Nod aloft. A natural shade to hide from brother sun. A concrete barrier to wall out sister water. Vampire metals to leech into sister earth. Who thought the gates to heaven hung above the industrial ghetto?

But this vision of light and energy was flawed.

Far, far, off to my left, where the strange, sulfurous paradise should have faded serenely into purple shade, I found an artificial void. Not a plain darkness. Not the ordinary patches of night and quiet that rise over city parks, or even the uncomfortable stillness of a block of abandoned houses; this was something larger and more unnatural. The center of the Benedict Main should have been a hive of life and light but it wasn't. Instead, my eyes found an empty space. A bleak place. A dark spot that ate light. It was at least several miles away, and my mind filled its darkness with a hundred fears. I remembered the man with the knife and the abrupt disappearance of my sunglasses. I wondered if I would see him again – the kind of plausible coincidence that could happen in a town the size of Akawe – and when he did, would he be wearing my sunglasses? Would he grin at me as he had at the planetarium? Would he pull his knife out at shove it into my gut? And had he gotten into my house? Had he been in my bedroom? Was anywhere safe? All sorts of hollow, haunted thoughts seemed to pour out of that darkness that marred the factory glow to our north. I didn't want to go anywhere near it. I wanted to get as far from it as I could.

"Let's go south," I said. "Let's try to go back the way we came."

92

Almost as soon as we set off, we passed a neat gray stuccoed house with dark green trim. Despite the cold, a man and woman stood in the driveway, admiring a motorcycle with flames running along its sparkling finish. The woman was wearing a woolly nightgown and fuzzy slippers.

"Yes ma'am," the man said, running his hand along the gas tank. "This is the best one, an' better than the rest. Say, can I step inside a minute? It's cold out here..."

"Uh huh," she said. "I guess. I keep that coffee hot all night."

The conversation seemed so utterly normal. It was the sort of thing I might overhear on Whitmore or Agit Street. And just like that, Hastings Boulevard seemed stripped of its hexed evil. It was a place to be careful maybe. I'd need to keep my eyes open. We were dumb to be out there alone. But it was, in the end, just a place where people lived and died and tried to make it from day to day.

We walked in silence for a while. For the most part, nobody bothered us. Hastings was busy with plenty of cars coming and going, some of them booming with bass. Once, some boys on a porch laughed at us, making comments I couldn't hear. Another time, a girl rolled down her car's window and yelled, "You lost, honkies?" before zooming away. Other than these brief contacts, people scarcely even looked at us as we passed by. I wasn't that worried about gangbangers. At least not while the streets were still crowded with people and cars. I kept my eye out for the man with the knife, though.

Eventually, we reached a broad, grassy triangle made where Hastings intersected two other streets that also crossed each other. The first was Valentine Street but I couldn't tell what the second was because the sign had gone missing.

"Is that –" Michael began.

"Yeah," said Adam.

The last year, with nine separate shootings, Valentine and Hastings had been dubbed the "Deadliest Street Corner in America."

"Bullshit!" said Adam, "Look at it. That ain't a street corner. It's a big triangle! No wonder, yo, it's more like three street corners!"

Some black teens – older kids – in dark sweats watched us from a bus stop. We walked past them without speaking.

"Were those Satanic Masters?" Michael asked when we were out of earshot.

"What?" asked Adam. "I don't know. Probably. This is their hood. Anyway, it's not Satanic Masters, it's Satan's Masters!"

"What's the difference?"

"It's a huge difference. 'Satanic' means you're evil, like the devil. 'Satan's Masters' means Satan is your slave; you enslave evil. That's what it means." Adam spun around so he was walking backwards in front of us, gesturing as he spat out the letters: "S A T A N S M A S T E R S. Strong And True Allies Never Surrender. Masters Aid Sinners To Embrace Righteous Sacrifice." He finished by crossing his arms across his chest.

"Curb," I said.

Adam spun around just in time to step off of the triangle and into the street.

I glanced over my shoulder. The kids at the bus stop were watching us as we walked away.

Michael's jaw was slack. "How do you know all that?"

Adam grinned. "One of my cousins is a Master. Not here but in Chicago. That's where they come from, you know."

"But I thought they were supposed to be a black gang."

"Yeah, they are, but so what? I mean, the Chalks are supposed to be a white gang. That don't matter much when a bunch of kids are growing up on the same block, spending all day together. I mean, it might matter to some people way high up in the gang, who think of the names and write the rules, but it don't matter to a bunch of kids trying not to get picked on."

Adam knew what he was about. He'd always been small. That's why the neighborhood kids had picked on him but usually left me alone. That's why Jay Flighting had broken Adam's finger years ago. *Is that why he lied to me?* I wondered.

We were onto the next block now, and I breathed deeply. I realized I'd been holding my breath as we'd crossed the grassy triangle.

Adam was just getting warmed up.

"Here's how you'll know the Satan's Masters. A few years ago, they all wore black-and-white, but then they started getting picked off street corners, so now they just dress like everyone else. But their symbols are the seven-pointed diamond, and a black knife and a white knife, or a black rose and a white rose. Or a black shamrock, because they were the Shamrocks in the beginning, like ages ago. Or, um, a comet with a skull. Or a martini glass. Those are their tags. You see them all over town. Not on the East Side at lot. Maybe not Ashburn Heights. But lots of places. 'Act with Class in Breath and Death.' That's their motto. And they get ruled over by the Nine Kingpin Senate, with two Stone Cold Consuls and a Trib for the soldiers and the shorties."

"What about the Chalks?" I asked.

"What about them?"

"What do you know about them?" I was thinking about Chalky, and the house Selby and I had seen in the Os.

"Not a lot. They split in two a few years back... one of their leaders was more racist and the other was less racist, so they split the gang into two pieces. The Pure Chalks were smaller. They most of 'em got busted up by Acheron PD. I mean, that's how small time they were. But the others, the Crazy Chalks, took over the Os, along with the Deadly Undertakers. But the Undertakers are a Chicago gang, just like the Mafia and the Masters are from Chicago... the Chalks are an Akawe thing."

"You heard about the Undertakers today?"

"Yeah, Kid Zero got shot? They was talking about it at the dance. He was a big deal, man. I always figured he'd be in prison. They had so much shit on him. Crazy."

"So you think that... that now there's gonna be a rivalry... like a war... between the Chalks and the Masters?"

"I don't know, but if there was, I'd put my capital on the Masters. There are millions and millions of 'em across the country. Practically every big city has a set or two. I don't even know if you can find any Chalks anywhere else... at least not outside Michigan. Then again, everyone in Akawe is kind of on their own. So I don't know."

"So..." said Michael. "You said the Masters were the Shamrocks before they were a gang?"

406

"Yeah, they were a bunch of black kids in a Mexican part of Chicago. They were a baseball team called the Shamrocks, which I guess was a weird name because they were black, but then they went to juvie together, got out, started the Satan's Masters."

"They were a baseball team?!" Michael was incredulous. "I don't get it. If they were just a bunch of kids, how did they spread all over the country?"

"Dooood," said Adam. "This didn't just happen. They ain't kids anymore. Some of them are old men. They been doing this stuff since my dad was a kid. Most of the big bosses are in prison. Yeah, they started the gang back before Vietnam, and then they started putting together these groups of kids to buy stores, and they got capital from the government to do it."

"No they didn't," I said.

"Look it up!"

"That's crazy bullshit!"

"They got a bunch of money from rich people. I think they even got some from the Olans. Those rich guys didn't know what the Masters were doing... all the murder and bribes and stuff. Or I don't know, maybe they did. But anyway, the Masters got all this money, and that's how they got big and rich and famous, and got everyone to join, and expanded out from Chicago."

"I don't believe that!" Michael shoved his hands into his pockets to drive his point home.

"It ain't a secret!" insisted Adam, eyes wide. "You can look it up. It was a big deal when the government found out what the money was being spent on. Anyhow, money got pulled, but the Masters were already big. And then they started gangbanging and running gambling rings and stuff, and that just meant more money. More capital. So yeah, they're a big deal."

"Are they like that here?"

"What do you mean, 'like that?'"

"Are they a big deal here?"

"They're a big gang here, yeah. But it ain't like they are in Chicago. Like I don't think they can get their people elected here or nothing. I mean, the Demonik Mafia was the same way... big gang out of Chicago, but the feds come in and arrest eight or ten of them in Akawe. That's enough to shut them down around here for long time. I mean it. The Mafia in Akawe is *over.*"

We walked in silence a little longer. Even while Adam was dropping the names of all the gangs he'd heard of, I was liking Hastings Boulevard more and more. The houses had gotten smaller, but they were in better shape. Fewer of them were boarded up, although more of them had bars on the windows and shining globes in the front yards. The bright lights. The frosted median. The soft sound of laughter and conversation coming from parked cars on this cold night. Sometimes the whiff of cigarette smoke floating off of some corner or stoop. It was a nice place to take a walk. I had started to enjoy myself. I was still worried about getting in trouble when I got home, and I was nervous about where things were headed with Adam, about what they'd be saying about him at school on Monday... about what they'd be saying about *me*... and *what are they going to do?*

But I was also sad that we were in such a hurry. I wouldn't have minded walking all night.

"Okay," said Adam, "I just thought of a story that will help you know what it's like... how we're all alone here in Akawe. 'Cuz everyone here really is kind of crazy. Even you, Michael. It's all crazy. So sometimes, if people from gangs in other cities are wanted for murder or something, they'll come here to hide out for a while. You know, Akawe isn't real close to anywhere... not even the D. And since the Masters are one of the gangs that founded the Kindred Nation, they'd protect people on the run who belong to other Kindred gangs. So there was this gang in Chicago called the Black Gunslingers, and they were Kindred. And they had a... um... a drug deal. With some members of the Chicago Demonik Mafia, and it went bad, and the Gunslingers slit the guy's throat. Everyone got caught but this one woman with the Gunslingers named Sister Ra. So she was running away from both the police and the Mafia. Got it? The Gunslingers get on the phone, make a few calls, and they decide it's best to pack her away to Akawe and get her set up with this house belonging to the Masters, so she can lie low for a while. Probably not too far from here. Hey, maybe the house was even *on* Hastings. Like, maybe it was *that* exact house."

Adam pointed at an overgrown Tudor with brown beams and mint green stucco siding. Michael picked up his pace. Adam went on:

"This happened I think six or eight years ago. It was when the crack wars were real bad. Sister Ra must have felt so relieved when she got in. Her boy with the Masters was there at the house, and the Gunslingers hadn't even told him the whole story because they were worried that if the word got out, the police would track her down. They just told him that Sister needed to lie low. So the boy had a day job but he told Sister Ra, 'Don't worry, my shortie'll take care of you while I'm out.' Well, that sounded fine to Sister Ra. Usually guys date girls in sister gangs, right? So she was sure this would all be fine. But she still wanted to play it safe, so she asked the girlfriend if she could search her, and the girlfriend said fine, and Sister Ra frisked her. Then Sister Ra checked all over the house for guns and didn't find any."

Adam waited. Michael and I realized we were supposed to respond, so we nodded. Adam continued:

"The shortie's name was Jailbait, because she looked real young. Actually, I think she was real young back then, like maybe sixteen. Actually, no, I think she was younger, like fourteen. Because my cousin was the one who told me this story, and she was only twelve back then... so if Jailbait was any older, who would my 'cuz have known to tell her the story? It's like –"

"What happened?!" burst Michael.

"Right. So Jailbait's alone in the house with Sister Ra, and Sister Ra's this big, strong woman, six foot three, muscles as big as... you are, Michael."

"Ha ha."

"That's pretty big, right? But Jailbait's just like a tiny little kid, like me. And she looks up at that big woman, a wanted fugitive, wanted for murder, and she says, 'Don't you worry, Sister Ra. We'll take good care of you.' She took Sister Ra into the bedroom and got her all tucked in like she was a little girl, even though Sister Ra was at least like ten years older than Jailbait. 'I got a headache,' said Sister Ra. So Jailbait got her a drink of water. 'It ain't gettin' better,' said Sister Ra. 'Go take a peep.' So Jailbait pulled the curtain aside and didn't see no one. No cops, no bangers, nobody. It was allllll quiet. Then Jailbait looked back at Sister Ra and said, 'When I have a headache, I just need a bit of dark. These curtains here ain't too thick. If you just put the cover over your head, maybe that'll help.' Sister Ra thought this sounded funny, but she'd been awake for days, and she was tired in her skin, her muscles, her bones, her brains. Her head had a splitting headache. Bang bang bang! Like a hammer was hitting her. So she finally gave Jailbait a nod and pulled the cover up over her head."

Adam took a deep breath.

"Just a minute later," he said, "there *was* a hammer. Jailbait had hid a hammer and a big rail nail inside the window. She knew that Sister Ra would ask her to look out the window, just like she knew Sister Ra would listen and cover up her head. But you see how hard it was? She couldn't put the point of the nail on Sister Ra's head and *then* swing the hammer... that would have given big Sister enough time to sit up, and then it would all be over. Jailbait had to be perfect about it. She had to start swinging the hammer even before she put the nail against Sister Ra's head!"

"Wait!" said Michael. "Jailbait wanted to murder Sister Ra?"

"Yeah. She wanted to. And she did. Like I said, she had to be perfect about it, and she was. She moved the head of the nail to where it needed to be right as the hammer came down and hit that nail into the side of Sister Ra's head. And Jailbait swung again and again, until Sister Ra's head was all crushed in and the rail nail went through the pillow and... and got stuck in the wood of the bed."

"Why did she mess with the nail at all?" I asked. "I think a hammer would've worked fine on its own."

"Shut up, John, it's my story."

"Did she get away with it?" asked Michael.

"Hell no. They caught her the same day. Her prints were all over everything, and anyway, Jailbait hadn't even gotten rid of the hammer and the nail. She was great at murdering someone, but real bad at covering up the murder. She's in prison now. She ain't jailbait anymore neither."

"But I don't understand," I said. "I thought Sister Ra went to Akawe to be safe."

"Right, well that's the moral of the story. I mean, it proves my whole point about Akawe. See the Gunslingers thought Sister Ra would be safe in Akawe because it's far away and... there aren't really any rules here. But..."

"There aren't any rules here."

"Yeah, that's right," Adam said. "The Satan's Masters in Chicago were allied with the Black Gunslingers. But Sister Ra had killed a Demonik Mafioso, and Jailbait was with the Demonik Mafia in Akawe."

"But," Michael said, "I thought you said that the Satanic Masters and the Demonik Mafia were biggest enemies!"

"There aren't any rules here," I said.

"In Chicago, they always are," said Adam. "In Akawe, yeah, they are here too. Enemies. But it's a small town. People know each other. Friends become enemies and sometimes enemies become friends. Jailbait's boy couldn't have known the risk, because the Satan's Masters weren't part of the original beef and the Gunslingers didn't tell him. But you *know* Demonik Mafia in Chicago was telling everyone in the gang about it, and just a day after Sister Ra disappears in Chicago, a big girl who looks just like her is hiding out with Kindred in Akawe?"

"So did the gang in Chicago blame the Akawe Satanic Masters?" asked Michael.

"Whose fault was it? If the Gunslingers had told the Masters what was going on, it might have all ended different. And anyway, what were they gonna do about it? That's kind of what I mean. We're crazy here. We're all crazy. Those Chicago and L.A. and Detroit gangs can't do a whole lot to control us. They sell us drugs, and we buy them. People are friends and shit, sometimes move there, move back here, but Akawe's its own thing. I think the Gunslingers knew that once they sent Sister Ra off to Akawe, they didn't really have any control over what happened next."

As Adam spoke, we passed a quiet, lush park filled with towering oak trees, their golden leaves grayed by the night. I knew that we *must* be in Quanla's neighborhood now, but I still wasn't sure exactly where her house was. We walked past several more blocks of prim, neat, split-levels. Then Hastings swung to the right, westward, and I realized we must have gone too far. The boulevard had changed, too. The grassy median had vanished and been replaced by a left turn lane, and the houses gave way to a string of businesses, most of them shuttered. A couple blocks ahead, we saw the shining McDonald's "M" rising above the street.

"I know we're in a hurry," Michael said, "but I'm starving."

"We don't have any money," I said.

"Guys, I got this," Adam said. "Just follow my lead. And John, keep reminding me that we don't have any money."

94

As Adam trotted ahead of us, almost skipping up the sidewalk, I marveled at how well I knew him and how much I didn't know him at all. I could predict his words, his tone of voice, his movements, and his intentions better than he could; the obvious consequence of keeping the same best friend for over a decade, from nursery school through grade school and on into junior high. But he'd kept a huge secret from me for a long time, and I wasn't even the first to guess it. Now I understood Elizabeth's exasperation when we had argued outside my locker.

I wondered too, a little bit, about my cousin. Michael – the quiet, awkward one, who didn't have any friends and who never stood up for himself – had been the only person to leave the dance and follow me to Akawe's most infamous street. Even more amazing, Michael seemed to be the one person other than me who cared what happened to Adam, and Adam had always treated Michael like shit. Christ, I had treated Michael like shit. I felt a kind of churning – a sickness – in my gut. It wasn't guilt. It was resentment. I resented that he made me feel guilty.

Adam hurried up to the door to the McDonalds, found it locked, frowned back at us, and circled around to the drive through.

"Should we run after him?" Michael asked.

"I don't think so," I said.

It took us a good minute to catch up and, when we got there, Adam was having some sort of a conversation with the cashier at the checkout window. But his posture was different. His left hand was clenched in a fist against his chest, his right hand was limp at his side, and his eyes seemed out of order... almost crossed.

"Hai wan' a schlu-shee," he said.

"Um," said the girl behind the register. "Um."

"Adam," I said, "We don't have any money."

The girl looked out the window at us.

"Oh, good," she said. "I thought he was out there all alone."

"No, he's just –"

"Hai wan' a schlu-shee!" Adam wailed.

"Do you know what he's saying?" the girl asked.

"I think he's saying he wants a slushy."

"It's real cold out."

"I know... he's, um... not... normal. And it doesn't matter because we don't have any money. Adam, we don't have any money!"

Adam looked at me, tears welling up in his eyes.

"John!" he whimpered, pawing at me. "John, why we walk so lawn? Why'ee wok so lawn!!" He grabbed at my jacket. "Haim tired! Hai wan' a schlu-shee!"

I put on my father's irritated voice. "Adam, no. We've got to get home. We're already in trouble, and my mom's going to kill me if we're any later. And I told you, we don't have any money!"

"But hai wan, hai wan, hai wan, hai wan!" He sat down on the drive through.

I looked up at the girl. She was looking at Adam sympathetically, as if trying to make up her mind.

"Get up," I barked at Adam. "You're acting like an asshole!" To the girl: "I'm sorry. I can't control him... I... he's just out of control."

"Just a minute," she said and closed the window.

Adam didn't break character. He crossed his arms petulantly, and resisted my attempts – which weren't "in character" – to get him back to his feet.

"Please get up," I said. "This is really embarrassing."

Michael stared at us, speechless.

The cashier opened the window again, beaming a bright smile. "This is on me," she said, handing out a big bag. "Please hurry home and get inside. It's cold and it's late."

"We're trying to get home just as quickly as we can," I said sincerely.

She shut the window.

She had given us two big boxes of fries and a cup of soft-serve ice cream.

"Schlu-shee!" squealed Adam.

95

We knew we'd gone too far, so we turned back.

"I think this is east," I said, pointing back the way we came.

When Hastings – which wasn't Hastings anymore; I just didn't know *what* it was – curved to the north again, we turned onto a side street that continued eastward. We ate as we walked, the wind died down, and the air seemed to warm a little. On our right, the city vanished into a wilderness of poplars, cattails, and tall grass. On the left, we skirted a subdivision of tidy brick ranch houses with birches and honeylocusts growing in the front yards and neat white bars affixed to the windows.

As the night deepened and the city quieted, I felt calmer and calmer. It had to have been far past ten by now. It may have even been after eleven, and yet I stopped worrying about what would happen when I got home. Whatever happened, I was sure it was a price worth paying for these still hours on foot in my city with my best friend and my cousin.

The longer we walked, the less we talked. Maybe we'd been talking about everything else – the city and its gangs – just to avoid Adam's secret, the ugly rumors we'd spread about Michael, and the shitstorm waiting for us at Radcliffe on Monday. Maybe we'd finally realized we didn't need to talk. Maybe we'd decided it didn't matter. Nothing we could say was going to change what was coming. We still had this night, these hours, these streets to ourselves.

That night felt like the negative mirror image of a drug. Not a proliferation of sense but its reduction to essentials. Night subtracts the number of colors, divides the volume of sounds, and what remains takes on a heightened importance. A secret energy, still in motion, fills the dark spaces separating things we are able to see and touch. Walking all those miles, all those blocks – feeling a dull pain in my feet and the sting of the air on my face – I felt sleepy and wide-awake at the same time. It was soothing and electrifying.

Eventually, the wilderness to our right gave way to broad fields with soccer goals and baseball diamonds and, in their midst, a looming brick structure, huge, penitentiary-style, with vertical slatted windows running its perimeter.

"Fuck," I said, breaking the silence.

"What is it?" asked Michael.

"That's Southern High School. We're way out. We're almost all the way out to city limits. I'm gonna be grounded for a month when we get home!"

"A month?" Michael laughed. "I'm gonna get grounded for a year!"

"A year?" laughed Adam. "Nobody even knows I'm out."

96

We continued eastward. As long as we could keep walking in the same direction, I knew that we would eventually hit Elmwood Road, and I could find our way back from there, even though it might be another several miles.

We'd entered a new neighborhood, one which looked more suburban than urban, even though I didn't think we had left Akawe. A clean, pale light fractured through liquid crystal panels inset into dark wood front doors. Shining black cars, still wet from the car wash, sat on sloping driveways, the drops slowly turning to ice. The glowing or flickering or shadowy second-story windows told us where someone was reading or watching TV or trying to get to sleep. The road undulated up and down hills, around curves, and passed cul-de-sacs, scattered gardens, neatly trimmed spruces, and silvery birches.

Another mile vanished under our feet.

97

And where the cemeteries and the farmlands and the forests began, the sky was robed in shades of purple moving toward black, and the stars glimmered like sequins overhead. And where the golden glow of houses and factories and streetlamps shone, they copied the hues of the setting sun.

Or of the rising sun.

I couldn't tell if the world was pretending to be dusk or dawn for us. I couldn't distinguish between the downward tilt of autumn and the upward climb of spring. But I was convinced that we were walking through a greater, grander planetarium than Suarez a few miles to our north. That we'd been taken away from earth for a while, into a new space, a multitude of spaces, to study a model of our world and universe in which everything was present and perfectly represented.

98

And the air tasted like snow.

And the steam from the basement furnaces fogged up out of the brick chimneys.

And the frost-kissed grass crunched beneath our dirty sneakers.

And all space turned above us as the dying city began to move again.

As if it wasn't even dying. As if it had been alive all along.

And we breathed as we went...

99

We finally got to Elmwood Road.

Ratty houses marched right up to the road and another dilapidated business strip stretched away to the left.

"There's a gas station," said Adam, pointing. "I bet they'll have a phone."

We crossed Elmwood and passed a brown, tired-looking bungalow. A garage connected it to a shuttered cinder-block business with a vacant lot on the far side. A sign on the side of the business read, "Akawe Tent and Tarp Shop."

"Wait a minute," I said. "Lucy said her house was next to a tent and tarp shop on Elmwood. This has to be Lucy's house. What else could it be?"

"Lucy who?" asked Michael.

"Lucy the Note Swallower! Lucy the Séance Supplier!" said Adam with a breath of awe, and in the next moment he had run up and banged his fist on the door.

It's over now, I thought. *This walk. This peace. It's all about to end.* I felt a dull ache spread through my chest.

Lucy opened the door. She was wearing a nightgown. When she saw us, her gray eyes went wide. Her gown rippled behind her. Her hair moved about her face in ghostly currents, but I don't remember feeling the wind myself.

"What's going on?" she said. "Tell me fast."

"Um. We got lost on Hastings, so we been walking," Adam said.

"You walked here from Hastings?!"

"Hastings over by East Street, I think."

"That's miles from here! What, did you go up there after the dance?"

"Yeah."

"Why?"

"Long story. Dumb story."

"Lucy?" someone called from another room.

"Just a minute," Lucy said, and hurried up the stairs.

We stood still and tried to overhear the conversation.

"They got lost," Lucy was saying. "No, they were just walking past... they remembered I told them I lived here. I know what I'm wearing, but I didn't know who it was. Anyway, I couldn't leave them outside!"

Each time Lucy stopped speaking, we heard the indistinct reply of a woman. Not so much calm as exhausted.

Finally Lucy came back and waved us up the stairs into the kitchen.

It was a humble, white-painted room with a white gold-veined linoleum floor, white cabinets, and a small white Formica table.

"Do you want to call home?" she asked. "For a ride or something? You just have to be kind of quiet. My brother is sleeping, and my mom's watching TV."

"What time is it?" I asked.

"A little bit after eleven... Eleven twenty I think."

I swore under my breath.

"We're going to get into a lot of trouble," said Michael despondently.

"Yeah, you probably are," said Lucy. "My mom would kill me if I was out right now. I don't think she'd ever let me go to school again."

Adam laughed. "For real?" he asked. "Can I have your mom?" His face was pale but I believed his smile. "Nah, it's all good," he said.

I called home first, and my father was so glad to hear that I was safe that he almost forgot to start shouting at me. Then, he remembered. "You are going to be in so much trouble for so long!" he bellowed.

"It gets worse," I said. "I need you to give Adam a ride... maybe to his sister's. And...Michael, too."

He didn't have much to say to that, so he hung up the phone.

"I can give you both rides home," I said to Michael and Adam. "Michael, you probably want to call Aunt Mabel."

Michael looked as though I had sentenced him to death, but he picked up the phone and dialed.

"Lucy, can I use your bathroom?" asked Adam.

"Um, sure." She gave a tired smile. "It's just around the corner to the left. Don't mind my mom."

A moment later, I could hear Adam chatting with Lucy's mom in the other room. She answered him in the same, tired monotone.

"So are you... in a lot of trouble?" asked Lucy.

"Yeah. Yeah, they aren't too happy with me. They thought I'd be at Taco Bell with my friends, and when I wasn't there, they started calling around. It was my father who picked up the phone. I wish it had been my mother. She doesn't get as mad."

Lucy chuckled. "Everyone else just called their parents 'mom' or 'dad,' or their first name."

"Huh?"

"You call your mom 'mother,' and your dad 'father.'"

"Yeah. I guess I do. It's something I started doing when I was a little kid."

I closed my eyes for a moment, then opened them. I know why I closed them; I was tired. I know why I opened them; I wanted to look at Lucy. When I opened my eyes, Lucy was watching me.

"What?" I asked.

"How was the dance?" she said.

"You weren't there?"

She shook her head.

"That's good. It was..." I searched for words. "Really weird. I'll tell you about it on Monday. Actually, I'm sure you'll hear about it at school. Why didn't you go?"

She thought for a moment. "Nobody invited me."

"I don't think it was that kind of a dance."

"I mean, you go to see your friends, don't you?" she said. "I don't have any friends."

"You *have* to have friends."

"I had some friends at St. Brendan's. They weren't close friends. They're all still going to school there. I went to Radcliffe."

"You've got friends."

"Do I?"

"What about us?"

"Ha!" she was amused at this. "None of you even talk to me unless you're breaking into an abandoned building –"

"I'm talking to you now –"

"– or lost off Hastings in the middle-of-the-night."

"You got me there."

We both stared at the floor for a moment, and listened to Michael on the phone, apologizing and distraught.

I yawned.

Lucy didn't yawn. She swayed lightly, rocking on her heels, not admitting her tiredness.

"It's okay," she said. "I needed to stay here anyway. I needed to watch my little brother."

"You're tired."

"No, I'm not."

"Yeah, you are."

"Oh, well. I can sleep in tomorrow. I don't watch the cartoons anymore. I sleep in on Saturdays."

"Why were you up so late tonight? We're lucky you were."

I thought again about what Chuck had said about coincidence being an easy thing in a city the size of Akawe. I had only been thinking of bad coincidences. Dangerous coincidences full of threat or murder. I wondered if this counted as a coincidence too. I mean, it wasn't a coincidence that we had passed Lucy's house. She lived on Elmwood Road, and that was the obvious way to get back home. That part of it wasn't strange at all. But was it a coincidence that I had remembered her description of her house, from one conversation we had had weeks ago?

"I don't know," said Lucy. "I don't go to sleep very early. Or sometimes I sleep, but then the train wakes me up."

"Me too. It's loud over by me."

"Oh yeah?"

"Sometimes when I hear the train, it sounds strange. Like it's a alive, you know? I mean, it doesn't sound like a train."

"Huh. That's weird."

We stood quietly for a moment. My Aunt Mabel, who'd I'd never seen really angry in my whole life, was getting wound up into a fury. I heard her voice building and building and Michael winced, holding the phone away from his face with a grimace.

Lucy looked at him. She looked back at me and gave a weary smile. Her eyes focused and unfocused. She blinked. She looked at the floor. She lifted her eyes to mine again.

Suddenly, I found her intense, and her intensity was one of the strangest things I'd ever witnessed. The immediacy of that look, almost like a ghost made flesh, entered me and made me shiver. Because anytime I wasn't with Lucy – wasn't speaking with her – I had a hard time remembering what she looked or sounded like. Her words weren't memorable. Her mannerisms weren't memorable. She'd said it herself: She didn't have any friends. She dissolved into the background, and nobody noticed her.

But now, looking at me, those two eyes fixed on me, her pupils shaped like orbits, like rotations and revolutions – she owned it. This glance was unique to her, and I didn't think that anybody else could glance at anything. Only Lucy was real right then, so I took in the angled shape of her face, the fake blackness of her hair, the gloss where she'd put Vaseline on chapped lips, the netted curl of her eyelashes, her everything. Her unobtrusive breathing. I felt my own breath and my pulse rush inside me. I felt like she could kill me by looking away from me.

"I think," Lucy said. "I should... go see if my mom wants anything."

"Yeah," I said. "My ride's gonna be here in a minute... so I guess... I'll see you in science.... Monday."

"Sure," she said. "Sure. Good night, John."

She turned to leave, and my pulse surged – it flooded – again – *don't go!* – and instead of being a shadow – an echo – of what I had felt a few moments before, this new current built and built until it was hard to breathe, and I felt like my mind and my heart had become unlinked, untethered, crackling with electricity, and I was about to emerge from myself and my skin – bright matter and sparkling energy, an impossible and radiant thing made of song and wings and flames and flight, a crest of wild atoms ready to break the chains of gravity and surpass all bond and limitation.

Lucy paused in the doorway.

"Was it nice?" she asked, looking back at me. "Being lost for a while? I mean, not having to go where someone else wanted you to? Not even having them know where you were?"

"It was perfect," I said. "But anyway, it's over now."

URBANTASM
Book 2: The Empty Room
by Connor Coyne

Available May 2019

URBANTASM
Book 2: The Empty Room
by Connor Coyne

Urbantasm: The Empty Room is the second book in the magical teen noir serial inspired by the author's experiences growing up in and around Flint, Michigan.

John Bridge is only two months into junior high and his previously boring life has already been turned upside-down. His best friend has gone missing, his father has been laid-off from the factory, and John keeps looking over his shoulder for a mysterious adversary: a man with a knife and some perfect blue sunglasses.

As if all this wasn't bad enough, John must now confront his complicated feelings for a classmate who has helped him out of one scrape after another, although he knows little about who she is and what she wants. What does it mean to want somebody? How can you want them if you don't understand them? Does anybody understand anyone else, ever? These are hard questions made harder in the struggling city of Akawe, where the factories are closing, the schools are crumbling, and even the streetlights can't be kept on all night.

John and his friends are only thirteen, but they are fighting for their lives and futures. Will they save Akawe, will they escape, or are they doomed? They might find their answers in an empty room... in a city with ten thousand abandoned houses, there will be plenty to choose from.

ACKNOWLEDGMENTS

I wish to thank God, who makes the impossible possible, my wife Jessica who has shown grace and patience with a project that has taken many years to complete, and my whole family, especially my parents Shannie and Gregory for teaching me the importance of education, curiosity, and perseverance, my late Grandma Coyne for teaching me the value of honesty and hard work, my daughters Mary and Ruby who give me a reason to leap out of bed each morning (even though they also ensure that I'm exhausted at the end of the day), and my mentors Jeffery Renard Allan and Jan Worth-Nelson who have kept alive my hunger for literature, conversation, and storytelling.

I also wish to thank the team that made this project possible. Although just one name appears upon the cover, books are a collaborative affair, and I could not have pulled this one off alone. I wish especially to thank Paul Lathrop, my oldest friend, who has supported *Urbantasm* from the very beginning and who has graciously produced this four-volume serial novel, Hosanna Patience who has edited *Urbantasm* through its many iterations, and Sam Perkins-Harbin who beautifully designed and illustrated the cover, map, and book interior. Further thanks to Darcie Rowan who, as publicist, has assiduously promoted *Urbantasm*, Reinhardt Suarez, who not only proofread the book but offered a wealth of insights into writing and publishing, and Andrea Cure, B. Alex Reed, Amanda Steinhoff, and Anemonë Zeneli who read advance copies of the book and offered their own valuable feedback. Gemma Cooper-Novack and Michael Kennedy have provided unflagging moral and spiritual support on days when this book felt like an unending wrestling match.

The Gothic Funk Press is an offshoot of the Gothic Funk Nation, a Chicago-based collective of dreamers that was active from 2004 until 2011; Skylar Moran, Elisabeth Blair, Amber Staab, Sean Conley, Hallie Palladino, Colin McFaul, Nora Friedman, Jen Kennedy Clara Raubertas, and many other friends involved in that project were and are an inspiration to me and I am grateful for their companionship on this journey. Ditto the Moomers crew, Scavhunt gangs (both Hot-Side-Hot and Cold-Side-Cold), UT crowd, and friends and teachers from the University of Chicago: Dr. Malynne Sternstein, Curt Columbus, Dr. Tiffany Trent, and Dr. Richard Kron, among others. I must also thank the students, faculty, and staff at the New School MFA program – especially Scott Larner, Marco Rafalá, and Helen Schulman – for their assistance with early drafts of Urbantasm. Twelve years later it is stronger as a result of their insight. Further thanks to Joe Loya (as an early writing mentor) and Michael Milligan (for brainstorming plausible physics with me).

It is indispensable that I thank my friends and family from Flint, Michigan, the Vehicle City, and especially Flint Youth Theatre, the Flint Literary Festival, the Flint Public Library, St. John Vianney Catholic Church, the Unitarian Universalist Church of Flint, the city's four high schools – Central, Northern, Northwestern, and Southwestern – as well as Powers High School, and the teachers I was blessed to learn under at Flushing High School. Shoutouts here to Katie Cawood, Joshua Aldred, Greg and Kathryn Nicolai, Demetrius Keone Thomas, Bree Lerner, Walter Hill, Bill Ward, Janet

Haley, Peggy Mead-Finizio, Jeremy Winchester, Jennifer Ramsdell, Bob Campbell, Leslie Acevedo and my wonderful students with the Flint Teen Writers Workshop, Father Tom Firestone, Melodee, Bob, and Ellie Mabbitt, Aly Condon and Connor Condon-Lathrop, Elizabeth Perkins and Donald Harbin, Emily Perkins-Harbin and Nathaniel Mosher, Carol and John Crawford (who let me live in their basement in 2002 when I was revising *Urbantasm*, and who provided a roof, food, and comfort for many kids who were lacking it otherwise), their daughters Sarah and Lindsay Crawford, John D. Martin III, Luna Slayton, Gordon Young, Andrew Highsmith (for brainstorming plausible urban renewal with me), Thad Domick (for brainstorming plausible organic chemistry with me), Katie Owen, Rebecca Williams (who helped me understand work at Michigan Radio), Ellie Sharrow, Donn Hines, Frank Polehanki, Miss Caroline Moore, Martin Jennings, Jeff Bean, Dick Ramsdell, Lottie Reed from the Golden Leaf Club (the *best* jazz funk you'll hear anywhere), and Jimmy and David Todorovsky from the Atlas Coney Island (the *best* coney anywhere for 37 years). And the City of Flint itself, that hard, passionate, stubborn, inventive, independent, big-hearted, beautiful city. *Urbantasm* is my humble (or possibly not-so-humble) attempt to tell *our* story and it is my deepest wish that I've made you proud.

This novel has been the work of 22 years, and it is simply impossible for me to individually thank every person who has contributed to its completion today, but you are all in my thoughts, dreams, and prayers, and my gratitude cannot be bound by words.

ABOUT THE AUTHOR

Photo by Eric Dutro

Connor Coyne is a writer living and working in Flint, Michigan.

His first novel, *Hungry Rats* has been hailed by Heartland prize-winner Jeffery Renard Allen as "an emotional and aesthetic tour de force."

His second novel, *Shattering Glass*, has been praised by Gordon Young, author of *Teardown: Memoir of a Vanishing City* as "a hypnotic tale that is at once universal and otherworldly."

His essay "Bathtime" is included in the Picador anthology *Voices from the Rust Belt*, edited by Anne Trubek.

Connor represented Flint's 7th Ward as its artist-in-residence for the National Endowment for the Arts' Our Town grant, through which artists engaged ward residents to produce creative work in service of the 2013 City of Flint Master Plan.

Connor's work has been published in *Vox.com*, *Belt Magazine*, *Santa Clara Review*, and elsewhere. He lives with his wife, two daughters, and an adopted rabbit in Flint's College Cultural Neighborhood (aka the East Village), less than a mile from the house where he grew up.

Learn more about Connor's writing at ConnorCoyne.com